A Summer Without Rain

Copyright © 2022 by Christie Gordon
All rights reserved.

No part of this publication may be reproduced, distributed, or transmitted in any form or by any means, including photocopying, recording, or other electronic or mechanical methods, without the prior written permission of the publisher, except as permitted by U.S. copyright law. For permission requests, contact Christie Gordon.

The story, all names, characters, and incidents portrayed in this production are fictitious. No identification with actual persons (living or deceased), places, buildings, and products is intended or should be inferred.

A Summer Without Rain – Second Edition
Cover Design by Christie Gordon
Editing by Catherine Chisnall
Proofing by Becca Waldrop

DEDICATION

To everyone who has had to fight for their flavor of love.

Trigger Warning: Because of the time and place in which this book takes place, there is quite a bit of prejudice.

CHAPTER ONE
SHANNON

S hannon peered at himself in the dusty mirror over his oak dresser in the bedroom of his parents' farmhouse, taking in his shoulder-length, almost black hair, and gray eyes under thick lashes, so much like his father's and his straight, pointed nose over full lips, so much like his mother's. He straightened the wrinkled, black-linen, button-down shirt covering his lanky frame and tucked it into gray trousers, worn thin at the knees and pockets. He rolled the sleeves up above his elbows and left the top buttons of his shirt undone, exposing a peek of his pale chest and long johns. He was the son of a long line of potato farmers. Money for new clothes didn't come easy. No matter, he liked his clothes dark. Dark things hid secrets, and of those, he had his share. It was too hot for a waistcoat and jacket, or even his scally cap. He didn't care how it looked. He was only going to see his best and only friend, Ciaran, next door.

He left his bedroom and strolled out a hallway, over plank flooring, and through the heavy, wooden front door of the house. His mother and father were out in town and couldn't bother him about his looks. They hated that he wore his hair so long, but he didn't care. He was different after all. More different than most people knew. His mother had started it, giving him an American name. After his mother's sister emigrated, she'd named her son Shannon and so his mother had thought giving him the name would be fashionable. Maybe she'd cursed him instead. He curled a smirk over his lips. He strolled past a dirt drive and to the path in the woods connecting his house to Ciaran's.

As he strolled, he looked down at the dust, kicking up like tiny, swirling ghosts under his black boots. He watched the shadow of his lanky, but graceful frame as it raced over bushes, his shoulders hunched, but his gait more determined than necessary. He straightened. *There, that's better. Now I look tough, invincible even.*

He peered at emerald woods bordering the dirt path ahead of him. Why didn't the whole damned world turn to dust? It hadn't rained for two weeks now. An Irish summer with no rain just didn't seem right. At the moment, lots of things didn't seem right. Like the cruel way Ciaran's mother just up and died the other day. How could it be that someone could be so alive and vibrant one day and cold and pallid the next?

Sweat tickled the tip of his nose and beaded over his lips. He swiped at it with the back of his hand and shook his head, causing small droplets to fling in every direction from his long bangs, just long enough to cover his eyes when he needed them to. The air stifled him. A full day of nothing but sun, left heat prickling over his skin.

He shifted his gaze down to his booted feet. No point watching where he went. After coming this way so many times, his body knew just where to go. Nearing the end of the path, he lifted his gaze back up to peer through verdant oaks and long shadows to see the outline of a battered barn.

Exposed cobblestones peeked out between cracks in plaster walls. A high-pitched, thatched roof told of better days. *How many times did I help Ciaran fix that bloody roof?* He spread a mischievous grin over his lips. Too many to remember.

He passed through a low stone wall in front of the barn and halted as a strange sound filled the air. Terns and jays chirped a familiar chorus overhead, but that was no bird. He turned in the dirt. It crunched below his boots while he listened, intent, gazing into the outside entrance of the broken building in front of him. The clear wail of sobs echoed off the barn's old walls and timbers. The faint silhouette of Ciaran, bent over the edge of a wooden pig stall, rushed at him. He whispered, "Ah shite, Ciaran…"

As he dashed into the barn, his heart thrummed in his ears. When he approached Ciaran, he slowed to a stop. Chickens clucked at his intrusion, but mournful sobs drowned them out. He looked Ciaran over, widening his eyes.

Mud splattered Ciaran's tan trousers and white, button-down shirt, covering wide shoulders, strong from working the farm all his life. He shook his shoulders over the pen, the waves of his blond hair bouncing around his face and over his ears.

Shannon's mind raced and his heart ached. *What should I do?* Well, he knew what he should do, but could he trust himself? He shouldn't touch him, should he? He never touched Ciaran. Touching him could set off things he shouldn't be thinking about. Maybe he should leave before Ciaran noticed him. *Yes, that's what I'll do…but still.* He let his gaze sweep over Ciaran's shorter, but well-built frame one more time. His heart beat faster, pounding out of control. He shifted from one booted foot to the next. His throat went dry, and he coughed, the sound echoing in the room.

Ciaran whipped around, straightening. As his gaze locked on Shannon, the sobs halted. "Shannon?" His lip trembled, betraying his emotion. He lunged forward, throwing his arms around Shannon's shoulders.

With a gasp, Shannon stumbled backward, then caught his footing. "C-Ciaran, wh-what are you doing?" His mouth dropped open and he stiffened, fisting his hands at his side. The heat of Ciaran's chest pressed against his, so close. His heart stuttered. Hot droplets spilled onto the nape of his neck, *Oh God, he's holding me.*

"I'm sorry, I can't help it." Ciaran buried his face into Shannon's neck and wept, tightening his hold.

"N-no wonder. You didn't cry at all at the bloody funeral yesterday." Shannon darted his gaze around the barn, forcing deep breaths through his lungs. He had to find a way to calm down.

"Father Brennan told me I had to be a man. I'm bloody eighteen now. But I can't. I just can't."

"That's nonsense. I'm a year older than you and if I lost my mother like that, I'd be bloody crying, too." *Ciaran needs me.* As Shannon closed his eyes, he slipped his arms around Ciaran's waist. The hardness of Ciaran's muscular chest thumped against his. Ciaran's intoxicating scent swarmed his senses. His heart quickened again, fear wrapping around him. He had to keep himself in check. Comfort him, but don't do anything more. *Don't think those sordid thoughts.* He brushed his hands in a timid trail up Ciaran's back. "Hush now. It'll be all right."

"Oh, Shannon, I-I know, but I can't stop," Ciaran said, his voice wavering. "I-I never told you what happened. How I found her." His breath hitched. "Her skin was so...gray. Her eyes, they were, they were...like the dead fish in the river." A fresh round of tears tumbled from his eyes.

"Don't think about such things. Try to remember how she was, how beautiful and green her eyes were." Shannon's vision blurred as his mind filled with the memory of Ciaran's delicate mother. Her eyes were so much like Ciaran's. His good looks definitely came from her.

"Without her, it's only me and Da. Th-thank God I have you. You're like a brother to me, you know."

A brother, maybe so, but I love him so much more than that. Shannon brushed his cheek against Ciaran's soft hair. He couldn't even think of a time when he didn't love him. Gentle breaths puffed against his neck while Ciaran cried, shivering over his skin, rushing heat into his groin, hardening his shaft. *God, no...It's not right to feel this way about Ciaran.* If anyone knew, he could be jailed or worse. He squeezed his eyes shut, savoring the feel of Ciaran in his arms. It was so good to finally have this moment, to smell Ciaran's sweet scent. He couldn't help it if being so close made his body hunger for more.

Shannon swallowed hard. *I have to think of something to say.* How could he calm him? How could he get Ciaran to release him before these improper feelings became known? He worried his lower lip. *Why did I have to walk by at this moment? Why didn't I leave just a little later?* Then he wouldn't be in this situation. He wouldn't have to be afraid of Ciaran feeling the arousal straining against his trousers. "Come on, that's enough. Let's go and see your da," he said in a husky voice, attempting to push him at the hips.

Ciaran's hold tightened.

God, please stop. Shannon wrinkled his forehead, his heart beating a frantic rhythm. He freed a long breath and wrapped his arms around Ciaran's waist again.

"My da...I think he's drowned himself in whiskey at the moment."

"Hush. He'll be okay." *Just a little more.* As Shannon tilted his head, he nuzzled into Ciaran's sandy-blond hair. If only he could run his fingers through its unruly strands. Was it truly as silky as it looked? He lifted a hand, but caught himself. *No, get away. Let go and get away from him.* Ciaran would be disgusted if he knew what he was feeling. Ciaran would shun him, wouldn't he? Just like everyone else did in their small, pathetic town. He'd learned his lesson. It's how everyone reacted after they'd found out he did those improper things with his male teacher, after all. "Uh, we'll be heating up the stew the neighbors brought over, tonight?"

Keeping his face hidden in Shannon's neck, Ciaran stopped crying. "Yes, I suppose." He held steady to Shannon's shoulders.

Shannon brushed his cheek over Ciaran's hair, breathing in the exquisite scent. As he closed his eyes, he drew Ciaran closer, trailing a slow circle over Ciaran's back. Only for a minute, a few seconds worth of bliss couldn't hurt. He could allow himself a tiny smidgen of what his heart begged for. His breathing became heavy.

With a lift of his head, Ciaran peered into his face. "Shannon?" He slowly spread a sly grin over his lips, as if thinking Shannon was playing some sort of joke on him.

As Shannon opened his eyes, he gazed deeply into Ciaran's face, raw desire filling every nerve ending of his body.

Gasping, Ciaran snapped his brows together. "What are you doing?" He blushed, searching Shannon's face.

Shannon shoved him away and stepped back, his chest squeezing. "I, uh, nothing."

"Doesn't seem like nothing." Ciaran's gaze focused on Shannon's groin.

Shite, the stiffy! Shannon rammed his hands into the front pockets of his trousers. Did Ciaran see? He cleared his throat, then glared at Ciaran. "It's nothing."

"Really now."

"Let's just bloody go." As heat flooded Shannon's cheeks, he turned and waited for Ciaran to follow. He ambled in silence with Ciaran behind him to the farmhouse, then looked it over. It was a smaller version of the barn, same cracked walls and dirty windows. He opened the door and stepped inside. The aroma of whiskey and cigarettes invaded his senses.

Ciaran flashed a knowing glance at him before brushing by. "Hey, Da, you ready for some supper?"

Mr. O'Kelly had thinning, brown hair and sat on a chair perched at a round, oak table in the center of the room. He lifted his head and dragged a blurry eye open to focus on Ciaran and Shannon. "What?"

"He's asking if you're ready for supper, Mr. O'Kelly. I think you might need a little tea as well." Shannon stood in front of Ciaran's father.

Mr. O'Kelly grunted, staring at the wall.

Shannon gestured for Ciaran to get started, while he went to a copper tea kettle by the fireplace. He shouldn't let Ciaran deal with his father in this state. It wasn't like Mr. O'Kelly to drink like this, but he supposed it was certainly understandable under the circumstances.

As he pottered around the small room, Shannon filled the tea kettle with water from a large pitcher at the kitchen dresser and set it in the range fireplace, centering the farmhouse. He built the fire up with a few more logs, then came back to stand with his back against a long butcher block table and watched Ciaran heat the stew.

After a few minutes, the whistle blew on the teakettle. Shannon grabbed it with a folded up towel and finished making Mr. O'Kelly and himself some tea. He brought mugs filled with steaming tea to the table and sat down across from Ciaran's father.

"Where were you, son?" Mr. O'Kelly lifted the mug to his mouth.

"In the barn with Shannon." Ciaran poured stew from a bowl into an iron pot.

"What were you doing in there?" Mr. O'Kelly took a sip of tea.

Shannon frowned. Mr. O'Kelly didn't need to know how upset Ciaran had been. "We were just tending to the animals."

"That's right, Da." Ciaran set the stew to cook in the fireplace. He walked back to the table and sat next to his father, dragging his chair a little closer to Shannon. "How's your tea, Da?"

"Fine, son."

The closeness of Ciaran's body engulfed Shannon. The embrace in the barn was toying with his head. He should focus on his surroundings to keep his mind off it, to keep from becoming aroused again. His gaze wandered to the fireplace inserted with iron pieces for cooking, tucked into the far wall. Two comfortable, but tattered green chairs sat in front of it and the familiar picture of Ciaran's parents on their wedding day hung above the mantle. His skin tingled as Ciaran's gaze focused on him, fixated on him. His own gaze caught on Mr. O'Kelly.

Mr. O'Kelly sipped his tea in silence, as if oblivious to any tension between the young men.

Shannon stole a peek at Ciaran, sitting so close.

Ciaran squirmed in his seat, studying Shannon.

What is going on behind those lovely green eyes? Shannon bit his lip. Something seemed different between them, or was he imagining it? "Ciaran, would you like some tea?" A distraction, that's what he needed.

"To be sure, that would be nice." Ciaran's intense gaze chased Shannon as he rose from the table.

Shannon fixed tea for Ciaran and came back to stand before him. His gaze met Ciaran's.

As Ciaran reached up and took the mug, his fingers rested over Shannon's.

With a gasp, Shannon yanked his hand from the mug.

Ciaran planted the mug on the table and lurched forward in his seat. "Are you okay, Shannon? Did you burn yourself?"

Shannon turned away and strode toward the kitchen dresser, opening the cabinet. "Um, no, I'm-I'm fine. I, uh, I'll get the stew since I'm up." He winced, struggling not to make a bigger deal out of his reaction. Ciaran's touch shook him more than it should. It was all too much, after the embrace in the barn.

"What's got you all hot and bothered?" Ciaran wore a mischievous grin.

Shannon fumbled through white, ceramic bowls, almost dropping one in his haste to bring them to the fireplace.

"N-nothing."

"Ah, come on, tell me." Ciaran shifted toward Shannon.

Shannon drew a deep breath and counted in his head, *one, two, three*. "I said, nothing." He forced himself to continue the deep breaths, attempting to calm the butterflies fluttering in his stomach. Ciaran had really got to him this time.

"Shannon—"

"Let him be, Ciaran." Mr. O'Kelly shifted and focused on his son.

Ciaran pouted.

Shannon found a ladle and poured the stew into bowls. If a simple embrace flustered him so, what would a kiss or a touch in the right place do to him? A shiver raced down his spine and lodged in his groin. *Don't think about it, not yet anyway. I'll have an evening to myself when I get home. Then my imagination can go wherever it wants.* He went back to the table and set a bowl with a tin spoon next to it, in front of Ciaran and another in front of Mr. O'Kelly.

Ciaran gazed up as if to question Shannon.

As Shannon glanced at Ciaran, he left to get his own supper. When he came back, he took a seat opposite Ciaran. He didn't want an errant connection of their bodies again. He stared down into his stew. *Just eat, Shannon.*

Ciaran leaned over the table with a spoonful of stew raised to his mouth. "Shannon, if you're not bloody eating, I know something's troubling you." He wrinkled his forehead.

"I'm not troubled." Shannon looked down at his stew and curled his lips into a faint grin. He shook his head once. Ciaran was a persistent bastard.

As he washed his stew down with some tea, Mr. O'Kelly leaned toward his son. "I said to let him be."

"But something's—"

"I'm not troubled." Shannon looked directly at Ciaran, letting a wide grin play over his face.

Ciaran smiled. "Sure you're okay?"

"Yeah." Shannon picked up his spoon, dipped it in his stew and shoveled it into his mouth.

"Mmm, this is very good stew. Almost as good as your mother's," said Mr. O'Kelly.

Shannon glanced at Ciaran. Would the reference to his dead mother upset him again? How would he respond? A clink sounded on the floor next to him and his gaze darted to Mr. O'Kelly.

Mr. O'Kelly peered down in his lap. His spoon rested on the floor by his feet. His face was slack, his lips parting.

"Yes, Da, she did make really good stew, didn't she?" Ciaran offered a sad smile. The fading light through the windows sparkled in his eyes as they filled with tears.

Shannon's heart ached for Ciaran. What could he do to make his grief lessen? He hated sitting here helpless, just watching Ciaran's sorrow eat away at him.

Mr. O'Kelly picked up his spoon. "Shannon, I need you to do something for me. That is, if you're able."

"Whatever it is, I'd be happy to, I'm sure." Shannon rested his forearms on the table. Maybe this was his chance. He could finally do something to help them. After all, Mr. O'Kelly was more like a father to him than his own father was.

"You see, there is this locket that belonged to my wife. It's a family heirloom of sorts and she really wanted it to be given to her sister. She, unfortunately, couldn't be here for the funeral with all that's going on. I'm afraid to send it through the post. Someone might steal it and I don't feel right sending Ciaran alone." Mr. O'Kelly glanced at his son. "Not with the Black and Tans all around." He released a heavy sigh. "Also, I don't want you taking the rail with all the problems there with the war. Some trains aren't running. Some rail workers won't transport munitions or British soldiers." He glanced between Shannon and Ciaran. "So, you'll have to take Missy and the cart."

Shannon nodded and shifted forward, fixating on Mr. O'Kelly. He'd heard plenty about the war, but it still seemed so far away from them. "Oh...and where does this sister live?"

"In Dublin—"

"Da. You mean crazy Aunt Iona?"

"Uh, yes, I suppose that is who I mean." Mr. O'Kelly dropped his spoon into his bowl.

Ciaran jiggled his leg with obvious excitement. "Shannon, can you go? Could you leave tomorrow?" He sat with his stomach flush against the table.

"Um, well, I suppose so." Shannon dropped his gaze to his lap. "It's not like my family would miss me any." They'd probably be happy to have him gone for a little while.

"Oh stop, they would, too." Ciaran's whole face lit up. "Shannon, this will be quite an adventure. Please, tell me you can leave in the morning. Please."

Shannon glanced at the table and thought for a minute. All of a sudden Ciaran's grim world seemed a little less grim. A trip to Dublin would be like a dream come true for him. They'd always wanted to see the city and they were finished harvesting most of the potatoes. He leaned further forward and looked directly into Ciaran's eyes. "Yes. Let's leave in the morning, first thing."

That evening, Shannon lay restless on his back in his bed. The heat from the day still lingered and he'd gone to bed in only his underwear.

His mother's muffled footsteps clopped out in the hallway from the heavy shoes she liked to wear. Why wouldn't she just go to sleep? Need built into a raging hunger inside his body. If she would just go to bed, he could let himself submit to it.

The slow creak of the door on the far wall filled the silence of his bedroom. Sighing, he turned his head to peer at it.

A soft glow illuminated the darkness from an oil lamp his mother held in her hand. She stepped forward, her long black hair spilling down over her shoulders, covering her bosom and white nightgown. "Shannon, dear, are you all right?"

"Yes, Ma. You know I am. You don't have to keep checking on me." He let out a loud exhale and turned his attention to the timbers in the ceiling.

"Don't use that tone of voice on me." She strolled through the room, sweeping the lamplight over its contents, his oak wardrobe and matching dresser, and over the foot of his mattress, across a dark, rumpled quilt. "I can't help wanting to tuck in my only child still living at home." The light stopped and headed toward him.

"I'm not a child. I'm a full-grown man now."

"Not until you marry and get out of this house like your sisters did." Her voice was sharp.

He groaned. "Stop it, Ma. I'm tired. I want to get some sleep before the trip tomorrow."

She stepped to his bedside and placed a hand on his cheek. She winced. "You bloody behave yourself now when you get to Dublin."

He twisted his head away from her. He knew what she meant. She didn't want him having any of those sinful urges she'd tried so hard to beat out of him, with the help of the town priest.

As she leaned over, she gave him a light kiss on the cheek.

"Goodnight, son."

"Goodnight."

She turned and left, shutting the door with a click.

He rolled to his side and looked out the small window into the moonless night. Was the constant checking she did really because she cared or was she just suspicious? It must be the latter. She was as suspicious as everyone else in the town. He wasn't right. Something was drastically wrong with him. He was tainted somehow, turned into a monster.

He stared off into the dark room, his mind filling with the O'Kellys. He let a faint smile creep over his lips. They were the only people who didn't fear him or view him differently after his affair with his teacher. *Mr. Flannigan.* His heart ached. What ever happened to him? He'd just disappeared without a word after they'd been exposed.

At first, he hadn't known what to think the first time his teacher kissed him. But it had awakened something inside him. He'd known for certain right then that he was different. All the strange feelings he'd always had made sense. In truth, he'd liked being with him, looked forward to it, asked for it even.

But then Father Brennan found out and tarnished his name, made even his parents think he was a monster. And the confessions, hours and hours of them denouncing everything he'd done, everything he'd felt. Was the priest right? Was he unholy?

But his beautiful friend could never know these things. *No, Ciaran will be repulsed if he knows.*

*Ciaran...*As he closed his eyes, he imagined himself in the barn again. Ciaran's muscular body pressed against his. His friend's faint breath teased the sensitive skin on his neck. He let out a soft moan, his cock hardening at the vision.

He rolled onto his back, reaching his hand under the covers to unbutton his underwear, then down between cotton and skin, into velvety black curls. Stroking lightly over his burgeoning erection, his need rose to a raw edge. Yes, the embrace in the barn definitely gave him something to think about for a very long time.

He took his other hand up and under the undergarment to his chest and teased a nipple into a hard nub, making his back arch while the delicious sensation rippled from his chest to his groin. A quiet pulse of pleasure rocked him. His cock ached for more. He pulled his hand off for a moment and spit an ample amount of saliva in it. Resuming his motions, he stroked with a slick and steady palm on himself.

Normally when he did this, he rushed. But tonight was special. He wanted to draw it out. He would make his body feel every second of his fantasy. His memories blazed with new sensations, new visions of Ciaran.

As he imagined his lovely friend pressed against him, he smelled him on his skin. Ciaran lowered his body slowly, sensually, sliding nimble fingers down his stomach until his lips met his erection. A mouth closed over his cock, sucking hard. The flicking of a tongue raced along his shaft. Pleasure seared through him. He freed a sharp gasp, tightening his hand and jerking his strokes. His palm became that beautiful mouth.

A low moan escaped him. He covered his mouth with his free hand to stifle it. He didn't need his mother hearing him. On impulse, he pushed two fingers past his lips and sucked. His tongue circled and flicked, mimicking the motions he'd use on Ciaran's shaft if given the chance. Ciaran's urgent moans filled his ears. The relentless thrusts of hips played in his mind.

He slid his fingers out of his mouth as a soft moan floated on his breath. He brought his slickened fingers down behind him and opened his legs. Tilting to one side, he reached the slippery fingers into the back opening of his underwear, and into his crevice. He circled his entrance in quick movements, while continuing to pump his cock with fast jerks of his hand.

A spasm shivered through his body. He was close. The tension in his groin hummed. His sensitivity heightened to a dangerous level. Slowing the pumps over his cock, he focused his attention on the fingers poised for entry. He pushed one in and another and circled, finding the internal spot that had pushed him over the edge so many times before. Sliding his fingers over it again and again, his body shook. Just a few more times and he'd surrender to the release beckoning him.

He drove feverish thrusts into his palm while his fingers pumped inside him. His sac grew tight. Urgent, soft gasps and the rustling of sheets filled the room with the raw edge of his climax. An intense sensation of pleasure melded from two points, causing an exquisite eruption over his hand. His teeth clenched and his toes curled, as he struggled to quiet his cries. Sumptuous contractions pulsed through him. He whimpered, "Ciaran..."

When it slowed, he lay panting in sweat-drenched sheets and snuck the hand up from his waning cock to lick the seed from it. He spread a devious grin over his lips. His mother would be obsessed with cleaning the sheets after he left tomorrow. Her little monster was busy doing those things again. As if other young men his age didn't do this. Well, he was sure they did, even Ciaran must.

He visualized the very pleasant sight of it. Except those poor young men didn't really know how it could be done. How it was done after having the unfortunate experience of having an older man teach them the many ways men can pleasure each other.

CHAPTER TWO
CIARAN

Ciaran blinked tired eyes while he stood in front of his house, busying himself with packing the small, horse-drawn cart. *I'm going to Dublin.* It would take two days, but so what. He was still going to Dublin. He quirked his lips in a quick grin. The morning sun warmed the top of his scally cap, filtering through to his hair, and the birds provided a symphonic melody floating overhead in the trees.

While he set pillows atop folded wool blankets, Shannon's behavior in the barn flooded his mind, the embrace, the look. What sort of a look was it anyway? It reminded him of something he'd read in one of his mother's romantic poetry books. And Shannon had a hold on him like one of the women he'd dated.

He strode over to bales of hay, piled at the side of the barn, picked one up and brought it to the cart. Although Shannon's behavior disturbed him, something else bothered him, too. It had forced him to confront Shannon yesterday. *Did I want something more from him, more than a comforting hug? No, that's absurd. Stop thinking about it. I'd just been upset is all.*

He threw the hay in the back of the cart and strode off to grab his suitcase, sitting by the door of the house. But Shannon had a stiffy, didn't he? Or was it just the shadows playing a trick on him? He frowned. It was hard to tell. Though, it wouldn't be the first time. He'd noticed Shannon getting a stiffy around him before.

He grinned. Damn, Shannon got more stiffies than anyone he knew. He tossed his suitcase into the cart and watched while it bounced on the pillows and landed next to a crate filled with food he'd packed earlier and his discarded jacket and waistcoat. It would be a hot day again.

As Ciaran patted down the blankets, he caught movement out of the corner of his eye.

Shannon strode out from the path connecting their houses, carrying a stuffed, white pillowcase, his dark linen shirt rolled up at the sleeves and tucked into his trousers, which were held up by braces. His boots clopped along as he walked.

Turning his attention to Shannon's gait, Ciaran smiled. He was always trying to look so tough. "Shannon, are you ready?"

Shannon ambled over and patted the hindquarters of the small, brown horse attached to their cart before coming to Ciaran's side. He peered into the back of the cart while tossing his pillowcase into it. "What's all this then?"

"Well, I packed us some bread and cheese, a few apples and some pickles in case we get hungry. And just in case we decide not to stay at an inn, I packed some blankets and pillows." Ciaran nodded once with a wide grin on his face. He'd made sure they were prepared for anything out there.

"Good God, Ciaran, you'd think we'd be traveling through the bloody wilderness with all that stuff. What about the money your da gave you? He didn't want us sleeping outside, remember?" Shannon gave Ciaran's hat a light ruffling.

Ciaran ducked out of his touch. "Uh, I know, but I sort of

feel it'd be wrong to use it. I thought maybe we could save it and get something special for him." He deserved it after everything he'd been through.

"Absolutely not, you know as well as I, there are bloody Black and Tans out on the road. How would you feel if that precious locket of your ma's got stolen? Or even worse, how would your da feel if you got killed?"

Hanging his head, Ciaran studied the dirt. Shannon always thought the worst would happen in every situation.

"No, he wants us staying close to the main roads and safe inside at night. That is what I promised him and that is what we'll do." Shannon huffed.

"Shite, Shannon, you're always doting over me like a bloody mother hen. You and my ma, when she was alive." Ciaran lowered his voice to a barely audible whisper, "Fine, then." He was a man now and people should start treating him that way.

"What was that?" Shannon dropped his head low to peer into his face.

Ciaran flared his nostrils, glaring at Shannon. "I said *fine*. But we're going into town before we leave, so I can get a book for the trip." Shannon hated going into town, but too bad. It would be a long trip and a book would definitely help.

Sighing, Shannon absently kicked at a rock. "Can't we just go? I'm sure you can pick up a book in the first town we get to."

"Oh, come on, you'll survive. If you'd just talk to people in town, maybe they'd see you're not so bloody terrifying after all." Ciaran grinned. Why did Shannon always have to pretend to be so mean all the time? He was scaring people, that much he knew. He also knew Shannon wasn't mean at all. In fact, he was sweet and caring when he wanted to be. "That and cut your hair." Though, he kind of liked Shannon's hair. The color was so dark, it shined blue when he wasn't wearing his scally cap.

"Hey, there is nothing wrong with my feckin' hair. I like it," Shannon said with a smile.

"Maybe if you'd wear some normal clothes and cut your hair, you'd get a girlfriend." Ciaran curved his lips into a playful grin. He'd never seen Shannon even look at a girl, which made teasing him about it all the more fun. He climbed up onto the seat of the cart.

Frowning, Shannon said, "You know nobody would bloody want me." He slowly followed Ciaran onto the cart.

Ciaran scoffed. He hated it when Shannon said things like that about himself. Shannon was a looker and was completely daft about it. "Why do you insist on reproaching yourself so?" He shook his head. "Ah well, good thing then. I can keep you all to myself." He grabbed the reins, lifted his arms, and flicked his wrists once. "Let's go, Missy." The horse lurched forward and broke into a trot.

Shannon chuckled. In a soft voice, he said, "You have more of me than you know, my dear friend."

With his brows furrowed, Ciaran studied him. What did that mean, exactly?

Mr. O'Kelly stepped out from the threshold of the farmhouse.

Waving, Ciaran said, "Bye, Da." He glanced at Shannon, his heart aching just a little. He knew he'd always have him by his side. Shannon didn't need to say things like that.

Mr. O'Kelly smiled and waved at them while they rode by.

As soon as they approached the town borders, Ciaran glanced at Shannon. How would he behave? Would he behave?

Shannon pulled his cap down low, letting his dark bangs fall over his eyes, and hung his head.

Ciaran glanced at the few straggly shops with living quarters above them, and cobblestone houses strewn on either side of the dirt road, then shifted in his seat and whispered. "Relax." He looked out over the street. Half a dozen people strolled the pavements under the warm morning sunlight and canopies of the occasional oak, nodding as they passed one another. Mr. Murphy, the pub owner, stared in his direction. He nodded at him and tipped his hat, smiling.

Mr. Murphy scoffed and continued walking.

Ciaran bumped Shannon's elbow. "Don't pay him any mind." He was a drunk anyway.

With his lips thinned, Shannon fisted his hands.

Ciaran stopped the horse and cart at the cream, plaster walls of a home turned bookstore on the ground floor. He climbed down from the cart and affixed the reins, then walked inside with Shannon following. He made a beeline past Mr. O'Connell, the bookkeeper, to an aisle of the store containing the classics. He looked up and down the rows. Which one should he choose?

Slouching beside him, Shannon tapped his foot on the hardwood floor.

"Relax," Ciaran whispered again, leaning close.

"He's staring at me. Hurry up." Shannon breathed in deeply, closing his eyes.

"What are you looking for, lad?" Mr. O'Connell, a balding man with an ivory tobacco pipe dangling out of his mouth, peered at them.

"*The Picture of Dorian Gray*. You have it?" Shannon glared at the man and smirked.

Mr. O'Connell scowled. "That's been banned. It's bloody indecent, it is."

Sniggering, Ciaran turned slowly toward Shannon. "Shannon, don't tease the man." He came in close, whispering. "My ma read that story...said it was good. Should have been a classic. I'd love to find it."

Shannon hung his head. In a low voice he said, "They banned it because they say that Oscar Wilde was a homosexual. They say the book could taint your young mind." He flashed his eyes at Ciaran, then studied him.

Ciaran scoffed. "Oh, bloody hell." He shook his head, chuckling, then his gaze caught on *Moby Dick*. "Oh, yes, I'll take that one." He reached up and grabbed a book off the shelf. He held it out for Shannon to appreciate.

"Of course." Shannon fingered the book's hardbound cover. "Maybe I'll read it when you've finished."

Ciaran grinned and gave him a deliberate nod. "Of course." Maybe they'd even read it together. He didn't mind reading out loud for Shannon after they had their supper and were in for the night. He stepped to an old, ornate wooden desk by the door, where Mr. O'Connell waited.

Shannon followed, keeping his gaze on his booted feet and his head lowered, lingering in the background.

"Oh, that's a good book, lad." Mr. O'Connell smiled at Ciaran, then glared at Shannon, his smile dropping.

"Hope so, we're going on a trip to Dublin. I'll be needing something to read while we travel." Ciaran paid for the book, then glanced at Shannon.

Shannon held his hands behind his back, his head so far forward that his scally cap hid his face.

Ciaran twisted his lips. *What on Earth is wrong with him? He's not paying any attention.* Ciaran poked him in the ribs.

As Shannon lifted his head, he narrowed his eyes and met the gaze of the older man straight on. "Uh, what?"

"Pay attention. I was just telling Mr. O'Connell here of our plans to go to Dublin." Irritation littered Ciaran's voice and he pinched his lips.

Shannon stole a quick peek at Ciaran, then glared at Mr. O'Connell and straightened himself up. Leaning over the desk, he put one hand on the edge and bent forward, closing the gap between him and Mr. O'Connell. In a low growl, he said, "That's right, we are." He watched, with a smirk, while Mr. O'Connell took a step back behind the desk.

Ciaran dropped his jaw, staring at Shannon for a moment. *No wonder everyone treats him so badly.* As he snatched the book off the desk, he turned for the door. "Come on." He stomped outside, leaving Shannon in his wake, to climb up onto the cart. He took the reins.

Shannon trotted from the bookstore to the cart and climbed into the seat.

Ciaran turned to sit sideways, glaring at him. His words were sharp. "No wonder people are scared of you, going around behaving like that. Why do you always have to act so bloody tough? You know, people can't believe it when I tell them how kind you really are. I don't understand you sometimes, not at all."

Shannon bowed his head in silence. His fingers wrestled with one another in his lap. "Can't we just get on the road and forget about this feckin' place, this life, for a little while?"

Ciaran studied him, his heart aching. He wanted more than anything to take away the pain he saw in his eyes every day. Could he comfort him here? He scanned around him. *No, too many people. Shannon doesn't like to be touched anyway. Except yesterday in the barn...* His heart warmed.

Ciaran gazed out at the scenery around him. The forest gave way to rolling, green hills as the sun spilled its rays low in the early evening sky. The scent of dry grass permeated the air. Visions of the day raced through his mind, chatting, reading, napping, and stopping to eat the food he'd packed on the roadside. Thank God he'd brought that food. Shannon had seemed ravenous after a few hours in the cart. He scanned the horizon. A small town off in the distance closed in on them.

"Ciaran, let's find lodgings up ahead there," Shannon said, ticking his head.

"To be sure, but nothing too fancy. I'd like to save at least some of this money Da gave me." Ciaran softened his voice, pain squeezing his chest. "It was supposed to be for their twentieth wedding anniversary." He closed his eyes tight and clenched the muscles of his jaw, trying to shut the memory out and keep the tears at bay.

"Are you all right?" Shannon turned toward him.

"Yeah, fine." Ciaran breathed through the lump climbing up his throat. Shannon didn't need to see him crying again.

Shannon kept his gaze affixed to him for a moment, his brows knitting, then straightened on the seat.

Ciaran directed the horse to pull up in front of the only inn he could see along the main street. He looked it over. A roof of dark shingles sat atop walls three stories high made of gray stones. White frames bordered the small windows, set in rows on each level and moss crept up the corners in small cracks.

"Uh, I'll get us a room then?" Shannon climbed out of the cart.

Ciaran slipped his hand into his front pocket and pulled out a wad of notes. He handed them to Shannon. "Here, and I have more. I'll bring our things in." He jumped down to the dirt and tended to the horse.

After leaving the cart, Shannon stuffed the notes in his front pocket and passed through a small door, painted blue.

When the horse was secured in a stable, Ciaran waltzed into the inn, holding his suitcase in one hand and Shannon's stuffed pillowcase in the other and found Shannon at a desk in the center of the lobby where a woman sat, writing in a ledger. His gaze roamed over the plain interior. Dark wood paneling lined the walls and an accent table sat against the far wall with a brass lamp centered on it. The stench of tobacco, beer and greasy food poured out of the dark tavern just across from him. "Good evening."

The woman looked up at him with large, brown eyes. She puffed a lock of red hair out of her face and gave him a forced smile. "Oh, you must be the friend?"

Shannon shifted his stance, frowning. In a soft voice, he said, "I-I'm only getting one room, s-so you can save some money." He peeked at Ciaran. "I-I told her we were, we're friends."

"Good." Ciaran looked Shannon over. He seemed tense. Why? "Yes, I'm the friend."

"Okay, then." She tugged out a drawer and came back up with a brass key in her hand. She held it out.

"Thanks." Shannon grabbed the key from her.

"You'll find it upstairs, second floor. The number's on the key," she said.

Shannon turned around and stood there. He parted his lips and the hand holding the key shook. He shoved his other shaky hand into his pocket, pulled out the remainder of the money and held it out.

"Thanks." Ciaran took the money and stuffed it into his front pocket, staring at Shannon's trembling hands. What was wrong with him? "Are you okay?"

"I'm fine." He huffed and thrust both hands into the front

pockets of his trousers. "Um, this way." He tilted his head toward the stairs.

The pair climbed a short flight of stairs to their room. Shannon unlocked and opened the door.

Ciaran looked into the room. Two beds rested against each wall and a shaky wooden table sat between them. A Tiffany lamp sat on the nightstand. A few cracks littered the plaster in the walls, but otherwise the room looked decent and clean.

They entered the room and raced for the beds.

Ciaran rushed to the far bed sitting under the room's only window. "I'll take this one." He threw his suitcase to the top of the bed. It would be cooler by the window.

Shannon frowned his displeasure. "Figures you'd take the one with the window. You'd better be prepared to have that thing wide open all bloody night."

Ciaran slid the small window open. "There, you satisfied?"

Grunting, Shannon stepped to the bed on the opposite wall and dropped his stuffed pillowcase on top of it. He unpacked a few items while Ciaran did the same. When he finished, he turned around. "I'm hungry."

Sighing, Ciaran set his suitcase on the floor at the foot of his bed. "Christ, Shannon, you eat enough for both of us." He went to reopen the door, turned around and grinned. "Well, let's get something to eat then." They had the rest of the night to enjoy.

CIARAN STROLLED into the stuffy tavern first and Shannon followed. "Jaysus, it's bloody crowded in here." He scanned through waitresses scurrying and patrons ambling about chattering, for an open table.

"There's a table over there." Shannon pointed to a table with one bench seat in the corner.

Ciaran nodded and strode over to the table with him close behind. He sat down next to a wood-paneled wall.

Sighing, Shannon took a seat beside him. He rapped his knuckles on the ragged table surface and jerked his knee up and down.

Ciaran watched him. Something was definitely bothering him. He looked like he would jump clear out of his skin if it wasn't attached. He should probably try to lighten whatever was going on inside him.

A pretty, young, blonde woman approached the table and looked them over. "What'll you have and make it quick. We're busy tonight, if you can't tell."

"Ah, I'll have a pint," Shannon said, rapping his knuckles harder.

"Me, too."

"All right, how about supper?" She tapped her pencil on her hip.

"What's good here?" Ciaran asked.

The waitress sighed as if they were taking too much of her time. "Most people like the shepherd's pie."

"Well, I'll have that then," Ciaran said.

"Same for me."

The waitress nodded and trotted off.

Ciaran leaned over to him. "She was pretty, wasn't she?" Maybe Shannon would finally have something nice to say about a woman. It was odd that he'd never even dated one. Maybe that terrible rumor about him and the teacher kept everyone from allowing their daughters to date him. It was sad, really.

Shannon wrinkled his nose. "I suppose. She was bloody rude though."

Ciaran shifted in his seat to look directly at him. "Do you ever find women you like?"

Shannon focused on his hand, still rapping on the table surface, and thinned his lips.

The waitress returned, setting pints in front of the young men. Pausing, she smiled at Ciaran before leaving.

Shannon peered at her and scoffed. He brought his beer to his lips and gulped down a good portion of it, set the pint down, then raised it to his mouth again and gulped the rest of it down.

Grinning, Ciaran's gaze followed the tilt of Shannon's pint. "Thirsty, aye?" He knew what Shannon was up to. He was drowning whatever was bothering him in beer. He'd seen it before. They were on an adventure. Maybe he'd join him.

Shannon's rapping on the table surface renewed along with the jerking of his knee. "You could say that." He held up his empty glass, catching the eye of the waitress. After a few minutes, another beer was set in front of him.

Ciaran watched the incessant jiggling, then sipped his beer. What the hell was going on? He could barely take any more. "Shannon, stop it, you're making me barmy."

"What? Why?"

Ciaran covered Shannon's hand with his own and looked directly into his eyes. "What on Earth is bothering you? We are on an adventure here. You can bloody relax." If this was the only thing that would stop it, then this is what he would do.

Shannon stared wide-eyed at their hands covering each other on the table and swallowed hard. "N-nothing's bothering me, really."

Ciaran brought a leg over the bench, straddling it, and scooted up close to him, putting him between Shannon's legs. His hand stayed over Shannon's, feeling the heat on his palm. Somehow, his touch was making Shannon less tense, and

Shannon wasn't shying away from it, like he usually did. Was it because of yesterday in the barn?

"Um, wh-what are you doing?" Shannon's gaze stayed on the hands in front of him.

Ciaran's gaze snagged on an object in Shannon's hair. "You have something in your hair. I wonder how long it's been there?" Ciaran reached up and plucked it off his head.

Shannon licked his lips and closed his eyes for a second, breathing heavily. As he opened his eyes, Ciaran shoved the object in his face.

"Look, it's bleedin' bark. You must have carried it all the way from home," Ciaran said, chuckling. He reluctantly removed his hand from Shannon's. He shouldn't do that too long in public. People might get the wrong idea, even though they weren't in Drimnagh anymore. He glanced around him, then inched closer to Shannon, his heart fluttering. *What is this feeling?* Being close to Shannon felt good. Before yesterday, he'd never been able to get close to him. Maybe it was the grief, maybe the feeling was comfort. He'd known Shannon ever since he could remember. He let his gaze roam over Shannon. He was so familiar.

Shannon's nonstop rapping and jerking ceased. He slowly brought his gaze from their hands to Ciaran's face and down to his lips, parting his own.

He's looking at me in the way he sometimes does. Ciaran released a soft gasp, softening his expression, letting his jaw grow slack, gazing deeply into his gray eyes. Shannon had the most beautiful eyes. Something stirred inside him, and heat shivered over his skin. His heart fluttered. "Shannon." His voice was a husky whisper.

Shannon blinked, then widened his eyes. "Um, I-I need to go and take a piss." He jerked up and jumped from the bench, then fled toward the door.

Ciaran scanned around him at the other patrons in the bar. *Shannon had looked at me like that in the barn. Why is he doing that? Why does it make me feel so strange?*

Ciaran fingered the edge of his pint. His relationship with Shannon was changing, wasn't it? It was as if an unspoken boundary had been broken, and he was comfortable touching him. In fact, he wanted to touch him and be close to him. It felt good. After all, his mother just passed and he needed the physical contact, right? That was all it was. Why had Shannon always been so adverse to it anyway? It was always such a bizarre trait of Shannon's, so unnatural. But for some reason, he was just like that.

The waitress walked up to the table carrying two plates of shepherd's pie. "Got your food here."

Ciaran smiled at her.

CHAPTER THREE
SHANNON

Shannon stomped outside and behind the building, letting his back rest against it. His head reeled with questions. Why did Ciaran sit so close to him? Why was Ciaran suddenly touching him all the time? And how the hell was he going to sleep in the same room with him tonight? Holding up his fists to his temples, he shut his eyes tight against his frustration. He'd just have to stick with his plan, get drunk and pass out.

With a shake of his head, he stepped into an outdoor privy and used the toilet. When he finished, he turned and halted. *One, two, three.* He tugged the door open, walked back to the tavern and stepped inside.

Damned Ciaran was carrying on with that waitress again. Heat pinched his insides. It was only a matter of time before he'd lose him forever to marriage. He shuddered. How alone and destitute would he be then? He strode to the table.

As the waitress gave Ciaran one last flirtatious smile, she sauntered away.

Shannon let a rush of air free from his chest.

"Food's here." Ciaran looked up.

Shannon took a seat at the end of the bench. He wouldn't sit too close to him this time. "Yeah, looks good." He gulped down his beer and held up the empty glass for another refill.

The two ate in silence for a moment. The waitress returned with Shannon's pint.

Shannon peered up at her, noticing her flirtatious smile at Ciaran. "Keep them coming." He huffed. She needed to get back to work. Wasn't it supposed to be bloody busy in here?

The waitress placed her hands on her hips. "Intend on getting bollocksed tonight, aye?"

Shannon glanced at Ciaran. "Yeah, well, we're on a bloody adventure, right, Ciaran?"

"Yeah, I hear you two are on your way to Dublin. That would be an adventure," the waitress said.

Ciaran gazed at her, smiling. "Keep them coming for me, too."

"Sure thing." The waitress trotted off into the crowd.

Ciaran shoved his plate close to Shannon's and slid in next to him, hips and shoulders touching. He shoveled mashed potatoes, ground beef and carrots, all held together with rich gravy into his mouth. The gravy kept smearing on his lips and he'd lick it off, or just not notice and it would stay there.

Shannon stared at him. He wanted to wipe off the spots of gravy but he knew he couldn't, so he focused on his food. *Just eat, Shannon.*

AFTER A FEW MORE BEERS AND conversation, Ciaran paid the tab and they both left the pub. They walked next to each other through the lobby, their gait unsteady.

Ciaran bumped into the table by the door. The lamp jostled

and tipped. He lunged forward and fumbled with it, caught it, and set it upright again. "Damn it, Shannon, help me out here, will you?"

"What do you want me to do?" Shannon said with a slur. He turned a little too quickly.

"Come here." Ciaran waved his hand at him.

Shannon stumbled to Ciaran, weaving in front of him. He stared at him. He hadn't the foggiest why Ciaran would request such a thing.

Ciaran straightened and wrapped a sloppy arm around Shannon's waist. "Help me." His voice echoed in the small lobby. He dropped his head to Shannon's chest.

The sudden heat of Ciaran's heavenly body pressed against Shannon pulled him out of his stupor, his senses reeling. The sweet scent of Ciaran floated into his nose. His pulse raced and a shiver worked down his spine. His breath caught, then he cleared his throat and regained his composure. At least the beer dulled some of his senses. He threw an arm around Ciaran's shoulders and assisted him up the stairs.

They stumbled every few steps, swore a bit, leaned on each other, and maintained an uneven gait to their room.

Once inside, Shannon shoved Ciaran away from him.

With a gasp, Ciaran fell into the dark room on the floor on his hands and knees between the beds. A glow from the hallway light illuminated him.

Snickering, Shannon covered his mouth with the back of his hand.

Ciaran twisted his neck, straining to look at Shannon from the floor, glaring. "Thanks a lot, you bastard."

"Oh come now. It's sort of a nice view, with your bloody arse pointed at me." Shannon gasped, covering his mouth again. *What the bloody hell did I just say?* He rushed to straighten up and feigned a cough.

Ciaran plopped his behind on the floor and studied him, furrowing his brows, rubbing at his forehead.

Shannon's chest tightened and his heart pounded. All this physical contact and the beer was indeed making him say things he probably shouldn't say. *Too late now.* Would Ciaran notice, or was he too bollocksed?

Swaying, though still seated, Ciaran stared at the floor, biting his lower lip. He opened his mouth as if to speak and shut it again. He climbed up to standing, clicked the lamp on and fumbled with his shirt buttons.

After closing the door, Shannon ambled to the side of his bed. His fingers worked at his own buttons.

Ciaran glanced at him, then tugged his arms out of his shirt.

As a droplet of sweat meandered down Shannon's forehead, he wiped at it. Oh God, Ciaran was undressing, right next to him. The room sweltered around him while he tried not to watch and struggled to keep his eyes fixated on his own buttons.

As he stole a peek at Ciaran, he fully digested the sight of Ciaran's broad back stretching his underwear and exposed shoulders. His heart pattered at the way the muscles tucked into his small waist. What he'd give to run his tongue along the smooth, toned flesh. *Stop it, Shannon.* Desire washed over him in a torrent of need and heat rushed his groin, swelling his cock. How could he possibly take his trousers off now? Ciaran was sure to see it.

Ciaran dropped his trousers, leaving only the underwear, and took another quick glance at Shannon, his face scrunching up. He shrugged and pulled the covers down. As he positioned himself to climb into bed, he took a double take at his suitcase lying open on the floor behind the footboard. He went to it, bent over, and picked up his mother's locket. He rubbed it between his thumb and fingers, closing his eyes, then brought it with him while he climbed into his bed. As he slid only the white sheet over him, he turned onto his side toward the wall. "Hurry up, will you?"

Shannon rested his hands on the button of his trousers. How the hell and exactly when was he supposed to take them off? His erection strained against the inside of his underwear.

A loud, sorrowful sob filled the room.

Is he crying again? Shannon whirled around, staring at Ciaran.

Ciaran's shoulders shook while sobs wracked his body.

Rushing to him, Shannon sat on the edge of his bed. He placed a hand on Ciaran's side, his heart aching for him. He had to comfort him somehow. *This is impossible to watch.*

Ciaran rolled onto his back, seized Shannon around the shoulders, and yanked him down into a tight embrace. "It...hurts...Shannon," Ciaran said, through hitched breathing.

Immediate heat caught his breath. Ciaran's muscled chest pressed sensually against Shannon's, hardening his nipples. His senses flooded with the scent of Ciaran and the emotion of the embrace.

A few broken sobs escaped Ciaran. "Oh, Shannon, I-I could see her, the morning before she died. Sh-she made me breakfast, just like always. Why didn't I see it? Why couldn't I have known that it would be the last time I'd see her like that. Alive...not gray and dead."

Shannon struggled to free himself. *I have to get away from him. I don't know what to say. I have to get away from his beautiful body.* Wriggling and squirming, he shoved himself partway up, his face dangerously close to Ciaran's, arousal swarming inside him. He gazed deeply into Ciaran's sad, wet eyes.

Widening his eyes, Ciaran gasped.

He dropped his head downward, crushing his lips against

Ciaran's. As he closed his eyes and wrinkled his brows, he relished in the forbidden kiss, taking all he could from it, letting it soothe the longing in his soul.

Ciaran widened his eyes further, inside a dark veil of hair. Slowly, they closed again.

Shannon let the kiss linger, the passion inside him building. He parted his lips and brushed against Ciaran's mouth with an insistent tongue. As Ciaran parted his lips, he drove his tongue inside, deepening the kiss. His pulse hammered in his chest. A lustful fire ravaged every part of him. He couldn't think, didn't want to think, just wanted to feel. He tasted the part of Ciaran he'd never had, but always craved.

Mimicking Shannon's movements, Ciaran pressed their lips closer still, tangling his tongue with Shannon's.

Ciaran's kissing me back! He let out a soft moan into silky flesh. Ciaran clung to his torso, pulling him downward, a never-ending spiral into an obsession he no longer had any control over.

Ciaran attempted to pull Shannon's body over him.

No! Shannon popped his eyes open. He wouldn't do this to him. He wouldn't violate him this way. He wouldn't be like Mr. Flannigan. He thrust himself up to sitting at the edge of the bed and whirled around, turning his back on Ciaran. He slapped his hands over his face. "Oh God, Ciaran, I'm sorry," he said, "I'm so sorry." His voice rose in pitch and cracked. He jumped from the bed and rushed to the door, popped it open, then lunged into the hallway, slamming the door behind him.

Shannon stood in the hallway, panting, pressing his forehead against the wall next to the door of their room. His body trembled. *What have I done?* Ciaran would surely hate him now, wouldn't he? The door slowly creaked open. An unexpected warm pressure wrapped around his wrist. He peeked at the doorway.

Ciaran gazed back at him, his eyelids hooding, his pupils dilating. He brushed his tongue over his lips, then gave a light tug on his arm.

Shannon turned and walked, allowing Ciaran to tow him back into the room. Why was Ciaran being so kind after what he'd done?

Once inside, Ciaran hauled him back to his bed, keeping his grasp on Shannon's wrist. He sat on the edge, peered up at him and tugged him forward and down. "Do it again," he whispered.

Shannon's will broke. He wasn't sure about anything anymore. Except, somehow Ciaran wanted him. He slid his dark trousers down and kicked them off, helped by his free hand, his cock hardening once again. Fixating on Ciaran's green eyes, he climbed into the bed, under the sheet, next to a Ciaran's near naked body, only their thin undergarments between them.

He caressed Ciaran's muscular arm with his fingers, reveling in the toned curves he'd admired only with his eyes. He leaned down and placed a lingering kiss on his willing lips while sliding himself over him, between his legs. Feeling Ciaran's arousal and taut body below him was delicious. Apparently, Ciaran wanted him, too. He closed his eyes and tensed his brow for a moment while he took in the feel of it. It'd been so long since he had any contact with another human being, and he savored every second of it.

He rocked his hips against Ciaran in a slow rhythm, then gazed into his eyes. Ciaran did want him, right?

Moaning, Ciaran parted his lips.

Shannon kissed him, unhurried and deeply. Would Ciaran stop him? Would he change his mind? Ciaran's erection thrust up against him, matching his pace and quickening it, knotting pleasure in his gut.

Letting out a soft gasp, Shannon thrust his hips against him, taking sweet friction from him, sensation building. "Ciaran," he whispered, breathless, while he brushed his fingers up along Ciaran's cheek. As he trailed his wet mouth along Ciaran's jaw and down into his neck, soft moans escaped Ciaran.

Ciaran ground his hips into him as if craving more.

Skimming his hand down Ciaran's side, Shannon became lost in the sensation of the thin fabric covering a muscled chest. Was he in a dream? Could this really be happening? A wave of pleasure jolted through him as pressure ground down on his cock. "Yes." He freed a choked moan. It must be happening.

Quickly, Shannon licked his palm and brought it down into thin sheets, then unbuttoned Ciaran's fly. As his hand reached between them, beneath the thin fabric, a shiver coursed through Ciaran's body. He found Ciaran's solid cock with his expert hand and stroked it.

A sharp gasp escaped Ciaran and he arched his back.

Shannon stroked harder, faster over his erection, swirling the tip with his thumb.

Bucking, Ciaran, freed a loud groan.

Shannon slid his slick palm with ease over Ciaran's seeping cock. As he circled the head of his shaft, Ciaran shuddered.

"Shite, that feels so good," Ciaran said inside a husky breath.

Oh, how I love the reaction I get when I stroke and tease him. Shannon gazed into his beautiful face, his heart aching, sensitivity heightening in his shaft. Did Ciaran really desire him?

Ciaran shut his eyes tight.

Does Ciaran enjoy being with me? Or were Ciaran's eyes shut because he imagined himself with some village girl? Shannon winced. Oh no, was Ciaran just trying to appease him somehow? But Ciaran's moans and rocking hips made his insides hum with desire and he couldn't stop, not now. He craved even more. He wanted to go inside him, but that would be too much. Ciaran was still a virgin. He pressed his lips onto the soft skin of Ciaran's neck, losing himself in the intoxicating scent that haunted him for so long.

Ciaran writhed below him, becoming more frantic with each stroke, trembling and jerking. He flashed his eyes open and looked up at Shannon's face. "Shannon, I-I'm going to—" An urgent thrust impaled Shannon's hand as his body grew rigid with the force of his climax.

Hot seed spurted out over Shannon's fingers. Ciaran's sharp moans swept over his ears. He almost smiled, but his own release rushed to the surface, teetering at a raw edge.

Panting, Shannon dropped his forehead onto Ciaran's chest. He thrust hard against Ciaran's thigh, again and again. The tension coiled. His sensitivity heightened. He freed a loud gasp as his peak hit, shuddering. He clenched his teeth and his toes curled, release surging through him, spilling inside his undergarment, pulsing over and over in delicious waves. He cried out with the pure power of it.

As everything slowed, Shannon relaxed his body over Ciaran's. He lay on his chest with his hair stuck in patches to his face while sweat rivulets dripped down his lean body. He roamed his hand up Ciaran's side, giving it a slight tickle. Ciaran's slow breathing raised and lowered his head over his chest. How Ciaran's heartbeat soothed him. *Tonight, I had a taste of what I've wanted my whole life.*

"Shannon?"

"Yeah?"

"That felt good, didn't it?"

Shannon tugged Ciaran into a desperate embrace, pressing his face into his chest, adrift in a hopeless sea of agonizing want, torturous guilt and unwavering devotion. Of course, it felt good. It felt too good in every way. But it still wasn't right. It had to end here. He'd have to find some way to put Ciaran back into his fantasies and daydreams. The thought ripped him inside and left a gaping hole. Tears pooled in his eyes. He rebelled against them, stuffing his feelings deep inside. "Y-yeah, i-it did." He dragged himself up and removed his underwear, then wiped himself off with it and grabbed a new one out of his pillowcase.

Studying him, Ciaran lowered his brows. "You're not going to leave me in this mess, are you?"

"What do you mean?" Shannon slid the new long johns on and climbed into his bed, lying on his side, facing him. He lifted his head from his pillow.

Ciaran slid out from under the jumbled confusion of sticky sheets, hung his legs over the edge of the bed and sat up. He wiped himself with the sheets, then looked around him for a moment as if reviewing the situation one last time, stood and treaded to Shannon's bedside.

With wide eyes, Shannon watched Ciaran.

Ciaran bent over and placed a hand on Shannon's sheets.

"Wh-what are you doing?" Shannon blinked a few times.

"Sleeping with you." Ciaran lifted a leg onto the bed. "You didn't really expect me to sleep in that slop, did you?" He let a small chuckle rumble in his chest. He pulled the sheets down, then climbed into the bed in front of Shannon, turning on his side, back to him. He turned off the lamplight, a clicking sound echoing in the room, and everything went dark.

Ciaran shimmied close to Shannon, with his back to his chest, grabbed his arm and pulled it tight around his side.

With a soft sigh, Shannon closed his eyes. Yes, it felt good. He snuggled in and drifted off to sleep.

First, a muffled thud filled the room. Then a loud groan, followed by whispered swearing. Shannon fluttered his eyes open in slow motion, unsure of the noises infusing his ears. He peered into the room in a daze. Sleep had yet to fully surrender his senses.

Ciaran's blond head poked up from the bedside and he glared at him with green eyes. "What did you do that for?"

Shannon opened his eyes completely. The light filtering in through the window lit the back of Ciaran's hair, making a halo around his head. It captivated him for a second. How his Ciaran looked so much like an angel. He smiled. "Do what?"

"Well, you shoved me off the bed for one." Ciaran rubbed back and forth along one side of his head, as if soothing a lump.

Memories flooded Shannon's mind. He thrust his chest forward, sitting up, and sent a loud gasp echoing into the room. *Oh God, I'm a monster.* He finally did the thing he promised himself he would never do. Well, although he hadn't done the thing, what he had done was bad enough. He swallowed hard and fixated on the cracks in the wall in front of him. "I-I'm sorry, I-I must have been sleeping. Um, I kind of th-thrash around sometimes wh-when I sleep." He held himself perfectly still.

"Ah well, I suppose that would explain it then." Ciaran stood with care. As he did, he studied Shannon, then widened his eyes and blushed. "I-I suppose I'll get cleaned up and dressed." He stepped to his suitcase and fumbled with the mismatch of clothing, pulling out a new white shirt and underwear. He snatched his tan trousers from the floor and marched out of the door to the shared bathroom at the end of the corridor.

Shannon sat stiffly in bed until the whining sounds of water pipes snaked into the room. As he released a loud exhale, he allowed himself to relax. He must stay away. He must make things go back to how they were, no contact, nothing physical to tempt him again. A sharp pain pierced his chest at the thought of never being close to Ciaran again—never holding him, never caressing his smooth skin, never tasting him. He grabbed his legs and pulled them tight against his chest, dropping his forehead to his knees. He rocked forward and back. How could he have done that? He should know better.

Now real memories will torture my heart instead of mere daydreams and fantasies. He released a ragged sigh, tears stinging the corners of his eyes. He clenched his eyelids shut, pushing the tears back into a mental closet, back where they belonged.

After a few minutes, he calmed and lay down in the bed on his side with his arms drawn up, clutching sheets around him, waiting for Ciaran.

CHAPTER FOUR
CIARAN

Ciaran leaned against the back of the closed bathroom door. He held his breath, then let it escape in a long sigh. He gazed around the room at the sterile white porcelain and chrome fixtures.

His gaze caught his reflection in the small mirror and wondered at the young man whose innocence was lost in a drunken moment by his best friend. What exactly was it they did last night? He rounded his eyes as the memories rushed his mind. Shannon actually wanked him off and came on his leg. What the hell would he do that for? Why? How did something like that even start? Shame wrapped around his heart. How could he have knowingly pulled Shannon back to his bed like that? They were both male, they weren't queer, were they?

But men did do things like this, didn't they? What about Oscar Wilde? Except these things happened in a far-off world somewhere, not here, not with his best friend. But still, something stirred deep inside him. He'd gotten aroused. Why had his body reacted that way?

It had to be a stray incident. They'd both been drunk,

hadn't they? He'd needed someone and Shannon had been there, maybe a little too there, but there anyway. *Oh, but it felt so good, fantastic even. How can doing that with another male feel that good? Am I tainted somehow?* Though, at least it was with Shannon, his best friend. At least he knew him better than anyone, probably better than he knew himself.

He stepped to the bathtub and turned the chrome tap. As the water flowed, he errantly brushed his hand against his hardening cock. He looked down at himself, blinking. Good God, even the thought of what happened last night was enough to arouse him still. Would he ever view Shannon the same way again?

AFTER CLEANING UP, Ciaran stepped out of the doorway of the bathroom, fully dressed, and went back to the bedroom. He took a quick glance at Shannon before going to his suitcase. How was Shannon feeling about all this? Was Shannon as confused as he was? "We'd best be off." He snatched his clothes from the floor and tossed them in his suitcase with the rest.

"C-Ciaran?"

"Let's just bloody go, okay?" Ciaran pressed his lips together. Did Shannon want to talk about it? What was there to say?

Shannon hung his head, clutching at the dark shirt over his chest, his breath catching.

Ciaran shut his suitcase with a click and stood, looking down on him, his heart aching. He didn't know what to do. "I'll meet you in the tavern. We'll get some breakfast." Shannon looked as pained as he felt. They should go on as if nothing happened. They had to be in public now. He forced a grin over his lips. He needed time to figure this thing out. He peered at Shannon again. He needed to go. He left the room and shut the door behind him.

SITTING at a round table in the corner of the dark tavern, Ciaran watched the entrance for Shannon. It was quiet this morning. Only a few customers sat in scattered positions in the room.

Raking a hand through his dark hair, Shannon strode in. He stopped and searched the room.

Ciaran held up his hand and waved. They should pretend nothing happened. It was the only way.

With a wave and a nod, Shannon walked to him. As he took a seat opposite Ciaran, he peeked over at him.

Ciaran shifted his seat, so it angled away from Shannon, setting an elbow on the table, gazing across the room. It was impossible to look at Shannon and not think about it. "I already ordered for us. Hope that's all right."

Nodding, Shannon said, "Yeah, that's fine." Sighing, he drew circles on the table in front of him with his finger.

A young girl with curly, brown hair in a long, blue dress came to the table with a tray filled with plates and mugs. She looked from Ciaran to Shannon while she set plates of food, mugs with tea, silverware, and napkins on the table. When she finished, she straightened, placing her hands on her hips. "Well, you two are sure in a somber mood today."

Shannon gazed at Ciaran.

With a glance at her, Ciaran said, "Yeah, got a little too bollocksed last night." And that's all he'd say about it. It was true, right? Maybe that was all it was. He frowned. Then why did it feel so good and why couldn't he stop thinking about it?

Shannon frowned and looked down at his plate.

She shook her head, chuckling. "Happens a lot 'round here." She turned and trotted off.

After picking up his fork, Shannon poked at his eggs. He glanced at Ciaran again, his brows wrinkling.

Ciaran cleared his throat and shifted his plate, so he sat with one leg out from the table. Why was Shannon looking at him like that and not eating? He picked up his fork and poked it into some eggs.

Silence and tension filled the air around them while they ate their meal.

IT WAS ALMOST NOON, and the sun washed the color away from the surrounding hills of grass and weeds. The young men sat in a veil of silent tension while the cart bumped and jerked along the road.

Ciaran thought back to the awkward breakfast they'd shared. The unusual silence between them had left him feeling distant. But what was he to say? He took in a glimpse of Shannon, sitting beside him. He wouldn't sit as close as he sat yesterday. Shannon didn't seem to want it. In fact, he seemed back to his normal self, being careful not to absently touch. But what did it mean exactly? Had what they'd done changed their friendship? He flinched. He couldn't lose him now, not when he needed him so.

Shannon glanced at him, then frowned. "So how are you today?" He flinched.

Raising his brows, Ciaran flashed him a glance. "What?"

"I, uh, just asked how you were." Shannon hung his head, then pressed his lips together. "I mean, you did tell the waitress about how much we drank last night and uh, well...does your head hurt as much as mine?" He winced while searching Ciaran's face.

With a frown, Ciaran knitted his brows, then scanned over the front of the cart. Did Shannon want to discuss what happened last night? *Is that why he's bringing up their drunkenness?* He turned on the bench seat, then lifted a leg between them and faced Shannon. "N-no, it doesn't hurt too bad. I'm okay, I suppose." The cart lurched sideways, and he tumbled, out of control, landing in Shannon's lap.

Shannon flung his arms around Ciaran, keeping him from falling any further. The horse whinnied with the abrupt strain on its harnesses. The cart straightened and he stared down into Ciaran's face, his breath quickening.

Lingering, Ciaran gazed deeply into Shannon's stunning gray eyes. His heart pounded. He closed his eyes for a second. *It feels good...His touch and his hold, I need this.* But he should get up. He sighed and placed one hand on the seatback and the other on the edge of the bench, then hoisted himself upright. When he straightened, he held his breath for a moment as their gazes locked.

Shannon flushed and turned his head, breaking the moment.

"Sorry about that." Heat flooded Ciaran's cheeks. *What the hell am I thinking?* They were best friends, always and forever. What happened last night wouldn't change that. He slowly let a chuckle rise out of him. It felt good to let the tension release.

Shannon smiled, then eyed him as if suspicious.

Ciaran's chuckles turned into full-blown laughter, filling the air around them. He couldn't stop himself.

Chuckling for a moment at first, Shannon burst out in hearty laughter.

"Ah, damn, Shannon," Ciaran said, his laughter slowing. He held the reins tight with one hand, then arched the other up and put it down squarely over Shannon's thigh. There was no reason not to touch him, not when they'd shared so much. Besides, it was natural to be close to your best friend like this, right? He gave Shannon's leg a solid squeeze and released it.

Shannon released a long sigh, then bit his lower lip. "Wh-what's so funny?"

"I don't know. It's just that I...nothing." He couldn't tell him what was going on in his head. Not yet. He still needed to think on it. He should change the subject. "Aren't you hungry yet? I can't believe it's been four hours and you're not whining, *I'm hungry, Ciaran, let's eat, Ciaran,*" he said, in a high-pitched voice, grinning.

"Shut up now, at least I'm still growing." Shannon gave him a wide smile and let the stiffness release from his shoulders.

"What's that supposed to mean?" Ciaran still grinned. "A bloody bean pole, you are. Just because I'm not as tall as you don't mean I'm short. I'm normal." That'd fix him.

Shannon leaned back and put a booted foot on the edge of the footrest in front of him, then rubbed his chin as if pondering Ciaran's words. "Uh, Ciaran? I am hungry," he said, "and I don't whine."

Ciaran held a chuckle, admiring Shannon's dark hair and light eyes. Shannon was a looker, that was for sure. And now, he had his friend back.

Batting at Ciaran's shoulder, Shannon said, "Stop it." He let a wide grin play on his lips.

THE PAIR FINISHED their meal at a tavern on the outskirts of Dublin. When two policemen entered, Ciaran watched Shannon stiffen.

The tall, mean looking blond and a mousy man with brown hair sat at a table two rows over from them. Their stiff black uniform shirts and beige trousers held the insignia of the Royal Irish Constabulary Reserves, the RIC.

Black and Tans. Ciaran wrinkled his nose. Although a rarity in Drimnagh, he'd heard the stories surrounding these men. Made up of newly solicited World War I British Army veterans, they were notorious for terrorizing Irish civilians. He studied Shannon. He'd better not try to be tough around them.

Shannon leaned toward him and in a low voice, said, "That blond policeman keeps looking at you."

Ciaran scoffed. "Why? We've done nothing. You're seeing things." Ciaran stood to leave. *Please don't say anything...We need to just leave, now.*

Shannon went to pay the bill.

The blond policeman rose up.

Ciaran strolled in the direction of the door.

The blond policeman swaggered toward Ciaran and slammed into his shoulder. "Bloody pissed Micks! Can't hold your liquor, ay, boy?"

Ciaran whirled around to face the man, rubbing the pain in his shoulder. "What?" He lifted his brows, dropping his mouth open. He certainly wasn't drunk. "I-I only had one pint."

The man chuckled. "Really, so, one pint and you're stumbling all over the pub, like a stupid git?" he said with a sneer.

Shannon lurched forward, grabbing a glass, his face menacing. He smashed the glass on the nearest table, making a sharp weapon, and darted between Ciaran and the policeman. He held up the jagged shard, neck level, with a wide stance. His voice was low, "Leave my friend alone." He glared at the man, flaring his nostrils, curling his lip.

"Shannon!" Ciaran snatched his arm. He was going to get them both killed.

Shannon yanked his arm free. "Stay out of this, Ciaran, it's between him and me now."

Ciaran watched the soldier's hand hover over a gun holstered at his side. People in the pub all around him rose up and stepped toward them.

"So, what do you think you're going to do with that?" The policeman gave him a wicked grin. "Maybe you should use it to cut your hair, you Irish pansy."

With a snarl, Shannon lunged forward.

Out of nowhere, the other policeman stepped in front of him, hands raised as if in surrender. "Now, now, that's enough. Billy, you don't want to be starting anything here, do you? Look around."

Billy took a quick scan of the men surrounding them. "What're you defending him for? Can't you see he's a bloody poof?"

Ciaran gasped. It wasn't true, was it? If Shannon was, then what was he?

Shannon held his position as if waiting to strike.

"Who made you the judge of that? He's an Irishman and we'll defend him to the death against the likes of you," a man called out from the crowd.

Shannon lowered his weapon a little, his gaze darting around him.

Ciaran scanned the crowd. All the other male patrons of the tavern stood around them, stern expressions on their faces. He noticed a few of them pounding their hands into their fists. Would they really defend him and Shannon? His gaze returned to the two policemen.

Billy stepped backward with his head lowered.

The brown-haired man made a slow circle, hands still raised. "Listen, we don't want any trouble here. Everyone, just go back to your tables and we'll let these fine lads be on their way." He nodded to them.

After dropping his weapon, Shannon seized Ciaran's hand. He hauled him out of the front doors and shoved him up onto the cart outside. "Let's go, now." He jumped in while Ciaran snatched the reins. With a slap of the reins and a shout, the horse startled, jerking forward at a canter.

Once they were well away from the tavern, Ciaran turned, facing him. "What the hell was all that about? Why'd they call you those names?" *How would they know what happened last night?*

Shannon held his head high. "It's just the Black and Tans, Ciaran, that's just how they are. You have to stay away from them. I'm surprised we haven't seen any until now. The bloody bastards." He huffed and relaxed his posture for the rest of the ride into Dublin.

CIARAN PLODDED along with Shannon dozed off, hunched over next to him, his dark hair swaying on his head. He slapped Shannon's thigh. "Look, Shannon, there it is, Dublin," he said, excitement ringing in his voice. It appeared they were already in the city proper. Tenement housing bordered the streets surrounding them. Children chased after one another under oak and ash lined pavements. Streetlamps hovered above them, hanging their glass heads as if in silent prayer.

Shannon opened his eyes and looked around them.

Straightening, Ciaran peered farther down the street. A large cathedral and ornate Georgian-style buildings with massive stone pillars stood like sentries along the larger boulevard. "Look at that, Shannon, wouldn't Father Brennan give an arm and a leg to preach in a church like that?" He pointed to the cathedral straight ahead of them, then tossed the reins to Shannon. "Here." He jumped into the back of the cart. They'd need the slip of paper with the directions.

"Uh, wh-what are you doing?" Shannon blinked a few times, then shifted in his seat. He pulled back to stop the horse at the entrance to the boulevard. Looking both ways, at a myriad of vehicles, he gritted his teeth as if anticipating some mayhem to come.

"Got it." Ciaran fumbled in his suitcase, stealing a glance at Shannon, then found it, holding up the wrinkled and scribbled-on paper in his hand. He peered into it. "Looks like we take a right."

"You've got to be joking. I can't even get out onto that damned street, there's too many motor cars." Shannon wiped his palms, one at a time, over his thighs.

"Come on, just do it, they'll go around you." Ciaran huffed. Shannon could be so timid at the worst of times.

"How do you know?" Shannon's voice rose.

Ciaran stretched forward, yanked the reins to the right and slammed them down on the horse's back. The cart lurched forward into the traffic of open carriages, riders on horseback and motor cars.

"Holy shite, Ciaran, remind me to clobber you when we get to your aunt's." Shannon took deep breaths as if fighting off nerves.

Ciaran looked out over squat brick buildings blended with the spires from cathedrals on either side of the tiny cart. Small shops with outstretched canopies hung out as if inviting them in. His gaze kept roaming the graceful curves of the occasional motor cars passing them by. He curled his nose up at the strange aroma of exhaust mixed with cooking and garbage. When a motor car's horn blasted, he jumped, then smiled. Now, this was an adventure. "Shannon, do you see that? There are so many shops here. I bet you can buy whatever you want." He spoke loudly over the noises of the city.

"Yes, but you'd have to have the money, first." Shannon wrinkled his nose.

Ciaran's gaze veered to the left. A canal came into view. The late afternoon sun sparkled on the water, sending shapes of light dancing on the arched bricks of the bridge above it. He found himself captivated by it.

Shannon's gaze followed Ciaran's. "Well, would you look at that? It's lovely here. Isn't it?"

"What?" Ciaran peeked at the paper. He'd better make sure they didn't get lost.

"Oh, nothing."

"Take a left, here!" Ciaran raised onto his knees in the back of the cart.

Shannon startled. "What? Here?" He jerked the reins as if afraid the horse would veer off their own side of the cobblestone boulevard.

"Yeah, here, here!" Ciaran's furious finger pointed down a side street. This was it. He was sure of it.

Shannon pulled hard to the left on the reins, keeping his gaze on the horse's head as it turned in the direction he intended. "Oh, thank God," he mumbled.

Ciaran looked out over a much smaller street with a few carriages rolling by them. He gazed up at the rectangular brick buildings lining either side of the street. How the hell did people handle living so close together?

As things wound down around them, Shannon relaxed his shoulders and sighed.

Ciaran glanced at Shannon, then out onto the pavement. A few people strolled in light conversation with one another, some carrying bags. A group of three women, about the same age as he and Shannon, came into view. People dressed a lot more fashionably here than back at home. The women's dresses were tailored and hugged their figures as if modesty were not an option. The sight stirred his senses.

Shannon studied the women, then cowered when the girls gazed up into the cart at them as if he were expecting something bad.

"Look at that, Shannon, there are lots of women here." Ciaran knelt behind and to the right of him, forearms resting across the seat back. Shannon shouldn't be so afraid of these women. They were nothing like the ones back home. Couldn't he see that?

Snickering, Shannon shook his head once.

One of the women pointed a shy finger at them and the trio giggled, turning towards one another.

Shannon widened his eyes, then focused on the horse.

A tinge of heat flared in Ciaran's chest. "Looks like that one likes you," Ciaran whispered over Shannon's shoulder. Would Shannon like her back? Did he find her pretty?

Shannon scoffed. "Don't be ridiculous."

"Shannon, we're not in Drimnagh anymore, there is no reason these women wouldn't like you." Ciaran patted a hand between his shoulders. "You know, you really aren't half bad to look at, sort of handsome actually." Something he seemed to notice even more after what had happened in the hotel room.

Shannon's face flushed, then a timid smile spread on his lips. The smile grew into a smirk. "Tell me something, how did your da know exactly where to go? I don't seem to remember him ever coming here."

"Oh, my da was born and raised in Dublin, my ma, too. They met here at school and moved out to Drimnagh after they got married. I suppose they didn't want to raise a family in the city. Too bad my ma only had me though. I know she wanted a large family." His heart ached with the memory of his mother.

Seemed he'd forgotten the reason they were here with all the excitement.

"Well, tell me a little bit about this aunt we're here to see." Shannon looked behind him, his gaze seeking out Ciaran's, then he grinned.

"I've only met her once when she came to visit us about ten years ago. There was some sort of a death, one of her close friends, I think. It wasn't spoken about too much. Anyway, she kept to herself mostly. Although she and my ma were very close when they were young. When I was born, they mostly just wrote to each other. All of what I know is stories my ma told me. She owns a pub and tends the bar. Anyway, she's supposed to be sort of a character, a bit political, too. I suppose any woman who would own a pub and live by herself would be a bit forward in her thinking." Ciaran let a faint grin curl his lips. It would be nice seeing her again, like a little bit of his mother was still here.

Shannon nodded. "How far now?"

Peering into the piece of crinkled paper he held, Ciaran said, "Oh, it should be just up ahead."

"What's it called again?" Shannon scanned the sides of the road at the shops on either side of them.

Ciaran read off the paper. "McFlynne's Whiskey River."

"Ah, there it is." As Shannon tugged the reins back, he steered the horse to a stop and stared toward the moniker and the building housing the pub.

Ciaran gazed at their destination. It mimicked the other buildings around it, reddish brick with small wooden windows, three-stories tall. It looked like it was well maintained. His aunt must be doing pretty well, despite the lack of a husband.

The two jumped off the cart. Ciaran grabbed his suitcase and Shannon's pillowcase while Shannon secured the horse.

Ciaran strode inside the pub with Shannon following. The warm evening air gave way to the cooler interior of the dank pub. There was a large, richly carved, mahogany bar to the left of him as he strode in. Various square tables with simple wooden chairs littered the plank flooring in front of them. Cigarette smoke and the smell of beer wafted on the air currents. Male voices spoke in hushed tones. He scanned the inside of the pub, turning his head as he went. A few patrons sat at leather stools in front of the bar and a middle-aged woman poured a pint of stout from a brass tap.

Pacing toward the bar, Ciaran eyed the woman. *Is that her?* He stopped at one end of it, waiting for Shannon to come up behind him. He looked at the thin, but well built, woman over. She had short, curly, red hair and a calming way about her. Dressed more like a man than a woman, she wore a tan, short-sleeved, button-front shirt, hanging untucked over her dark trousers. She wasn't much like his mother, but he still got a good feeling from her.

She gazed beyond the two young men and set the pint down in front of a burly man. Her second glance came quickly, as if recognizing them, and she studied them for a moment. A wide smile broke out over her lips, while she sauntered toward them. "My, my, Ciaran, is it? I've been expecting you. Your da's telegram came this morning," she said, "You look just like your mother."

"Uh, hello, Aunt Iona," Ciaran said, taking her fully in.

Stepping sideways and out from the behind the bar, she greeted Ciaran with arms outstretched. "Give us a hug, you dear sweet boy." She wrapped her arms around his shoulders.

Ciaran stiffened at her sudden touch, but slowly wrapped his arms around her waist. He didn't expect her to hug him like this, but it felt good after everything. As his heart ached and his eyes stung with the threat of tears, he gritted his teeth.

"I'm so sorry about your mother. She was a good woman and a wonderful sister to me," she said, with a gentle honesty. "I wanted so badly to come to the funeral, you know. But we were ransacked by the RIC the day I was to leave, bloody Black and Tans."

Ciaran's vision blurred and he peeked at Shannon, then bit his lip. This woman who'd spent so much time with his mother, knew her maybe more than he did, was right here. But his mother was gone forever.

Hanging his head, Shannon took a step backward.

She released Ciaran, but kept her hands on his shoulders, looking him over once more.

Ciaran tilted his head forward. He was struggling not to break down right then and there.

"It's all right, luv. Have a seat with your friend here and I'll have Kelly stable your horse. Can I get you both a pint, maybe?" she asked.

Ciaran looked to Shannon as her hands dropped from his shoulders. What would Shannon want to do? He'd seemed uneasy. Would he want to stay or go to their room?

Shannon shifted on his feet, then nodded.

"Come on, then." Ciaran lifted his chin. He walked to a table in the corner with Shannon following, then set their belongings down and took a seat.

Shannon sat in a chair next to him, eying him closely while Iona's voice snaked out of a back room, barking orders to someone. "You okay?"

"Yeah, it's just, seeing her is so...it all makes it seem so real somehow." Ciaran's voice cracked and he wrinkled his forehead, his vision clouding.

Shannon thinned his lips, then reached under the table and squeezed Ciaran's hand, resting over Ciaran's thigh. Keeping a tight hold on it, he brushed his thumb over the top, fixating on Ciaran.

Searching his face, Ciaran gazed deeply into Shannon's gray eyes, then focused on his lips. How soft they were last night and how warm Shannon's hand felt now. Would he ever be able to kiss him again? Would Shannon let him?

Shannon yanked his hand away.

"Ahem." Aunt Iona coughed, looking over the scene before her, then set three pints down on the table. She spoke in a light tone while she sat down across from Ciaran. "So, who is your friend here?" She tipped her head toward Shannon.

"My name is Shannon, ma'am." Shannon's voice wavered. He peeked at her through the dark hair covering his eyes under his cap, then sipped his beer.

She smiled a warm, inviting smile at Shannon, who visibly relaxed.

She lifted her pint to her lips. "Shannon, my boy, according to the telegram I've received from Ciaran's da, you've been a very good friend to my nephew."

Blushing, Shannon averted his gaze, his face tensing. "Yes, ma'am."

"Oh come now, just call me Iona. It is my damned name, you know." She snickered.

"Y-yes ma—I mean, Iona." Shannon appeared to let down his guard and gave her a broad smile.

"So tell me about your trip." She set her pint back on the table.

"Well, there were Black and Tans in a tavern we ate at today. They tried to pick a fight with us." Ciaran's gaze caught on Shannon. He smiled and gestured to him. "But Shannon here stood up to them." He wouldn't mention the names they called him.

Shannon took a large gulp of beer and his face reddened again.

"Oh, did you now?" She asked.

"Yeah," Shannon said.

"And so, how did you get away unharmed? I know those bloody bastards. If they're looking for a fight, they don't give up easily." She took a sip of beer.

"The other men in the tavern all gathered round and said they'd defend us. Then the soldiers just stood down." Ciaran gulped his beer, studying Shannon, then set his glass back down. Why was Shannon looking so embarrassed? He should be proud of himself.

"Oh, I see. Maybe there was some Irish Republican Army in the pub with you then. You were lucky," she said.

Shannon nodded his head before taking a large gulp of beer.

"Other than that, there's not much to tell, just a bloody long, boring ride. Although, we did get a little pissed last night." Ciaran nudged him. "Isn't that right, Shannon?" What would he say to that?

Shannon's breath caught and he widened his eyes, staring at Ciaran.

"Yeah, Shannon here had to help me up the stairs to our room." Ciaran took a sip from his pint, throwing him a knowing glance. He wanted to do that again, that much he knew.

She chuckled. "Well, isn't that just like a couple of boys from the bog. Get them out and they go off and get bollocksed first thing." She slapped Ciaran on the thigh. "I've got a pot of stew upstairs if you're ready for supper."

Shannon leaned forward in his seat, focusing on her. "Oh, I'm ready."

Ciaran smiled at him. *Always hungry.* "You'll have to excuse my friend, Aunt Iona. Seems his stomach is as big as a whale's."

Grinning at Shannon, she rose up from her chair. "Well, that's just fine. Always liked a boy with a healthy appetite." She walked over to the bar and spoke to a husky man before coming back to the young men. She waved her hand at them. "Come on then, upstairs, and bring your things."

They followed her up a flight of stairs and through a doorway, into a small room. The smell of simmering beef and vegetables hit Ciaran immediately, causing his stomach to growl. Maybe he was as hungry as Shannon. He looked around her flat. It was nicely furnished with traditional oak furniture. It had a relaxed and comfortable feel to it. There were soft cushions on a greenish couch and heavy, yellow, striped curtains hung around the windows.

Showing the young men into a hallway, she pointed to a room at the end of it. "Here you go, Ciaran, you can take the guest room." She stood sideways to allow him to enter. Ciaran's heart skipped and he thinned his lips. They wouldn't be in the same room tonight. He threw his suitcase on the bed, then strode back out to join them.

"Come along, Shannon," she said, waving her hand again. She passed by a bathroom and stopped at another door. She pointed into it. "You can stay in the study. I'm sorry it's not as comfortable as the guest room, but there is a bed. I'm used to having guests, you see. Owning a pub sometimes means you need to, how shall I say it, house people." A soft grin played over her lips.

"Of course, thank you, very much." Shannon entered with Ciaran behind him.

Ciaran took in the small room. A writing desk sat against the far wall under a window and a single bed with a dark quilt draped over top of it rested to the left. A circular rug covered plank flooring and a small glass lamp sat on the desk.

Shannon dropped his stuffed pillowcase on the floor behind the bed, then glanced at Ciaran. They strode out and ambled through the main room and an open archway into the dining area and kitchen of the flat.

Aunt Iona poured stew into brown stoneware bowls.

Ciaran took a seat at an oval walnut table, big enough to sit six people comfortably. What stories might this table have to tell? Probably of friends sharing laughter and meals around it.

After dropping into a seat next to Ciaran, Shannon folded his hands on the table.

She served each of them, then got her own meal and sat down across from them. "So, you boys are very close?" She raised a spoon to her full lips and blew air across hot lumps and liquid.

"Yes, Shannon is my best friend. He's like a brother to me," Ciaran said, grinning at Shannon.

"Really, a brother?" She raised her brows.

Shannon studied her, pursing his lips.

"It's not often I see two boys from the bog so...close." Looking them over, she smiled. "It's nice, there is obviously something very special between you."

Shannon choked on his stew, sending bits and pieces flying out onto the table. He stared at the table, his face going white.

"Shannon!" Ciaran jumped at the table, and patted Shannon's back. Why would he react that way to her comment? Was there some unspoken innuendo that only Shannon understood?

"I-I'm sorry!" Shannon lurched forward in his haste to wipe up the mess with the napkin from his lap.

She chuckled. "My, my, a bit touchy, are we?"

"No, I just, I just..."

She reached across the table and placed her hand on Shannon's forearm, resting on the table. "It's okay, dear. There is nothing wrong with being *close*."

Stilling, Shannon brought his gaze to her and dropped his jaw open. "Uh, that's not why I—"

As she slapped the table, she pitched herself back in her seat. "Well then, I insist you stay a couple of nights. I love having company. Especially company as endearing as yours." She sniggered.

Shannon plopped down in his chair, searching the table as if it held the answer to something. He chanced a look at Ciaran.

"Of course, we'd be delighted to stay for a couple nights." Ciaran smiled at her. That might give them some time to explore more than just the city.

Drawing deep breaths, Shannon focused on his stew.

THAT NIGHT, Ciaran lay in his bed in the guest bedroom. It was too girly for him. He frowned. Doilies rested on the nightstand next to the bed and a lamp with—he shuddered to think of it—red feathers. Who on Earth would decorate a room with feathered lampshades? It didn't seem like his aunt's style, judging by the way the rest of the flat was decorated.

He turned onto his side, absently placing his hands between his thighs, and exhaled with a sigh. It was late and he couldn't sleep. Memories of last night tugged at him. How soothing it had been to drift off in Shannon's arms, listening to his steady breathing.

His mind flooded with the rest of it, Shannon's hand touching him, caressing him, stroking him. It sent a shiver through his body. He pressed on the erection already straining inside his underwear. A wave of pleasure washed over him. *It's not right, is it, to think of your best friend this way? Isn't it a sin even?* But deep down, what he wanted, no, needed, was more of what only Shannon could give him. *No, that's not really true, is it? What would Shannon think if he knew? Still, if I could just be with him, I could finally sleep. Yes, I'll just go to him and tell him this.*

Surely, he'd let him into his bed.

He climbed silently out of bed and padded through the darkness into the hallway. He stood motionless, listening for any signs of his aunt. When only silence surrounded him, he tiptoed down the hallway.

CHAPTER
FIVE
SHANNON

Shannon was desperate in his attempt to sleep. His mind filled with memories of the illicit act he'd engaged in with Ciaran last night and how he'd reacted to his touch. His hard cock ached with need. Maybe he should give in to his urges? But how would he keep himself quiet? He couldn't, not with the new memories and sensations to fuel his activity.

Ciaran's silhouette emerged in the doorway, bathed in errant light filtering in through the window from a streetlamp outside. It cast a light glow to his hair.

Lifting his head off his pillow, Shannon sat up on one elbow on his side. "Ciaran, what's wrong?"

"Shh…" Ciaran stepped to the side of his bed and looked down on him, his wide eyes glinting.

Shannon's heart pounded and his breath quickened.

"Move over," Ciaran whispered.

"But why? What are you doing?" Shannon creased his brows. He'd already barraged himself with reasons why he shouldn't go into Ciaran's room and now he stood before him.

With his heart thrumming in his ears, his gaze roamed over Ciaran, so gorgeous, and stopped at his groin. It couldn't be, could it? The thin cloth of his underwear gave way to something solid underneath. A jolt of desire twitched his own hard cock. What he'd give to feel that beautiful erection in his palm again. But it was wrong, so wrong. "No, Ciaran, we shouldn't," he whispered.

Ciaran frowned, then pursed his lips. "I-I just, am feeling so alone and I need someone to sleep with, that's all," he said softly. "Please, Shannon."

Shannon's heart ached with love for him. He couldn't deny the request. He backed up in the bed and flung the sheet down. "All right then, come on," he whispered.

Ciaran slid in beside him, lying next to him on his back. He looked up to meet Shannon's gaze. "I don't know what happened. I just couldn't sleep, and I-I slept so well with you last night."

This is almost intolerable. Shannon snapped his brows together. How he wanted to press his lips against Ciaran's and force himself on him again. But tonight, he hadn't had nearly the same amount of beer. Tonight, he had some wits about him. "It's okay, just turn over and I'll be right here."

Ciaran hesitated and let out a sharp exhale, then rolled onto his side.

Pressing his chest against Ciaran's back, Shannon wrapped an arm around him.

Ciaran entwined his fingers in Shannon's, tugging his arm tightly around him.

As Shannon breathed in the sweet scent of Ciaran, he closed his eyes. He was on fire again. Sure, maybe Ciaran found this comforting, but it was going be pure torture for him. He wanted to rock his hips forward, to relieve the ache in his groin. But there was just no way he could allow it tonight.

Ciaran rolled his hips backward, pressing his buttocks against Shannon's erection.

With a soft grunt, Shannon reluctantly pulled his hips away. "Stop, Ciaran," he whispered over his neck.

Ciaran buried his head into the pillow he shared with him, clenching his eyes shut and releasing a soft moan. "I'm sorry."

The silence and darkness closed around the pair as two sets of eyes found it difficult to close. Two bodies ached to increase their contact and two sets of lungs breathed quicker than usual.

SHANNON WOKE to the aroma of bacon wafting into the room. A warm body snuggled against his chest and he drew it closer. He nuzzled into a tuft of blond hair, breathing in deep. The scent of Ciaran flooded into him. How he loved this smell. Caught up in the moment, he pressed his lips to the top of Ciaran's head, giving him a tender kiss.

Stirring, Ciaran rolled to his back. "Mmm, Shannon."

"Hush, you don't want Iona to hear you, do you?" Shannon whispered. He watched while Ciaran's eyes fluttered open and attempted to focus on his face. Oh, what he'd give to have those sweet lips pressed against his. He grinned at him. Having him close like this would have to do.

Widening his eyes, Ciaran searched over Shannon's face, then parted his lips. He reached a timid hand up and brushed across his cheek with his fingertips.

Shannon let out a soft gasp. What was Ciaran doing? The way he looked at him, his actions, they were all things a person does when they have feelings for another. Not just friendly, brotherly feelings, but real feelings. His heart swelled and ached. He averted his gaze and took a hard swallow. If he allowed himself to go down this path and was wrong, his heart would be thoroughly broken. He needed to get out of here before things progressed. "I, uh, we should get up now." He scrambled over Ciaran and off the bed. With his hands shaking, he snatched his dark trousers and slid them on. He straightened and took one last hesitant glance at Ciaran, looking so beautiful in his bed, then rushed from the room.

STANDING AT A CREAM-COLORED GAS STOVE, Iona held a silver spatula in her hand. A tattered white robe wrapped around her small frame and equally tattered slippers covered her feet. "Sleep well?"

Yawning, Shannon sat at the dining table. "Yes, of course." The truth was it had taken him hours to finally fall asleep. Every little movement or involuntary muscle spasm of Ciaran's had been a shock to his system.

She grinned. "Could've fooled me."

Ciaran trudged into the room. He'd dressed in tan trousers and a white, cotton shirt. With his head lowered, he moved deliberately across the wood floor. He sat down next to Shannon, stretched his arms up over his head and sighed.

Iona glanced at Shannon, then stared at Ciaran.

Shannon focused on Ciaran.

Looking up, Ciaran glanced at Aunt Iona, then on to Shannon. "Good morning?"

"Morning, Ciaran, how about some sausage and eggs? There's some soda bread and butter on the table." As she turned around to her stovetop, she mumbled, "Suppose I'm the only one getting any sleep around here."

Ciaran's intense gaze flared over Shannon's skin. He faced him and smiled. Ciaran's leg pressed up against his shin. His nerves jolted and he cleared his throat. The look on Ciaran's face was something he'd never seen directed at him before. It held a yearning, a craving. He'd seen that look before, yes, but only directed at women, like that rude waitress at the inn. Ciaran's leg moved sensually up and down his shin. He should pull away, but he didn't want to. Heat flooded his cheeks and his cock stirred. He fixated on Ciaran's lovely face.

"Here you go, eat up." She slapped plates full of sausage, eggs and beans, and cups filled with tea on the table in front of them. She started back to her stove, stopped, and did a double take of the young men as they eyed each other. "I said eat up!" She shook her head while turning back to her stove.

Shannon startled, pulled out of his trance by her gruff demand. He shoveled food into his mouth, one forkful after another. He dared a glance at Ciaran. He was doing the same.

She made herself a plate before sitting across from the young men, same position as last night. "So, I have a favor to ask of you two today."

"Really, what is it?" Ciaran asked.

"Since you have that cart, Ciaran, dear, I would be grateful if you could go across town and pick up some supplies for the pub. If it's not too much trouble," she said, with a calculating tone.

"Of course. Shannon, we can see a bit more of the city." The edges of Ciaran's mouth twitched, and he jiggled his leg up and down.

Shannon nodded with a mouth stuffed with eggs.

"Ah well, I had a different plan for Shannon. You see, I need some help with the pub today and was hoping he would help me tend the bar." She placed a forkful of eggs into her mouth.

Wrinkling his brows, Ciaran pursed his lips, then freed a soft huff. "Oh."

Shannon peered at her. There was definitely something under the surface of her smug demeanor, something suspicious. He wasn't sure he liked Ciaran going out by himself. But he had no other choice than to agree. He was, after all, a guest in her home. He swallowed down his food. "Yes, I'll help you with the bar. You'll be all right on your own, won't you, Ciaran?"

Ciaran shoved bits of egg and beans around his plate with his fork, pouting. "I suppose so."

"Just stay away from any of those policemen. I won't be there to protect you this time." Shannon watched him. Would he take his advice?

"Yes, listen to Shannon now. I'll give you a map that'll take you on a route where you shouldn't have any problems." She sipped some of her tea.

Ciaran shifted on his chair. He curled his lip and glared at Shannon. "I can take care of myself, you know."

Chuckling, Shannon shoved another forkful of egg into his mouth, then swallowed it all down. "Yeah, right." Ciaran hadn't had the experiences he'd had. Ciaran had never had to fight the way he had.

SHANNON WAVED GOODBYE TO CIARAN, as he rode off alone on the cart down the small street, Iona's map in his hand.

As Shannon watched him leave, his chest pinched. Fear gnawed at him. The encounter they'd had with the Black and Tans played over in his mind. What the hell would Ciaran do if faced with the same situation all alone? He'd known that if he hadn't faced them right then and there, that man would not have backed down and Ciaran could have been arrested. *If someone was going to get arrested, it would be better if it was me.*

He turned to Iona, standing next to him in a white linen shirt and tan trousers. "You sure he'll be all right?"

She waved her hand at him. "Oh, he'll be just fine. He's an adult, you know. People have to start treating him like one," she said, heading for the pub entrance.

He followed her to the door, then stopped, holding the door open. He twisted his head for one last look at Ciaran's back while he departed, huffing. She'd better be right or she'd have him to deal with.

When he walked into the cool air of the pub, Iona stood behind the bar at a porcelain sink, washing glasses. He strode in until he stood beside her, rolling up the sleeves on his dark cotton shirt. It was eleven in the morning and a few patrons mulled about in various positions around the room, having their first beer of the day. He waited patiently for her to give him some direction.

"Let me tell you something, Shannon. I've been tending bar for a long time, and when you do that for as long as I have, you get to see inside people really well. You sort of know things about people just by looking at them. And there are two things I know when I look at you. The first is, something hurt you pretty bad in your short life already." She searched his face as if to see the effect her words had on him.

He hung his head. So it showed, everything showed. He fidgeted with the edge of the sink below him.

"The second is, you're in love."

Gasping, he glared at her, wrinkling his brows. "But I-I—" Tears flooded his eyes. The hurtful memories of brutal confessions and pain of a love unrequited raced to the surface. He clenched his jaw, attempting to quell the emotion swarming inside him.

She placed her wet hand on his forearm. "It's okay, luv, you don't have to tell me about it."

He took a long swallow, forcing the tears back. "Wh-what do you see when you l-look at Ciaran?" With his gaze affixed to hers, he studied her, trying to see even what she didn't say.

"Ah well, he's a bit innocent, that one. My sister, God rest her soul, she overprotected him. He's a good kid, don't get me wrong, he's got a great heart. But then, you already knew that, didn't you?" As she leaned forward, she narrowed her eyes at him as if to prove a point. "He's in love, too, just doesn't know it yet." She removed her hand from his forearm.

He shifted his gaze in the opposite direction, unable to meet her words head on. His breath hitched. His heart hammered. His lower lip trembled. Was it true, what she said? Could Ciaran possibly love him back? She'd been so right about his own situation, why wouldn't she be right about Ciaran? Could he dare allow his feelings to be known? The room blurred. He shut his eyes tight against it. A single, hot tear tumbled down his cheek. He swiped it away with the back of his hand, and opened his eyes again.

She looked out across the pub as if in reflection. "My dear Shannon, love comes in a variety of flavors, sort of like ice cream. There are those most people like and accept, you know —vanilla, chocolate, strawberry. But then there are those people don't like so much, mostly because, maybe they just seem strange, or they don't want to try something new. Sort of like, mint, I suppose. There's nothing wrong with mint, but for most people, it's just not for them. Of course, some people would even steer you away from it, would tell you there's something wrong with liking it even. But if you like mint, so what? You like mint."

As understanding bloomed in his chest, he widened his eyes. He was different, not evil, not a monster, just different. His taste in love was just different from most people. And if Ciaran's taste could be the same, then there was hope after all.

As terror surged into him, he gripped the edge of the sink so tight his knuckles went white. He'd never talked about his deep, dark secret without some sort of punishment. "S-so what's the chance of two people both liking mint?" His voice wavered.

She tipped her head across the pub to two large gentlemen sitting across from one another at a table. "See those two big burly men over there? That's Colin and Dave. They both like mint," she said with a smug smile and a quick nod.

"Oh." He squeaked and coughed into his palm. "Oh." As he stared out across the pub, his mind reeled. She told him it was all right to be what he was, and he wasn't alone. There were others, men who by all outward appearances were completely normal. They just liked a different flavor of love. Warmth flooded his chest.

"So come on over here and I'll show you everything you need to know about tending a bar." She gave him a hard slap between the shoulders.

He jerked with the force of her slap, pulling him out of his thoughts. He threw her a wide smile, maybe the first true smile he'd allowed himself in many years.

As Shannon attempted to pour a pint from the brass tap, he watched the dark liquid fill the glass in front of him. He tilted it, just as she'd instructed, to keep the foam from being too thick. As the glass filled and he straightened it, the foam grew thick again.

"Aye, that's too bloody much foam, boy," a man with brown hair said from a barstool behind him.

"I-I'm sorry, sir. I'll try again." Shannon poured the beer out over the brass drain. Where the hell was Iona anyway? She had abandoned him and left him ill prepared, damn it. Half an hour wasn't nearly enough time to figure this all out. And now, all these customers were staring at him. How could he possibly get this right when they were all looking at him like this? His palms were sweaty while he started another pour. A presence warmed his back.

"Let me help you there."

Shannon looked down to see two male arms reach around him while a body pressed up against his back. He took a hard swallow. Who was he? Why was he so close? Warm hands fell over his and guided him through the process, filling the glass at a tilt to three-quarters full from one tap, then letting the beer cascade before topping it off with another tap. When they'd finished, the foam top had just the right thickness.

The man let go.

Shannon turned and looked the man over. It was the same man Iona had told to stable Ciaran's horse. What was his name, Kelly?

"Go ahead, serve him," Kelly said smiling, his eyes a bright blue, his blond hair falling over his forehead.

Shannon brought the pint to the man at the bar. "Here you go."

"Ah, perfect pour. You bloody got it that time." The brown-haired man gave him a coy grin, raising his glass.

"Um, uh, thank you." Shannon sighed.

"So, my name is Kelly. You must be Shannon." Kelly held out his hand.

Shannon took Kelly in. He was maybe a few years older than him. He seemed pleasant enough, like someone he already knew well, even though they'd never met. What a strange feeling for him to have. Certainly not one he was used to. He gave Kelly's hand a firm shake. "Uh, yeah."

"Yeah? Is that all, just yeah?" Kelly's gaze held a certain playfulness. He nudged Shannon in the ribs with his elbow.

Heat rushed Shannon's cheeks. What else was he supposed to say?

"Come on then, tell me something about yourself." Kelly leaned sideways on the bar, propping on an elbow.

"Well, uh, there's nothing much to tell, really."

"I hear you're from Drimnagh?" Kelly let a smug smile play on his face.

Shannon's words were slow and deliberate. "Yes. We came here to, to bring a necklace to Iona." He attempted to meet Kelly's gaze, but failed. It was not something he normally did, but Kelly seemed different somehow, nice.

"I used to live in the bog myself. Coming to Dublin was a wonderful thing. Ciaran's aunt, she sort of took me under her wing and actually pays me to spend time in her pub." Kelly chuckled. "Can you bloody believe that?" He playfully batted at Shannon's arm.

Shannon forced himself to look into Kelly's eyes, his chest tightening. *What the hell does he want from me?*

"My, you are a quiet one." Sighing, Kelly grabbed a brown rag from the back bar counter. "Gotta watch out for those quiet ones, my ma used to say." He wiped the top of the bar.

A bald man stepped up and sat at a barstool.

Shannon turned to him. "Can I get you something?"

"Yes, a pint please," the bald man said.

Shannon peeked at Kelly.

"Oh no, you've got to do it yourself now. Just go on up there and tilt it like I showed you." Kelly ticked his head toward the tap.

Shannon grabbed a glass from a shelf under the bar, held it under the first tap and poured, then waited and topped it off from the second tap. He bit his lip, doing his best to keep the foam under control. It came out perfectly. *I did it.* Grinning, he glanced at Kelly.

"See? You did a bloody great job on that one," Kelly said.

Shannon straightened his shoulders, puffing out his chest just a touch. He hadn't felt like this in years. He set the glass down in front of the bald man. "Here you go."

The bald man glanced up. "Thanks."

Shannon took a step toward Kelly.

"Son?" a voice said from behind him.

Shannon turned around to the man he'd just served.

"Good pour." The bald man smiled.

Shannon held his head up higher as he went to clean some of the dirtied glasses.

"So, you're from Drimnagh, aye?" the brown-haired man asked.

"He doesn't talk much, Patrick," Kelly called out from the end of the bar, still cleaning.

Shannon grinned, giving his head a slow shake. "Yes, I do talk. Just not to strangers. Didn't your ma ever tell you that?" He snickered. Too bad Ciaran wasn't around to hear what he just said.

Straightening, Kelly put his hands on his hips. He stepped closer. "My, aren't we a witty one when we want to be."

Shannon laughed outright, his chest filling with warmth. "Yeah, suppose I just don't get much of a chance normally." He looked at Patrick. "Yes, I'm from Drimnagh."

"Get many of them Black and Tans out your way?" Patrick asked, sparking the interest of the bald customer.

"No, not usually. Crossed them on the way here though, bloody bastards." Shannon dried one of the glasses he cleaned.

"You did now. How'd that go?" the bald man asked.

Shannon shrugged. "Well enough, I'm still bloody alive,

aren't I?" He smiled while the men at the bar laughed, clinking their glasses together at his comment.

SHANNON PARKED himself just outside the entrance of the pub on a chair he'd taken from inside. A few people meandered by. Probably on their way home to supper, as it was early evening. An unusual quiet filled the warm air surrounding him. He looked to the cloudless sky. Would it ever rain? He shifted his gaze up the street. Ciaran should be back by now. His heart quickened.

His mind filled with memories from the day—pouring numerous beers, cleaning glasses and chatting with customers. It'd been exhausting, especially talking to customers. It wasn't like him to make small talk with people or for him to talk to anyone he didn't know well. The circumstances back home had pushed him into a shell. But as the day wore on, he'd found himself coming out, spreading his wings. Even now, he was nodding at a few of the passersby when they caught his gaze and the anxiety he usually felt was gone.

He spread a wide smile over his lips. At some point, it had been actually pleasant. He'd even laughed with a few of the men, and felt right at home in there behind a bar. Who'd have thought? But no one here knew what happened. No one thought of him as defective. Even Iona, she knew he liked men and she didn't care.

Iona must have a plan. There was a definite reason she made him stay by himself and tend the bar. Just like there was a reason she sent Ciaran out on his own to pick up supplies. Ciaran needed to be an adult, to figure out he could handle complicated situations by himself.

A horse pulling a small cart emerged down the street

As he stood, Shannon peered at the young man, squinting to see more clearly. Blond hair, white shirt, it was Ciaran all right. But what was all over the front of his shirt? As Ciaran came closer, the stains on the front of his shirt became sharper. Distinct dark, reddish-brown splotches came into view.

Shannon turned his focus to Ciaran's face and hurried toward him. Something dirtied his face as well. "Oh my God, Ciaran. Are you all right?" he said, while grabbing the horse's bridle and directing him to the alley next to the pub.

CHAPTER SIX
CIARAN

Ciaran swayed with the motion of the cart, giving Shannon a lop-sided grin. "Yeah, I'm great actually." He straightened his shoulders. He'd shown the bloody bastard. He could be just as tough as Shannon.

"What's happened to you? Is that blood on your shirt?" Shannon stopped the horse at the side door to the pub and raised his hand to Ciaran as if attempting to help him down.

Ciaran slapped Shannon's hand away. "I can get out of the bloody cart." He wasn't that hurt after all. He lumbered down.

As soon as Ciaran stepped on the ground, Shannon seized him, yanking their bodies together. He buried his face against the side of Ciaran's head. "What happened? How bad is it? Did you come up against more Black and Tans?"

"What's all this then?" Iona stepped out from the side door to the pub.

Shannon freed Ciaran and spun around to face her, glaring. "See? He shouldn't have gone alone, he's hurt!" He creased his brows, pointing at Ciaran.

"Just a minute now. Ciaran, are you all right? What happened, sweet boy?" she asked in a calm voice.

Ciaran swept a wide smile over his face, his body twitching with energy. "I won. That's what happened. You should have seen it, Shannon. This bloody awful man was shouting at this poor woman. Well, I wouldn't have none of that. So I got between them and I told the man, *leave that woman alone*. And he told me to make him. So you know what? I bloody well did." He cackled, his mind filling with the memory of the fight. He'd won and that was all that mattered. He'd saved that poor woman.

"What do you mean, *you did?*" Shannon stared at him, the corners of his lips twitching.

"Um, he swung at me first and well, I got a bit of a bloody nose." Ciaran swiped at his nose, unable to stop smiling.

Shannon gasped, looking him up and down.

"But you should have seen me, Shannon. I clobbered him good, twice even, and he ran off," Ciaran said, puffing out his chest.

Iona grinned. "Well, I'm proud of you, Ciaran. You did a good thing." She nodded her head in encouragement.

Shannon threw a glare at Iona. "What do you mean? He could have got himself killed."

"Hush, Shannon, don't be such a mother hen. Be proud for your friend," she said with a curt nod.

"But, I—"

"See? Don't be a mother hen." Ciaran snickered. She was right. Shannon always doted over him.

Grunting, Shannon grabbed Ciaran by the arm. He hauled him into the side door of the pub, up the stairs and through Iona's flat into the bath. He hurried to wet a washcloth. He swiped the washcloth in harsh dabs over Ciaran's face, cleaning the dried blood from it.

"Shannon." Ciaran searched his face. Why was he behaving this way? It was only a little blood.

He dabbed.

Furrowing his brows, Ciaran said, "Shannon."

Harder, he dabbed.

Ciaran snatched Shannon's furious arm by the wrist. "Stop." He looked directly into Shannon's stunning gray eyes.

Frowning, Shannon creased his forehead, and met Ciaran's gaze. He whined, "You could have been killed, Ciaran." His breath hitched.

Ciaran softened his expression. He must have scared Shannon. He'd never seen him this upset. "Listen, I didn't kick off. I didn't even come close to kicking off. I'm fine, really. I'm sorry. I didn't mean to scare you."

As if seeing him for the first time, Shannon searched his face.

Ciaran parted his lips. What was going on between them? Something was different. He'd never seen Shannon look at him this way. Something had changed between them. His heart swelled with emotion. Could Shannon be feeling the same way he did? Was it possible?

Jerking his wrist free, Shannon flung his arms around Ciaran's shoulders, yanking him close. He clung to Ciaran as if desperate, as if loosening his hold would mean losing him altogether. He whispered, "No, Ciaran, I'm sorry. I have to trust you. I have to have faith in you."

Ciaran lost himself in the soothing embrace. Being in his arms felt heavenly. Could he tell him? "Shannon, I—"

After releasing him, Shannon stood in front of him, studying his face. His hands hung loosely on Ciaran's hips. "You what?" His gaze darted between Ciaran's eyes.

What if I'm wrong? Fear jolted Ciaran's chest. He shifted his gaze to the wall. "Nothing."

Shannon leaned forward, pressing his forehead onto Ciaran's temple, shutting his eyes tight. He sniffled and clenched his jaw. "Okay," he said softly. He drew a deep inhale, then released Ciaran and stepped out of the bathroom, swiping at his eyes.

Standing alone, Ciaran examined the white tiles on the floor. What was he about to say to Shannon? What was this feeling, this ache that kept gnawing at him? *Is it*—he shivered—*Love?* But he'd known Shannon all his life. He was his best friend. How could he be in love with him? And if he was, which he certainly wasn't entirely sure of, why now? Or, had he always felt this way about him, his feelings just needed the help of a drunken night in a hotel room to surface? He scratched his head, twisting his lips. There were so many questions, and he had such little experience with which to draw answers.

Shifting his weight onto one foot, he lifted the other to press the toe of his brown boot into a crevice in the tile. So what, if anything, should he do about the current situation? Shannon was certainly behaving differently, too. Holy shite, he'd actually hugged him for once. He was certainly emotional. Did it mean he had feelings for him, too?

But then why had Shannon been so eager to perform a forbidden act on him the other night, but not last night? He didn't even allow him to push against him. It was baffling. Clearly the hardness he'd felt pressed against his bum last night meant Shannon wanted to do something, meant he'd aroused him in some way. So why would he not do anything? And why did he feel the need to leave so quickly this morning?

Shannon had rejected him, plain and simple. Of course, he could argue with himself about how he shouldn't be doing those things with his best friend anyway, and shouldn't want those things from another man. But the reality was, he did. For whatever reason, it tempted him. To think of it excited him in a way he never thought possible. If it was immoral, then he wanted to be immoral.

Maybe he wasn't forward enough, maybe he had to make his intentions clear. He smirked. Maybe Shannon was struggling the same way he was?

He turned to the door. Well, maybe the best course of action was no action at all. It would all work out in the end. It had to, right? He sauntered out of the bathroom to the stairs.

CIARAN APPROACHED Shannon and Aunt Iona, sitting at a table in the bar. A bottle of whiskey rested on it with a few shot glasses. Were they getting drunk? "Might I join you?" He flashed Shannon an uncertain glance. Why was he drinking like this? Did it have anything to do with what happened?

"Of course, sit down next to your friend there," Iona said, her hand outstretched to the empty seat beside Shannon. "I've got Kelly and a friend of his to tend the bar for a few hours, so we can all drink together."

Ciaran sank into the offered seat, then turned to fixate on Shannon. Maybe a bit of teasing would lessen the tension. "Drinking whiskey now, Shannon? You better eat something settling before you get going on that. You know what happened the last time you drank that stuff." Ciaran spread a playful grin on his face.

Shannon froze with his hand around the glass still on the table. "Quiet, you don't need to tell the whole world." His cheeks reddened and he scowled.

Iona focused on Ciaran with an inquisitive, but smug grin. "Oh, Ciaran, please tell."

Shannon flared his nostrils, then glared at Ciaran, giving him a slow shake of his head.

Ciaran chuckled, turning to his Aunt. *He can't scare me with his nonsense.* "Well, I finally got Shannon to go to a pub with me in town about a year ago. He started drinking whiskey. I've no bloody idea why. Suddenly, he just up and vomits all over the bar." He made a face of disgust and waved his hand in front of them. "It was the damnedest thing and a bloody awful smell."

"Oh my." Iona broadened her lips in a wide grin and sniggered.

"I told you I didn't want to go to that place, Ciaran. I told you I didn't belong. That was why I drank the bloody whiskey." Shannon intensified his glare.

Ciaran continued waving his hand. "Bloody awful smell, Shannon. I've no idea what the hell you ate for dinner that night." Ciaran snorted.

"Shut your trap. I didn't bloody well eat, that's why and you know it." Shannon let a slow grin thin his lips. "Okay fine, it was sort of funny, wasn't it?" He sat forward. "I mean, I made such a mess, practically the whole pub had to clear out. And do you remember how it went all down Seamus' shirt? He deserved it, the feckin' bastard." He snickered.

Iona watched, smiling, as the young men reminisced. "Well then, I'll go and fetch us some supper. I wouldn't want a repeat performance." She raised her brows, then slapped her hands to the table and stood, heading for the bar. When she returned for a brief moment, she set another shot glass down in front of Ciaran, winked at him and left for the front door.

After they'd all filled up on fish and chips Iona bought from a nearby tavern, the whiskey shots flowed again, but this time at her dining table in the flat.

Her arms drew an arc around her. "It's so nice to see young love flourishing here in my home." She laughed.

The young men ceased everything and stared at her.

"What?" Ciaran widened his eyes.

"Oh, did I say something to upset you, dear?" Her laughter slowed to a stop.

Ciaran blinked and looked at Shannon. Why would she say something like that?

Shannon gave her a knowing glare.

Ciaran drew his attention to her. Something was up between them.

Through his teeth, Shannon said, "We're not in love." He placed an elbow on the table as if challenging her.

She met Shannon's glare head on, straightening in her chair. "Oh, really? Prove it then."

"What do you mean? What's going on here, Shannon?" Ciaran darted his gaze between Shannon and his aunt. Why were they suddenly behaving this way? Why did Shannon look so angry? What had she said...*Something about love?* He stared at Shannon. Did Shannon have feelings for him and didn't want to admit it? *Certainly not in front of his aunt...*But he wanted to know. Did Shannon feel the same or not?

"Oh, nothing really. I've just noticed *something* going on here between you two. I think it's love." She let a soft smirk grace her lips.

Ciaran huffed out a laugh. He should dispel this discussion right away. Shannon did not look happy, not at all. "Now why on Earth would you say something like that? It's ridiculous. Shannon's a boy and, well, he's just my best friend, that's all. Right, Shannon?" A lump formed in his throat as his gaze caught Shannon's for a split second. *It hurts to say that. Why?*

With his voice cracking, Shannon said, "Right, we're not in love." He stared at the table, his jaw muscle bulging.

"Okay, prove it then." She motioned with her hands for them to move closer together.

"Prove it how?" Ciaran scooted his chair closer to Shannon's.

"Let me see you kiss each other. If you're not in love, it will surely show in your kiss." A teasing tone laced through her voice. She looked between them both as if waiting for something to happen.

"No." Shannon gripped the arm rail on his chair tight.

She nodded once and chuckled. "Oh, come on now, Shannon, one bloody kiss can't possibly hurt anything."

Is this my chance to find out? "Come on, Shannon, let's just do it and shut her up." Ciaran offered him a sly grin, then placed his hand on Shannon's arm. "Just do it." His heart ached. Now he *needed* to know. If she could tell from their kiss, then he'd make Shannon do it.

Shannon glanced at Iona, pursing his lips. "I said n—"

Jumping, Ciaran seized Shannon's head, driving their lips together in a brutal and passionate kiss.

Shannon widened his eyes. He clawed at his chair.

Ciaran kept a solid hold on the back of Shannon's head. He thrust his tongue against Shannon's teeth, trying to gain entrance. Shannon struggled in his hold, but he wouldn't let him go. *Not now. I need this, even if it's the last time I'll ever have it.*

Shannon's struggling stopped. He parted his lips and drove his urgent tongue into Ciaran's mouth, sliding it along Ciaran's.

Ciaran softly moaned into Shannon's mouth. The kiss

ignited his desire, sending a rush of heat into his groin, making his cock harden. It was too much in front of his aunt. They had to stop before he was unable. He released his hold on Shannon, and sat in a daze in his chair, his lips and groin tingling. He wiped his mouth with the back of his hand. "So, what do you think?" He forced himself to focus on Aunt Iona.

Blinking a few times, Shannon touched his lips, then lurched in his chair, facing Iona. "She doesn't think anything, do you, Iona?" Menace threaded through his voice. Leaning toward her in his seat, he glared at her.

She gave him a warm smile. The hint of a twinkle played in her eye.

"Shut up, Shannon, let the woman speak." Ciaran shifted in his seat, leaning in closer to his aunt. He needed to hear what she had to say. What he'd been feeling had to have been something more than friendship, it just had to.

Shannon softened his expression, tilting his head and wrinkling his brow as if trying to plead with her with only his eyes, turning his lips down.

Rounding her green eyes, she studied Shannon, then opened her mouth as if to speak, but closed it again. As she pitched herself forward in her chair, she slapped her hands on the table and laughed. "Gotcha!" She glanced from Shannon to Ciaran. "I can't believe you actually did it. Oh, my gosh, I was only joking. You two are so gullible."

Shannon freed a frustrated exhale and leaned back in his chair. "It's getting late. I'm heading off to bed." He stood, leaned over her, and whispered in her ear.

Straining to hear, Ciaran watched the exchange. There was definitely some secret between them.

She grabbed Shannon's hand, giving it a gentle squeeze. "Whatever do you mean?"

Shannon furrowed his brows, then focused on Ciaran.

Staring at them, Ciaran hung his mouth open. What in God's name was going on? Why would she think any of this was funny? It wasn't a joke, not to him.

Sighing, Shannon headed for the bedrooms.

Ciaran's attention drew to his aunt. Now that Shannon was gone, should he ask her the truth? Would she tell him?

Freeing a heavy breath, she rose from the table and looked at him. "Go on now, off to bed. We have things to do in the morning."

He caught his lip with his teeth, then nodded and quickly made his way through the flat, into his room and flicked on the feathered lamp, then sat down on the edge of the bed. Placing his elbows on his thighs, he leaned over to let his hands cover his face. His head was swimming, not only from the alcohol flooding his veins. His mind flooded with the illicit act in the hotel room, with Shannon's reaction when he was hurt, to whatever secret Shannon shared with his aunt. *And that kiss...*It was driving him mad. It had inflamed him in a way he'd never thought possible. He wanted more, no, needed more. His hardened cock pushed against the confines of his trousers. Without thinking, ran his palm across the smooth cloth covering the solid flesh, sending a delicious shudder through him.

Quick footsteps clomped in the hallway.

Ciaran looked up, then stood.

Shannon appeared in the doorway. He slammed the door with a thud behind him and watched, panting, a hungry glint in his eye.

"Sha—"

In a flash, Shannon fused his mouth with Ciaran's. His kiss was brutal in its quest for flesh, devouring everything in its wake. As it threw Ciaran backward, he captured and bound his prey. He tore at Ciaran's shirt, ripping it out of his trousers. He thrust his hand underneath, opening buttons to ravage the soft skin of his chest. He shoved his hips forward, pressing his erection hard into Ciaran's hips. As a moan escaped Ciaran, he joined him with a sharp gasp.

Ciaran's heart pounded. Desire hummed over his body. He craved more this time, as much as Shannon would give him. He'd let Shannon do whatever he wanted.

Shifting to Ciaran's neck, Shannon's mouth sucked and licked impatiently at sensitive skin in a track from Ciaran's jaw to his shoulder, reddening it.

Ciaran thrust his hard cock against him, through their trousers, while Shannon walked them both to the bed.

"Oh, God, I want you, Ciaran," Shannon said in a husky voice through the war he raged on Ciaran's body.

"You have me," Ciaran said between ragged breaths. He shoved his hand up between them, making a frantic attempt to unbutton Shannon's shirt, then underneath to unfasten the buttons of his undergarment. He'd do to Shannon what was done to him. As he tapped his fingers over Shannon's chest and down his stomach, Shannon's body shivered.

Shannon released a loud moan. "Keep going." A raw urgency threaded through his voice.

Dashing his hands to Shannon's belt, Ciaran hastily unbuckled it while Shannon continued to lick and suck with insistence on his neck. His body shuddered from the attention, and he closed his eyes for a second. He yanked Shannon's belt free. Finding his fly, he unbuttoned it and hesitated. "I-I'm not sure, what do I do?" He wanted more than anything to pleasure Shannon.

Shannon drove them both down onto the bed.

Ciaran landed on his back with Shannon falling on top of him.

While inflicting a steady stream of persistent kisses and supple bites on Ciaran's neck, Shannon rolled his body enough to unfasten Ciaran's trousers. He ran his mouth down over Ciaran's underwear, stopping at a nipple, coaxing and biting until the nub hardened through the thin fabric. He shoved his hand into Ciaran's trousers.

Sensation pulsed Ciaran's hard cock with Shannon's insistent touch. Moans of building need escaped him while Shannon palmed the moist depths of his groin.

Shannon opened more buttons and freed Ciaran's shaft, pumping steadily over it, then slowed, panting, and gazing deeply into Ciaran's eyes.

As need built to a peak, Ciaran bucked. It wasn't enough. He was right there. Why did Shannon slow down? "F-faster, p-please," he whined.

"Shh..." Shannon pressed a finger to his lips, halting his actions all together. He sat up on his knees and peeled his shirt away, then flung it to the floor. He shimmied out of the top of his undergarment, then looked down at Ciaran.

Hunger flared inside him while he gazed at Shannon's bare chest. *He's definitely a man and I still want him. I don't understand and right now I don't care.*

Shannon, turning his attention to his own trousers, slipped them down with his undergarment to his knees, then sat on the bed and removed them. He threw them to the floor with his shirt and gazed at Ciaran.

Ciaran focused on Shannon's erection, standing tall against his stomach, a bead glistening at the tip. His breath quickened, lust coiling inside him, then he roamed his gaze up Shannon's pale chest to catch with Shannon's.

With a wicked grin, Shannon said, "Do you want to touch it?"

Nodding, Ciaran brushed his tongue over his lips.

Shannon lay down on his side, next to Ciaran.

Ciaran surrounded Shannon's cock with his hand, barely

touching it. As he stared at it, he moved his palm softly, elegantly, up and down his shaft.

Moaning, Shannon arched his head back. A shiver shook him, and he lowered his head to crush his lips to Ciaran's.

Opening his mouth, Ciaran let their tongues engage, probing each other. Shannon's reaction to his touch had his cock aching. He wanted to do more to him. If only he knew how.

Shannon caressed Ciaran's cheek, then pulled away, taking a quick breath. "Ciaran, I uh, is this okay? I mean—you want this?"

"God, Shannon, do you have to ask?" He huffed. Why would he ask something like that *now*? Wasn't it obvious?

Shannon spread a quick grin across his lips as he repositioned himself over Ciaran's waist. He pulled Ciaran's shirt open, then the top of his undergarment and lowered his head into the soft skin of his taut stomach. He licked and teased the sensitive area, causing Ciaran's muscles to flex.

Ciaran placed his hands on the back of Shannon's head, his tongue tickling over his skin. He pressed on it, pushing him further down. If his hand felt so good on him, what would his mouth feel like? Would Shannon do that?

When Shannon reached the top of Ciaran's trousers, he pushed his slick tongue just under the waist of his undergarment.

Desire pulsed through Ciaran's body and a deep groan escaped from his throat.

Shannon set his palm on the thin covering of Ciaran's undergarment, over his erection, and with just enough pressure, slid it sensually up and down. He stopped his hand and felt the lip under the head with his fingers. He ran small circles with his thumb in just the right spot.

Ciaran's cock pulsed with sensation. He freed a drawn-out

moan and thrust against Shannon's fingers. Damn, Shannon knew just how to touch him to drive him mad.

Tugging at the top of Ciaran's trousers, Shannon said, "Take these off."

Ciaran shimmied out of the top of his undergarment, then raised his hips enough to allow Shannon to pull everything down and off.

Shannon sat on tucked legs between Ciaran's thighs, gazing upward to Ciaran's exposed groin. He curled the edge of his mouth into a coy grin, then licked his lips.

Tensing his brows, Ciaran raked his teeth over his lower lip.

Shannon glanced into Ciaran's face, then his attention refocused on Ciaran's groin. He surrounded the base of his cock with his palm and lowered his head between Ciaran's thighs, then licked slowly and sensually up Ciaran's shaft.

"Oh, God." Pleasure jolted through Ciaran. He slapped his hands to the back of Shannon's head, urging him on. God, he wanted this. He'd only heard of these things and certainly never thought he'd ever have it. Not before marriage. Tension coiled deep inside his gut, tightening his sac. He gasped as Shannon's tongue moved over him.

Shannon took the head of Ciaran's erection into his mouth and swirled his tongue around it, then licked his shaft.

As sensation built, Ciaran pressed harder on Shannon's head. "Damn, Shannon, keep doing that."

With a groan, Shannon stroked himself a few times before driving his mouth all the way over Ciaran's shaft, taking him to the back of this throat.

Ciaran jerked his hips, unable to control them. Pleasure tingled and shivered over his whole body. He choked out a growl.

Shannon bobbed his head up and down with an insatiable appetite, while he worked himself with his palm.

With his peak building inside him, Ciaran thrust and shook. What should he do? Should he push Shannon off him? *Oh, but it feels so good.* "Shannon...Shannon!" His body shuddered. He couldn't hold it. He pushed on Shannon's shoulders, rocking his hips back.

Undeterred, Shannon kept his pumping mouth over him.

Ciaran clutched dark hair in his fingers and surrendered, surging his seed into Shannon's mouth in delicious waves.

Devouring the hot fluid spilling into him, Shannon eagerly lapped and swallowed as much of it as he could manage.

As it all slowed, Ciaran grabbed him by the shoulders and pulled him upward.

Shannon stopped the quick strokes on his own erection and raised himself to rest at Ciaran's side. His heavy breathing filled the air. His eyelids were hooded, his pupils wide, and his body trembled.

God, what awful thing did I do to him? Ciaran darted his gaze between Shannon's eyes. "I-I'm sorry, Shannon. I didn't mean to, um..."

Shannon twitched the edges of his mouth as if attempting a smile, then gazed shyly down at Ciaran's chest and drew a small circle on it. "It's okay, I uh, like that."

"You do? You mean you've done that before?" Ciaran widened his eyes. Were the rumors about the teacher true? What else had Shannon done? Had he done these things with anyone else? Heat flashed in his chest. No, he wouldn't.

Shannon's cheeks reddened and he buried his face in Ciaran's neck. "Please, I don't want to talk about it."

Wrapping his arms around him, Ciaran said, "Then we won't." If the rumors were true about Shannon having an affair with Mr. Flannigan and then Father Brennan dealing with it, what sort of horrors had Shannon gone through? Maybe someday, Shannon would tell him. He turned his head into Shannon's and pressed his lips against his cheek. He held the kiss for a moment before pulling away. He needed to give Shannon some release from his arousal. He slowly snuck a hand between them and stroked gently on Shannon's still very hard cock.

Shannon tensed his brows and let out a soft moan.

"Tell me what to do," Ciaran whispered. Desire flashed inside him. He liked making Shannon feel good.

"J-just k-keep doing that, but harder maybe, a little faster, too," Shannon said inside deep breaths.

Ciaran increased the pressure and speed of his palm on Shannon.

"Just a minute." Shannon pulled Ciaran's hand back up by the wrist, looked him straight in the eye, and ran a seductive and saturated tongue along Ciaran's palm.

Ciaran stared back, swallowing hard, his own cock stirring back to life.

"Okay, now try," Shannon said.

Ciaran gazed deeply into Shannon's eyes while he placed his wetted palm on his erection. It slid with ease over the stiff shaft.

Groaning, Shannon bucked in obvious pleasure.

Ciaran guided Shannon onto his back, engaging him in heated kisses, stroking his shaft, feeling it pulsate in his hand. Doing this to Shannon was too intoxicating for words.

Surrendering to Ciaran's control, Shannon melted into the mattress. He explored Ciaran's mouth with his tongue while his hips thrust insistently upward with each stroke of Ciaran's palm. His body trembled and his hip thrusts became erratic. He broke Ciaran's kisses and shut his eyes tight, his face tensing, his teeth clenching, then buried his face into the crook of

Ciaran's neck, as if holding on for dear life. The moans started deep in his throat, rushing to be released. As Shannon's climax came, he drove hard into Ciaran's palm, his body growing rigid, seed erupting over Ciaran's palm and between them. A cry escaped him.

Ciaran softly covered Shannon's mouth with his clean hand and shushed him. Could Aunt Iona hear Shannon? *God, he looked so blissful. Did I do that to him?* As it subsided, he released his hand from Shannon's mouth and rummaged in the sheets, cleaning them both off.

As if searching for something, Shannon looked up into Ciaran's eyes.

Ciaran spread a faint smile on his lips and cupped Shannon's face in his hand. It was time for answers. "I like this, Shannon. I like being with you this way. But what exactly is this?" His gaze roamed Shannon's face. Would he finally hear what he wanted to hear?

Shannon's throat dipped with a hard swallow. He looked away for a moment, then came back. "I-I don't know, I suppose it can be whatever you want it to be," he said softly.

"Well, what do you want it to be?" Ciaran held him tightly. He would get his answers.

Shannon whined, "I don't know, Ciaran." He shifted under Ciaran's body, attempting to look away again.

Ciaran pressed on Shannon's chin, bringing him back. Was the secret Shannon shared with his aunt how he felt about him? Is that what was going on? He should just ask. Surely, Shannon would tell him. "Is it what Iona said, you suppose? Could we be in love?" He pressed his lips together, his heart hammering in his chest. What would he say?

With wrinkled brows, Shannon searched his face. He opened his mouth to speak, then shut it again.

Maybe he doesn't feel the same. Maybe I'm wrong. His chest ached. He needed to get out of this somehow. He spread an anxious smile over his lips. "That's silly, isn't it? To think we might be in love with each other. I mean, sure, I love you. But you're my best friend. So of course, I'm going to love you, in a way. But guys don't love each other, do they, Shannon?" He forced a grin.

Shannon's eyes glistened and he twisted his head away, then took an audible swallow. "Yeah, I suppose we love each other like friends." He huffed a quick chuckle. "It would be silly to think we'd be in love." He turned onto his side, away from Ciaran, and curled himself into a tight ball.

Shifting in the bed, Ciaran leaned over Shannon's side, caressing his shoulder. Was Shannon about to cry? A lump formed in his throat. Why wouldn't Shannon just tell him if he loved him more than a friend? "Are you all right?" What could he do to make him feel better, to make him trust him?

"Yeah, just feel a little sick all of a sudden." Shannon's voice cracked.

He's not ready. I won't push him. "I knew you shouldn't have drunk all that whiskey." Ciaran lay back down and hesitated. What should he do? He should comfort him as best he could. He wrapped his body around Shannon's in a desperate embrace and placed a lingering kiss on his back. "Goodnight, Shannon. Let me know if you need to be sick, okay?"

A light sniffle escaped Shannon. "Yeah, okay. Goodnight."

Ciaran reached for the nightstand, flicked off the lamp with the red-feathered shade and went back to Shannon. He positioned himself as close as possible, making sure no gaps existed between them, giving him a brief but pure squeeze. He closed his eyes.

Shannon's breathing became rhythmic in his hold.

CHAPTER SEVEN
SHANNON

Shannon dreamed. Feeling strangely content, a presence surrounded him. He tried to seek out a face, but there was none. A soft voice drifted over his head, swirled around his ears, and lingered in his heart. It spoke words he'd longed for, ached for, and searched for, words of acceptance, of compassion and love. Yearning to hold on to it, he reached out, grasping emptiness.

Popping his eyes open, Shannon looked around him. Ciaran's green eyes gazed back at him. He squinted, attempting to focus.

Ciaran let a smile play on his face.

They both lay on their sides, facing each other. Ciaran had rested his hand on Shannon's cheek and his gaze searched Shannon's face.

Ciaran parted his lips. "Thought you'd never wake up."

"Oh? And how long have you been watching?" Shannon's gaze roamed over Ciaran's lovely face.

Dropping his gaze to Shannon's lips, Ciaran caressed his cheek with his fingers.

Shannon's pulse skipped a beat.

Ciaran brought his face close.

As Ciaran pressed his lips to his own, Shannon closed his eyes. He swooned, even this early in the morning. As Ciaran broke the kiss, Shannon took a moment to refocus.

"Long enough to see you make a bunch of silly faces while you sleep." Ciaran grinned.

Shannon let out a sharp gasp. "I did not." He spread a smile across his lips.

"Yes, you did. What were you dreaming about anyway?" Ciaran looked him over.

"None of your business," Shannon said with a sly grin.

"Were you dreaming about me?" Ciaran lifted his brows and bit his lip.

"Maybe." Shannon averted his gaze. Yes, Ciaran was the one he'd reached for in his dream. If only he'd been able to hang on.

Ciaran beamed. "I hope so." He leaned in, placing a deep, lingering kiss on Shannon's lips.

Rapping sounded at the door. "Boys, time to get up," Iona said in a lighthearted shout from the other side of the door.

They both jumped and pulled apart.

"Shite, Shannon, do you think she knows what we did last night?" Ciaran said, hustling to get out of bed and put his discarded clothes on.

"I'd say she definitely knows something." Shannon already had his undergarment on and hopped on one leg to push through his trousers. As soon as he threw his dark shirt over his shoulders, he glanced at Ciaran.

Ciaran's trousers were already in place, and he was buttoning the top of his underwear.

Shannon reached for the door and thrust it open.

She stood at the doorway, her hands resting on her hips, a smug grin on her face. "Well, having a little fun, were we?"

"N-no, ma'am." Ciaran rubbed his neck and frowned.

Hanging his head, Shannon attempted to hide his smile. *She did this on purpose.* Too bad Ciaran wasn't privy to their ice cream conversation yesterday.

Ciaran fidgeted with the hem of his shirt, hanging from his hands. "Ah, we were, we were just—"

"Stop, Ciaran. Come in here and have a seat at the table." She turned and strolled into the kitchen.

Ciaran followed with his head lowered, clenching, and unclenching his fists. As he twisted around, he wrinkled his forehead, peering at Shannon.

Shannon snatched Ciaran's hand.

Lifting his brows, Ciaran took a deep inhale while Shannon led him to the dining table.

Shannon tightened his hold on Ciaran's hand as they sat down beside each other. He'd calm him the only way he could, given the situation.

After the young men sat down, she set mugs of tea in front of them. While getting one for herself, she picked something up from the counter and came to the table with a small, ornate, silver picture frame in her hand. She took a seat opposite them, the same place she always sat. She frowned as she gazed into the frame for a moment, then placed it in front of the young men, the picture facing them.

Shannon and Ciaran leaned over, getting a good view of the contents the frame held.

That must be Iona. Shannon took in the photo. She looked youthful. She stood with her arm around a young woman with dark, wavy hair. The woman was pretty, very feminine looking. She wore a long skirt and a frilly top. Both women stood in front of the pub entrance, smiling. After seeing enough, he shifted his gaze up to meet hers.

Her eyes glistened with tears.

Shannon's breath caught.

"That, my dear boys, was my partner. And I think you both know what I'm talking about, not just a business partner, mind you." She sniffed the unshed tears away.

Shannon glanced at Ciaran, watching her with his mouth hanging open, then he focused back on her.

"Her name was Sinead. I met her at university. She was... my best friend and my lover. She died about ten years ago."

Nodding slowly, Ciaran took a hard swallow.

Shannon's heart ached for her. How terrible it must have been.

"It's a hard road you may be traveling, especially in a small town like Drimnagh. Please, be careful with yourselves when you go home today. Not everyone is as understanding about the very special thing you have with each other. And it is special. Don't ever let anyone tell you otherwise." She flashed her gaze between them as if to drive her point across.

Ciaran slowly turned to face Shannon. He opened his mouth as if to speak, but closed it again.

The wheels are turning furiously in Ciaran's head. Shannon squeezed his hand a little harder and gauged Ciaran's reaction.

Staring at their entwined hands, Ciaran pinched his lips, then gazed at Shannon with longing in his eyes.

Iona stood and went to the stove. With her back to them, she said, "So what'll it be today? Omelettes maybe?" She held her head high.

"Uh, yes, that sounds wonderful." Shannon glanced at her, then turned his attention back on Ciaran. What was going through his lovely head?

Ciaran dropped his gaze to his lap and fidgeted with the bottom hem of his shirt with his free hand.

She moved efficiently around her kitchen, pulling out pans, eggs and cheese. "Don't you two need to pack?" An unexpected cheer filled her voice.

"Come on, Ciaran," Shannon said softly. He stood and pulled him along. Why was Ciaran so quiet? His behavior unnerved him. Was Ciaran having second thoughts about what they were doing? *God, I hope not. It would kill me.* He towed him to the guest room.

Once they were inside, Ciaran whirled around, throwing his arms over Shannon's shoulders, yanking him close.

Gasping, Shannon wrapped his arms around Ciaran's waist.

"Oh, Shannon, is it true? Is this special?" Ciaran said against Shannon's neck.

Shannon tightened his hold on him. "Yes, it's very special, to me anyways." How he longed to tell him everything—how in love he really was, how he'd always been in love with him. He inhaled and opened his mouth to confess it all. A shock of fear tore through his heart, catching the words in his throat. He fisted his hands behind Ciaran's back. He clenched his jaw. Why did he still fear rejection when Ciaran did nothing but give him signs otherwise? What was wrong with him? Had he been so polluted by what happened to him, he was unable to say what needed to be said? A heavy ache filled his heart. He clung to him, unable to do anything else.

Lifting his head, Ciaran gazed deeply into his eyes. "Shannon, I—" He tensed his face. "It's special to me, too." He buried his face in Shannon's neck.

Ciaran's breath whispered, warm and tickling, against the sensitive skin of Shannon's neck. He tilted his head and brushed his cheek over Ciaran's soft hair. *Say something soothing at least, Shannon.* Words refused him. Surrendering to his fear with a sigh, he skimmed his hand up Ciaran's back and smoothly raked his fingers through his silky hair. A vision of the sorrowful embrace in the barn flooded his mind and how he'd longed to do just this. It was another lifetime ago.

Home. Shannon softly sighed. How would they ever go back there, to their old lives? His heart stammered, squeezing his chest. He pushed Ciaran's head deeper into his neck, drawing him in closer. He swayed their bodies in a barely noticeable dance. The words screamed inside his head to be released. *I love you, Ciaran, I've always loved you and I always will.* But tucked somewhere deep inside is where they stayed. He shut his eyes tight.

"Breakfast is ready," Iona called from the kitchen.

Ciaran dragged himself away from Shannon's arms. He narrowed his eyes and ducked down to search up under the long bangs covering Shannon's face. "Are you okay?" Ciaran whispered.

Wincing, Shannon said, "Yeah." It was a simple lie. He released Ciaran and walked out of the room with his head lowered. He had to gather himself before reaching the table. He dropped into a chair at Iona's large dining table, then let out a heavy sigh. He slid his forearms over the surface, gazing at his hands, while his fingers meshed, each trying to dominate the other.

Iona turned from her place at the stove and frowned. She brought a plate filled with the mixture of eggs and cheese over to Shannon, then set it down, leaned over and opened her mouth as if to say something.

Ciaran bounded into the room.

Shutting her mouth, she focused on Ciaran.

"Aunt Iona, I can't believe I almost forgot to give you this." Ciaran said, excitement radiating from his voice. In his outstretched hand was the gold locket, the sole reason for their journey.

She walked toward him, smiling. "Oh, thank you, luv. I must say, I'm honored your dear mother thought to give it to me. It does mean a great deal."

Ciaran dropped the locket into her extended palm and took a seat beside Shannon. As he fixated on Shannon, he wrinkled his brows.

As Shannon watched Iona, she unclasped the mechanism on the locket's chain and put it around her neck. When she let go, it hung midway into her bosom. Using a delicate touch to probe it with her fingers, she appeared to be in deep thought for a moment before going back to her stove.

Shannon picked at his food, hearing the sound of a chair dragging across the floor.

"You don't want to go home, do you?" Ciaran whispered into his ear.

Shannon slowly shook his head, staring at the fork making sluggish, deliberate circles on his plate. He wished it was the only problem he had at the moment.

Ciaran draped his arm around Shannon's shoulders and gave him a firm squeeze.

Closing his eyes, Shannon let Ciaran's touch comfort him.

Iona set a plate with an omelette on it in front of Ciaran and peered at Shannon. "My, not eating, are we?" She planted her hands on her hips, spatula hanging limp at her side.

Shannon lazily put the fork into a bit of egg and raised it to his mouth. He didn't feel like eating or talking. Couldn't he just be left alone to sulk in peace? He deserved to sulk, didn't he? Not only was he going back to that horrible place, but now he seemed to finally have what he wanted for so long and he couldn't bring himself to say the words he needed to say.

She left again to put an omelette on a plate for herself.

When she returned, she sat opposite the young men. She dug into her eggs, but stopped periodically to turn a puzzled gaze to Shannon.

Ciaran ate, keeping an eye on Shannon, brushing their legs together.

When they finished eating, Iona promptly cleared the table.

Shannon walked in silence back to his room to gather his things. Once inside, he placed bits of clothing into his pillowcase, sighing while looking around the room. He became aware of a presence in the doorway. He turned.

Furrowing her brows, Iona stood in the doorway, her arms crossed over her chest.

Shannon hung his head, hiding under his bangs.

She stepped into the room and stopped directly in front of him, then placed a hand on his forearm. In a soothing voice, she said, "Shannon, dear, I expect you may be a bit frightened. Sometimes it's hard to get what we've wanted our whole lives. The reality doesn't always follow the fantasy, does it?"

"I, I love him, so much," he said, barely audible, but saying the words out loud. To his surprise, the floor he examined blurred, and his breath hitched. With his shoulders shaking against his will, he bit his lower lip, stifling a sob. He wouldn't cry.

She pulled him forward into her soft body, holding him in a strong embrace. "I know it hurts, luv. But that's just how it is. Take the chance. It's worth it, it really is. I know you'll be careful. Please remember this, if you ever need anything, let me know." She released him and left the room.

He ambled to the edge of the bed and sat down with his arms resting on his thighs. The threat of tears dissipated, but the feeling of trepidation wouldn't soften. He'd have another day to deal with it at least. Maybe they could stay in the same inn they stayed at on the way here. This time it would be different, much different.

SHANNON SAT BESIDE CIARAN, holding the reins and saying their final goodbye to Iona. She'd given them monstrous hugs and they'd thanked her. She'd provided much more than just a place to stay.

"Take care of yourselves, and remember to please be careful. I'll miss you both terribly." She waved at them.

With a flick of the reins by Ciaran, the horse clopped down the narrow cobblestone street. "I'll miss you, too. Maybe we can come back some time?" Ciaran called.

"Anytime, luv," she yelled.

Shannon nodded once, watching her with sadness eating at his heart, while she faded from view.

SHANNON LOOKED at the countryside surrounding their small cart, noticing patches of brown in the green hills. The patches weren't there the last time they came through here. Would everything finally just dry up? The late afternoon heat sweltered around him, making sweat form on his brow and upper lip. He shifted his gaze ahead of them. The small town they'd stayed at on their trip out was coming into view.

It's time to talk to Ciaran. Shannon chanced a peek at him. He'd been thinking over and over about Iona's warning to be careful since they left Dublin, but Ciaran had kept holding his hand and giving him absent kisses while they'd plodded along alone. Although it was like a dream come true, he had to make Ciaran understand the full consequences of someone seeing him do those things. "We need to talk about something." His voice was low and firm.

Ciaran spread a wide grin over his lips, playfully knocking his shoulder into Shannon's chest. "Oh really, you mean you finally have something to say?" His body bumped along in the cart.

"This is bloody serious." Shannon held Ciaran's hand between them and gave it a sharp squeeze.

"Ow." Ciaran startled and wiggled his hand.

Shannon held tight and didn't let go.

Ciaran huffed and glared at him.

Shannon furrowed his brows. "We really have to be careful when we get back home. If anyone sees or even suspects they see something between us like this." He held up their entwined hands. "Well, it would be bloody awful."

Raising his brows, Ciaran twisted his lips. "What do you mean, it would be bloody awful?"

"I mean awful, as in, it's illegal, Ciaran." *He better not question me as to how I know these things.* He glanced at the horse, then focused on Ciaran, studying him. Would he have to disclose his illicit affair with Mr. Flannigan? He couldn't, not yet.

Ciaran let a faint smile play on his lips. "You mean they'd put us in jail for holding hands?"

"Don't be daft. It would mean our special thing here would be over." Shannon scoffed. Should he tell Ciaran how he, himself, would be driven from the town, if not killed? Should he tell Ciaran how he'd be forever shunned? No, it'd surely bring up the situation with the teacher.

As if in deep thought, Ciaran examined Shannon's face.

Fear jolted Shannon's heart. He looked away.

"But, how do y—"

"Just know I'd never see you again." Shannon breathed deeply. This conversation must end, here, now.

"Don't even say that. I'd never let that happen." Ciaran frowned.

In a low and spiteful voice, Shannon said, "Yeah, well, sometimes you don't have a bloody choice." He unwrapped his fingers from Ciaran's and rested his hand in his lap as they approached buildings and townspeople.

Ciaran pursed his lips and tensed his brow, then scanned their surroundings. As the inn came closer, he steered the horse to the front entrance.

"Listen, I'll check us in and bring our things up to the room. Then I'll meet you in the pub." Shannon climbed off the cart, focusing his attentions on pulling Ciaran's suitcase and his pillowcase out of the back.

Flashing a quick smile at him, Ciaran said, "Hungry again, are we?"

Shannon returned the smile. "Yeah."

Shannon strolled into the smoke-filled tavern after taking care of his tasks to find Ciaran sitting at the same bench they'd sat at the last time they had supper here. "Feeling a bit nostalgic, eh, Ciaran?" He let out a faint chuckle. He took a seat next to Ciaran and raked a hand through his hair, scrutinizing the room. A fair number of patrons filled the tables and sat at the bar. The place must be doing very well. A hand warmed his thigh, startling him. He tossed Ciaran's hand off, then glared at him. "Didn't you hear what I said earlier?"

Peering at him, Ciaran creased his brow. "Of course, but nobody could see that and besides, we're not home yet."

Shannon leaned in close. "You never know who may be around. You think people from our town might not have traveled here? You think rumors can't spread from here to Drimnagh? Besides, you have to get used to keeping your hands to yourself now." He searched Ciaran's beautiful face. Did his words hurt Ciaran? But he had to get through to him.

Ciaran frowned, then hung his head.

Ah, shite. Shannon's chest ached. This was terrible. Maybe he shouldn't have been so harsh.

Turning his head away, Ciaran stared toward the far wall of the tavern, thinning his lips.

Shannon pressed his chest against Ciaran's side. "I'm sorry. I shouldn't have been so hard on you. It's just—"

Ciaran whirled around to face him. "What happened, Shannon? Why is it you know all these things?"

Lurching back, Shannon gasped, then opened his mouth to speak.

"What would you like then? Couple a pints maybe? Seemed to really enjoy the beer the last time you were here." The waitress gave Ciaran a flirtatious smile. She tapped a pencil on the side of her blonde hair, swaying slowly.

Shannon lowered his head, hiding under his hair. He darted his gaze across his lap. His heart hammered in his chest.

"Uh, yes, a pint for me and my friend here. And do you have the shepherd's pie tonight?" Ciaran asked the waitress.

"Of course, every night." She eyed them both as if curious.

"We'll have that again, too," Ciaran said.

The waitress trotted off.

Shannon's mind raced. *How can I answer Ciaran's question?*

Ciaran placed his hand on Shannon's forearm. "Shannon, please, let's just eat and get to our room, okay?"

The two sat in silence while they drank beer and ate their supper. Shannon glanced over at Ciaran, feeling his leg resting lightly against his own. How was Ciaran ever going to be able to control his behavior? He knew Ciaran. He was impulsive. It made him anxious. What if Ciaran did touch him inappropriately and someone saw? The intense scrutiny he was always under would surely worsen.

Shannon shoveled mashed potatoes, gravy and ground beef into his mouth, thinking of the town priest, Father Brennan. He'd taken it upon himself to handle the situation between himself and Mr. Flannigan. He was the one who'd told his parents what happened, who'd made his parents believe he was tarnished, a thing to be feared and kept under control.

Shannon gulped down his food with a sip of beer, then snarled his lip. Father Brennan always pretended to be so sympathetic to him. But he'd always seen behind the guise. He knew what the priest really thought of him. He'd seen the loathing and revulsion in his eyes.

Shannon narrowed his eyes. *The bastard even told me what happened to me was evil. He said Mr. Flannigan was an evil person, possessed by some demon.* He shifted in his seat and swallowed more of his supper down. He'd been made to go to confession and relive everything in great detail. The priest delighted in making him feel as if he himself were evil, after he admitted to liking Mr. Flannigan's attentions. Those terrible things made him feel horrible about himself for years. *Oh, how I hate that priest.*

Sighing, Shannon played with the mashed potato on his plate with his fork. *And whatever became of Mr. Flannigan? He simply disappeared without a trace. Although I never loved him, I was fond of him. It was painful when he disappeared without so much as a goodbye.*

"I said, aren't you going to finish your food?" Clear irritation flooded Ciaran's voice.

"Huh? Yeah, I am." Shannon shoveled his dinner into his mouth at a quick pace.

Chapter

Eight

Ciaran

They'd finished eating, Ciaran paid for the meal and followed Shannon back to the room.

Shannon pushed the key into the lock, his hands trembling, then opened the door and entered the room. He walked to the nightstand and turned the lamp on.

After stepping inside, Ciaran shut the door with a creak. It was time to find out what happened to Shannon. Judging by his shaking hands and the way he'd been behaving, it was something terrible. Now that they were alone, he would comfort him as best he could. He gazed at Shannon's back, then went to him and hooked his arms around Shannon's waist from behind.

Tilting his head back, Shannon held onto Ciaran's arms.

Ciaran placed soft kisses at the back of his neck, nuzzling into dark hair. Desire shivered over his spine. He wanted Shannon more than anything, but first he needed to know his deep, dark secret.

After turning around in Ciaran's arms, Shannon gazed deeply into his eyes.

Ciaran searched his face. What did he see there? How much pain he held in his eyes. He pressed his lips against Shannon's, in a tender kiss. Was he ready to talk about it? "Shannon, I need to know something."

Shannon's breath caught. He clutched at his chest. He stared at Ciaran, dropping his mouth open.

Darting his gaze between Shannon's gray, pained eyes, Ciaran asked, "What happened with Mr. Flannigan? I need to know exactly what he did to you."

Shannon's eyes flooded with tears. He wrinkled his forehead and his lip trembled. He blinked, sending thick tears tumbling down both cheeks. He opened his mouth as if to speak, but only a choked sob came out. He balled his hands up into fists held straight down at his sides, as if the action could build a barrier between himself and his emotions.

With his chest aching, Ciaran yanked him into a firm embrace. *Oh, God, the whole thing must be more horrible than I thought.*

Shannon's shoulders shook with heavy sobs. His breathing hitched.

"It's okay, Shannon, I'll understand, I promise. I just need to know." Ciaran held firm and kissed the side of his head. How could he alleviate his pain? He tugged him even closer, shushing him.

Shannon unclenched his fists and clung frantically to Ciaran, burying his face in his neck, weeping out of control.

"Oh God, it must have been awful. I'm so sorry...so sorry." Ciaran swayed them both back and forth, then brought his head back for a moment, studying him, pain piercing his chest. He'd never seen Shannon outright cry before, not since they were children. Tears formed in his eyes. He quickly blinked them back and placed a gentle kiss on the side of his head. How could he help him?

Shannon wept for a few minutes in Ciaran's steady embrace and soothing kisses. Soon, he quieted, let him go and took a seat on the edge of the bed. He peered down at his loose hands sitting in his lap.

Ciaran sat next to him and draped an arm around his shoulders, pulling him close.

Relaxing into Ciaran's body, Shannon turned and rested his head in Ciaran's neck. He sniffled. A new round of tears pooled in his eyes and one rushed down a wet trail on his cheek.

"Please, talk to me." Ciaran's voice was thick. He swallowed a lump climbing up his throat. He had to be strong for Shannon now, he couldn't give in to his own emotions.

Shannon drew a deep breath. "Ciaran, h-he...we did th-things, bad things, behind the schoolroom."

Heat surged in Ciaran's chest. He snarled and said, "He forced you, didn't he?" *The bloody bastard.*

Shannon let a short sob escape. "No, he didn't," he said in a soft voice, "I mean, at first, I suppose he did a little. But I wouldn't say it was forced, maybe just a strong suggestion."

Ciaran gasped and widened his eyes. "Wh-why did you let him?"

Flinching, Shannon drew himself back. He bit his lip while another tear tumbled down to his jaw. "I-I don't know, Ciaran." He took a deep inhale. "Maybe I was just curious."

Ciaran tightened his grip on Shannon's shoulders. *I'm not saying the right things. What am I supposed to say?* "I'm sorry. I didn't mean to accuse you."

"But you might as well. I was just as bad as he was. I w-was just as terrible. The first time I was a little scared, but I should have known better. I knew it was wrong and I didn't stop it, never even told him to stop. Then after, I thought about it, all the time. I couldn't wait for it to happen again. And it did, many times. Each time he did more to me, showed me more about what men can do with each other. And I enjoyed it, asked for it even. You see, Ciaran, it seems I've always had feelings for men. Well, for boys, a certain boy, in fact. All I ever thought about was you while we did those sinful things." Shannon's shoulders shook again while more tears gathered and made their descent down his cheeks. "A-and now, I-I've gone and done the same thing to you that he did to me. I-I'm a m-monster, aren't I, Ciaran?"

Ciaran took a sharp breath. *That's not right. What he's saying cannot be right.* He drew him nearer as Shannon released soft sobs into his shoulder. "No, you're not a monster. It's not the same, not at all, because I love you, Shannon. Not like a friend, not like a brother even, but like a lover. I honestly love you with all my heart." His own tears mingled with dark hair.

Shannon's crying came to an abrupt halt. He was quiet for a second and pulled away, peering with intense longing into Ciaran's eyes. He placed a palm on each of Ciaran's cheeks, searching his face.

Ciaran lost himself in Shannon's stunning gray eyes. Yes, what he said was true. He loved him. He'd probably always loved him.

Shannon traced arcs across the soft, wet skin with his thumbs, tenderly brushing away Ciaran's tears. His scanning gaze stopped, and he widened his eyes as if finally understanding him fully. "Ciaran, I-I love you, too. I've always loved you, ever since we were little. Even when I was with Mr. Flannigan, it was you I loved, you I dreamt of being with. It was always you." He fixated on Ciaran's face.

Lunging forward, Ciaran crushed Shannon's lips with an urgent kiss.

Shannon tumbled backward onto the bed with a grunt, then kissed back with an intense hunger, struggling to reposition himself on the bed with Ciaran on top of him. He clawed at Ciaran's shirt, lifting it from its confines. He plunged beneath thin fabric to open buttons and ravage the soft skin. He thrust his hips upward.

As Shannon's erection met with Ciaran's, it sent a pulse of pleasure bolting through his system. Ciaran's senses were full of his lover, his Shannon.

Moaning, Shannon greedily consumed him. He moved his lips across Ciaran's jaw and down onto his neck, sucking and nipping tenderly at the sensitive skin.

Insistent groans ripped from Ciaran's mouth. He writhed, grinding into Shannon, trying to gain as much friction as possible through the restricting fabric of their trousers. He roamed hands over Shannon's lean body through the thin cotton dress shirt, unable to take the time to undo buttons or get underneath, then down to his buttocks. "Shannon, do it all to me, everything." He needed this, needed him. It was all so perfect, there was nothing left standing between them. All the barriers and confusion were broken down completely.

Shannon continued his rapid assault on Ciaran's neck, shuddering against him. "Do you want to enter me?" he asked between increasingly heated bites and licks on Ciaran's chest, thrusting his hips against Ciaran again and again.

Ciaran popped his eyes wide open. *What exactly is he asking me?* He slowed his actions and looked down on him.

Arching his head back, Shannon peered up at Ciaran.

Ciaran searched his face.

"What's wrong?" Shannon asked through ragged breathing.

"I don't know what you mean." Ciaran did his best to maintain a look of calm while apprehension wound in his chest.

Shannon kissed Ciaran on the mouth, pushing his tongue deep into him as if to show him with his mouth what he wanted him to do. He broke the kiss. "I want you, Ciaran. I want to feel you inside me."

Ciaran pulled away. "I'm sorry, I just don't see how—"

"I'll show you."

Furrowing his brows, Ciaran stared at the wall. What did that mean exactly? Men had sex with other men? But he'd never even done that with a woman.

Shannon placed his palm on Ciaran's cheek and guided him back. He kissed him gently on the mouth. "You're not ready."

Biting his lip, Ciaran hung his head.

"It's okay, I'd never want to do something you're not ready for. I can wait, there are so many other things we can do, and I want to do it all with you." Shannon rolled to the side, grasping the bottom of Ciaran's shirt. He drew it up and moved to allow him to shimmy out of it and the top of his undergarment. As he leaned over him, he gave Ciaran a warm, lingering kiss. It quickly turned heated. The previous intensity between them resumed as he opened his mouth to accept Ciaran's tongue. He roamed his hand down Ciaran's bare chest and unfastened Ciaran's trousers, then lightly ran his fingertips over Ciaran's muscular abdomen, stopping over a nipple. He teased, giving it a light pinch, hardening the nub.

Sensation shivered over Ciaran, from his nipple to his shaft. He tensed his brow with a groan. He'd no idea doing that could make him feel so good. Shannon definitely knew what he was doing. He wanted to give Shannon the same pleasure. He raced a hand along the front of Shannon's shirt, unbuttoning it with quick jerks of his fingers, then unbuttoned the undergarment. He couldn't wait for skin-on-skin contact. As soon as Shannon's shirt and undergarment were open, he plunged his hand onto Shannon's chest, sliding over and across his skin. He couldn't touch enough of it. He snuck his hand down between

Shannon's legs and stroked hard on his erection through his trousers.

Shannon bucked and pulled away from Ciaran's mouth, moaning urgently. "Touch me, Ciaran." He found Ciaran's chest with his mouth and resumed his assault on Ciaran's nipple with his teeth and tongue.

Pleasure surged through him, making him shiver. He unfastened the buttons on Shannon's trousers, fumbling with it. He wanted to touch him, to feel him in his palm.

Shannon reached down and placed his trembling hand over Ciaran's. He gazed deeply into Ciaran's eyes, then swiftly unfastened his trousers, and rolled onto his back to remove the rest of his clothing.

As Shannon turned onto his side, Ciaran slickened his palm and wrapped it around Shannon's arousal with a fierce grip. He marveled at the soft skin covering the hard shaft, so much like his own, but different in such an enticing way.

As Shannon engaged in deep kisses over Ciaran's lips, Ciaran stroked Shannon.

Releasing a loud, long moan, Ciaran pressed his hardened cock against Shannon's hips. Sensation pulsed his cock and coiled in his gut.

Shannon pushed urgent thrusts into Ciaran's slick palm.

More, I want more of him. As lust quivered over his body, Ciaran crawled down between Shannon's legs and kissed and sucked the inside of his thighs, sniffing at the heady scent of him. Shannon's shaft brushed against his cheek. He lifted his head over Shannon's erection, studying the perfection of it, the glistening pre-seed at the tip, then glanced at Shannon's face. Could he do this? God, how he wanted to. He could make Shannon feel so good. The power of it became almost overwhelming.

Shannon looked down at him with raw need filling his eyes. He brushed his tongue over his lips and whimpered.

Plunging his head down, Ciaran grabbed the base of Shannon's seeping cock with one hand, running his tongue up the outside of his shaft.

Shannon bucked as Ciaran's tongue slid sensually up and down, over and over, each time Shannon's cock pulsed, and his body shuddered.

Ciaran slid his tongue faster and faster. He lifted his head and plummeted again, placing his entire mouth over Shannon's erection, taking him in completely. Oh, the feeling it invoked in him, the aching need it produced in his own cock. He needed this, needed to do this to him.

Arching his back, Shannon let out a loud groan. He clasped the bedcovers, shutting his eyes tight, his hot shaft pulsating inside Ciaran's relentless mouth.

Ciaran kept on him, moaning and writhing, rapt in the act and the sudden power he held over Shannon. He became bolder, flicking his tongue over the head of Shannon's erection.

A new round of insistent moans ripped out of Shannon and into the room.

Ciaran slid his mouth back over Shannon's throbbing cock and heightened the pressure and speed, making Shannon's body tremble. He was lost in Shannon's reaction, in his obvious urgency.

"Uh, Ciaran, stop," Shannon panted, "Stop, I-I'm...Stop!" Shannon shoved Ciaran off him, then held himself still, breathing heavily. He shuddered and his cock jerked off his stomach. As his breathing slowed, he gazed down at Ciaran.

Ciaran lay on his side, over one of Shannon's legs. Had he done something wrong? Did he hurt Shannon somehow? Tension hummed inside him. "Why did you push me away?"

He raised up over Shannon's waist on his elbows, his chest pressing onto Shannon's weeping cock.

Shannon's face flushed. "Because I didn't want to, um, I didn't think you'd want me to um—"

"You did it to me." Ciaran shrugged his shoulders. "I think I can handle it." In fact, he craved it even. What would he taste like?

"Really? Are you sure?" Shannon winced, then widened his eyes, licking his lips.

Ciaran lifted a corner of his mouth, then dived down over Shannon's cock, gliding his mouth back over it. God, he tasted good. As he took him in fully, he moaned against his shaft, resuming his motions with renewed intensity. He was determined now. He would take him to release.

As if in surrender to every lick, every suck of Ciaran's mouth, Shannon arched his back. A loud cry tore from his throat while his climax spurted into Ciaran in waves of pulses. He thrust erratically between Ciaran's pumping lips.

Ciaran kept a tight hold on Shannon while his seed surged into his throat. With unexpected eagerness, he drank it all in. The act fed his desire. His body trembled with a sweet tension. As it finished, he rose up, plunged his hands down and stripped off his trousers and underwear. He needed to finish, now. He sat up again, hung his head, then positioned his saliva-soaked palm over his solid cock and pumped fast and hard. As sweet tension surged inside him, he panted and let sharp gasps break from his throat.

After lifting up on his elbows, Shannon watched Ciaran. As he pushed up to sitting, he placed his palm over Ciaran's frantic, pumping hand.

Ciaran slowed his actions, looking into Shannon's eyes as a ravenous need swept through his body.

"Let me," Shannon said softly.

Ciaran gazed at Shannon, pleasure tingling inside him, while Shannon gently directed him to lie on his back.

Shannon climbed between Ciaran's legs. Keeping his gaze affixed to Ciaran's, he placed a sensual lick up the outside of his shaft.

Gasping, Ciaran shuddered. Tensing his brows, he let out heavy breaths. "Oh, God, Shannon, I'm so close." If he didn't hurry, he was sure he would climax without any more stimulation.

Shannon let a sinful smirk play on his lips. He ran his slick tongue up Ciaran's erection again, circled the head a few times and waited.

As his cock pulsed, Ciaran gasped. "Ah, what are you doing?" He was going to drive him to lose his damn mind.

Shannon grinned and slid his wet fingers up Ciaran's shaft, then pushed his thumb onto the spot just below the lip of his cock and circled.

The action sent sensation thrumming through to the ends of his body without giving him what he needed for release. He squirmed and writhed.

Shannon continued the motion, waiting, gauging the reaction.

"Shannon, oh, God, give me more," Ciaran pleaded.

"Now?"

"Y-yes, n-now."

"Not yet." Shannon's cock came to life once again. He loosened his grip on Ciaran, licked his palm, and stroked hard and fast on himself. He shut his eyes for a second, releasing a soft hiss.

Ciaran glared at him, lifting onto his elbows. He whined, "What do you mean not yet? You're driving me nutty."

"I thought you could handle it?" Shannon said through ragged breathing. He jerked his hand over his reddened cock and tensed his face, as if wanting to catch up. As he bit his lip, he closed his eyes again.

"You are wicked, you know that?" A taunting tone laced through Ciaran's voice. Sighing, he dropped back to the bed.

After a minute, Shannon stopped the hand on his cock and sat on tucked legs, then leaned forward over Ciaran, running his tongue up and down his shaft. He resumed the pumping of his own erection with quick jerks.

Letting out a sharp moan, Ciaran rocked his hips. He ensnared the back of Shannon's skull with his hands, gripped his hair tight, and kept him there while he thrust into the wet heat of Shannon's mouth.

Shannon attempted to lift his head as if to protest, but Ciaran shoved him back down.

"I'm not letting you back up until you finish, my wicked lover." Ciaran's release surged to the very edge again.

Shannon let out a faint chuckle as if thoroughly enjoying the comment, then took Ciaran's solid cock back into his mouth.

Ciaran gave a brutal thrust upward with his hips as Shannon gave him what he needed to rip his release from him. His body quaked and shivered as his climax surged through him. Delicious spasms of pleasure followed, his frustration pouring out of him. As he held tight to Shannon's head, he freed a loud cry.

Shannon sucked and lapped at Ciaran's seed, jerking over his own erection in a furious motion. As Ciaran's climax slowed, Shannon's seed spurted between his fist. He gasped, shutting his eyes tight. After it finished, he licked the slightly sticky fluid from his hand and tossed himself up next to Ciaran.

Still in a post-climax haze, Ciaran looked at Shannon. "Bloody hell, Shannon, I've never felt anything like that." His breath came in heavy inhales and exhales. It was wonderful. He'd had no idea his body could feel that way.

Rolling sideways, Shannon wrapped himself around Ciaran.

Ciaran surrounded him with his arms.

Shannon turned his head as if looking at Ciaran's profile. He rolled a slow smirk across his lips. "I never imagined you would talk dirty like that, my wicked lover."

A soft grin graced Ciaran's mouth. "Yeah, well, you sort of brought it out of me, that and a lot more." With a long sigh, he turned his focus to the ceiling. "Wouldn't it be nice if we could stay just like this, in this room, with only each other?" Longing threaded through him.

Shannon nuzzled Ciaran's neck. "God, I wish we could. I'd never go back to Drimnagh if I didn't have to."

Tightening his hold on Shannon, Ciaran leaned his face into his dark hair. He planted a tender kiss on his head. "I never understood why everyone treated you so badly and why you seemed to build such a wall around yourself. Da and Ma refused to talk about it when I asked. But now that I know what really happened between you and Mr. Flannigan..." He let out a puff of air. What a terrible thing and he'd never known. "How did everyone find out anyway?"

Shannon frowned and pursed his lips for a moment. "It was Mrs. O'Boyle. She found us back there one day. Damn, did she get an eyeful. She screamed bloody murder, too."

"Oh, shite, Shannon. What were you doing?" Ciaran shut his eyes tight against the heat piercing his chest. Why did he have to ask that?

"Um, well, we were—"

"Stop, I don't think I want to know." Ciaran gave him a squeeze. "I can't believe you didn't run off."

"Of course, I didn't run off. I couldn't leave you. You were the only thing that kept me going." Shannon traced an imaginary circle around Ciaran's chest with his fingers. "I can't live without you, Ciaran," he said softly. He reached an arm around him, pulling himself in.

"Hush, don't say that." Ciaran's heart ached. He'd never want to find something like that out.

"It's true."

Ciaran rested his fingers on Shannon's chin and gently guided his face toward him.

With glistening eyes, Shannon gazed at him.

Ciaran placed a tender, but intense kiss on Shannon's lips. "I'll make sure you'll never have to live without me then."

Releasing a long exhale, Shannon loosened his hold on Ciaran.

Ciaran's gaze searched the ceiling. How were they going to handle things when they got back? How could he not be with Shannon like this after sharing so much. It would be painful, that he knew. "It's going to be hard, isn't it?"

"What?" Shannon took a quick breath.

"Going home tomorrow, I mean. We won't be able to be together like this, will we." Ciaran swallowed hard, the reality of the situation falling on him like a dead weight.

"No, I suppose not. It's not like we ever slept at each other's house, even when we were kids." Shannon looked to Ciaran's face, the corners of his mouth twitching as if trying to lighten the mood.

Ciaran glanced at him, then returned his attention to the ceiling. He couldn't accept it. "We have to think of something. There has to be a way for us to be together, like this."

"We can't push it, the consequences would be unthinkable." Shannon buried his face into Ciaran's neck.

Ciaran drew a deep inhale. What would the consequences be exactly? "What ever happened to Mr. Flannigan?"

Squeezing him, Shannon said, "I don't know. I just never saw him again."

Ciaran cut his gaze to Shannon's face, wrinkling his brows. "Did you love him?"

Shannon puffed out a breath. "No, I told you, you're the only one I've ever loved." He squirmed in Ciaran's hold as if uncomfortable with the conversation. "I suppose I cared about him, in a way, but I never loved him."

A light smile played on Ciaran's lips. *That's what I wanted to hear.* "Don't worry, Shannon, we'll think of something, and no one will ever know." There had to be a way to be together like this. There were places they could hide.

"God, I hope so." Shannon reached over Ciaran and turned the lamp off, then snuggled into him. "Goodnight, wicked lover." He grinned.

Ciaran let out a faint chuckle. "Goodnight."

CHAPTER NINE
SHANNON

Shannon found himself in a hazy room, unable to see the walls surrounding him though he sensed their presence. The bed was soft beneath him, and the warm embrace of Ciaran surrounded him, comforting him. His chest tightened. *Something is there...*

A figure materialized out of the haze. Glowing red eyes searched him out, surrounded by a grotesque, white mask, reminding him of a marionette with an evil and bulbous face. His heart hammered as if it would break free from his chest. He seized Ciaran closer and shook him, his voice a frantic whisper. "Ciaran? Ciaran, please wake up. Please, you have to. Please, wake up, please..."

Ciaran kept his eyes shut, breathing steady in slumber.

Shannon clutched and groped at Ciaran's body. Panic lit up his spine. He plunged his face into Ciaran's chest, shaking with fear. The figure's sharp gaze pricked at his skin as it neared. He gathered enough strength to peek up.

The figure stood, in black billowing robes, terrifyingly close to the bed. It reached an arm out, much too long, much too daunting. With a crooked finger, it pointed at him accusingly.

Shannon veiled himself behind his long hair, but was unable to take his gaze off it.

"Look what you've done. Fornicating with another male, it's evil, Shannon. You are evil, possessed," it said with thundering clarity.

Father Brennan? "No, I'm not." Shannon whimpered.

"You must repent for your sins, Shannon," it said, in a voice hissing with malice.

"I-I won't, it's not a sin. W-we love each other. It's not a sin!"

"You must confess. We must burn the demon out of you!" The voice thundered in his ears.

"No. I'm not possessed. There is no demon!" Shannon's voice was shrill. He succumbed to tears, breaking down in silent weeping.

The horrible figure came closer until it loomed directly above him, hunched over.

Trembling with fear, Shannon snatched at sheets and flung them around him, trying to bury himself. The figure groped for him with crooked fingers. It clutched him by the shoulders and shook him violently. He shrieked with fright.

Shannon opened his eyes. He flung upright in the bed. For a second, the horrible white mask and red eyes glowed at him in the dark of their room. He screamed.

Sitting on tucked legs, Ciaran shook Shannon by the shoulders, facing him. "Shannon? Wake up, please, it's just a dream!" He brought his face close, staring at Shannon, then threw his arms around him and held on tight.

Shannon seized him in desperation, Ciaran's warmth surrounding him. He trembled and buried his face in Ciaran's soft neck, holding his breath to stifle tears, fighting off the memory of the ghastly figure.

"Hush, it was only a dream." Ciaran rubbed his hand up and down the back of his head in a soothing gesture.

"It, it was terrible Ciaran, just awful." Shannon sniffled. "F-

Father Brennan, he was, he was pointing his finger and telling me to repent. He told me I-I was possessed by a-a demon." His chest squeezed, like an invisible vice wreaked havoc on him. He tried counting the pressure away. *One, two, three.* It was better, but the dream was too terrifying this time. "Ciaran, I need you. Please, just hold me." Urgency threaded through Shannon's voice. Ciaran tightened his arms to the point of being painful.

"I'm here. I won't let you go, not ever." Ciaran rocked him forward and back, placing a tender kiss on the side of his head. "Hush, it'll be all right. I won't let anything happen to you."

After a few minutes, Shannon relaxed. *How long will this sense of dread last this time?* Reluctantly, he loosened his hold on Ciaran and lay down on his side. While he lowered himself to the bed, Ciaran kept his hands on him, continuing to apply comfort. He curled up into a ball.

Ciaran lay behind him, wrapping himself around Shannon.

Sniffling, Shannon drew Ciaran's arm tight around him. As Ciaran ran soft swirls over his forehead with his fingers, he entwined his hand in Ciaran's free hand.

"Shh..."

Shannon closed his eyes once again.

WARMTH LIT up Shannon's face. He fluttered his eyes open. Sunbeams ran in a straight line from the window, up the bed and onto his cheek. He shut his eyes again and mumbled softly while he searched in an absent manner for the familiar arms of Ciaran. When he found them, he pulled them tight around him, snuggling into the embrace.

A slow, insistent push and something solid pressed against Shannon's backside. He whispered, "Mmm, Ciaran." The push came again, a little firmer this time while soft lips brushed against the back of his neck. He slowly rolled over, letting Ciaran bring him into his chest. He tilted his head up, meeting Ciaran's warm mouth in a lingering kiss.

Inside a breath, Ciaran said, "I want you." He placed a soft kiss on Shannon's forehead and caressed up and down Shannon's arm, then around to his back.

As Ciaran drew him closer, his erection pressed solidly against Shannon's. He released a soft moan.

Shannon spread a slow, half-grin on his lips. So, Ciaran wanted to do that. He roamed his hands over Ciaran's well-built frame. "So soon?"

"Soon? Are you bloody joking? I can't get enough. I don't know what nasty spell you put on me, Shannon Sullivan, but I definitely can't keep my hands or other things off you." Ciaran placed a palm on Shannon's cheek, then his kisses turned hungry and heated.

Shannon moaned against Ciaran's mouth. The contact and persistent rocking of Ciaran's hips against him had need humming inside him. He slid his erection sensuously between the soft skin of Ciaran's pelvis and stomach. Sensitivity heightened. He pulled away from Ciaran's exploring mouth. "Ciaran?"

Ciaran drew ragged breaths. He gazed at Shannon with pure desire. "Yes?"

Shannon looked with longing into Ciaran's green eyes, the pupils dilating with arousal. Was Ciaran ready to take him completely? He yearned to be filled with the one he loved. He ran a timid finger up Ciaran's arm, watching goosebumps break out over Ciaran's skin. "I, uh, do you think, maybe, um..."

"What? For God's sake, Shannon, just say it so we can get on with things." Ciaran spread a warm smile over his lips.

He rolled in the bed, putting his back against Ciaran's

chest, then pushed his fingers into his mouth, and slicked them with an ample amount of saliva. He drove his wet fingers behind him and ran over his entrance, making it slick. He grabbed Ciaran's wrist, then pulled him tight against him, pushing his behind into him. Ciaran's erection nudged into his crevice, against his moistened entry. He shuddered and let out a deep moan. It felt so good to have Ciaran's erection so close to where he wanted it.

Inside a gasp, Ciaran said, "Wha—"

Shannon flung his arms to the headboard, then shoved, driving the head of Ciaran's hard cock into his passage. He released a sharp gasp with the burn of being filled, arching his back, clenching his eyes shut. Ciaran's body grew rigid behind him, and a hiss of pleasure washed over Shannon's ears.

Jerking his hips back, Ciaran withdrew himself. "Shannon, what are you doing? What was that?" Shock and desire laced his voice. He pawed at Shannon as if unsure if he should continue or pull away completely.

Shannon wriggled and squirmed, frantically trying to reposition his entrance over Ciaran's erection.

Rolling to his back, Ciaran pushed Shannon away.

A shiver rushed up Shannon's spine. Was this all Ciaran would allow him? Trembling, he rolled himself over to his other side, facing Ciaran. He propped his head on his hand, elevated by the elbow. He winced as his gaze caught Ciaran's face. Didn't Ciaran like it? Was it too much for him?

Ciaran searched the ceiling as if it held some sort of mysterious power, raking a hand though his unruly bangs.

Shannon grabbed Ciaran's raised arm. As he gently lowered it back to Ciaran's side, Ciaran twisted his head, redirecting his gaze toward him.

For a moment, they studied each other as if transfixed.

Did I push Ciaran too far? Shannon's chest tightened and his heart ached. What if Ciaran questioned their new relationship? What if he made Ciaran afraid of being with him the way he wanted? He shouldn't have done that. He darted his gaze over Ciaran's stunning face. "C-Ciaran? D-do you still want me?"

Startling, Ciaran dropped his mouth open. He rolled to his side and cupped Shannon's cheek. "Oh, God, Shannon, yes. Yes, of course. I-I just didn't know what you were doing. I thought maybe I hurt you somehow or-or did something I shouldn't."

Shannon exhaled a held breath, giving a soft smile of relief. "No, Ciaran, it's exactly what I wanted you to do." He relaxed.

"Why on Earth would you want something like that?" Ciaran widened his eyes, staring at him.

As heat rushed his cheeks, Shannon looked away. How could he tell Ciaran the act he found so strange was exactly what he craved? He swallowed hard and peeked at him, searching for meaning behind his expression. "Why wouldn't I?"

Continuing to study him, Ciaran caressed Shannon's cheek. He lifted his brows as if he understood. "Y-you mean, that is what m-men do?"

Shannon gave him a shy smile. Ciaran was naïve, maybe more than he'd thought. He reached around him to trace circles on his lower back. "Yes, that is what they do," he said with a nod of conviction.

Ciaran glanced at the far wall and came back. "But doesn't it hurt? I mean—you looked like you were in pain. You don't have to do that just for me, you—"

Pressing his index finger to Ciaran's lips, Shannon said, "Stop. It feels good and I like it. I enjoy it even." It was obvious that Ciaran didn't understand the act was not a sacrifice to be made. Pulling him near, he gave him a quick kiss. He put a solid hold on the back of Ciaran's head while sliding his face so close their noses touched. "I want to feel you inside me." His voice was husky with need. His cock pulsed and hardened. How good would it feel to have Ciaran do that to him? He licked his lips as his gaze lowered to Ciaran's mouth.

Ciaran tensed his brows for a second, then his lustful expression returned. His breathing quickened and grew heavy. "Well, I have to admit it felt pretty damn good to me, too."

Shannon lunged, unable to hold back anymore. He locked his mouth on Ciaran's, giving him a heated kiss. He thrust his tongue into his mouth and flicked sensually inside Ciaran's teeth.

Groaning in response, Ciaran pressed his erection firmly into Shannon's hips.

Anticipation flared through his body, setting Shannon ablaze.

Ciaran pulled him into a hasty embrace, then pushed him away, guiding him back around so Shannon's backside was exposed to Ciaran's hard cock.

A low moan left Shannon's throat while he pulled Ciaran's hand around, up to his mouth and sucked sumptuously on his fingers. They dripped when he pulled them from his lips and led them to his behind. As the hard flesh of Ciaran's erection pressed against his backside, he wet his passage again and slipped two fingers inside, stroking.

Ciaran remained still, as if fascinated. while Shannon maneuvered his fingers. He pressed his forehead to Shannon's back, then placed a solid grip on Shannon's shoulder. He nudged Shannon's entrance with the tip of his cock, replacing Shannon's fingers. "Tell me what to do, I don't want to hurt you."

Shannon released a loud moan, then pushed on the headboard and shoved his hips down onto Ciaran, making his cock enter him. "G-go in s-slowly." Heat seared through him. An exquisite and intense pressure teased his insides.

Gasping, Ciaran drove his hips forward. "Like that?"

"Y-yes." Shannon moaned. Letting impulse control him, he seized Ciaran's hip. He guided him back out, repositioned himself and tugged him back in. Heat exploded inside him, giving way to delicious pressure. "Go faster."

Ciaran drove in and out of Shannon as if it was instinctive. "Oh, shite, Shannon, I-I've never felt anything like this," he said through ragged breathing. He filled the room with loud gasps with each insistent thrust of his hips, his body shaking.

After adjusting himself just right, Shannon ground onto Ciaran, feeding his internal spot of pleasure. Each thrust sent jolts of sensation through to his aching cock. He stroked hard on his seeping erection, working at a frenzied pace while Ciaran continued to drive into him.

"Sh-Shannon, I-I'm going—"

"Keep going, d-don't pull out." Pleasure strained his voice.

Ciaran stiffened behind him.

Oh God, Ciaran's coming. Shannon rocked faster, harder with his hips.

Ciaran groaned as his climax surged inside Shannon, filling him.

Closing his eyes, Shannon let the delicious tension release in his groin as his peak slammed through him. His seed poured out over his jerking palm as sweet contractions rocked through his body. Moaning, he shuddered and submitted to it all.

Ciaran wrapped his arms around Shannon from behind, then drove inside him one last time and held it, drawing him close.

Hot puffs of air brushed the sensitive skin of Shannon's neck as Ciaran panted behind him. He clutched at sheets with sticky fingers and wiped himself off.

"Oh God, Shannon, that was unbelievable." The remnants of desire laced through Ciaran's voice.

Shannon shivered with a post-climax pulse. "Yeah, it was." He snuggled in closer to Ciaran, letting his eyes close. Taking in the momentary daze, he relished in the moment he'd just shared with him. He let a faint smile cross his lips. Only a week ago, he'd never have dared to think all this could be possible. But it was. Here they were and he was happy, maybe for the first time in his life. He pulled up Ciaran's hand, entwined in his own, and placed a gentle kiss on the back of it. His words were soft. "I love you, Ciaran, so much."

Giving Shannon a quick squeeze, Ciaran said, "Not as much as I love you."

*No, that can't be...*Shannon snuggled into Ciaran's embrace. If that was what he wanted to believe, then he'd let him, for now.

"Hey, Shannon."

"What?"

Ciaran's words were slow. "Does this mean I'm not a virgin anymore?"

Shannon chuckled and tugged on his arm. "Yes. I suppose I just took your virginity." He nodded his head once in satisfaction.

Ciaran freed a short gasp, then kissed the back of his neck. "I'm glad it was you."

"Me, too." Shannon closed his eyes once again and dozed off for a few minutes.

Ciaran stirred and spoke in a low voice. "Shannon, we have to get going."

An ache tore through Shannon's chest. He wasn't ready to go back to that place, to deal with those people in their town again. He wasn't ready to leave the comfort and safety of the bed they shared in this room or his beautiful Ciaran's arms. He buried his head in his pillow and let out a sigh, then a heavy groan.

"Shannon, I know it's hard, but we still have all day together. Let's make the most of it, okay?" Ciaran lifted his head to peer over Shannon's shoulder as if gauging his reaction.

No, not yet. Shannon held still. He still wanted to bask in the warmth of what they'd just shared.

"Are you okay?"

I better say something, or Ciaran will keep questioning me. "I'm okay. I know we need to get going. Just give me a bloody minute, will you?" Shannon winced. The words poured out of his mouth with more irritation than he intended.

Ciaran slid farther back on the bed, tugging on Shannon's shoulder.

Reluctantly, Shannon allowed Ciaran to guide him onto his back. He peered up into his face.

Ciaran gazed down on him, wrinkling his forehead. "You know I have to get back to my da. I'd much rather stay here like this, too, but my da needs me. You know how upset he was, Shannon. Don't get mad at me for that." Frustration filled Ciaran's voice.

Shannon studied his face. "I know, I'm sorry." He seized him and yanked him down on top of him, giving him a tight hug. Finally, he could be open with Ciaran about his problems with the townspeople. Finally, he would understand everything. "They all hate me, Ciaran. Ever since I was caught with Mr. Flannigan, everyone looks at me with disgust. I think they're scared of me, too, like I'm going to go around raping everybody or something. It's bloody horrible. I don't feel safe or comfortable anywhere. Not even with my own parents, in my own bloody house." Tears rushed to the surface, threatening to overwhelm him.

"Hush now, I'm sure your ma and da don't think that way about you. They are good people."

"No, you don't understand. They treat me bloody horrible. They never even allowed me to speak about what happened. It was never to be brought up again, they said. My ma, she won't even hug me anymore. My da, he won't stay in the same room with me. They don't act that way so much when you're around. They have to keep up appearances, you know. But when we're alone, it's very...cold. Why do you think I spend so much time at your house? Aye?" Tears invaded his eyes and a lump climbed up his throat, but he struggled against it. *It's so difficult to admit these things to him, even now.*

Ciaran tensed his brows as if in deep in thought. He lifted up, propped on his elbows, and gazed deeply into Shannon's eyes. He brushed a lock of black hair from his forehead. "I-I don't understand, how could everyone blame you for what happened? Didn't the blame lie with Mr. Flannigan? I mean, he's the one who started it, right?" He thinned his lips.

With his heart aching, Shannon clenched his jaw. Surely, Ciaran knew how the society of their small town worked. How protected from it could he have possibly been all these years? Why didn't he understand what he was telling him? Anger lodged in his gut. He glared at him. "It doesn't matter, Ciaran." He rolled to his side and climbed out of bed.

Ciaran stared at him and dropped his mouth open.

Shannon snatched his undergarment and trousers, threw them on, and trudged down the hall into the bathroom. He slammed the door shut, locked it, and leaned his back against the inside, taking deep breaths to calm himself. The lump in his throat returned. His vision clouded. He blinked and a hot tear raced down his cheek. He'd been so sure Ciaran would see his point of view now. *But Goddamned Ciaran lives in some perfect world where things are fair and just, where people are always upfront and respectable.* He just refused to see the darker side of people. A torrent of fierce pounding jostled the door, rippling throughout his body.

"Shannon, don't you shut me out. I might not understand everything, but that's no reason to behave this way!" Ciaran's angry voice carried through the door.

Shannon closed his eyes and stilled. The brutal pounding thundered again.

"Damn it, Shannon, if you don't come out, I'm going to bust the bloody door open!"

Shannon maintained his position, focusing on taking deep breaths. Maybe Ciaran couldn't understand and would never understand. He'd just have to accept that. He bit his lip and blinked back more tears. He should open the door. "Give me a minute." He wiped up with a towel, then pushed through his undergarment, buttoned it, and slid his trousers up his legs and fastened them. He sighed and unlocked the door.

The door creaked, cutting through the tension. Ciaran stood in the doorway, wearing only his undergarment, half buttoned, hanging his head. As he lifted his head, he clenched and unclenched his fists. He gazed at Shannon and chewed his lower lip.

Shannon focused on Ciaran's face, willing himself to keep control over his emotions.

"Don't shut me out, ever." Ciaran pursed his lips.

The words stung Shannon and he dropped his gaze to the planks of the wooden floor. Slowly and clearly, he said, "I want, no, need you to believe me when I tell you what it's like for me back in Drimnagh. I didn't ask to be treated this way and I certainly am not imagining it." He straightened his head and locked his gaze on Ciaran's. Would there be any understanding at all?

Ciaran took a few careful steps toward Shannon and

wrapped his arms around his waist in a soothing embrace.

Lowering his cheek onto his shoulder, Shannon surrounded Ciaran with his arms.

"Shannon, I'm so sorry. I had no idea how bloody terrible things were for you. I have to admit, I always sort of thought you brought a lot of it on yourself. You know, with how tough you're always trying to act. I never fully understood why you were so bloody unfriendly to everyone." Heavy emotion weighed in his voice.

"They were unfriendly to me first," Shannon said softly. "I didn't believe it in the beginning either. But I started noticing people whispering behind my back. Or they just wouldn't answer me when I talked to them. Then when I went into town, they'd cross the street in front of me so they wouldn't have to walk by me." He gritted his teeth. An old, familiar rage swelled within him. "It makes me so angry to think about it, even now."

Ciaran tightened his hold with one arm, then stroked down the back of Shannon's hair with his hand. "I know. Sometimes anger helps hide the hurt, doesn't it?"

Nodding, Shannon squeezed Ciaran.

Ciaran placed a gentle kiss on the side of Shannon's head. "Well, you have me. We have each other, and that's all we really need, right?"

"Right." Shannon pressed his lips together. But how he wished things were different. How he longed to feel normal again, like he belonged, especially after spending time with Iona behind her bar. Finally, he'd felt like himself there, like it was all right to be himself there. Something inside him had come out from hiding, was set free. Squashing it again for the sake of protecting himself from the cruel townspeople of Drimnagh would be difficult. But he had to do it, if for no other reason than he couldn't possibly leave Ciaran's side.

Ciaran released Shannon and peered into his face, his hands falling to Shannon's hips. "So, are we okay again, you and I?" He wrinkled his brows.

Forcing a smile, Shannon said, "Yeah. I could never stay mad at you for very long." He spread a smirk over his lips.

Ciaran gave Shannon a smug grin. "I know."

Shannon chuckled. "What do you mean, you know?"

Cocking his head, Ciaran said, "I just know. Let's get going, before they charge us for another night."

SHANNON TURNED the silver tap on the tub, starting the water for his bath. Good thing Ciaran decided to wait in bed while he cleaned up. He could finally think through how he would handle being back in their hometown. As he peered at himself in the mirror, he went through the tedious motions of shaving. How would he ever be able to look Father Brennan in the face again? Would the priest somehow see the sin in his eyes while he sat in church on Sunday? Would the love he shared with Ciaran somehow shine like a beacon to everyone in the town?

He finished the last stroke with his razor on his chin, watching the dark particles dissipate under a cascade of liquid from the tap. He turned his attention to the lukewarm water in the claw-foot bathtub. It was so hot already, a cool bath would be just what he needed.

He dipped his fingers in the water. It was nice and cool, perfect for a hot day. He removed his trousers and underwear, stepped into the tub and lowered himself in. It felt so good. The water surrounded his body, removing the remnants of sweat and lovemaking. He frowned for a moment. Ciaran's scent would be washed from his skin, too. He twisted his torso to grab the soap.

CHAPTER TEN

CIARAN

Ciaran stepped into the doorway of the bathroom and locked it, enjoying the view of Shannon as he climbed into the tub. He'd been in luck and Shannon had forgotten to lock the door. He dropped his trousers and underwear to the floor and stepped out of them.

Shannon startled. "Damn, you scared the shite out of me." He spread a sad grin on his face. "How did you get in here?"

"You forgot the lock." After padding over to him, Ciaran picked up the small bar of soap. He'd wash him. It might be his only chance.

"Oh...What are you doing?" Shannon lifted his brows.

Ciaran slid into the tub, positioning himself directly behind Shannon. With his legs spreading out on either side of him, the cool water enveloped him. "I was just lying there, thinking how I should be spending every second with you while we're here. You know, since we won't be able to be like this when we get home. And so, I decided to help you wash." His voice was soft as velvet. He couldn't shake this feeling of loss at going home. All he wanted was to keep Shannon close. He slid his slick hand and the bar of soap in circles across Shannon's back.

Shannon leaned into Ciaran's touch, moaning softly, then closed his eyes and relaxed into him.

"Don't get any ideas, my wicked lover. We still have to get out of here in the next half hour." Ciaran smiled as his gaze caught on Shannon's half-aroused shaft.

Shannon cleared his throat, then sat upright. "Yeah, right." His voice was hoarse.

Ciaran caressed Shannon's chest and abdomen with the soap. Desire shivered down his spine, swelling his cock. He brushed the soap over Shannon's nipple, watching it harden.

"Maybe I should let you wash me when there's more time." Shannon's voice wavered. His erection stood tall against his stomach.

Smirking, Ciaran dropped his hand to find Shannon's erection. There was no way he wasn't touching it, at least.

Shannon took a quick inhale.

"I told you we don't have time." Ciaran bit his lip inside a smirk. He'd make time for this. Everything felt too good again. He pressed his lips to the nape of Shannon's neck.

Shannon shivered, then another more urgent moan escaped him.

Sliding his hips forward, Ciaran pressed his erection firmly against Shannon's lower back. Sensation pulsed over him.

Under Shannon's breath, he said, "Damn, Ciaran, you're making this impossible." He lowered himself backward, leaning against Ciaran's chest.

After seizing Shannon's erection with a slick hand, Ciaran pumped him with urgency and speed. Sharp breaths escaped his throat. He came at Shannon with hungry kisses and rocking hips, struggling for friction on his own aching cock.

Shannon rocked his hips in time with Ciaran's hand. As he

closed his eyes and tensed his brows, his second climax of the morning came rushing to the surface. He seized the sides of the tub, hanging on tight. Loud, sharp gasps echoed off the tiles as his seed burst into the cleansing water. His shoulders heaved, and he drew deep breaths as if trying to calm himself.

Ciaran pushed desperate thrusts against Shannon's back, attempting to force his release. He was so close. Just a little more. His breathing was ragged, and his limbs shook. "Shannon..." His voice quivered with need. He threw his arms around Shannon's waist, pulling him closer against his hard cock as he ground forward.

Shannon lifted Ciaran's arms from around his waist, then turned himself around in the tub. As he gazed deeply into Ciaran's eyes, he placed a passionate kiss over his lips. He grasped the soap from him and rubbed it in his palms, making his own hands slick, then reached down and stroked Ciaran's erection.

Resuming the rocking of his hips, Ciaran whispered, "H-hurry, Shannon." He needed it hard and fast, the same way he'd given it to Shannon.

With a faint smile, Shannon squeezed Ciaran's cock and jerked his palm over it. He dropped his face toward him for a deep, penetrating kiss. "How's that?"

Ciaran bucked. His body trembled. "G-good." His voice was barely audible. He clenched his eyes shut, furrowed his brows, and moaned in pleasure, sensation building in his cock. His shaft grew even stiffer and pulsed in Shannon's palm as release surged over him. He thrust hard into Shannon's hand, pawing at the sides of the tub while his seed spilled out of him. The small room filled again with the sounds of desire as he succumbed to his climax.

As it finished, Shannon leaned forward and gave him a deep kiss. As he pulled away, Ciaran opened his eyes.

Ciaran's body relaxed in a post-climax haze. "I wasn't going to do that," he said, "I was just going to wash you." He let a faint chuckle rumble in his chest.

Shannon freed a soft laugh. "Well, I'm not sure if I'm clean or not now, but we'd best be on our way."

CIARAN LOOKED out over the horizon from his viewpoint in the churning cart. The rolling hills gave way to trees and brush, the beginnings of forest. The changing scenery was a sure indication they were much closer to home. *Home*...what would it be like when they got there? Would they really have to stop everything they'd started? How terrible would it be if they were caught? The hot day just began to surrender to cooler tones.

Shannon's stomach grumbled. He glanced at Ciaran, sitting directly next to him, as if he couldn't get close enough. He squeezed their tangled hands, sitting in his lap. "Ciaran, don't suppose there's a town up ahead where we could grab some supper?"

Smiling, Ciaran turned to face him. "Hungry again, are we? You ate enough to feed a cow this morning." It was already late afternoon though. He was surprised Shannon hadn't said something sooner. His gaze shifted out to the pothole-littered road in front of them. "Yeah, I think there's something just up ahead. Shouldn't be too long." It seemed like they'd been on this lonely stretch of road forever. He'd been wanting to talk to Shannon, but didn't know how to broach the subject of their return. He gave a quick squeeze of Shannon's hand.

Shannon nodded.

Ciaran shifted in the seat, then focused on Shannon and opened his mouth, then shut it. How should he say this? He furrowed his brows.

"What is it?" Shannon studied him.

Ciaran pursed his lips. *Out with it.* "I, uh, was just thinking about something." He wrinkled his brows, his heart quickening. He might not like the answer he was about to get.

"And?"

"And, well, how bad is it, exactly? What we're doing, I mean." Ciaran turned in his seat to face Shannon directly. He searched his face, locking onto his eyes.

Staring at him, Shannon dropped his mouth open.

"Shannon?" Ciaran tensed his face. Was it so bad he couldn't even talk about it?

"Uh, well, it's pretty bad, I suppose. You know Father Brennan calls it an abomination." Shannon cringed, fixating on Ciaran.

Ciaran's heart lurched. That couldn't be. It didn't properly describe how he felt about Shannon, not at all. He loved him. How could it possibly be an abomination? He stared off in the distance beyond the horse, his eyes stinging with tears.

Leaning forward, Shannon squeezed Ciaran's hand. "Remember what Iona said. What we have is special. You know, there were other men there, in her bar. Men just like us, who love each other the way we do. It's not like we're the only ones in the world. Just maybe the only ones in Drimnagh." He unwrapped his fingers from Ciaran's hand and draped his arm around his shoulders.

Ciaran buried his face into Shannon's neck. It didn't make any sense. He'd listened to Father Brennan his whole life about everything. *He comforted me when ma died.* "Then why would Father Brennan say something like that? I mean, wouldn't he know?" Heavy emotion dripped from Ciaran's voice.

Shannon flinched, then drew a quick inhale of breath. In a voice almost low enough to be a growl, he said, "No, he wouldn't know. He's bloody afraid, that's all. Afraid of something he doesn't understand, something that's different. The love we have is just as sweet as the love between a man and a woman, Ciaran. It's just not as common."

After lifting his head, Ciaran toyed with one of the buttons on Shannon's shirt. He ached to have him close. He didn't want them to be anything but what they'd been the last few days. He dropped the reins and flung both arms around Shannon's shoulders, holding him tight. "I love you, Shannon."

Shannon returned the impulsive embrace, pulling Ciaran's head closer to his neck, then sniffled. "I love you, too, so much," he whispered.

"Then we'll just have to keep it our little secret, won't we?" Ciaran released Shannon and searched quickly for the discarded reins. They'd find a way. It wouldn't end when they got home. He sniffed the tears back while righting the reins and swiped his eyes with the back of one of his hands.

Watching Ciaran, Shannon lowered his brows as if pondering his lover's internal emotions.

Ciaran steered their horse and small cart to the front of a tavern located on the lower floor of a rather large masonry building. The town they were in was only a few hours from home. Giving the reins a rough yank, he stopped the horse. "Here you go, Shannon. I'll go and find us a table and meet you inside." It was Shannon's turn to take care of the cart, after all.

Taking the reins, Shannon slid over while Ciaran climbed down from the cart.

Ciaran strode to the heavy front door of the establishment, opened it, and stepped inside. He peered through the smoke filling the dingy main room for an open table. Quite a few were empty and he walked toward a round table tucked into the corner. As he sat in a chair, he gazed toward the front door. When it opened and the light from outside shone on Shannon's dark locks, he lifted his arm and waved.

Shannon nodded once and stalked to the table, then placed both hands on his hips. "Sitting in the corner again, Ciaran?" He spread a wide grin over his lips, then snickered. "Suppose we should. I never know when you're going to decide to fondle me or worse." He dropped into the chair next to Ciaran.

Leaning in with determination, Ciaran gave him a coy smile. "It only happened once, and we were safe inside our hotel room."

Shannon shifted his chair closer. "And how about you kissing me in front of your aunt?" He arched a brow.

Heat flushed Ciaran's cheeks and he straightened, shifting his gaze to the table. He rested his forearms on the table, then smirked. "That was a challenge. I had to take it."

A frail, anxious-looking man came to the table, waiting eagerly for the young men to notice him. When he snagged their attention, he said, "What'll it be today, boys?"

"Oh, ah, a pint for me and my friend here. What's the special of the day?" Ciaran rubbed his leg against Shannon's. Would the man notice?

Shannon threw him a quick frown.

"Well, we're mostly known for our fish and chips," the waiter said.

"Why don't you bring us two orders then." Ciaran watched Shannon and ran his hand up the inside of Shannon's thigh beneath the table. "Is that okay, Shannon?" If he didn't notice before, he'd notice now.

Shannon nodded with a dumb smile playing on his face.

The waiter walked off with Shannon's acknowledgement.

Shannon attempted a glare at Ciaran, but it quickly fell away to a wide grin. "Stop it." He made a feeble attempt to sound serious.

Letting a playful grin spread on his face, Ciaran moved his hand sensually up Shannon's thigh, brushing it against his burgeoning erection. Desire shivered up his spine. "You ready for more?" he whispered. He definitely was. He couldn't get enough of him.

Shannon scanned the crowd as if nervous and leaned in close to Ciaran. "You have got to stop this. I'm serious, Ciaran."

Sighing, Ciaran dragged his hand away. Shannon was right. This could be bad for both of them. He planted his elbows on the cracked tabletop and rubbed his palms over his face. "I can't help it. I don't know what's got into me."

Shannon smirked and leaned toward Ciaran. "You've turned into a sex fiend, that's what."

With a slow shake of his head, Ciaran let out a soft chuckle, then sat back. "So I have." He looked directly at him. "Bet you didn't know I always was— just didn't have anyone to fool around with before." His cheeks heated.

"Good lord, what have I got myself into?" Shannon sniggered.

Ciaran slapped him hard on the arm just as the waiter came back with two glasses filled with amber-colored beer and heaping plates of greasy fish and chips. He watched while Shannon stuffed fish and potatoes into his mouth. "Slow down, you'll choke yourself."

Shannon carried on as if Ciaran hadn't said a word.

The young men finished their meal, paid the bill, and rose from their table to head for the front door.

As Shannon opened the door, a blustery wind swirled dust and leaves past him into the tavern.

Ciaran blinked his eyes against it, the rough bits of dirt scratching against the insides of his eyelids. "Damn, Shannon, when did all this bloody wind pick up?"

Shannon stood behind him and crossed his arms on his chest. "Don't know. Hope it settles down a little." He strode through the doorway toward their now dusty cart. Another gust licked at his face, making his hair dance.

Ciaran tugged at the collar on his white dress shirt in an attempt to shield himself from the onslaught of wind. He followed Shannon to the cart and unfastened the reins. "Do you suppose it might finally rain?" he called out over the groans of turbulence. He climbed up into the cart, sat beside Shannon and held the reins out. An uneasy feeling washed over him, making him shiver, though it wasn't cold.

"Doesn't smell like it. Sure doesn't seem right though." Shannon darted his gaze to Ciaran, his breath catching.

"What?" Ciaran blinked at him through the swirling dust. He looked spooked.

Shannon pulled his shirt tighter around him. "We have church tomorrow morning." He thinned his lips.

Patting his back, Ciaran said, "It'll be fine. It will." He'd make sure it was fine. No one would ever say or do terrible things to Shannon again.

Shannon focused on the road, almost indistinct as dust blew and billowed over it, while Ciaran steered the horse.

CHAPTER ELEVEN
SHANNON

An hour into the ride, Shannon had gone to the back of the cart and grabbed blankets for them both. Now he and Ciaran were hunched over, clutching the warm wool around them. He marveled at the wind. They were almost home, and it never stopped. It might have even got worse and now it was cold. It could at least rain if it was going to be like this.

"I think I see the house." Ciaran's blond hair twirled as he spoke, and the dark blanket flapped around his brown shoes.

Shannon looked ahead. A definite shape took form among the dancing trees, but darkness surrounded them, and no light came from it. "Looks like your da's not home," he shouted over another furious gust. He drew his gaze to Ciaran.

Ciaran slouched in clear disappointment.

Shannon's heart ached for him. Poor Ciaran probably worried in secret about his father the whole time they travelled. He leaned in close, letting loose his blanket and wrapped an arm around his shoulders. "I'm sure he's just fine."

"Yeah, I know." Ciaran tucked his body into Shannon.

The horse hauled them along through swirling tendrils of debris until they reached the front of Ciaran's barn.

Shivering, Shannon released his protective hold on Ciaran, then rewrapped his blanket around himself and followed him off the cart. He helped him detach the horse and watched as Ciaran ambled off, bridle in hand, guiding the horse to its waiting stall. What should he do now? Should he follow him into the barn, or should he bring his things into the house and make it comfortable for him? Better bring the things in the house.

Shannon picked up Ciaran's suitcase, his pillowcase and the pillows and blankets from the jumble of detritus flying around in the cart, then strode to the front door of Ciaran's house. As he entered, a stale smell rose up to surround him. Was Ciaran's father really all right? He dropped his blanket and the other items from the cart by the door and scanned his surroundings.

Shannon ambled to the table and lit an oil lamp sitting on top of it. The lamp fluttered a warm glow into the main room. His gaze snagged a piece of paper trapped under a glass on the table and he picked it up. Mr. O'Kelly's handwriting was scrawled over the surface. The wind spoke in high-pitched whistles through the house while he read.

Dearest Ciaran,
I am in town at the pub. Hope your trip was pleasant. Please don't wait up.
Love,
Da

Shannon freed a heavy breath. Why was he so tense? Must be the wind. It always made houses sound like they were alive when it blew this hard. *Kind of creepy, really.* A sudden burst of air, a swirl of leaves and a thud reached out from behind him, making him shiver again. He turned to see Ciaran's sad face in the doorway, his hair a flurry of blond locks. He strode to him, holding up the note in his hand. "Your da is just in town. I'm sure he'll be back shortly."

Ciaran nodded.

An eerie howl rustled the eaves of the house.

"You okay?" Shannon shuddered, not from the cold this time, and studied Ciaran. He seemed off.

"No. Shannon, will you stay with me?" Ciaran's pleading gaze met his.

Shannon's heart ached. He drew a still-blanketed Ciaran close. "Uh, my ma, at least, might get worried if I don't get home soon." How he dreaded going home, but his mother would have expected him home already.

The whistle of another gust rushed through the empty rooms. A loud clap broke through the whistle and air currents snaked over the young men.

Ciaran startled and trembled. "What was that?" His voice shook.

Shannon drew deep breaths to calm his nerves. "I-I think a window must have blown open, that's all." It was getting creepier by the minute in the house, but he couldn't show his fear to Ciaran. "Let's go and check it out, okay?"

Grunting, Ciaran released him, dropped the blanket, and groped around until he found Shannon's hand.

Once Shannon had a firm hold on Ciaran, he towed him toward the direction of the sound they'd heard. It had come from Mr. O'Kelly's bedroom. As he crept toward it, a cool draft brushed against his skin. It strengthened the closer he came to the room. When he reached it, he peered inside the doorway.

The window was wide open. A rush of air made his hair flutter as another gust picked up. He turned to Ciaran.

Ciaran had shut his eyes tight.

"Your da's window is open, see? Just like I said." Shannon pointed at it.

Ciaran opened his eyes wide and focused on him, his lower lip trembling. "Y-you don't think a ghost could have opened it, do you, Shannon?"

"What? Why on Earth would you say something like that? It's obviously the bloody wind." Shannon pressed his lips together. Was he thinking about his dead mother?

Ciaran flushed and dropped his gaze to the floor, then shrugged and made a weak attempt at a smile. "I don't know. It's just a bit strange around here with Ma gone. Suppose I'm imagining things."

A loud crack pierced the wind. They both jumped.

Sharp pain raced up Shannon's arm. He looked down. Ciaran crushed his hand. "Ah! You're hurting me." He wriggled out of his grasp and sped to the window. It was loosened from its runners and dangled free in its frame. He slammed it shut and slid the locks to secure it.

Ciaran wrapped his arms tight around his chest and stared with wide eyes while Shannon fixed the window.

Rubbing his hands together, Shannon strode back to him.

Ciaran focused his attention on him. "S-so the window just broke? Like that?" he asked as if he wouldn't believe his answer anyway.

Shannon surrounded him with his arms. "Yes, it just broke. It's an old house with old windows. We haven't had wind like this in a long time. I'm sure your da would have fixed it if he'd known it was about to break." He ran his fingers up Ciaran's back and twined his hand in his soft hair.

"Please stay with me, Shannon, please," Ciaran said in a soft whimper.

Shannon sighed. There was no way he could leave now. Not with how frightened Ciaran was and the strange comment he'd made about a ghost. "Okay, I'll stay." He broke his hold on him and returned to the table. As he put down the note, still clutched in his fingers, his gaze caught movement by the hearth. "What are you doing?"

Ciaran set up blankets and pillows in front of the fireplace. As he flashed a mischievous grin, he halted primping the blankets. "I thought we could have a roaring fire and maybe lie down while we wait."

"A fire, aye? Well, it's definitely cold enough for one." *He's smiling like he won a prize.* "Don't get any bloody ideas now. Your da will probably be home soon." Shannon stalked with his hands wrapped behind his back to Ciaran's nest of blankets, sprawled over the plank floor.

Ciaran fluffed one of the pillows. "Don't you trust me?" He looked up as Shannon crouched down in front of him.

"No." Shannon flinched as Ciaran gave him a playful punch in the shoulder. "Ow." He rubbed it.

"You deserved it." Ciaran grinned in satisfaction. "So do you want to make the fire, or shall I?"

"I'll do it." Shannon set about finding the things he needed to build the fire. Once the fire started, he sat back, gazing at his handiwork. He'd made a fine fire. The whole house seemed cozy now, not cold, and empty like it was. He crossed his legs on the arranged blankets.

Ciaran sat beside him.

The warmth from the fire brushed along Shannon's cheek. He sighed. "You know, the scariest thing in this house right now is you. Talking about ghosts and fixing blankets for us in front of a fire." He locked his gaze on Ciaran's. "Funny, I never knew this side of you before." He searched his stunning face, the light from the fire dancing across it, and stopped to gaze at his full lips.

"Do you like it?" Ciaran asked in a husky voice.

Shannon leaned in, supported on one arm. "Um, yeah." He wanted so badly to kiss him. But should he?

Ciaran shoved Shannon backward with the force of his body, then drove him into the blankets. His kiss was urgent with need as he opened his lips to penetrate Shannon's mouth with his tongue. He shimmied on top of him, clawing at the bottom of Shannon's shirt, trying to pry it from its constraints. He ground his hips downward as if to crush him against the floor.

Melting into Ciaran's ravenous kiss, Shannon lost himself and his whereabouts for a moment, surrendering to the sweet taste and touch of his beautiful Ciaran. *Bloody hell, we're in Ciaran's home. Mr. O'Kelly could come through that door at any moment.* He shoved Ciaran upward.

Ciaran's stunning face hovered above Shannon's and his hips rolled against him, his erection finding friction on Shannon's.

As sensation swept through him, Shannon panted. "We can't do this here. What if your da comes home?"

Ciaran tensed his brows and mumbled something incoherent, then rolled onto his back.

"What did you say?" Shannon sat up and turned to face him.

Ciaran sent a blank stare to the ceiling, holding his bent arms over his chest. "I said, it bloody well figures." He thinned his lips.

The eaves shook and howled with a strong gust. A shrill noise like a screech pierced the air around them. Ciaran thrust up and dived against his chest. "Shite! What was that?"

"I'm sure it's just the feckin' wind knocking something around outside." Shannon's nerves prickled with alarm. He wrapped his arms around Ciaran's shoulders and held him in a solid embrace. "What's wrong? Why are you so afraid? You know it's just the wind." He scanned the room for the strange noise, resting his gaze on the window. He could faintly make out the angular shapes of tree branches just outside. He nodded toward it. "Look, it was probably just a tree branch falling against that window there."

"Don't you find it just a little bloody scary?" Ciaran gazed up into his face with wide eyes.

Shannon met his gaze. How should he answer that? If he agreed, it might frighten Ciaran more.

"I don't know why, but ever since my ma died, I just get these, um, creepy feelings around the house. It's like she's still here sometimes with us."

Shannon pulled him closer and peeked into the fire. "Well, maybe she still is? Maybe she's keeping an eye on you."

"You think?" Ciaran released a soft chuckle and squeezed him. "I bet she'd be turning in her grave if she saw us kissing just now. She'd probably give me a thrashing."

Shannon thought back to Mrs. O'Kelly. She had always looked so happy. He couldn't imagine her ever being upset or disciplining anyone. *Maybe that's how Ciaran got to be so spoiled.* He let a smirk race over his lips.

"What are you smiling at?" Ciaran quirked his mouth in a wide grin.

"Oh, just thinking about how you never got punished for anything."

"Did so. Don't you remember that time we tied Seamus up to the tree by the barn and left him there all night? My da just about killed me for that." As his gaze rested on Shannon's mouth, he licked his lips. Desire played in his eyes.

His lips are so close. Shannon ached to feel them again. "Yeah, well..." He came close and gave him a gentle kiss, but filled with passion.

Ciaran broke the kiss and fixated on Shannon's lips. "Do you think it will rain?" Seduction laced his husky voice.

Shannon tried to smile, but a hungry fire burned inside his body. His hard cock strained against the inside of his trousers. He furrowed his brows as he attempted an answer, but words wouldn't form. All he could think about was tasting Ciaran again.

Closing his eyes, Ciaran pressed his delicious lips onto Shannon's. The kiss was eager, insistent this time.

Shannon opened his mouth, allowing Ciaran's tongue to enter, to probe and search out the moan waiting to be released from his throat. As his pulse quickened, he reached his arms around Ciaran. He craved the feeling of Ciaran beneath or on top of him, which one didn't really matter.

A burst of wild wind and twirling leaves spun around the young men. A loud bang rang out in the room. They startled and released each other to stare at the door.

Shannon dropped his mouth open, his gaze snagging on Ciaran's father, swaying in the doorway.

Mr. O'Kelly's face scrunched up as if confusion muddled his mind. His hair was a mess of thin wisps. He teetered a step forward and stopped again. The door hung wide open, letting another strong gust blow swirls of debris in behind him.

"D-da!" Ciaran jumped to standing. He sped forward, slammed the door shut and embraced his father.

Mr. O'Kelly hesitated, then wrapped his arms around his son. He sent Shannon an uneasy glare.

Shannon darted his gaze to the jumbled folds of blankets beneath him. His chest tightened. What had he seen? He chanced another peek at Mr. O'Kelly.

Mr. O'Kelly's head rested on his son's shoulder. "You didn't have to wait up," he slurred, "Aren't you tired from your trip? I'm surely tired."

As trembling started inside Shannon, he watched from his position on the blankets.

Ciaran assisted his father toward the table.

Did Mr. O'Kelly see anything? Or more likely, how much did he see? Shannon was paralyzed. He wouldn't move until his question received some sort of answer.

Ciaran attempted to guide his inebriated father into a kitchen chair. Mr. O'Kelly wavered and stumbled. The chair toppled backward with a loud crack as it hit the floor.

Ciaran seized his father around the waist, holding him steady and keeping him from falling backward. He straightened and let out a frustrated sigh. "Da, let's get you into bed." He flashed a worried glance at Shannon. "Get over here and help me."

Shannon stood at once and paced to them.

As Shannon wrapped an arm around his torso, Mr. O'Kelly gave Shannon an accusing glare.

Ciaran got a secure hold on the other side of his father, and they hauled him into his bedroom.

Both of them assisted Mr. O'Kelly into a sitting position at the edge of his bed.

Shannon's gaze caught Ciaran's.

Creasing his brows, Ciaran bit his lip.

Shannon straightened his shoulders and stepped back.

"Just go and wait for me. I'll get him settled and be right out." Ciaran raked his hand through his hair. Letting out a puff of air, he turned his attention to his father again.

Shannon made his way back out to the fireplace. He paced before it, reviewing what precisely they were doing when the door blew open. This was exactly what he was afraid of. Why didn't Ciaran ever listen to him? He furrowed his brows in frustration and fisted his hands at his side. If Mr. O'Kelly had seen them kissing, would he ever be allowed to see Ciaran again? His breath hitched. He covered his mouth with his hand. Was it all over, just like that? *Shannon, you're worrying yourself into a panic. Take deep breaths, one, two, three.* His pacing halted as Ciaran appeared from the hallway, striding in his direction. "Is he all right? Did he say anything?"

Huffing, Ciaran threw his arms down, rolling his eyes at him. He shoved his hands into his front pockets as he approached and stopped just in front of him, then looked up. "He's fine. He just passed out. He didn't say a word."

"But do you think he saw anything?" Shannon studied his face, impatient for answers.

Ciaran yanked his hands from his pockets and placed them squarely on Shannon's shoulders. "If he did, he surely won't remember it in the morning." He leaned in and planted a quick kiss on his mouth.

Shannon bolted back, flinging Ciaran's hands off his shoulders. "Stop, Ciaran, that's what almost got us into bloody trouble in the first place." He was angry and he would let him know it.

Creasing his forehead, Ciaran said, "But I wanted you to stay. He's asleep now, he can't see or hear us." He gave him a shy look and stepped forward again, then ran a light finger down the front of Shannon's shirt. "Don't you want to finish what we started?" His voice was low and sensual.

Shannon's desire hummed and heat rushed his groin. No, it could only lead to more trouble. "Ciaran, get a hold of yourself. My God, we nearly got caught and we've only been home a few hours. What if your da remembers, aye? Then what? What excuse could you possibly have for kissing me, sitting on blankets, in front of the fire? Have you no idea how that must have looked?" He kept his voice soft just in case Mr. O'Kelly could hear them. Heat flared in his chest. He had to drive this point home or there was no hope for them.

"But he's—"

"No, Ciaran. Not tonight, not ever with someone in the house, not ever when there is a chance of someone coming home, not ever when there is any way we could be seen." The volume of Shannon's voice increased, despite his attempts to keep it soft.

Ciaran whirled around and stood stiff, clenching his hands in fists at his side. He stared at the floor. "Fine. Then go home."

"Ciaran, I—"

"Go home," Ciaran said with a snarl.

Hanging his head, Shannon looked at his boots. Would Ciaran ever understand how dreadful it would be to be found out? Would he ever understand the terrifying experience of being forced into confession, of seeing loathing and fear in the eyes of everyone who came upon him? He turned and took slow steps toward the door. When he neared it, he rested his hand over the knob and hesitated. "Shall I come collect you for church tomorrow?" An unintentional waver shook his voice. A whistle raced overhead from the wind just outside. He'd almost forgotten about it.

Ciaran whispered, "Yes."

Shannon nodded once as if Ciaran could see him. He grabbed his stuffed pillowcase, then opened the door to the tumult of rushing air. He stepped outside and slammed the door shut behind him. He stood for a moment on the stoop, letting the wind chill his bones. It lashed his skin as fragments from the dry brush collided with his face. He blinked. The path in front of him blurred as the dust mixed with unshed tears. *It's all right. I don't need to see the path to get home.* He took off in a dash across the open space in front of the house, passed the barn and set off into the woods.

He ran hard. His feet flew over rocks and sticks. His pillowcase whipped back and forth. Wetness streaked across his cheeks. He paid it no mind as the cold chilled it. He panted. Fire burned in his lungs. His house came into view, desolate and dark up ahead of him. He couldn't stop until he got there. If he stopped, he feared he might not make it.

His feet hit the solid wood of the step on a small front entry. He quickly turned the chilled knob and opened the door, then entered his house. It wasn't really a home, just a place to keep his things. He glanced around the small kitchen and main room in front of him. Their long, plank dining table stood bare between two benches by a butcher-block and a kitchen dresser. A rumpled couch sat under a long window at the far end, next to the hearth. As he walked into the room, a faint glow caught his gaze.

His mother entered the room from a short hallway, squinting as she held an oil lamp up. "Shannon? Is that you, dear?"

His gaze roamed Ma's dark, wavy hair. It ran all the way down the length of her back. She wore her long pajamas, the ones that reminded him of a flour sack. He strode toward her. "Yeah, Ma. It's me."

She frowned and wrinkled her brows, the lamplight reflected in her gray eyes. "Are you okay, son?" She squinted and brushed the back of her hand over his cheek.

He flinched, pulling away, remembering the cold streams on his face when he'd run through the forest. He swiped at his cheeks, clearing them of wetness and dust. "I'm fine. I'm going to bed." He brushed by her and trudged into his room.

Once inside, he dropped his pillowcase, shut the door, and quickly undressed. He slid under cool sheets and his dark quilt.

The fresh scent of outside air rose up from the sheets. He turned over onto his side, facing the door. His mother had indeed washed them after he left. Anything to keep her son clean. Anything to keep the dirty thoughts from returning.

The sound of her soft footsteps crept in from outside his door. She paused for a moment, the lamplight glowing on the floorboards underneath. The shadows from her bare feet fluttered in the faint light. *Go to bed, Ma.*

He shut his eyes for a moment, envisioning Ciaran. He tried to imagine himself in front of the fireplace, with Ciaran's sweet kisses. In his head, Ciaran caressed him and reached down between his legs. He hardened.

The light from beneath the door faded and his mother's footsteps padded away into nothingness.

He let a faint smile hover on his lips. He snuck his hand down to unbutton his undergarment, then placed slow strokes over his erection. His breathing quickened. As he increased the pressure and speed, flashes of memory invaded his fantasy, all culminating in Ciaran's harsh voice telling him to leave. An ache rose up in his chest. He halted the stroking over his arousal, then buttoned his undergarment and tucked his hand under his pillow. He ached, but he just couldn't bring himself to enjoy it tonight. It wasn't the same, not having his beautiful Ciaran here with him. It was lonely and unsatisfying.

He peered out his window. What was Ciaran doing now? Did he also look out of his window into the blustery night? Was he thinking of him just as he thought of Ciaran? Would he pleasure himself, fantasizing about their trip?

He wanted to go back. He imagined himself running through the woods again, but this time to Ciaran's home. He'd tap on his window and be let inside. They'd make love, falling asleep in each other's arms. He missed him terribly. Much more than he ever thought he would.

He pushed his face into his pillow and shut his eyes tight. He'd see him tomorrow and everything would be fine. It had to be.

FAINT RAPPING FILLED Shannon's bedroom. He rolled over and pulled his pillow up over his head. *Just go away.*

"Shannon, dear, time for breakfast," his mother called from outside his door.

More rapping sounded, insistent this time.

A hard knocking shook the door. "Get yourself up, boy. Your ma's made you a nice breakfast and you'll eat it," his father's gruff voice thundered from beyond the door.

He flashed his eyes open. Da sounded irritated. He rolled over, focusing on the door. "I'm coming, Da." Angry voices carried in from the other side of the door. His mother and father were already at odds over him.

He slowly rose from the bed, a lumpy mattress sitting in a simple frame, and padded to his oak wardrobe at the far end of the room. After opening it, he perused his clothing. It was all pretty much the same, different shades of dark gray and black. He changed his undergarment, then pulled out a newer dress shirt and slid his arms into it. Finally, he tugged into a pair of black slacks and sat on his bed to push into his socks and boots. He raked his fingers through his hair, then grabbed his scally cap and ambled to the door. With one last look around the sparse room, he left. As he made his way to the kitchen table, his gaze snagged on his rather thin father sitting at one end.

Mr. Sullivan wore a tan, three-piece suit and held a leather-bound book in his hand. His brown hair was neatly pressed to the top of his head.

Shannon watched his father. Seemed Da was all prepared for his big morning at church.

Mrs. Sullivan stooped over the fireplace insert in a flowery house dress and red apron. She clanked pans and spatulas around while she worked.

As Shannon neared, the gaze of his father's deeply set brown eyes darted away from him. He sat down on the bench seat next to his father and placed his cap in front of him.

Mr. Sullivan grunted and rose up from the table.

Frowning, he watched from under his long bangs as his father ambled toward the hallway and into his parent's bedroom. He turned his attention to his hands, wringing in his lap. His heart ached with disappointment. He'd been gone six days and his father had barely even looked at him.

A messy plate of eggs, sausage and beans and a cup of tea was set down before him on the table. He peeked up at his mother.

Mrs. Sullivan studied him, her gray eyes wrinkling with worry. "So how was your trip?" She gave him an anxious smile.

She's trying too hard. "It was fine, Ma." He didn't feel like talking to her. He never really felt like talking to her. He picked up his fork and lifted a lump of eggs to his mouth.

"Dublin must have been exciting. Did you see any of the sights?" Her voice sounded cheery, but the lines of worry remained on her face.

"No." He really hadn't seen much of anything there, had he? But he'd learned a great deal. "I'm going to church with Ciaran this morning." He shoveled food into his mouth. His mother would leave him alone if he started eating. It always worked.

She sat down across the table from him. "We're worried about you, Shannon."

He stopped the fork midway to his mouth and peered

across the table at her. Nausea clouded his stomach. *Not this again, please.* "I'm okay. You don't have to worry about me." His gaze roamed her face as he waited for her response. The one he knew was sure to come.

She leaned forward, speaking in almost a whisper as if to keep his father from hearing her in the next room, "You're spending all your time with the O'Kelly boy and no time at all with any of the girls in town. When are you going to start acting like a normal boy?"

He stared at his plate and frowned. *A normal boy.* What the hell was that anyway? Maybe one who didn't make love to his best friend? He spread an uneasy smile over his lips, despite himself, and shifted in his seat.

"What is it?" His mother leaned in closer to him.

"Nothing, just don't worry about me." He steadied himself and shoved a forkful of beans into his mouth. He should at least appear normal for his mother, and normal young men ate their breakfast, right? She seemed determined today though.

She came back in her seat and rested her hands in her lap. "While you were gone, I spoke to Mrs. O'Doyle. You remember her, don't you? She was the one who got your sister that nice platter for her wedding. She said her Melissa wouldn't mind it if you called on her. Do you think you could do that?" She fixed her gaze on him.

His breath caught in his throat. She'd never taken it this far. Of course, she'd chosen a girl from another town, someone who'd not heard all the rumors swirling around him. He picked at his food again, then fixated on her. "Ma, I don't need you playing matchmaker for me."

She scowled and knit her brows. "You won't do it yourself. Frankly, I was hoping you might meet someone on your trip. But it appears, as usual, you were too wrapped up in that O'Kelly boy."

"Ma!" Startling, he slapped his hands on the table. "Don't you dare say anything about Ciaran." He glared at his mother.

His father appeared in the hallway, holding his book with a firm grip to his chest. He pinched his lips, lowering his brows. In a low voice, almost a growl, he said, "Don't you talk to your mother that way, boy."

Shannon jumped from his seat, grabbing his scally cap, stared at his surprised mother's face and rushed to the front door. He stopped with his hand on the knob. *Da won't even say my name.* Pain coiled in his chest. He yanked the door open and sped down the path, back to his Ciaran and away from the hollering voices behind him.

His feet flew as he ran down the trail. The dry dirt kicked up behind him in clumps. Halfway, he slowed, out of harm's way. The morning sun peeked through the trees and lit patches like stars in the night sky all around him. Cool air surrounded him, refreshed him after the long days of sun and heat. Yesterday's windstorm must have cooled the air. How eerie it was. He scanned the thick blanket of trees around him. A few broken and downed branches hung from the canopies and poked about from the underbrush.

He winced. *Oh no, there's a whole other situation to agonize about now.* A clear vision of the glare he'd received from Ciaran's father after being caught kissing by the fire filled his mind. Would Mr. O'Kelly remember? Would Ciaran still be mad at him? Picking up his pace again, he came to the edge of the woods. His gaze caught on Ciaran walking out toward the barn.

Shannon searched the area between the barn and house for a sign of Mr. O'Kelly and strode in Ciaran's direction.

CHAPTER
TWELVE
SHANNON

Ciaran stood at the far end of the barn at the horse stall. Chickens clucked all around him. What were they so upset about? He twisted his head and took Shannon in, walking toward him. *He looks anxious. Is he still upset after last night? I have to make things right.* He let a wide smile play on his face. "Morning, wicked lover."

Sighing, Shannon relaxed his shoulders.

Ciaran left the horse and approached Shannon. He looked good in his Sunday best, delicious even. But that would have to wait. As he got close, he hooked his arms around Shannon's shoulders and buried his face in his neck. He took a deep breath. "I'm sorry, Shannon."

Shannon draped his arms around Ciaran's waist and rested his cheek on his hair. "It's okay. It was just a bloody strange night." He lifted his head to peer into Ciaran's face. "Did your da say anything?"

"No. He doesn't remember a damn thing." *Poor Shannon worried about nothing.* They could have had another night together. But maybe he was right...He pulled apart from

Shannon and hung his hands on Shannon's hips, then spread a wide grin on his face. "He was so bloody pissed last night, he's still having a hard time getting around."

"Will he be going to church with us then?" Shannon scanned his face.

"Think so. He is getting dressed, at least." Ciaran released Shannon's hips, then leaned forward for a quick kiss, desire shivering over him. How he'd wanted more of this last night. They'd definitely have to find someplace to go after church.

Shannon moaned softly into Ciaran's mouth, then jerked away, clearing his throat. "Ciaran, do you think I could clean up here?"

Gazing at him, Ciaran knit his brows. "Why?" He ran his fingers along Shannon's cheek. "You're a bit stubbly, but you look clean enough."

Shannon bowed his head. "I didn't get a chance at home. My ma started in on me. She gave me the whole *you need to find a girl* talk." Sadness threaded through his voice.

Heat pierced Ciaran's chest. "And what did you tell her? Did you tell her you already had one?" Ciaran grabbed his hand and swung it playfully between them. *Shannon with a girl...*He snorted.

Grinning, Shannon gave Ciaran a shy look. "No." He huffed. "She set me up with a girl from Johnstown Bridge. I'm supposed to call on her." He pursed his lips.

Ciaran looked Shannon up and down, wrinkling his nose. He'd have to refuse. "And you won't, will you?"

Shannon let out a nervous chuckle. "No, of course not. I mean, not unless she makes me."

"She won't make you." Ciaran relaxed his stance then pinched his lips. "Even so, you wouldn't, right?" He narrowed his eyes at him. What would he do if Shannon called on a girl? He couldn't, not now.

With a shrug, Shannon said, "I don't know. If my ma really presses me on it, I suppose I'll have to."

Ciaran faced him. Pain wrenched his chest. He was a man now. No one could force him. "You can't. You're with me now. I don't care what your ma says or does, you don't have to go along with it."

Lifting his brows, Shannon squeezed Ciaran's hand. "Are you jealous?"

Ciaran turned away from him, tearing his hand out of his grasp, and scoffed. *Is that what I'm feeling?* "No, of course not. Why would I be jealous of some girl you've never met?"

"Look at me, Ciaran."

Ciaran stood his ground.

Yanking on Ciaran's arm, Shannon forced him back around.

Ciaran threw a glare at him, then clenched his jaw. This wasn't fair, not at all.

Shannon stared at him a moment as if taking it all in. "You know I only love you. I'd never, ever, do anything with anyone else." He searched Ciaran's face.

He said he only loves me. Ciaran relaxed with a groan and grasped both of Shannon's hands, shaking them once. "I know, but I still don't want you calling on anyone." He let a faint grin play on his face. "Except me."

"Yeah, okay." Shannon shifted his weight, exhaling a breath of air. "Can I please get cleaned up now? We'll be late."

CIARAN WAITED IN THE CART, watching Shannon hold the front door to the house open for Da.

"Thank you, Shannon. You're such a pleasure to have around." His da gave Shannon a pained grin, then walked with forced steps to the waiting cart. Wrinkles littered his black suit and the undocked tail of his white shirt peeked out from under his black belt.

Shannon followed his da and helped him onto the bench seat next to Ciaran. He climbed in the back and sat behind them, facing backward.

Ciaran gave the reins a quick flick and the horse took off down the drive.

During the ten-minute ride into town, Ciaran let his thoughts wander to everything Shannon had told him. It seemed, even in church, where judgments should be withheld, they still ridiculed him. His body jolted on the seat as it bumped over a pothole in the road. He glanced at his father, slumped in the seat next to him. He should be more mindful of the road.

The three of them plodded along in silence into town.

Ciaran smiled as they passed the bookstore where he'd bought his book for the trip. He didn't get much time to read it. He was too busy paying attention to Shannon. He drove the cart through an old cemetery, over a gravel drive and to the front of the church.

Townspeople milled about and a pair of men in their finest Sunday clothes came to great his father.

Ciaran looked over the men. He didn't recognize them as they helped his father from the cart. He jumped from the cart, then turned his attention to hitching the horse alongside Shannon. "Thanks, Shannon." Ciaran gave him an intentional glance while they walked from the now-tethered horse through dry grass and moldy gravestones.

"You're welcome. Always glad to be of service." Shannon grinned at him and held his head high as they walked.

Studying him, Ciaran strolled beside him. He seemed different today, like his shoulders were lighter, like he had confidence. He smirked. Maybe it had something to do with the love they held for each other.

Ciaran's attention drew to the small church of their town. It was a stone building, dating back a few hundred years. Ivy, probably as old as the church itself, had scaled the walls steadily over the decades to shroud a good portion of it in glossy, heart-shaped leaves. He looked up in amazement at the church's square tower and spires sitting atop each corner over the entrance.

After climbing a short set of stone steps to an open red door, Ciaran strolled inside. He gazed at the graceful curves of the tall windows. As he walked into the church beside Shannon, he peered over the numerous rich paintings of Christ and Mother Mary lining the walls. To think someone actually took the time to so carefully and methodically paint perfectly plump cherubs and flowing robes in such vivid hues boggled his mind. He'd always wanted to reach out and run his fingers along the smooth surface, to feel if there were any tiny bumps still left over from the artist's brush.

Ciaran took a seat at a shellacked wooden pew in the very back with Shannon following to slide in next to him. They waited for Father Brennan to take his position in a grandiose pulpit. Large, ornate ceramic vases filled with white roses sat on pedestals at either side of the podium. Voices spoke in whispers around them. A lone baby teetered on the verge of tears.

Ciaran pressed his leg against Shannon's. Even here, he still wanted to feel him close. It couldn't be what Father Brennan had told Shannon. No love could be bad, could it? He took in the familiar musty scent of the church with a deep inhale.

Smiling, Shannon gazed at Ciaran.

With a sheepish grin spreading over his lips, Ciaran rubbed

his leg suggestively against Shannon's, then fixated on the pulpit. *No, it's not wrong to love Shannon.*

Leaning over, Shannon whispered, "Ciaran, have you no shame?"

Ciaran came close and gave him a playful bump with his shoulder. "No."

Mr. Sullivan turned around a few rows ahead of them and flashed a disapproving glare.

Dropping the grin from his face, Shannon hung his head, then wrapped his arms around his waist. The foot of his free leg tapped a nervous rhythm on the dark, wooden floor.

Ciaran watched the exchange. It was as if all of Shannon's confidence was sucked out of him with one look. His heart ached for him. How terrible it must all be for him.

The congregation around them stood, and they did the same.

Father Brennan's voice filled the room as the service began. They read scripture, sang hymns, and bowed in prayer along with everyone else. A few times, Ciaran gave Shannon a playful poke to rouse Shannon when he started to doze off, but Shannon never let his eyes drift back up. It was as if the old Shannon had returned, not the one who'd changed so much back in Dublin.

Communion started and Ciaran stood, waiting in still silence beside Shannon for their turn to proceed up the center aisle for their wine and wafer. A man next to him stepped into the procession. Ciaran needed to do something to get the old Shannon back. He gave Shannon's hand a quick squeeze, then flashed a mischievous grin at him and stepped to the man next to him.

Dropping his mouth open, Shannon let out a soft gasp and brought his head up. He scanned the people around him.

Everyone around them continued their journey to the pulpit, caught up in ritual.

Ciaran stepped up the aisle with Shannon following. It might have been risky, but it got Shannon to stop his ruminating. He stopped in front of Father Brennan and got down on his knees to accept his sacrament. Was he a sinner now? Maybe, but God wasn't striking him down. In fact, everything went on just as it always had. He watched Shannon as he finished.

Shannon went through the motions without looking at Father Brennan. His gaze shifted to peer anywhere, but at the priest.

Ciaran frowned. Shannon was obviously still uneasy.

ONCE THE SERVICE ENDED, Ciaran walked out of the church door with Shannon following, into the fresh open air. Relief washed over him as the sun warmed the top of his head and shoulders. It was over and he had the rest of the day to spend with Shannon.

Out of nowhere, Father Brennan materialized right before him. Short, wiry, gray hair covered the sides of the priest's balding head. His eyes were shocking with how blue they were. The priest's cheeks and nose were reddened. Did the good Father imbibe in a little too much communion wine?

Shannon halted in place, his skittish gaze growing wide. He hung his head and slumped his shoulders as if to appear smaller.

Father Brennan gave Shannon a sly smile. "Shannon, my boy, I hear you went to Dublin with Ciaran last week." His black robes hung at his sides, hitting the ground as if his stout frame was too short for them.

"Um, yeah." Shannon fixated on the ground. He clenched

and unclenched his fists, rushing a quick, nervous glance to Ciaran.

Why is he asking about that? "We did and it was wonderful. We got to see my Aunt Iona and Shannon here even tended her pub. Ah, the cathedrals there are something to behold, Father." He forced a grin at Father Brennan.

The priest's attention focused on Shannon once again. "Oh, did you now, Shannon? I'm sure you must have met some very interesting individuals there." He stood with his hands clutched behind his back, swaying.

Shannon narrowed his eyes, looking up to meet the priest's gaze straight on. "Uh, they were interesting, you know, like most people in the city might be."

"I'll go and fetch the cart." Something didn't sound right in the priest's voice. He should get Shannon out of here. Ciaran turned and bound off.

CHAPTER THIRTEEN
SHANNON

S hannon's chest squeezed and his hands trembled. *Damn it, Ciaran!* How could he leave him alone with Father Brennan like that? Shannon bowed his head and waited. *Hurry please...*

"Have you need for confession today, Shannon?" Father Brennan said in a low voice.

Shannon's nerves frayed and his hands trembled harder. "Uh, n-no, not today."

The priest leaned close and spoke in almost a whisper, "Are you sure, my boy? Seems you might at least have had some thoughts on your trip that might not have been, how shall I say it, pure?"

Shannon gave a slow shake of his head. "N-no, I didn't. I-I was good, very good." He hung his head as he spoke. A cold sweat broke out on his skin.

Moving closer, Father Brennan bowed his head down to Shannon's level. "Well, Shannon, your father seems to think maybe that's not the case. Is there something you might want to tell me?"

"N-no, of c-course not. I-I've no idea why my father would think that." Shannon drew a deep inhale. *Damn my father.* Where was Ciaran with the bloody cart, anyway?

Father Brennan seized his arm, just above the elbow.

Shannon startled. *No, please...*

"Come now, Shannon, I'm sure there's something you need to confess." Father Brennan applied a forceful tug to his arm.

It's gone too far. His father had requested a confession and there was nothing he could do about it. With a heavy sigh, Shannon let the priest haul him back to the church. The disdainful stares and condemnatory whispers from churchgoers flooded his veins with humility as he passed by them.

After striding in through a side door of the church, they walked to the draped confessional box. Shannon reluctantly went inside and sat down. Rustling filtered through the box as Father Brennan took his seat.

The panel slid open between them.

"You may begin, my child," the priest said.

Shannon's heart pounded and sweat formed on his brow. Nausea balled up in his gut. He couldn't possibly admit what he had done with Ciaran. He had to lie. Would he be struck down dead as soon as he left the church? Tears stung the corners of his eyes. He searched the familiar interior of the booth and the cracks in the wooden surface he'd studied through the tears of past confessions. His throat went dry, and he licked his lips. "F-forgive me father, f-for I have sinned." He blinked. A hot tear raced down his cheek and his lip trembled. He swallowed hard, feeling like he might suffocate. "It-it's been a month since my last confession, I-I..."

"Go on."

He glanced at the partition. Only the faint outline of Father Brennan's lips showed through it. His breath hitched in his throat. He struggled to keep from weeping outright. He opened his mouth, furrowing his brows. "I-I got angry with Ciaran. I-I wasn't very nice to him." He relaxed a little. Maybe he could get away with something simple after all.

A sigh from the priest floated through the partition followed by creaking as he shifted in his seat. "Seems to me there's something much larger than that bothering you, son."

"N-no, there isn't." Shannon struggled to hold his voice steady. He had to sound convincing.

"Don't lie to me."

"I-I'm not."

Father Brennan's voice took on a smug tone. "You are and I know it. I feel it. You need to confess, son, or you'll never be absolved."

Shannon bit his lip. Another tear rolled down his cheek. "B-but I—"

"You and I both know why you're here. Let's be out with it." The priest's words were sharp.

Oh no, he wants that. Shannon glanced at the ceiling inside the booth. Why did it always come down to this? Why must the priest always put his sexuality on display inside the confessional booth? What could he tell him that wasn't too damaging? He darted his gaze around the inside of the booth as if it held the key to his release.

"Come on then. I haven't got all day."

"O-okay, I-I had unclean thoughts. I couldn't help it. I-I touched myself. I pleasured myself." Shannon felt dirty and shamed as the words left his lips. "P-Please, forgive me for sins that I have forgotten." He swallowed again, fighting back more tears. A lingering moment of silence filled the booth. Would it be enough or did the priest want more? He clenched his fists in his lap and pursed his lips.

"Did you think about men or women when you did these things?"

Gasping, Shannon covered his mouth with the back of his hand. A sob caught in his chest. His eyes filled with fresh tears, and he hunched over in his seat with his other arm wrapped around his waist. His voice cracked. "Women."

"Ah, Shannon, my boy..." Father Brennan shifted in his seat, sending the sound of swishing cloth through the barrier.

Shannon's whole body shook. He shut his eyes tight and held his breath.

"That'll be five Hail Marys, for each time." Father Brennan sighed. "You are forgiven and dismissed, my child."

Shannon jumped up and sped from the booth, leaving the curtain swinging in his wake. As he swiped at his face, he ran through the church and out of the front door. Once outside, he scanned the cars and carriages for Ciaran's cart. A waving arm caught his attention. "Oh, thank God."

With a wide smile on his face, Ciaran sat in the cart, waving to him.

Shannon ran to Ciaran and jumped up into the seat beside him. He struggled to steady his breathing. "Where's your da?" His voice wavered still.

Wrinkling his brows, Ciaran turned in the seat and studied him. "Shannon, where were you? You look like you've been crying."

Shannon wrapped his arms around his own waist and gazed down at his feet, frowning. "I'll tell you later. Can we please go home?"

Shannon remained still, not speaking the whole way home while Ciaran drove the cart and pulled up in front of the barn. Thankfully, Ciaran had the good sense to leave him alone. He climbed down from the cart and helped Ciaran tend to the horse, then walked with him into the barn while Ciaran guided the horse to its stall.

Ciaran secured the horse, then turned to him. He threw his

arms around Shannon's shoulders, holding him tight. "Tell me what happened."

Shannon melted into the comfort of his embrace. "Oh, Ciaran, Father Brennan made me go to confession."

"He what? You didn't tell him anything, did you?" Ciaran shifted his head to search his face.

"God, no. It was bloody awful though. My father requested it, the bastard." A calming wave swept through Shannon. All he needed was to be right here in Ciaran's arms.

"What did you tell him? Why were you so upset?" Ciaran wrinkled his forehead.

Shannon buried his face into his neck. There was no way he could admit to him what he told Father Brennan. It was too embarrassing. "Nothing, just hold me."

Tightening the embrace, Ciaran said, "It doesn't seem like nothing. You just don't want to tell me, do you?" He huffed a soft exhale. "You know, my da is gone for the rest of the afternoon. He's at the pub again getting a bit of the hair of the dog." Seduction laced his voice, and he gave Shannon a lingering kiss on the cheek.

Shannon's desire flared. "Really? Are you sure he won't be back?"

"Very sure. He's coming home with Mr. Flaherty and he never misses the poker match directly after lunch. We have plenty of time." Ciaran gave Shannon's bum a quick squeeze.

Shannon's hips pushed against Ciaran's. The distinct hardness of Ciaran's erection pressed against his groin. *Everything else be damned.* He wanted him, now. "Where shall we go?" His breath quickened. He kissed the soft skin of Ciaran's neck.

A shudder rolled through Ciaran's body. "Oh, Shannon." Ciaran moaned softly. He stepped away, grasping Shannon's hand, then hauled him outside and to the front door of his house. He tore the door open, glanced back with a smirk and led him into his bedroom.

Shannon stood next to Ciaran's brass bed and watched him close the door.

Ciaran gave him a coy smile and came to stand in front of him. "Take your clothes off." His voice was husky.

"Just like that? You expect me to just do as I'm told?" Shannon smiled, looking Ciaran up and down.

"Yes. Well, if you won't, then I'll go first." Ciaran undressed, slowly, sensually, keeping his gaze affixed to Shannon's while he unbuttoned and removed his shirt and unfastened his trousers, then his underwear.

Shannon caressed Ciaran's shoulder.

Ciaran slapped his hand away, offering him a playful grin. He shook his head slowly. "Uh-ah, you can look, but don't touch, not yet, anyway."

"What sort of wicked thing are you planning?" Shannon's pulse raced. He never imagined Ciaran taking things under control like this. He took in Ciaran's taut stomach and muscular arms.

Ciaran sat on the dark quilt covering his bed and removed his shoes. He stood and pushed his trousers and underwear down and off.

Straightening, Ciaran stood completely bare in front of him. He stepped forward and placed his hands on Shannon's hips, giving him a soft kiss.

Shannon moaned into the kiss. The faint pressure of Ciaran's hard cock pressed against the cloth of his slacks. "Can I touch you now?" Need filled his soft voice and sent heat into his swollen cock.

Ciaran trailed his tongue down his neck. After pushing Shannon's shirt aside, he sucked seductively on his collarbone.

"No, not yet," he said, his voice muffled as his lips grazed his skin.

Shannon tilted his head back. His fingers twitched. How he ached to feel Ciaran's soft skin. "Can I kiss you?" he asked, in a low, raw voice.

"No, not yet." Ciaran positioned his hands over Shannon's belt, unfastened it and slid a hand down the front of Shannon's slacks. Ciaran brushed his fingers against Shannon's erection.

Sensation teased Shannon's groin. He rocked his hips, craving more friction.

Lifting his hand out, Ciaran ran delicate fingers across Shannon's shaft, through the fabric of his slacks.

Shannon moaned as Ciaran's fingertips moved harder up and down, running circles around the head of his stiff cock. Shocking pleasure washed over him with the way Ciaran's hand worked on him through his slacks. He tensed his brows and hung his mouth open, needing to be filled with whatever part Ciaran he could get. "P-please Ciaran, let me kiss you."

Teasing in silence, Ciaran smiled against his neck. He reached his hand under Shannon, between his legs, and curled a finger to give an enticing push into the crevice of Shannon's bum, circling, running all the way under his sac and around to the head of his erection again. Ciaran squeezed through the thin fabric and rubbed hard with his index finger and thumb.

Shannon released a sharp gasp as a wave of sweet sensation rolled over him. What was Ciaran doing to him? How did he ever learn something like this? His need rose to an unbearable level. He yanked Ciaran into his chest and buried his head in Ciaran's neck, ravishing the soft skin in front of him with kisses and soft bites.

"N-no, Shannon, stop." Ciaran shoved hard on his chest.

Shannon stepped back in a daze.

Naked and panting, Ciaran stood before him.

Shannon fisted his hands at his side. "What are you doing? Are you trying to drive me bloody mad?" His desire hummed and ached inside him with no outlet.

Grinning, Ciaran nodded his head. "Yes. I am." He took a determined step toward him again.

Shannon held out his arms and stopped Ciaran before he continued his attack, resting his hands on Ciaran's shoulders. "Where did you learn this? I thought you never did anything before our trip?" He had to have an answer. There must be an explanation for his sudden aggressive behavior.

"Simple. I've done that to myself." Ciaran cocked his head and eyed him as if curious.

Shannon spread a knowing smile over his lips. So, his lovely Ciaran did do those things. He released him. "Too bad I wasn't around to see it."

Ciaran let out a soft chuckle. "That could be arranged." His voice held a playful seduction and he rocked from side to side. He clasped his hands in front of him, then looked at him and straightened. He brushed his tongue over his lips in a slow, sensual circle, then turned and padded to his oak nightstand. He opened the drawer and produced a small bottle of mineral oil.

Shannon freed a short gasp. His cock swelled even harder as he watched Ciaran pour the slick oil in his own palm.

Turning around, Ciaran gave him a coy look. He backed up to his bed and lay down at an angle on his back, propped by a pillow. His gaze fixed on him while he reached down and placed a slow stroke up and down his erection with his slickened palm. He wrinkled his brows and thrust his hips as he pleasured himself.

Shannon moved to the bed and leaned over Ciaran, supporting himself on straight arms on either side of Ciaran's hips. "You have no idea how many times I've imagined you doing just that." He came down and placed a passionate kiss on Ciaran's open mouth. It was time to participate.

Giving him heated kisses, Shannon climbed onto the bed, and straddled him on his hands and knees, then unbuttoned his shirt and undergarment. He straightened over his knees, pulled out of the sleeves, and threw his shirt to the floor. His attention shifted to his slacks. He unfastened them and shoved them down, undergarment and all. He fixated on Ciaran, moaning, and thrusting beneath him while continuing long, even strokes over his thick cock.

Shannon grasped Ciaran by the wrists, pulled them up over Ciaran's head and lay down on top of him, entwining their fingers. Ciaran's slickened erection slid against his stomach. With slight fumbling, he kicked his slacks and undergarments the rest of the way off. He wrapped his arms around Ciaran's head while still binding his arms and supporting himself on his elbows. He crushed Ciaran's lips with deep kisses.

Opening his mouth, Ciaran thrust his tongue urgently inside. He rocked his hips with Shannon's in an insistent, but slow rhythm, rubbing their erections together.

A wave of sensation pulsed through Shannon's body. He had what he craved. "I want you, Ciaran," his husky voice whispered against Ciaran's mouth.

"Do you want to go inside me this time?" Ciaran thrust harder against him.

Shannon swept a faint smile over his lips. "You mean you'd let me do that?"

Ciaran nodded.

"You sure you're ready?" Shannon ached. Would Ciaran really let him go inside already? After all, it took at least a month with the teacher before he agreed to it. "It hurts. At first, I mean." He should prepare Ciaran first.

"So, lots of things hurt." Ciaran flicked his tongue sensually against his lips. "I just want to try it. You said you liked it, right? You said it felt good."

"Yes, well, I'm used to it." Shannon came down to claim Ciaran's taunting mouth again. He kissed him hard, and Ciaran moaned in response.

Ciaran broke the kiss. "Are you trying to talk me out of it?"

Shannon stopped his rocking hips and kisses. "God no. If you want to try that, I'd be more than happy to oblige you." He offered a soft grin and rolled off him, then reached over to the nightstand and grabbed the bottle of mineral oil. He turned back around to face Ciaran.

With wide eyes, Ciaran drew a deep inhale.

"You sure you want to do this?" Shannon searched his face. He looked scared.

Ciaran nodded, but his eyes betrayed a hint of anxiety.

"I'll be gentle, don't worry." Shannon guided Ciaran onto his side, facing away from him. He put an ample amount of oil in his palm and hissed as he brought it down over his erection. An exquisite slickness and heated pressure enveloped his hard cock. Desire hummed inside him and grew to a painful level with anticipation. He rested his face against the back of Ciaran's neck and nipped at the soft skin. "You ready?"

Ciaran took heavy breaths. "Y-yes."

With slickened fingers, Shannon ran a light trail down Ciaran's side, watching as Ciaran's body quivered from the sensation. He continued down into the crevice of Ciaran's behind. With care, he ran slow circles over Ciaran's entrance and waited for his response.

Ciaran pushed his hips back into his slick fingers. Letting out a soft moan, he closed his eyes. "Harder."

Increasing his pressure, Shannon slowly pushed a finger inside. It barely went in before he pulled it back out. "You okay?" He looked over Ciaran's shoulder.

Ciaran resumed stroking his erection with quick jerks of his hand.

"Hey, be careful. I want you to wait for me."

Ciaran panted. "Hurry up then. It doesn't hurt."

Shannon released a soft chuckle. Ciaran was so impatient, even now. He circled Ciaran's entrance again and pushed a finger all the way in.

Bucking, Ciaran gasped.

Shannon circled his finger and stroked inside Ciaran, finding the spot that made him shiver.

"Damn, what was that? Do that again." Ciaran pushed back into his finger.

Shannon inserted a second finger and brought them in and out, stroking the spot over and over, then halted his actions.

Letting out a loud moan, Ciaran arched his back. He stopped the quick strokes on his seeping cock and panted. "Do it, hurry." His voice held a seductive urgency.

Shannon pulled his fingers out and nudged his erection against Ciaran's entrance. He pressed his forehead against Ciaran's back and grasped Ciaran's hips while he drove slowly inside.

Ciaran's body stiffened and another deep moan ripped from his throat.

Delicious heat and pressure surrounded Shannon's cock as he drove into Ciaran. He let out a soft gasp as he pulled out and drove back inside. A rush of pleasure pulsed through him. Ciaran's body tightened around him as he drove into him.

Closing his eyes, Ciaran tensed his brows. He pumped over his rigid shaft while filling the room with desperate gasps, his body shaking against Shannon's.

Shannon tugged Ciaran's hips close and reached around to cover the hand stroking Ciaran's erection. He pushed it away, wrapped his own palm around Ciaran's shaft and stroked while thrusting into him. His climax built to a delicious tension and hummed in his groin.

Ciaran groaned and his body stiffened.

Hot seed spurted over Shannon's hand. A peak of intense sensation rippled through him, release erupting from him. He surrendered to exquisite spasms, filling Ciaran. He panted and cried out with each pulsing wave. He seized Ciaran, pulling him close while it slowed to a blissful end.

"Now I know why you like that so much." Ciaran's voice sounded far away.

Shannon withdrew his cock from Ciaran while still holding him in a tight embrace. "It feels incredible, doesn't it?" He spoke against Ciaran's back, unwilling to lift his head for the moment.

"Yeah, that's a good word for it." Ciaran let out a lazy chuckle and drew Shannon's arm tighter around him. "Ah, I could sleep so well right now."

"Why? Didn't you sleep well last night?"

"No, not after our little fight. Truthfully, I got sort of used to sleeping with you next to me," Ciaran said. "I missed you last night." He nuzzled into the pillow they shared.

Shannon squeezed Ciaran. "I missed you, too."

"Ciaran?" Shannon nudged Ciaran, sleeping soundly next to him. He listened to his deep, steady breathing and looked out over the drawn-out shadows in the trees outside his bedroom window. It must be afternoon. Hunger pangs gnawed at his stomach.

Ciaran stirred.

"Come on, your da will be home soon. I don't want a repeat

of last night." Shannon unwrapped himself from around Ciaran's body and shimmied to the edge of the bed.

"Where're you bloody going?" Ciaran peered at him.

Shannon stood and picked up his clothes. "I'm getting something to eat. I'm famished." He slid his undergarment and slacks up his legs, fastened them and pushed his arms through his shirt and buttoned it. He opened the door. "Do you want anything?"

Rolling onto his back, Ciaran rested his forearm over his face. "I'll have whatever you're having." The gravelly tones of slumber filled his voice.

"Okay, hurry up." Shannon strode out into the main room and into the kitchen area. He crouched down and opened the door on the dresser. A loaf of bread sat next to a bowl filled with potatoes. He grabbed the bread, set it on the counter and opened the door of the icebox. A block of cheese rested on the shelf. He pulled it out and placed it next to the bread. He scanned the counter for a knife. He let a slow smirk cross his lips as he came across a knife sitting by the sink. He grabbed it and set about cutting the bread and cheese into slices and putting them on a small platter. When he finished, he turned.

Ciaran stood at the table, gazing at him, his hair a blond mop and his bare chest creased with bed wrinkles. He took a seat at the table.

Shannon set the platter down in front of Ciaran and sat across from him. He spread a slow smirk over his lips. "You'd better clean up a little more than that before your da gets home."

Still groggy, Ciaran looked up at him, and yawned. "Shannon, although I love you dearly, you are such a fussbudget. Will you please relax?" He grabbed slices of bread and cheese and made a small sandwich. He devoured it in only three bites.

Shannon widened his smirk into a broad grin as he watched Ciaran eat. Who cared what names Ciaran called him? At this point in time, he was in heaven. Maybe he should pinch himself to see if it was real. *Ciaran is my lover. Not my friend, not my little brother. Ciaran loves me and he let me have him completely.* What more could he ask out of life? He made himself a cheese sandwich and kept his gaze fixed on him while he ate it.

The rumble of a motor car approached the house. His heartbeat quickened. Mr. O'Kelly must be home. "Come on, Ciaran, go and put your shirt on and fix your hair. Please? For me?"

"Fine." With a heavy sigh, Ciaran rose from the table and trudged to his bedroom.

A doorknob clattered and Shannon turned his head toward it.

Mr. O'Kelly cracked the door open.

"Good afternoon, Mr. O'Kelly. Did you have a good time at the pub?"

Mr. O'Kelly took a few steps into the room with an unsteady gait and closed the door.

Shannon's chest tightened. What would Ciaran think of his father's condition? At least it wasn't as bad as the night before.

Mr. O'Kelly came back around to focus on him. "Indeed, I did. Where has Ciaran gone off to?"

"Right here, Da." Ciaran strode out from the hallway leading to the bedrooms. His white shirt hung open over his undergarment and down over his slacks, untucked. His hair was brushed, but a lock of it popped out on the side of his head.

"Would you like some bread and cheese?" Shannon pushed the platter toward Mr. O'Kelly.

"Thank you, Shannon, but no. I'd like to get out to Nessa's grave and was hoping you boys would accompany me." Mr.

O'Kelly walked over and put his hands on the back of a chair while he waited for an answer.

"Of course, Da." Ciaran winced and stepped toward his father.

Shannon bit his lip. How close they were. Not at all like he and his father. They were never at odds, and were always polite and respectful. A stab of pain plunged into his heart. He shifted his gaze to his hands, resting on the table surface.

Mr. O'Kelly left the chair and strolled toward the hallway leading to the bedrooms. "I think I left my pocket watch in your room this morning," he mumbled, passing his son.

"You will go with us, right, Shannon?" Ciaran walked over and stood directly in front of him at the table.

Shannon gave him a sad smile. "Of course. If you want me there, I'll be there."

Mr. O'Kelly ambled back into the kitchen, shoving a silver watch into his pocket. "Well, let's be off then." He walked to the door, opened it, and stopped.

"Um, I need to get my shoes." Shannon stood from his chair, trotted into Ciaran's room, and entered it. His heart jolted as he scanned the rumpled sheets and bedcovers. *Oh no, Ciaran's father was just in here looking for his pocket watch.* Slowly, his gaze rose to the nightstand. He gasped as he took in the bottle of mineral oil, still opened, sitting right out on the nightstand. Would Mr. O'Kelly have any idea what they had done with it? If he asked, what sort of an excuse could he give him?

Shannon strode to the nightstand, capped the oil, and tucked it away in Ciaran's drawer. He turned his attentions to the bed and straightened it, then grabbed his shoes and socks and sat on the bed's edge. With trembling hands, he slid his shoes on. He slowly shook his head. They had to be more careful. They had to stop doing things in Ciaran's house.

Shannon stepped out of Ciaran's room, hanging his head, and stuffed his hands in his front pockets. What should he expect when he returned to the main room? If his own father had seen those things in his room, he'd be thoroughly beaten, if not worse. He certainly would never be allowed to see Ciaran again. But those were *his* parents, the ones who always scrutinized every little thing he did. The ones who inspected his room every chance they got. He entered the main room and snapped his gaze up.

Ciaran held the door open as his father stood, waiting, on the front stoop.

Looking Ciaran over for a second, Shannon searched for any indication things were not right.

"What?" Ciaran furrowed his brows, shifting his stance.

Should I say anything about the oil? Shannon glanced at Ciaran's father, standing near to Ciaran. No, not yet, Mr. O'Kelly was too close and it appeared, for now, all was well. "Nothing, I'll tell you later," he whispered, walking past Ciaran and out of the door.

The three strolled in silence down the drive and turned at a path between two fields. Fledgling plants waved at them from their beds of peat and dirt as they passed. A warm breeze picked up and ruffled the shirts and hair of the three men. Ahead stood a tall oak tree, its canopy branched out at least twenty feet in all directions.

Shannon gazed up at the tree's branches. This tree was Mrs. O'Kelly's favorite. He'd seen her sitting beneath it many times reading books of poetry. His chest ached. She'd never read those books again. His gaze fell to the fresh grave at the base of the tree's trunk. At least she'd always be here, under her tree.

The trio stopped at a grave marker carved out of stone. A Celtic cross with a ring surrounding the crucifix stood tall out of a square base. A small insignia centered itself in the crucifix. The base held Nessa's full name, etched in intricate writing, along with the dates of her short life.

Shannon bowed his head and formed the sign of the cross with his index finger, from shoulder to shoulder and forehead to chest, along with Ciaran and his father. He stole a glance at Ciaran and Mr. O'Kelly, standing next to him.

They stood still, like statues on guard. Ciaran sniffled and bit his lower lip.

The urge to reach out and hold Ciaran engulfed Shannon. He couldn't, it would look suspicious.

"So, Nessa, your locket is safe with your sister." Mr. O'Kelly turned to glance at Ciaran. "Your son seems well." He glanced at Shannon. "And Shannon is even here to see you," he spoke in a soft and steady voice.

"Hello, Ma. I've missed you." Ciaran's voice wavered. "Iona was very nice—" His breath hitched.

Shannon lurched sideways, reaching out for Ciaran, then snapped back. What would he normally do? He pursed his lips and his mind raced as Ciaran's grief consumed him once again. He ached to hold him. But should he?

Whirling around, Ciaran flung his arms over Shannon, burying his face in Shannon's shoulder, succumbing to quiet weeping.

Shannon freed a soft gasp. What would Ciaran's father think? He glanced up from behind Ciaran's shoulder to peek at Mr. O'Kelly.

Mr. O'Kelly wrinkled his brow as if pained.

He placed a timid hold around Ciaran's waist. He didn't see any sign of disapproval from his father.

Mr. O'Kelly stepped to the young men and laid a gentle hand on his son's shoulder as if to help comfort him. "It's all right, son." Emotion laced his voice.

Shannon closed his eyes. He couldn't look at Ciaran's father anymore. If he did, would their new feelings show? Would some trace of intimacy seep out of him? He buried his face into Ciaran's neck, holding him tighter. It seemed like a lifetime before Ciaran broke the embrace.

Straightening, Ciaran wiped his eyes with the back of his hands, then gazed deeply into Shannon's eyes and leaned forward, closing the gap between their lips. He halted and pulled back, feigning a nervous cough into his hand. He turned to his father. "Da, can I go back now?"

Mr. O'Kelly gave his son a quick hug and stepped back. "Yes, you can go." He glanced at Shannon and nodded his head.

Shannon went to take Ciaran's hand. *Don't, Shannon.* He jerked his hand back. He hung his head and strode beside Ciaran, leaving the gravesite. He looked ahead, strolling with his hands clasped behind his back. Ciaran's house loomed off in the near distance.

"I'm worried, Shannon."

Shannon's heart quickened. He stopped. "About what?" He held his breath, studying Ciaran. Did Mr. O'Kelly say something about how they left the bedroom after all?

Ciaran stopped next to him. "About my da. He's drinking a lot." He pinched his lips.

Exhaling, Shannon relaxed. "Shite, Ciaran, you scared the crap out of me." He let his arms fall loosely to his sides and gave him a faint smile.

"What the hell did you think I was going to say?" Ciaran lifted his brows and stepped closer to him.

"Well, that maybe your da saw the mineral oil and messy bed in your room. That maybe your da suspected something. How's that? We shouldn't have left it like that. He went in there, you know, to look for his watch." Shannon let his smile fade, then pressed his lips together.

"Oh, relax. He wouldn't think anything of it. He probably thinks we were in there fixing something."

"With mineral oil?" Shannon's voice rose in pitch. Ciaran wasn't the least bit concerned about it?

"Well, I don't know, maybe we needed to...oil something up."

"Like what? My willy?" Shannon huffed out a laugh. This conversation was ridiculous.

Ciaran freed a strained chuckle. "Yeah, your willy and my arse." Ciaran turned and started toward the house again. "Christ sake, Shannon, what a thing to say."

Shannon jogged to catch up to him and followed him into the house and to the kitchen table. Ciaran took a seat and he did the same, at a chair right next to him.

Fixating on Shannon, Ciaran leaned toward him, and rested his forearm across the table. "I'm telling you, Shannon, my da is drinking far too much. I'm worried about him."

"Maybe there's just something he has to sort through. He really loved your ma, you know. It might just take some time for him to get over losing her." He caressed Ciaran's arm on the table.

"What if he doesn't get over it? What if he turns into one of those drunks, like Mr. Doherty or something?" Ciaran scrunched his face up.

"He won't end up like that. Your da is bloody better than that. He'll pull out of it. Just give him time." Shannon's stomach growled. It must be getting late. "What'll we do about supper tonight?"

Ciaran looked at him like he had worms crawling out of his mouth. "Supper? Is that all you think about?"

Shannon spread a devious grin over his lips. "No."

Sitting back, Ciaran slapped him on the shoulder. "Quit

thinking about the mineral oil. You wicked boy." He let out a soft chuckle.

CIARAN BOILED potatoes and cabbage and heated some corned beef that the neighbors had dropped off. He looked up while setting a few bowls filled with food on the table and sat down.

Mr. O'Kelly came in through the front door and shut it. "Begorra, what a pleasant surprise."

Beaming, Ciaran placed the final dish on the table and took a seat beside Shannon.

Stepping to the table, Mr. O'Kelly sat beside him. With a faint smile, he looked over the food for a moment, tilted his head forward and lifted his hands in prayer.

Ciaran and Shannon prepared for grace.

Mr. O'Kelly let out a faint cough. "Bless us O Lord, and these Thy gifts, for which we are about to receive, from Thy bounty, through Christ, our Lord, Amen."

"Amen," the young men said in unison.

Ciaran dished out food onto his plate and dug into it, then his breath caught. "Shannon, want to go fishing tomorrow?"

Shannon looked up from his plate, his mouth brimming with cabbage. He gulped it down. What fun that would be. "Uh, yeah. We haven't done that since last summer, have we?"

"Nope. Wouldn't it be good to have fresh fish for supper tomorrow, Da?" Ciaran glanced at his father.

"Sounds wonderful." Mr. O'Kelly pushed a fork of boiled potato into his mouth.

"Want to go with us?" Ciaran knit his brows, stopped eating and focused on his father.

"Uh, not tomorrow, son. I have some business to attend to

at the pub." Mr. O'Kelly ate his food as if unaware of the tension filtering off him.

Ciaran glared at his father.

"That's okay, there'll be more fish for us then." Shannon focused on his plate of food. Ciaran was not going to be happy with that answer.

CHAPTER
FOURTEEN
SHANNON

Shannon rolled over in his bed, squinting as the sun shone in through his bedroom window. *Morning already?* His mind drifted back to the previous evening. He remembered sitting in the comfortable chairs by Ciaran's hearth and reminiscing over too much tea with Ciaran and his father. It was pleasant enough. At least Ciaran's father wasn't drinking. And for once he'd come home to a dark house. No one to bother him, he just went to bed. He'd been so tired last night. The eventful day wore him out. A soft knock broke through his memories.

"Shannon, dear, are you awake?" His mother called out from the hallway.

"Yes, Ma. I'll be out in a minute." He slid to the edge of his bed and dropped his legs over it, then stopped to wipe the sleep from his eyes and rose to dress.

He entered the main room and focused on his mother.

She wore another dull housedress and sat at the kitchen table, looking up at Shannon. "Do you have anything else to wear besides black?" She tipped a red and green flowered teacup to her lips.

"What?" *What was she getting at so early in the morning?* He lifted his legs over the bench and sat across from her. Her stare crept over his skin.

"You're going into Johnstown Bridge today with your da and I want you to look your best." She set the teacup down on its saucer, in front of her.

He leaned forward as if then he would understand better. "What are you talking about? I'm supposed to go fishing with Ciaran today."

She stood and walked to the hearth. "No, you're going with your da. Melissa is expecting you." She placed some eggs and toast on a plate and came back around to face him. She waited, a finger tapping the edge of the plate as if she knew he'd be upset.

"I told you I didn't need a matchmaker. I am not going to Johnstown Bridge. I am going fishing," he said, his chest heating more and more with each word. He glared at his mother.

She slapped the plate down on the table in front of him. Her piercing gaze fixated on him. "You're going to do as you're told."

His father entered the room from the hallway and took a quick inventory of the scene in front of him. "Hurry up and eat. I expect you'll clean yourself up a bit better, too."

Shannon clenched his teeth and looked down at his plate, hiding under his long bangs. "I have to go and tell Ciaran then." His voice was soft, but sharp. He had to give in. He had no choice. There was no arguing with his father.

"I'll talk to Ciaran. You need to get going or you'll be late." His mother stepped to a large bowl and busied herself with the morning dishes.

Shannon kept his attentions on his father, waiting by the front door.

Scowling, his father opened the front door and left the house.

Shannon glared at his mother. "What have you set up for me, Ma?" He forced his breakfast into his mouth.

She spoke with her hands in the bowl and the sound of lapping liquid and clanking glasses. "You're meeting her for lunch at the tavern. She'll be there with her da. After you're properly introduced, your da and Mr. O'Doyle will walk the town to leave you two be."

"You've got it all planned out, haven't you?" He fought to keep from sounding too distressed while he spoke. He fisted his free hand under the table. What would Ciaran think? Ciaran would have to understand. He didn't have a choice. He'd just go and get it over with. Then maybe his parents would leave him alone for a while. It was guaranteed this girl wouldn't like him anyway, right?

His mother turned from the bowl and stepped toward him. She stretched her index finger out in front of her. "You listen up. It's about time you got married, Shannon Sullivan. It's about time you started pretending like you have some interest in girls. Do you hear me?"

He hung his mouth open and dropped his fork to the table, then stared at his plate. He wanted to crawl inside a hole somewhere. Did she know he didn't like women? Did she know he wasn't forced to do those things with Mr. Flannigan?

She stabbed her finger at him. "Answer me!"

"Y-yes, Ma." He rose from the table and padded to his room. Once inside, he closed the door and covered his face with his hands. He bit his lip, forcing tears back. If his father saw he'd been crying, the ride to Johnstown Bridge would be hell. He sucked in a deep inhale and calmed. *Ciaran has to understand.* He went to his wardrobe and put his only white shirt on, a present from his eldest sister, and left to get more water to shave and clean up.

Shannon walked to the front door, hanging his head, nausea gnawing at his gut. The rumble of an engine starting up sounded from the front of the house. He furrowed his brows. Had his father borrowed a motor car for the trip? He opened the front door and looked outside.

His mother stood next to a beaten up, black lorry. A few dents marred the side panels and rust made splotches on the roof.

Shannon strode outside and stopped next to his mother.

"What do you think, Shannon?" His father called out through the open window. He sat behind the wheel in a brown suit with an air of pride surrounding him.

"Well, uh, it's, uh—"

"We bought it while you were in Dublin. If you'd stuck around long enough yesterday, you'd have seen it." His mother hung her hands on her hips. She spoke as if it were completely normal for a farmer to just go out and by a motor car.

He widened his eyes. "It's nice." What else could he say? He grabbed the door handle and pulled. It gave a satisfying sound as it clicked open. He climbed into the passenger seat. The memory of Ciaran and their fishing trip flooded his mind. "Ma? You'll tell Ciaran where I've gone right away, won't you?"

She wore a forced smile. "Of course, dear. You just go and have some fun, okay?"

Shannon peered over the hood of the lorry, then focused on his mother. He tugged the door closed and gave her a weak wave.

His father pushed the clutch and let it out slowly.

The lorry lurched forward a few times, jerking Shannon's head forward, before it smoothed and started down their drive.

He watched his father with fascination as they pulled onto the road. "Da, I didn't know you knew how to drive."

"Well, I just learned last week as a matter of fact. Mr. O'Doyle taught me when I bought the lorry." His father kept all his focus on the road in front of him.

"So, you bought it from him then?" Shannon tried to sound happy.

His father nodded.

It all makes sense now. Shannon thinned his lips. His father had bought the lorry from the O'Doyles, and in return, their daughter had agreed to be called upon by Drimnagh's notorious Shannon Sullivan. She surely wouldn't want anything to do with him. He leaned back and made himself comfortable for the hour-long ride into Johnstown Bridge.

SHANNON GAZED at the landscape of trees and brush rolling by outside his window, listening to the soft chatter of unseen things clinking inside the lorry. There was nothing more he could say to his father. The breeze from the open window ruffled his hair and blew in a myriad of wildflower scents. He thought back to Ciaran. His mother better keep her word and tell Ciaran where he was. Ciaran would understand. This trip just couldn't be helped. They'd made him leave so suddenly. They'd forced him to do this.

The car slowed and he looked out over the buildings lining the street ahead of them. Although Johnstown Bridge was a little larger than Drimnagh, it looked pretty much the same. Two and three story buildings jutted out between trees, their walls the color of fresh dairy cream. He straightened in his seat as they pulled into a space in front of a tavern. He read the sign on the brick building, *O'Donnell's*. He spread a smirk over his lips. At least it didn't say O'Doyle's. It was bad enough they'd bought the O'Doyle lorry. They didn't need to be eating in their tavern, too.

His father parked the lorry, glanced at him, then opened his door and climbed out. He buttoned his tan suit jacket, then waited at the curb for Shannon to join him.

Shannon strode, hunched over, hands in his front pockets, to his father. The bright, midmorning sun made him squint.

As he approached, his father said, in a low voice, "Listen, I'll introduce you, then I'll be on my way."

Shannon nodded, turning to enter the tavern. A sharp tug pulled on his sleeve. He stopped.

His father grasped his shirtsleeve. "Be nice, Shannon. If I hear you've upset this girl, I'll have your bloody hide. Do you understand?"

Wincing, pain stabbed Shannon's chest. How could his father say such a thing? Why did his father think he'd upset her? Did his father really think him so monstrous? He swallowed the negative thoughts deep in his throat. He wouldn't let them eat away at him, not now. He had enough to deal with.

His father released the restraint on his sleeve.

With his father right behind him, Shannon strode into the smoky tavern. He scanned the contents of the sparse square tables littering the floor with a few patrons sitting around them. The place was clean and bright. The food smelled delicious. His gut ached with hunger. Thanks to his mother, he hadn't got a chance to eat much of his breakfast.

A young woman sat beside an older man toward the center of the room, his curly blond hair cut short on his head, his light blue gaze snagging on Shannon.

That's Mr. O'Doyle. Shannon's breath caught. He hadn't seen him in four years, since his sister's wedding.

The young woman, also blonde, gazed directly at him.

Shannon walked toward the O'Doyles, sliding his cap off his head, and holding it in front of him. Mr. O'Doyle hadn't changed at all. Was that the same brown suit he wore to the wedding? He attempted to get a good look at the young woman as he walked to the table. She was pretty enough, but her light blue eyes burned right through him. His pulse quickened and he dropped his gaze to the wood planks on the floor, then stopped, just in front of them.

His father strode up behind him with all the confidence of a prize fighter.

Mr. O'Doyle stood and walked around the table to his father with his hand outstretched and a nervous smile. "Good morning, Mr. Sullivan."

"Good morning." Mr. Sullivan shook the outstretched hand. "This here is my Shannon." He gestured to Shannon.

Shannon gave the young woman at the table a shy glance and nodded at her father.

"Well, pleased to meet you, Shannon. This here is Melissa." Mr. O'Doyle tipped his head toward the young woman and held out a hand to Shannon.

Shannon took Mr. O'Doyle's hand and gave it a firm shake, eying Melissa from under his bangs.

Melissa stood and curtsied for him. A low-cut, cream-colored blouse left the top of her full breasts exposed and spilling out while a long, teal skirt covered her narrow hips. She lifted her head and looked directly at him with intense blue eyes, tilting her head as if curious. She placed a delicate hand on the chair beside her. "Hello, Shannon, nice to meet you. Won't you take a seat, here, next to me?" Her voice held a softness and unusual sweetness.

"Um, yeah. Nice to meet you, too," Shannon mumbled, sitting in the chair she pointed out. He glanced at his father.

Was he really going to leave him here with her? What on Earth would he say to her?

His father frowned at him. "All right then, we'll be off. See you in an hour or so." He turned to leave with Mr. O'Doyle.

Shannon studied his hands, wringing in his lap. He needed to say something.

"Nice day, isn't it?" she asked.

"Yeah," he said, softly. Why did he have to be here? Why couldn't he just be fishing with Ciaran? His gaze rose to Melissa's blouse and shifted back to his lap. Could he even look at her? Those eyes might see inside him, might see his sins. Her small hand rested over his. His breath caught. Why was she touching him? They'd just met.

"You're shy, aren't you?" She squeezed his hand.

She seems curious, not mean, and certainly not intimidating. He chanced a glimpse directly into her face. Her eyes captivated him for a second. He shifted in his seat and focused on their hands. "I, uh, suppose I am, a little."

She chuckled. "A little, aye?" She released his hand and sat back in her chair.

He let his gaze wander up to look at her fully.

She flung a long lock of hair off her shoulder.

He studied her. She wasn't scary after all, just a woman, no more, no less.

"You don't want to be here, do you, Shannon?" She spread a smirk over her mouth.

He widened his eyes and parted his lips. Was it that obvious? He leaned forward and forced himself to meet her gaze head on. "No, I do. I just…I was supposed to go fishing with my friend today. My ma didn't tell me about our meeting until this morning." He searched her face. What did she think of him?

"Oh, I see." She gave him an innocent smile. "And who is this friend of yours?"

He freed a long breath, relaxing while he imagined Ciaran's beautiful face. "Uh, his name is Ciaran. Ciaran O'Kelly."

"You mean the boy who just lost his mother?" She shifted closer to him as if fascinated in what he had to say.

"Yes, how did you know?" He laid his forearms on the table in front of him.

"News like that travels fast around here. I heard she just fell over dead in their field. Is that true?" Her words were quick and sharp.

He winced. "Yes, that's true." He cut his gaze to his hands, his chest tightening. He should be careful with her.

She covered his hand with hers once more. "I'm sorry, maybe that wasn't such a good thing to say. Did you know her well?"

"Yes. Ciaran is my best friend." He straightened his spine and faced her head on. Would she have something ugly to say about that?

She pulled her hand back and set it in her lap. "And who else are you friends with over there in Drimnagh?"

"No one."

"No one? Come on, no girls?" A playful twinkle showed in her eyes.

He gave her a slow shake of his head. "No, no girls, I..." He took a hard swallow, staring at his hands. What could he say to that?

"I can't believe you don't have any girlfriends, Shannon. A nice-looking, pleasant boy such as yourself, you should have lots of girlfriends." She winked at him and gave him a flirtatious smile.

He focused on her. Did she really think of him that way? He didn't think he could believe it. His chest squeezed and he gazed around the room. *Where's the damned waitress?* "Um, let's order something."

Leaning in close to him, she whispered, "Do I make you nervous, Shannon?"

He twisted his head toward her. She was close, too close. "N-no, not at all. I-I'm just hungry."

She placed her hand on his arm and caressed it. "I can make you feel good, Shannon, really good."

"W-what?" *Holy shite, what does she mean by that?* He yanked his arm away and flagged down a waitress.

A woman with long, chestnut hair in a green dress strode over to them and stood before their table. Her brown eyes studied them. "Can I get you something?"

Melissa shifted in her seat.

"Y-yes, I'll take a pint and some stew, please." He shifted his attention to Melissa.

"Oh, I'll have the same." She gave him a warm smile.

"Sure thing." The waitress trotted off.

"So where were we?" She leaned in close again.

He moved his hands to his lap and stared at them. "W-we were just, um—"

"Talking about what I could do for you." Her voice became softer, sensual.

"I-I don't need you to do anything for me." He trembled. *Where's the privy in this damned place? Maybe I can go hide in there until the food comes.*

"Why not? Don't you like me?" She covered his hand again, placing a smooth caress over his fingers, resting on his thigh.

What did Ma get me into? His heart thumped in his chest. Did she have any idea this girl was so forward? Maybe she did, maybe this is why his mother had chosen her. Sure, she seemed innocent enough at first, but now she'd become some sort of temptress. "I-I, sure I like you well enough." He struggled to keep his voice steady.

"We could go out the back, you and I." She ran her palm up

his thigh, brushed his groin and brought her hand back down.

A shiver ran up his spine. He closed his eyes, his heart pinching. She brought her lips so close to his ear, it tickled.

She whispered, "You see, I don't believe in waiting when you have an attraction to someone."

"A-an attraction?" His voice rose to an unnatural pitch.

"Aren't you attracted to me? Most men are." She traced circles on his thigh with her fingers.

The waitress walked to their table and set two pints and bowls of steaming stew in front of them. She hesitated, giving them the once over, and strode off again.

He let out a nervous chuckle. "Uh, l-let's just eat for now, I'm starving." He took a large gulp of his beer and started in on his stew.

She pulled her hand back and sat upright in her chair, then waited for a moment, picked up her spoon and dipped it into her stew.

He rushed a nervous glance to a clock on the wall over the bar as he blew on a spoonful of stew, perched in front of his mouth. They still had a good half hour before their fathers returned. How would he fend off her advances that long?

As he finished his meal, he set his spoon into his empty bowl with a clink, then grabbed hold of his pint and downed the remainder of it. As he set the glass back down, he glanced at her.

She searched his face. "So, you want to go out the back, or not?"

"Wh-what? No, I don't want to go out the back." His pulse quickened. Why was she so insistent on this?

She flinched and drew her gaze to her half-eaten stew. "Not many men would turn me down. But then you're not like most men, are you?" She locked her gaze on him.

His heart jumped. What did she mean by that? "I, uh, no

I'm not, I guess."

"I have to admit, I've heard some rumors about you." She smirked.

"What sort of rumors?" He watched her. Did he really want to know? He had to at least ask.

"Well, that you were, how shall I say it." She flashed her eyes at him. "Not all that interested in women."

He forced a chuckle, his hands starting to tremble. "Oh, that's ridiculous, what else would I be interested in?"

"Men."

He gasped and caught himself, then came forward, glaring at her. *My father be damned.* "What sort of a thing is that to say? I don't like people going around spreading bloody stupid gossip like that. Of course, I like women, just not women like you. I like nice women, women that wouldn't want to just take you into some bloody alley after you just met. You should be ashamed of yourself, really." He huffed, crossed his arms over his chest and came back in his chair, staring at the table.

"I'm not really like that, Shannon." Her voice changed again. Her soft, approachable manner returned. "I took a dare. My friends and I wanted to know if the rumors were true, so we came up with a plan to see if you'd go into the alley with me. I'd never have done anything. Just wanted to see if it was true, that's all."

He furrowed his brows, glaring at her once again. An ache spread into his heart. It was cruel, what she did to him. He'd let himself believe maybe she did like him, maybe someone besides Ciaran could actually find him interesting and attractive. But it was all a malicious joke. He rose up from the table, his chair groaning across the plank floor.

She focused on her stew.

Shannon trudged into the privy, then paced. He scanned over the white, tiled walls and dirtied fixtures. How could he have been so stupid? How was it the rumors of his town spread so far? Or maybe, he wondered, maybe his sister said something to her? She did know these people, after all. He steadied himself and did his business. After washing his hands, he exhaled a rush of air and entered into the tavern, then sat down next to her. "So, what does this mean exactly? What will you tell your friends?" Sarcasm and resentment laced his voice.

She searched his face, narrowing her eyes. "I have to admit, I do like you. But I'll have to tell them the truth. You wouldn't do anything with my advances. They can take that any way they want." She gave him a smug grin.

Heat swelled inside his chest. He clenched his teeth. How could she so callously play upon the situation? It greatly affected him, his life, and yet she acted as if it were all a game. He jumped up, seized her wrist, and jerked her up out of her chair.

"Wh-what are you doing?" She rounded her eyes, feebly attempting to resist.

He glared at her, flaring his nostrils. "What I'm doing is, I'm giving you what you bloody wanted. You think I don't like women, right? Well, I'm going to show you that's not the case." He hauled her through a side door, out of the tavern and into the alley. To his surprise, she seemed happy to go along with him.

He shoved her up against the outside wall of the building, hovering over her, glaring into her blue eyes. He propped his hands on her hips.

She seized him around the shoulders and tugged him downward.

Does she like being treated this way? He came down, giving her a harsh kiss.

She licked across his lips as if attempting to drive him further. As she drew him in closer, her breasts pressed firmly against his chest. She probed and prodded with her tongue for entrance. She clawed at him, thrusting her hips into his.

Oh God, I've become the prey and she's the aggressor. He surrendered for a moment, allowing her to kiss him, to violate him. Should he struggle against her advances? But would she then tell everyone he liked men? *And what of Ciaran?* It had already gone too far. He parted his lips, letting her tongue enter, then broke the kiss and stood, panting, in front of her. Heat rushed his cheeks. He forced himself to look at her.

She smiled at him with moist, reddened lips, her eyelids hooding. "Shannon, you are a good kisser, to be sure. But why don't I arouse you?" she said, smooth and seductive. She pressed her hips against him, proving her point.

His head swam. What could he say to that? He couldn't will himself into arousal, could he? He had to think quickly. "Maybe I just need a little more coaxing." He could think of Ciaran, just close his eyes, and pretend she was his Ciaran. Why didn't he think of it before?

She pulled his head down, pressing her soft lips against his. Her tongue entered again, penetrating him.

He closed his eyes, slipping into fantasy. He blocked out the soft body moving against his and replaced it with a hard muscular one. In his ears, he only heard Ciaran's sensual moans. On his lips, he only felt Ciaran's urgent kiss. He hardened and drove his erection into her. If feeling his arousal were the proof she required, he'd make sure she felt it.

She broke the kisses and gazed up at him. "Shannon, you surprised me. I was sure you only wanted men. Does this mean I'll see more of you?" She gave him a coy grin, then playfully touched the tip of his nose with her index finger, swaying their hips together.

Guilt crashed into him at full force. *I am Ciaran's and Ciaran is finally mine.* There was no way he'd see her again. "No, you won't." He pried himself loose from her grasp, turned away and raked a hand through his hair. He refused to see what new manipulations she'd use on him.

"Oh really, well then, tell me, Shannon, why did you use me this way?"

He wheeled around to face her. "I used you? You have got to be bloody joking. I don't believe for one minute you're really a nice girl. In fact, I don't know what story to believe, and I don't care." He stomped to the door of the tavern and yanked it open.

"Shannon Sullivan!"

He went inside and slammed the door shut behind him. He had to get away from her. The whole thing was crazy. He strode into the tavern, sighed, and his gaze caught on his father standing with Mr. O'Doyle at their table.

Mr. Sullivan's and Mr. O'Doyle's gazes searched the room.

The door slammed behind him.

She trotted up to walk beside him.

Shannon bowed his head. Whatever she had in mind now couldn't be good. He approached the table. His father's anxious stare ground into him.

"Melissa? You okay?" Mr. O'Doyle asked, wrapping an arm around his daughter.

His father spoke gruffly in his ear, "Shannon? What have you done?"

Shannon peered at his father. "I haven't done anything, Da." He darted his gaze to her. What was she going to do?

She dropped her head against her father's shoulder, wrinkling her forehead.

Heat flared in Shannon's chest. He had enough of her games. "Tell them, Melissa, tell them nothing happened. We just talked is all."

She flashed him a sly grin. "He's right, Da, nothing happened. He just said we should go out back to talk, well, but then he kissed me." She wrinkled her brow and locked her gaze on her father's, then bit her lip. "He wouldn't stop, I had to shove him off me. His hands were everywhere, and he even pressed up against me." She buried her face in her father's chest, her father tightening his hold.

"Shannon, you bloody apologize this instant." His father shoved him hard, positioning him right in front of Melissa and her father.

Shannon darted his gaze from her to her father. "I-I'm sorry. Really, I am." His voice shook, despite his attempts at keeping it level.

"Mr. Sullivan, I don't think I'll be letting my Melissa see your son again," Mr. O'Doyle said.

"But, Da," she whined.

Mr. O'Doyle snapped his brows together, hanging his mouth open, focusing on her. "No, that's final." He shifted his attention to Mr. Sullivan. "Please excuse us. It's been a pleasure doing business with you anyway." He hustled his daughter off and out of the front door.

Shannon snickered. Seemed her plan backfired on her. He was free of her for good. His father's sudden tight clutch sent shooting pain through his arm. He flinched.

His father hauled him out of the door of the tavern. When they reached the lorry, he opened the passenger door and tossed Shannon inside.

With a loud crack, his head hit the top of the doorjamb as his body flung onto the seat, landing on all fours. Pain jolted through the top of his skull. He cried out, then struggled to right himself, rubbing his palm over the top of his head.

His father entered the driver's seat. The engine roared to life and the lorry jerked backward. He missed the gear, making the transmission groan. "Shite!" He shoved it forward, catching the correct position with the shifter.

Shannon cowered in his seat. What was his father going to do to him?

As the lorry sped down the road, they sat in complete silence for a few moments, then his father smacked him on the side of his head.

Shannon's head jerked sideways and burning lit up his ear. "Ah! Da, what was that for?" He rubbed the side of his head.

"That was for doing exactly what I told you not to. What's the matter with you? You don't pay any attention at all to women, then you get one alone and you practically rape her? Honestly, have you no bloody morals at all?" His father's voice was livid, bouncing in the small cab of the lorry. He glared at the road stretched out in front of them as if he were too angry to look at his son.

"No, Da, I didn't. She was lying," Shannon said in a whine. Tears stung the corners of his eyes. If he let them fall it would only make things worse.

"Oh, so you didn't kiss her? You had the girl out in the alley, and you just talked to her?" Sarcasm laced his father's voice.

"N-no?" Shannon watched his father step hard on the brakes, making the lorry lurch. He thrust his arms straight out in front of him, bracing himself, barely missing being thrown into the dashboard. He trembled. *Da might just kill me.*

The lorry tires screeched and slid on the pavement and the lorry came to an abrupt stop. His father turned in his seat to face him. His gaze blazed as it roamed over Shannon. "You going to start crying now? You're a bloody baby—you know that? Who the hell are you anyway? You can't possibly be my son. No son of mine would have allowed a bloody teacher to fondle him the way you did."

"Da!" The tears spilled over. He gritted his teeth. Cowering, he covered his face with his hands and rocked, soothing himself. For a few minutes, only his soft weeping filled the cab.

His father never talked about the molestation. It felt as if the scathing words had hacked his heart into tiny pieces.

His father twisted forward and slapped his hands to the steering wheel.

Startling, Shannon peeked at his father through dark locks.

His father growled. "I'm sorry, Shannon. I never should have said something like that to you. It's just bloody frustrating to know what that man did to you." He held up his hands in fists. "I could have killed him myself." He dropped his hands to his lap. "Your ma, she won't let anyone bloody talk about it. She thinks then we'll all forget. But I see how people treat you. I know what they think." He turned to his son, his leg resting on the seat between them. "Truth be told? I was bloody proud you took that girl in the alley and did whatever you did. Sure, it wasn't right, but at least it means you're not queer, for Christ sake." He gave his son a thin-lipped grin.

Shannon stopped the tears and sniffled. "Y-you were p-proud of me?" He couldn't believe it. He never thought he'd hear those words spoken out of his father's mouth. His eyes filled with tears again. *He's proud of me...*

"Well, yeah. Like I said, it wasn't right though." His father patted him on the thigh.

Is this real? Shannon widened his eyes and took in his father fully. A warm feeling enveloped him. He felt closer to his father right now than he had in years. And all it took was a stolen kiss with the wrong girl in an alley. He huffed a soft laugh. How could something so wrong turn out so well? Not only did he have an excuse for never seeing her again, his father was actually proud of him. He wiped his eyes and sat back in his seat, gazing with wonder at his father.

His father put the lorry back into gear. This time, the lorry started smoothly toward home.

• • •

Shannon watched his father maneuver the lorry as they pulled up in their dirt drive. Clouds of dust billowed behind them and spindly shadows from swaying trees played against the sides of the house.

Shannon gazed out of the window toward the path between his house and Ciaran's. Was it afternoon already? It must be, seemed like he'd been gone forever. *Ciaran.* Where was he? Did he go fishing today after all? As soon as the lorry slowed to a stop, he shoved the door open and ran out.

"Where you going?" His father called out.

Shannon waved, keeping his focus on the path. He had to see Ciaran, had to feel him in his arms after being forced to be with that woman. He moved fast over the rocks and grit on the familiar path between their homes. The melodies of terns poured out of the surrounding trees. He barely registered them. *Ciaran.* He wanted him so badly he could almost smell his sweet scent.

He slowed his pace as he neared Ciaran's disheveled barn. He studied every inch of the area, hoping to catch a glimpse of him. After not seeing him anywhere, he strode to the front door of Ciaran's house and gave it an impatient knock. A minute passed and the door creaked as it opened.

Mr. O'Kelly stood, wavering before him.

The smell of liquor on his breath almost bowled Shannon over. "Mr. O'Kelly, is Ciaran around?" He panted and searched around him.

Mr. O'Kelly flinched as if the sun were too bright, even in the shadows of the afternoon. "Shannon? Why yes, he's in the barn." He pointed an unsteady finger to the ramshackle building across the dirt clearing from them.

He whirled around, hurrying to the barn. His vision flooded with Ciaran's silhouette at a rugged and worn workbench near the far end of the barn.

CHAPTER
FIFTEEN
CIARAN

Earlier that morning, Ciaran whistled and strode up the path connecting his house to Shannon's. A fishing pole dangled over one shoulder and a wicker basket swung in his hand. It would have been nice to get his father away from the pub, but he looked forward to spending some time alone with Shannon. He spread a mischievous grin over his lips. Hopefully they'd do a lot more than fish.

He looked up the dusty path to see the outline of Shannon's house. He roamed his gaze over cracks in the plaster. It even appeared as if it might fall away in some spots. How did Mr. Sullivan miss it? The man was too meticulous to allow their house to fall into any type of disarray. The thatched roof always looked perfect. The wood on the front porch was always oiled. Neat and tidy, that was how Shannon's parents kept things.

His own house, on the other hand, was anything but neat and tidy. Even when his mother was alive, it always needed a little dusting or sweeping. He smiled. *My ma was more of a free spirit, too spontaneous for the drudgery of organized housework.*

He bound up the stoop and used the black iron knocker on the door to announce his presence. After a few raps, he waited.

The door opened and Mrs. Sullivan stood before him.

He looked her over, knitting his brows. Where was Shannon? Shannon always answered the door when he came over. "Uh, good morning, Mrs. Sullivan. Is Shannon home?"

She planted her hands on her hips and eyed him. "Morning, Ciaran. No, he's not. He won't be fishing with you today. He went with his father to Johnstown Bridge." There was an overly cheery tone in her voice.

Pain filled his chest. Wasn't that where the girl his mother set him up with lived? He glanced at his feet, shifting. *Should I ask if Shannon was indeed calling on a girl?* Would that look suspicious? His gaze met with hers. "So ah, what is he doing there?" He did his best to keep his voice light.

She smiled as if satisfied. "He's calling on a girl, of course."

He reeled inside. *That bastard did it.* He didn't even have the decency to come tell him. "Thank you," Ciaran fought to keep his voice steady. He turned, the click of the door shutting behind him filling the silence, and started back toward his house. He hung his head and took deep breaths. Why did it feel like he was drowning? *Is this what jealously feels like? Or just pure betrayal?*

He wandered along the path, kicking at rocks, in the direction of the river. Where was Shannon right now? What was he doing with that girl? Pain spread inside him and focused to a pinprick inside his heart. A vision flooded his mind of Shannon sitting on a couch next to a beautiful woman, gazing into her eyes. Shannon taking her hand in his. Shannon leaning over and kissing her, giving her the same hard and penetrating kisses he relished and craved.

He shook his head. The rock he kicked became blurry. He swiped at his eyes. *It really hurt, too much.*

LATER IN THE DAY, Ciaran dragged a knife through the center of a fish, cleaning it, then glanced at the metal bucket sitting beside him on the bench.

"Ciaran!"

Shannon? Ciaran turned to face him, frowning. Heat flooded his chest and his heart squeezed. Shannon had left him to call on a girl. He pushed a lock of hair out of his eyes with the back of his wrist, a heavily serrated, curved knife dangling from his hand. He watched Shannon run to him.

"Ciaran, I—" Shannon stopped, looking Ciaran up and down.

Ciaran flared his nostrils. *It wasn't right to leave me like that. We'd had plans today. And now he thinks he can just walk in here like nothing happened?* Pain pierced his chest. He wrinkled his forehead.

"What's wrong?"

"What's wrong? You know bloody well what's wrong. We were supposed to go fishing today. But instead, you decided to go and call on that...that girl! Your ma told me all about it when I went to collect you." Ciaran stabbed toward him with the knife. "You know I didn't want you to call on her. You knew how I felt about it. I bet you thought I'd just get over it and you'd be able to just come prancing in here like nothing bloody happened. Just like you are now, didn't you?" he said. "Let me tell you, Shannon, that was bloody mean and dirty. I don't know how I'll ever forgive you." He twisted around and dropped the knife on the half-cleaned fish. He spread his hands on the bench, hanging his head. The anger in his chest built.

Shannon stepped toward him and placed a gentle hand on his shoulder. "Ciaran, I-I'm sor—"

Growling, Ciaran spun around, and shoved him backward.

Shannon staggered, almost falling on his backside before catching himself.

"No, Shannon, you can't just apologize this time and make it all right." Ciaran glared at him. He wouldn't let him off this easy. They had something between them now.

Shannon's eyes glistened. "Ciaran, I-I couldn't come tell you. My ma and da, they made me leave early this morning. I thought my ma would come directly here to tell you. I wasn't trying to hide anything." He held out his open palms in front of him. "I didn't want to go, you know that."

Ciaran hung and twisted his head away from him. Could he believe him? But this was Shannon he was thinking this way about. He'd never done something like this before. He wrinkled his nose. Would Shannon give up what they'd started for a chance to be with a girl? *I don't know...*

Stepping toward Ciaran, Shannon timidly reached for his hand, attempting to entwine their fingers.

Ciaran tore his hand away and stomped into the center of the barn, putting distance between them. *It still hurts.* He crossed his arms over his chest, turning his back toward him. With a low, soft voice, he said, "What did you do with her then?"

"N-nothing, I swear it. We, we just talked and ate some lunch, that's all." Shannon said, his voice wavering.

Only the soft clucking and scratching of chickens filled the space between them for a few minutes.

"Well, at least you didn't kiss her or something." Ciaran scoffed. *As if Shannon would kiss a woman.*

Shannon choked out a loud gasp.

Wheeling around, Ciaran narrowed his eyes. "You didn't, did you?"

Shannon's throat dipped with a slow swallow and he rubbed his palms on his dark trousers. "N-no, of course not.

Don't be ridiculous. Why would I do something like that?" His words were fast. He offered a thin-lipped grin, then let out an anxious chuckle.

Ciaran stalked toward him, inspecting him. *Something's not right. I know it. I feel it.* "Why are you so nervous? I know you, Shannon Sullivan, something happened, didn't it?" He walked a measured, deliberate circle around him.

"S-stop this, Ciaran, I don't even like girls, you know that." Shannon turned to face him. "It's just that I had to spend a lot of time alone with my da. It wasn't very pleasant, is all." He stepped to him and grabbed Ciaran's hands, then widened his eyes as if surprised that Ciaran allowed it. In a shaky voice, he said, "Please, hold me, Ciaran."

Ciaran yanked his hands free, then flung his arms around Shannon's shoulders in a firm embrace. He buried his face into Shannon's shoulder, his heart swelling with emotion. "Don't ever do that again. It bloody hurt to think about you being with someone else, even if it was arranged by your ma…even if it was with a girl."

"I'm sorry, Ciaran, I promise it won't happen again. Next time, I'll tell my ma to go to hell." Shannon tightened his hold on him.

Ciaran smiled, releasing a soft chuckle. "Jaysus, Shannon, you don't have to go that far." He lifted his head and looked directly into his eyes.

Shannon smiled back at him. "I don't, aye? Well, what if she finds some other bloody girl to set me up with then?"

"I'll just have to kidnap you or something." Ciaran came in and placed a lingering kiss on his lips, his shaft swelling. They were all alone. He could have him again. He pressed his erection into Shannon's hip. Now he'd know what he was thinking.

Shannon moaned against Ciaran's mouth. "How about you kidnap me right now?"

"Gladly." Ciaran started a soft assault on his neck. He pushed Shannon backward, toward the wall of the barn.

Shannon's back hit the hard plastered surface of the wall and he lifted his hands, entwined with Ciaran's, over his head. He rolled his hardening cock into Ciaran, then trailed soft bites on Ciaran's neck.

Ciaran's body shuddered. Being with Shannon again like this felt so good.

Shannon startled, then shoved him away.

"What are you doing?" Ciaran stumbled backward, then wrinkled his brows.

"Your da is just in the house, we can't do this here," he whispered as if Ciaran's father could hear them.

"Oh, come on, he's probably passed out by now." He turned his lips down. "He's been drinking again, you know." There seemed to be nothing he could do to keep his father sober. Not even fishing would keep him from the pub.

Shannon drew him close again, leaning on the wall.

Ciaran fell against his chest, wrapping his arms around Shannon's waist, relishing in the feel of Shannon's hold.

"Yeah, I know. I knocked on the door and spoke to him before I came in to see you." Shannon stroked the back of Ciaran's hair.

"He was bad, wasn't he?" Ciaran's words were almost lost in the cloth of Shannon's shirt.

"Hush now, I'm sure he'll be all right. Just give him some time." Shannon tightened his hold and placed a gentle kiss on the top of his head.

Ciaran reluctantly pulled away, but kept his hands on Shannon's hips. With a long sigh, he gazed into Shannon's stunning face. "I'm going to go and check on him, I'll be right back." He turned and left for the house.

A SUMMER WITHOUT RAIN

Ciaran slowly opened the front door and peered into the main room of the house. "Da? You okay?" He scanned the contents of the room as he entered, leaving the door open behind him.

The low rumble of snoring came from the direction of the hearth. He tiptoed toward the sound and stood in front of his father slumped over in a plush chair in front of the fireplace. *He's passed out all right.* It pained him to see his father suffering, so alone. He must help him somehow, but how? A huge divide had come between them. His only solace now was Shannon.

Shannon. He spread a grin across his lips and took careful steps through the room to the hallway and into his bedroom. He pulled the nightstand drawer open and grabbed the mineral oil bottle. This would surprise Shannon. His cock hardened again. How good it felt to be inside him or filled by him. He closed his eyes for a moment, palming his erection through his trousers, sending a shiver through his body. He had to have him, right now...all of him.

CHAPTER SIXTEEN
SHANNON

Shannon stood in the barn, waiting. He tipped his head back, gazing at the cobwebbed rafters in the roof. He chuckled. Should he pinch himself? He didn't think he'd ever get used to knowing Ciaran was really his. And now he was actually waiting for Ciaran to return so they could make love? It was all too much. He huffed a laugh. The sound of it echoed in the barn.

"What's so damn funny?" Ciaran stepped through the doorway with a grin on his face. He stalked playfully toward him.

Heat flushed Shannon's cheeks and he straightened. "Oh, I don't know. Maybe you're driving me mad." He ambled toward Ciaran, his gaze catching on the bulge in his front pocket. He pointed to it. "What's that? It's a little bloody short to be your, ah—"

"No, it's not, it's a surprise." Ciaran widened his grin into a full smile as he stopped in front of him.

What could it be? Shannon cocked his head and attempted to shove his hand into Ciaran's pocket.

Ciaran jumped away. "Oh my gosh, you are a nosy one."

"What is it? Tell me." Shannon bit his lip inside a grin.

Ciaran walked to him and hooked an arm around his waist, pulling him close. He planted an urgent kiss on his lips. "I'll show you when the time is right."

Shannon pushed his hips against him, feeling the hard, cylindrical object. *It's the oil.* "You are wicked—"

Moaning, Ciaran dropped hard kisses over Shannon's mouth. He groped at Shannon's shirt, backing him up to the wall again, kissing and sucking the soft skin on his neck along the way.

As Shannon stepped backward, he exposed his neck in eager surrender to Ciaran's advances. Wet heat slid over his neck, sending waves of desire all the way through to his groin. "Wh-what about your da?" he asked through ragged breathing. He'd almost forgotten.

Ciaran whispered against the skin of his neck, "He's passed out like I said he would be."

Shannon freed a low groan.

Skimming his hand down between Shannon's legs, Ciaran cupped his erection and stroked sensually and slowly over his trousers.

"But what if he wakes and comes out here?" Sensation coiled inside Shannon's gut.

"He won't wake for a bloody long time, trust me. Stop asking so many questions." Ciaran stroked quicker over Shannon's firm cock, obviously not dissuaded. He ground his hips against Shannon, pressing him hard into the wall.

Overcome with need, Shannon submitted to the pleasure pulsing through his body. He snuck a hand into Ciaran's trousers, bypassing his belt and anything else in the way. He craved the feel of him in his palm. He stroked his erection, pressing his fingers into just the right spots to get what he wanted.

As expected, Ciaran bucked and moaned with desire. He twisted his hips, with Shannon's hand still trapped in his trousers, and unbuckled Shannon's belt. He worked with quick fingers, to unfasten Shannon's trousers, then lifted Shannon's hand out of his own. He left his neck, only for a moment, to tug Shannon's trousers down to just above his ankles, then unbuttoned his undergarment and exposed his erection. He plunged to his knees, placing his mouth and fist over Shannon's upright cock, stroking, sucking, and lapping at it.

Shannon arched his back, his head still snug against the wall, and savored the delicious sensation. He searched for something to hang on to, groping at the plaster behind him, then he gave up and clutched at Ciaran's hair.

Ciaran worked him with his palm, lips, and tongue without mercy.

Waves of pleasure rocked through Shannon, one after another. His sensitivity rose quickly. Release built to a raw edge. "C-Ciaran, I-I'm close." He clenched his teeth, writhing, trying to keep his climax from reaching the surface. Ciaran had brought the oil, and he would use it, damn it.

Ciaran pulled off him, peeked up at him and gave him a devious grin. "Like that?"

Nodding, Shannon was unable to use his voice.

Ciaran rose up and locked his gaze onto Shannon's. His eyes hooded and his pupils widened. He gently brushed Shannon's cheek with his fingers. In a low, seductive voice, breathing heavily, he said, "I love seeing you this way, all worked up and wanting me." With one arm around Shannon's waist, he reached his hand down and pumped hard on Shannon's still slick cock.

With a few strokes, Shannon grew sensitive again. Gasping, he struggled against letting go.

Ciaran stopped his hand.

Shannon furrowed his brows. *We have better things to do.* "I-I thought you wanted to use the oil?"

"Yes, but I thought I'd give you a little of your own medicine first. Remember what you did to me in that bloody hotel room?"

He spread a faint grin over his mouth, then bit his lower lip.

"You tease." Ciaran jerked his hand over Shannon's erection.

A jolt of pleasure seared through Shannon's body. He closed his eyes and let a loud moan tear out of his throat, filling the barn. He fisted Ciaran's shirt, holding on for dear life. Just as his release neared the edge, Ciaran stopped. He opened his eyes.

Ciaran watched him as if mesmerized.

Crushing Ciaran's lips with his own, Shannon tangled his tongue with Ciaran's. He couldn't take any more.

Ciaran freed a deep moan into his mouth.

Probing, Shannon slid his tongue deeper, penetrating Ciaran's mouth.

Ciaran dragged away, reached into his pocket and took out the mineral oil bottle. He opened it, poured some into his palm and gazed at him with another lust-filled grin.

What would Ciaran do now? His body hummed with desire, having been brought to the brink so many times. Why wasn't Ciaran lowering his own trousers? He let a lazy smile grace his lips. Maybe he'd have to take things into his own hands.

Ciaran capped the oil and tucked it into his pocket.

Fixating on Shannon, he stepped to him and placed his slick palm over Shannon's shaft.

As Ciaran's delicious palm rubbed the front of Shannon's erection and made quick circles over the tip, he gritted his teeth. A sweet pulse rippled through his body, and he shuddered. He didn't want to climax yet, but Ciaran made it almost impossible. He arched his head back and tried to pull his hips away. "Ciaran, s-stop, I-I can't take it," he said, through ragged breathing.

Ciaran stopped.

Shannon stole a peek at him.

Stroking himself, Ciaran rubbed his other hand up and down in his own trousers.

Shannon let a wicked grin spread over his lips. So, Ciaran really enjoyed watching him teeter on the edge.

Ciaran leaned in for a deep kiss. "Seems I'm a quick learner, aye, Shannon?" Ciaran unbuttoned his shirt and underwear, unfastened his trousers, and brought everything down and off in one quick motion. He gazed at Shannon and drew close for another deep, lingering kiss.

Shannon whispered, "Take me now, Ciaran, I beg you."

Biting his lower lip, Ciaran motioned to the floor.

Shannon nodded, removed his clothing, then got down on all fours. He felt wholly exposed like this, but it would be worth it. He took a brief scan of the room. Thankfully, the chickens were gone. While he waited, fumbling sounded behind him. Something soft, yet hard, nudged solidly against his entrance. A rush of desire coursed through him, and he pushed into it. He wanted to be filled, now. "Come on, Ciaran, no more teasing." He looked behind him

Ciaran was on his knees, directly behind him, eyes shut, stroking himself with oil.

Shoving backward, Shannon drove Ciaran partially into

him, clenching his teeth as the burn turned into an exquisite pressure.

Ciaran freed a sharp moan, then leaned over him and wrapped his arms around Shannon's waist. He drove himself into Shannon, in and out, slowly and maddening.

Shannon made a small adjustment to his hips and Ciaran's hard cock hit the bundle of nerves inside him, making him cry out. He hung his head between straight arms, unable to take the weight of it any longer. Ciaran drove harder, faster with his hips, urging his climax back to the surface. He was so close, if anything so much as brushed against his shaft, he'd erupt. He waited in delectable agony for Ciaran to catch up.

Ciaran began to shake with the promise of release. He rested his chest on Shannon's back and reached around him, grasping Shannon's erection with his still oiled hand, and pumped.

Arching his head up, Shannon let out a loud, low moan. The sweet tingling of climax came on hard and relentless. Intense contractions pulsed through his body, spurting his seed out over Ciaran's fingers onto the ground below him.

Ciaran gave one hard, deep thrust, then groaned. His body became rigid. His release spilled into Shannon's passage, his thrusts slowing. The heaving of his chest pressed against Shannon's back.

"Damn, you are a wicked one, aren't you?" Shannon relaxed, spent.

Ciaran panted. "Only for you, Shannon Sullivan, only for you." He pulled out of him, lifted up and stood carefully. As he began to dress, he took a quick glance at Shannon, still exposed on his hands and knees. "Hold on." He rushed to the workbench, grabbed an old rag, came back to Shannon, and cleaned him.

"Uh, thanks, it was a bit messy, wasn't it?" Shannon

released a soft chuckle. He must look ridiculous, bent over naked with his soiled arse sticking out. When Ciaran finished, he stood and dressed. He glanced at Ciaran, standing back at the workbench with his knife. "So, you went fishing after all?"

"Yeah, it at least took my mind off what you were doing." Ciaran pressed his lips together.

Shannon walked up behind him and wrapped his arms around Ciaran from behind. He placed a tender kiss on Ciaran's neck. "I'm sorry."

Ciaran twisted his head toward Shannon. "It's okay. Let's just forget about it," he said. "So, help me out here, we're having fish for dinner."

Smiling, Shannon came around to Ciaran's side at the bench. He peeked over the top of the silver bucket. At least five more fish were suspended in the murky water. He lifted his brows. "Jaysus, you did pretty bloody well today."

"Yeah, you missed out, for sure." Ciaran sliced the fish he worked on into filets.

Shannon reached in the bucket and lifted out another fish. His hand stopped midair. He looked at Ciaran. "What did you do with the oil?" he said, in a mocking tone.

Ciaran spread a quick smile over his lips. He gazed into Shannon's face and tapped his front pocket with his elbow. "Don't you worry now, got it right here."

CIARAN FRIED the fish at the hearth while Shannon sat at the dining table. Potatoes boiled in a large, white pot next to where Ciaran flipped the fish over in a cast iron skillet.

Shannon took a deep sniff of the air. The aroma was lovely. He glanced at Mr. O'Kelly, just rousing from his slumber in his chair by the hearth. He stood and walked over to him. "Mr.

O'Kelly, can I get you something?" He stopped in front of the still groggy man.

Mr. O'Kelly blinked a few times before directing his gaze at Shannon. "Why, yes, some tea would be wonderful. Is that fish I smell cooking?" He straightened in his seat and fussed with the collar of his shirt.

"It is. Seems Ciaran did quite well today at the river." Shannon did his best to make light conversation. Hopefully, it would lessen Ciaran's revulsion with his father's condition.

"Yes, well, seems Ciaran's become quite a cook, too." Mr. O'Kelly wiped his palms over his face.

Shannon walked into the kitchen and filled the teakettle with water from a pitcher, then strolled to Ciaran and handed it to him so he could heat it. He remained next to Ciaran.

Ciaran flashed a worried glance to him and leaned toward him. "See, he's sloshed, isn't he?" he whispered.

"Hush, Ciaran, he'll be all right. Let's just get some tea and food in him and get him to bed." Shannon let himself lean harder into Ciaran for a moment, relishing in the brief contact. He longed to kiss him, if only Mr. O'Kelly hadn't been in the room. With a sigh, he stepped to Mr. O'Kelly and held out his hand. "Can I help you to the table?"

"Oh, I think I can manage, thank you." Mr. O'Kelly grunted as he hauled his body up out of the chair, then ambled toward the table with an unsteady gait.

Shannon followed with his arms held out in front of him, preparing in case Ciaran's father took a tumble. He stopped and waited, watching the older man maneuver himself into a chair and rest his forearms on the table.

The shrill whistle of the kettle blew, and he went to retrieve it.

Mr. O'Kelly winced at the sudden noise.

Shannon made them all tea and set the filled cups on the

table. Afterward, he helped Ciaran with the fish and potatoes. He brought the plates, brimming with fried fish and buttered potatoes, to the table while Ciaran brought the silverware. He sat down between Ciaran and his father.

Ciaran gazed at the empty chair across from him, knitting his brows.

Shannon frowned. *Ciaran's thinking about his mother again. Will he be all right?* For a moment, they all ate in silence. He startled. *Da bought a bloody lorry!* "Oh my gosh, Ciaran, I forgot to tell you."

Mr. O'Kelly jumped and focused on him with difficulty.

Ciaran widened his eyes, hanging his mouth open. "What, for God's sake?"

"My da bought a bloody lorry. Can you believe it?" Shannon's gaze darted from Ciaran to Mr. O'Kelly, and back to Ciaran.

Ciaran blinked hard and shifted forward in his seat, resting his full fork on his plate. "You mean a motor car, with a bloody engine and everything?"

Shannon spread a proud grin over his face. "Yes, Ciaran, it has an engine, obviously."

"Oh, shut up, you bloody well know what I meant." Ciaran lifted his fork to his mouth and sat back.

"Well, your da must have had quite a good crop this year," Mr. O'Kelly said.

"Um, suppose so." He slowed his chewing. Jaysus, he'd distanced himself so far from his family, he had no idea how well the crop did last year.

Ciaran came forward in his seat. "Let's go and see it, right after supper, okay?"

Shannon smiled. "Yeah? Let's." He dug back into his food. He'd like to see his father, too, now that their relationship had taken a step toward healing.

"Da, would you like to go with us?" Ciaran asked.

Mr. O'Kelly shook his head. "No, I think I'd rather just spend a quiet evening at home, if you don't mind. I'm not much up for such things these days. I'm sure I'll see it soon though." He pushed the last bit of potato onto his fork from his almost empty plate.

Ciaran frowned, then slid a bit of fish into his mouth.

After eating, Shannon helped Ciaran clear the table and clean the dishes. While they cleaned at a bowl, Ciaran bumped him from the side.

Smiling, Shannon peeked at Ciaran. "What are you up to?"

Ciaran kept his gaze on the plates in the bowl in front of him. He let a smirk play on his lips. "Nothing."

Shannon bumped Ciaran back. He leaned in close to Ciaran's ear and whispered, "You thinking nasty thoughts again, Ciaran O'Kelly?"

Ciaran glanced up at him. "Maybe."

"I thought you wanted to see the lorry?"

"I do, but it's still early."

"Oh, you nasty little bugger."

CHAPTER
SEVENTEEN
CIARAN

Ciaran walked hand-in-hand with Shannon down the path connecting their houses. It'd been a long time since they'd come this way together. It seemed they'd always spent their time at his own home. He took in the darkness just starting to creep its way into their forest. The trees always had an ominous way about them this time of day. Subconsciously, he squeezed Shannon's hand tighter. A vision of all those dark fingerlike tree branches reaching out for him, like in some fairy tale, flooded his mind. *Don't be so silly, Ciaran, you're an adult now.*

As they neared Shannon's house, Shannon pulled his hand away from Ciaran's and quickened his pace. He scanned the surrounding open area between the house and barn. "I wonder where they've hidden it?"

"Maybe it's in the barn?" Ciaran searched for the lorry, but didn't see it.

"No, there's no room. Let's just go ask." Shannon turned and strode in the direction of his front door.

Ciaran followed.

Once on the front porch, Shannon turned the knob and opened the door. He looked toward his mother from the doorway, knitting his brows.

Ciaran stepped up beside him.

Mrs. Sullivan sat on a dark, paisley sofa with a book. A delicate cup and saucer sat in front of her on a walnut coffee table. "Oh, Shannon, dear. You decided to come home for once? And you brought Ciaran with you, I see." She nodded to Ciaran.

Ciaran brushed by him, entering the house. "Hello, Mrs. Sullivan." He smiled at her. It'd been a while since he'd seen her though she pretty much looked the same.

"Ma, where is Da and the lorry?" Shannon frowned and scanned the room.

"Not here to see me?" Chuckling, she shifted in her seat. "Your da had some business to take care of in town. I suspect he won't be home till late. You're welcome to stay with me awhile though."

"No, I think we'll just head back to Ciaran's place." Shannon pursed his lips and headed for the door.

Ciaran studied Shannon. What on Earth was wrong with him? Why did he look so anxious all of a sudden? "What do you mean? Why not wait? We haven't seen your lovely mother in a long while, have we?"

"Oh, thank you, dear, you're always such a sweet boy." She beamed at Ciaran.

Shannon huffed and grabbed Ciaran by the elbow, then lugged him through the still-open doorway.

"Hey, Shannon, what the..." Ciaran stared at him and walked out with Shannon.

"Shannon, that is no way to treat your friend," she shouted from inside.

Once out in the open and off the front porch, Ciaran jerked his arm out of his grasp. "What the bloody hell are you doing?"

Shannon leaned close to Ciaran's face, locking his gaze onto Ciaran's. In an angry whisper, he said, "I think she already suspects, and I can't have you doing something stupid with her around."

What? Heat flooded Ciaran's chest. He placed his hands on his hips, taking a step back from him. "Shannon. Number one, how the hell would she bloody know anything? And number two, I'm not so sure I like you accusing me of doing stupid things." He glared, standing his ground.

Shannon put an index finger to his lips and glared equally hard at Ciaran. "Shush. Just believe what I'm telling you for once."

"What's the matter? Having a tiff, are we?" She leaned on the doorjamb, smirking.

Shannon focused on his mother and straightened his shoulders.

Ciaran whirled around. He'd show Shannon he was wrong. He opened his mouth to speak. A hard jab poked his back, thrusting him forward a step. He twisted his head and threw Shannon a quick, furious glare.

Shannon widened his eyes and lifted his brows at Ciaran while nodding once.

He's really serious about this. Ciaran sighed and relaxed his shoulders, then twisted to face her.

"No, Ma, just trying to make a decision, that's all. And we've decided to head back to Ciaran's house. Right, Ciaran?" Shannon poked Ciaran's back again, not so hard this time.

Ciaran nodded his head. He'd go along with it, for now. "Guess I'll visit you another day, Mrs. Sullivan." He gave her his best smile.

She hesitated, nodded, and strolled in the house.

Shannon watched the door click shut. "Let's go." He turned in the dirt and headed for the path.

Ciaran glanced at the house and chased after him. "Hey, hang on." He jogged to meet up with Shannon's steady pace. "What was that all about? Why did you say you think she suspects?" He needed to know the full story. With quickening breath, he fought to keep up with Shannon's long-legged strides.

"Because, why else would she all of a sudden start setting me up with women? Plus, she's sort of said some things that made me wonder." Shannon slowed his pace a little and relaxed his shoulders.

"Okay, so what did she say?" Ciaran grabbed his hand.

Shannon stopped and faced him. "She said I needed to pretend to be interested in women, that I was too interested in you. And that I shouldn't spend so much time with you, I should start spending time with women." He creased his brows, searching Ciaran's face.

Ciaran winced, his heart pinching, and he shifted his gaze to their hands, entwined between them. "Oh."

"Look, I'm sorry. Maybe I shouldn't have said anything." Shannon wrapped his arms around Ciaran's shoulders, drawing him close.

Sighing, Ciaran returned the embrace. He'd always thought well of Shannon's parents. The fact that they might be trying to take Shannon from him was a little hard to hear.

Shannon kissed the side of his head.

"It's okay, I guess it does appear sort of bad, the fact that you've never dated anyone and we're always together. Let's just go back to my house." Ciaran dragged himself away and grabbed his hand again. They'd both just have to find a way around it.

Shannon fixated on Ciaran while they strolled back to the O'Kelly household.

Ciaran hung his head and drooped his shoulders while

they walked. How many more times would he have to put up with Shannon calling on a girl to keep people from being suspicious? How were they both supposed to pretend nothing had changed between them to their families and friends? Just as they approached his front door, he stopped and turned to Shannon. He gazed deeply into Shannon's eyes, then leaned in for a lingering kiss. He wouldn't let anything come between them.

Shannon balked at first, but surrendered to the deep kiss and returned it.

Ciaran broke the kiss, opened the door, and peered into the main room of his house. "Da? You still up?"

His father leaned out from behind the chair he sat in by the hearth. "Yes, but not for long. Come on in, boys, and tell me about this lorry."

Ciaran noticed the short glass his father held in his hand and cringed. Caramel-colored liquid splashed as it moved. Anger swarmed inside him. He stomped toward his father. "Da, why are you getting bloody pissed again?" He flared his nostrils.

Shannon followed him into the room and stopped a ways back.

His father startled and gazed up at his son, raising his brows. "Whatever do you mean? It's just a little something to help me sleep."

"No, it's not, Da. This has got to bloody stop. You're drinking far too much." Ciaran furrowed his brows and clenched his teeth. It wasn't fair. It was like he'd lost both his mother *and* his father.

Shannon shuffled his feet, chewing his lower lip. "Uh, Ciaran, I'll just wait outside, okay?" He turned to leave.

"No, Shannon, you stay. Tell him, please, tell him he's

drinking too much." He huffed. Maybe Shannon could talk some sense into him.

His father focused his attention on Shannon.

Shannon's face reddened. "Uh..." He glanced at Mr. O'Kelly, then at Ciaran and stared at the floor.

Ciaran stabbed a finger at his father. "Tell him, Shannon."

Bowing his head, Shannon took slow steps toward Ciaran's father. He neared them both and stopped, his gaze darting between them. "Mr. O'Kelly? Firstly, I guess I want you to know that I think very highly of you." He paused as if gauging the reaction to his words.

His father shifted uneasily in his seat, but kept his focus on Shannon.

Ciaran waved his hands, goading Shannon on. He needed Shannon to do this for him. He needed his help here.

"Um, but, I do think maybe you're taking in a bit too much of the drink. I, um, understand, you know, how the situation must be so painful for you and all." Shannon gave him a sheepish grin.

He's not going to do it. An angry fire burned in Ciaran's gut. Without thinking, he shoved Shannon, propelling him backward.

Shannon stumbled and almost fell, then caught his footing and hung his mouth open, staring at Ciaran.

Panting, Ciaran faced Shannon, glaring back at him. He needed the tough Shannon right now, the one he'd seen so many times in town. "No, you tell him the truth. You tell him how he has to stop all this. Now." His voice broke.

Shannon tensed his brows, then moved his mouth as if forming words.

Mr. O'Kelly lunged at his son and threw his arms tight around Ciaran's torso from behind.

"No, Da! Stop it, stop it I say!" Ciaran flailed in his father's arms.

"Hush now, Ciaran. It's not your friend's fault. Stop all this and settle yourself," Mr. O'Kelly said.

"No, let go, let go..." *I have to get through to him.* Ciaran fought to free himself.

Mr. O'Kelly held his son tight.

Gradually, Ciaran calmed. As he lowered his head, he hung his arms limply at his sides. His eyes stung with the threat of tears. It was no use. His father had always been a strong man. Apparently, the drinking hadn't changed that.

Ciaran's father released him.

Shannon covered his mouth with his hand and fixated on them.

"Sit down here, both of you." Mr. O'Kelly sat in the chair.

Ciaran sniffled and sat opposite his father in a matching upholstered chair.

Shannon strode over to the kitchen table and grabbed a chair, then placed it between Mr. O'Kelly and Ciaran. He lowered his gaze to his hands, gripping his thighs.

"Boys, I will admit my drinking habits have been a bit abnormal lately. But Shannon is right, it's only because of losing your mother, Ciaran. Now, that said, I'll have no more of this bloody talk, do you understand?" He scowled, eying Ciaran.

"Yes, Da."

"Yes, Mr. O'Kelly."

"Good. Now, tell me about this lorry Shannon's father bought." His father returned to a more relaxed position in his chair, then picked his glass up from the hearth and brought to his lips as if defiant for a quick sip of his whiskey.

"There wasn't much to see. Shannon's father was out with

the lorry." Ciaran kept his gaze on the embers in the fireplace, slumping his shoulders.

"Well, then, suppose there's not much to bloody tell either." His father rose from his chair, grunting, and left the two young men while he ambled in the direction of his bedroom.

Ciaran watched him, along with Shannon. What the hell was that, then?

His father stopped in the hallway for a moment, turning back to the young men. "Goodnight." He proceeded down the hallway where his bedroom waited.

Ciaran shifted his attention to Shannon. "I think my da's gone completely daft."

Letting out a soft chuckle, Shannon brought his hand up to cover his mouth. "Maybe, but at least he's not bloody falling-down hammered tonight."

Ciaran sat back in his chair with a huff. "That's not funny, Shannon."

Shannon placed his hand on Ciaran's arm, above the elbow. "I'm sorry, I didn't mean nothing by it."

"I know." Ciaran groaned in frustration, shaking his head. He focused on Shannon. "I'm just so worried. What if he doesn't bloody stop? What if he gets worse even? I can't handle losing him, too." As his voice faded off, his lower lip trembled, and his eyes filled with tears.

Shannon squeezed Ciaran's arm, then leaned forward and kissed his cheek.

Ciaran's heart ached. "Oh, Shannon, stay with me tonight, please." He placed both hands on Shannon's forearms. All he wanted was to sleep in Shannon's arms again.

Slowly shaking his head, Shannon leaned back. "No, Ciaran, you know I can't do that. You know it will only lead to something we can't control. What if your da sees or hears something? He may be pissed, but he didn't seem too bad off tonight."

Ciaran dropped his head. With emotion filling his voice, he said, "Please, just this once. I need you."

Shannon brought his face close, then whispered, "God, Ciaran, you know I'd like to, I'd really like to."

Lifting his head, Ciaran glared at him. He was only asking for this one simple thing. Other young men their age stayed the night at each other's houses, why wouldn't Shannon stay with him tonight? It wasn't that unordinary. Especially when things had become so strained, especially when he needed him so? His words were sharp. "But you won't, will you."

Shannon gasped, staring at him. He came close again. "Think about what you're asking. Think about the consequences. If you need me, I'm right here, but I won't let you talk me into something so foolish." He huffed and flared his nostrils.

Ciaran snatched his wrist and rose up, then hauled Shannon up and across the room, continuing until they stood at the front door. He tugged the door open, took him onto the front stoop and slammed the door with a thud.

Shannon peered at him.

Hooking his arms around his waist in a tight hold, Ciaran buried his head into his shoulder, clinging to him like a frightened child.

As Shannon held him, he brushed his hand up and down Ciaran's back. "I'm sorry. It'll be all right," he said softly.

"I miss you so much, miss sleeping with you. I wish it didn't have to bloody be this way. I just wish we could be together like we were on our trip. Why does it have to be so hard?" Ciaran's voice shook with emotion. Pain lingered in his chest.

"Because people don't understand what we have. It scares them, I suppose." Shannon tightened his hold on him.

Ciaran pulled away, keeping his hands on Shannon's hips, and peered into his face. "Just this once, stay with me. We can just sleep. I promise. I won't start anything."

Shannon released a heavy sigh and opened his mouth to speak.

"We can sleep in the main room, in blankets on the floor. We wouldn't even be in my room. That's not bloody suspicious now, is it?" Ciaran lifted his brows. He could talk him into this, he knew he could.

Shaking his head once, Shannon pursed his lips.

"It's not suspicious at all. Believe me, Shannon, my da will not suspect a thing. He'll just think I was upset, like I am, and you stayed." He studied Shannon's face. Was it working?

Shannon knit his brows. "And what about my ma? What will she think when I don't come home?"

"Oh, so what. Who cares what she thinks. You can just tell her you were tired after the bloody trip she made you take into Johnstown Bridge and you fell asleep." Ciaran smirked. That would fix her for making Shannon call on that woman.

"Damn it...fine then." Shannon drew away from Ciaran and raked his fingers through his black bangs. He turned away for a moment, then faced him again. "You better be right about this." He bit his lower lip.

Clutching the front of his shirt, Ciaran jerked him forward for a quick kiss. "Come on then." He let a wide grin play on his face. *I won.*

Shannon followed Ciaran into the house and helped him get blankets and pillows from his bedroom and a chest in the hallway. They set the blankets up on the floor in front of the hearth. But away from each other, not close like they were on that windy night when they'd first returned home.

Shannon shut off the lamp on the table and returned to the blankets, then glanced at Ciaran, unbuttoning his shirt. He reached out to him. "Stop, Ciaran, I don't think we should undress, it looks too planned."

Still smiling, Ciaran nodded. As long as Shannon stayed, he'd do whatever he wanted.

Shannon lay down on his blankets on his side, removed his boots and tried to get comfortable.

Sliding up behind him, Ciaran wrapped an arm around his waist. Shannon was here and would be with him all night. Arousal ached inside him, swelling his shaft.

Shannon twisted his head. "You think this won't look suspicious?"

"Just let me be close to you for a little while."

"Don't you dare fall asleep," Shannon said.

Ciaran placed a sensual kiss on the back of his neck.

Shannon let out a soft moan, then stifled it.

A lustful fire raged inside Ciaran. He yearned to ravage Shannon right then and there. He moved his hand slowly and deliberately down Shannon's chest, over his belt and onto his trousers, then played with Shannon's stiff cock through his trousers. *He's feeling the same way I am.*

Shannon thrust forward as if attempting to gain more friction.

Ciaran pressed his hardened cock into his backside, rubbing along Shannon's shaft, then stopped to squeeze and circle the tip. Maybe he should stop, but he couldn't. It all felt too good.

A soft gasp escaped Shannon's throat.

Ciaran stroked his palm harder against him, pressing his own cock against Shannon's back end, sending a shudder through his body.

Shannon reached around at the back of him and mimicked

the motions Ciaran used on him. In a whisper, he said, "You sure are good at that."

"Mmm..." Tension coiled inside Ciaran. That's what he needed, Shannon's hand on him. He choked out a soft moan. He rubbed faster, more insistent over Shannon's cock while grinding onto his hand. His groin hummed with sumptuous friction.

Shannon stilled his hand on his backside, caught between them.

Ciaran thrust against Shannon's open palm and fingers. His breath became ragged. His need and sensitivity heightened.

Shannon's hips rocked in time with the fondling of Ciaran's hand. His body shook. He groaned, low and urgent. With his brows tensed, eyes closed, his whole body grew rigid, then he slapped his free hand over Ciaran's and pressed hard on his erection.

Shannon's arousal pulsed under Ciaran's hand. *He's coming.* Ciaran's body jerked as a peak of sensitivity pulsed through his groin. His climax pushed close to the surface. He thrust harder, faster into Shannon's flattened hand. Sweet release washed over him. Stifling himself, he bit his lower lip. Delicious contractions spilled his seed, wetting his undergarment. He let out short, soft gasps while the waves of climax washed over him. Shuddering, he thrust hard, one last time, as it all subsided. "Oh, God, Shannon. What you do to me..." he whispered, pulling his arm away from Shannon's waist and rolling onto his back.

Shannon smiled and turned onto his stomach, propped on his elbows, and faced him. He winced, then held his arm out straight in front of him as if his arm hurt. "Oh really? No, I think it's what you do to me. You really like that bloody through-the-trousers stuff, aye?" He leaned over and nudged him with his shoulder.

Chuckling, Ciaran raised his hand to his forehead. "Yeah well, it's convenient when you don't have time or are in a place where you might get caught." Shannon should know these things, he wasn't exactly innocent.

Shannon knit his brows and glanced at him. "And what sort of situations are you talking about?"

Heat flushed Ciaran's face as he rolled away from him for a few seconds, then came back to his side, facing him. He glanced at Shannon and returned to his back. It was too embarrassing to admit to his own deviant behavior. "I don't want to tell you."

"Come on, I'd tell you."

"No, you wouldn't."

"I would," Shannon said, his voice rising in volume.

"Ah." Ciaran furrowed his brows. After all, Shannon did tell him all about his affair. *I guess I should tell him some of it at least.* "Um...well, sometimes, and granted this was all before our little trip, when my ma would take me into town, I'd go to the privy at the tavern and watch the girls through a little hole in the wall."

"You didn't." Shannon widened his eyes, a smirk growing on his lips.

Ciaran nodded his head, offering a coy grin. "Seamus told me about it. Sometimes he'd do it with me." Seamus was a devious bastard sometimes. Probably why they'd been friends in school.

"He what?" Shannon leaned closer as if to see his face in the faint, ambient light. "You didn't do anything *with* Seamus, did you?" He winced.

As Ciaran studied Shannon's face, he let his smile fade. Did that hurt Shannon somehow? "Why, you jealous?"

"Yes, I'm jealous. Why wouldn't I be? You told me you hadn't done anything with anyone else, remember?" Shannon huffed and wrinkled his nose.

Ciaran let a soft grin play on his lips. He had to make Shannon understand it was nothing like what they were doing now. "No, I didn't touch Seamus and he never touched me. We just looked through the hole together."

"Must have been a big hole." Shannon's body relaxed.

I should probably tell him all of it. Then maybe Shannon would see that he's not the only one in town doing immoral things. "And then sometimes, I went to Noleen's house and watched her through her window." Ciaran said, studying him.

Shannon let out a soft gasp. "You mean the Noleen that lives on the other side of your house? The one that never married? Isn't she a lot older than you?" He dropped his mouth open.

Ciaran gave him a smug nod.

"You bloody little pervert, you. I suppose you took Seamus with you for that, too." Shannon scowled.

"Nope, just me," Ciaran said with a smirk.

"Jaysus, and I thought I was bad. Did you ever confess those things to Father Brennan?" Shannon stared at him as if stunned.

Ciaran frowned. "Yeah, he'd always give me a ton of Hail Marys for it. It didn't stop me." Though, it sounded like his confessions paled in comparison to what Shannon had gone through.

"Anything else I should know about since we're on the subject?" Shannon smiled as if amused.

"No, well..." Heat surged in Ciaran's cheeks. Should he tell him the rest? The thing no one had ever known?

"Oh my God, what else?" Shannon studied him.

Why not. "I did it at school a few times." The heat in Ciaran's cheeks heightened.

"At school? Where, for God sakes?" The edges of Shannon's mouth twitched.

"I hid by the girl's privy, and did it while they were in there." Ciaran let out an anxious chuckle. He placed his hand over his face, hiding his shame. That was it. He'd told him everything. And Shannon had thought *he* was bad. He'd never thought he'd ever tell a soul about that last bit.

Shannon shook his head, releasing a puff of air. "Ciaran?"

"What?" Ciaran's palm muffled his voice.

Shannon pulled Ciaran's hand down from his face, then leaned in and placed a lingering kiss over his mouth. He gazed deeply into his eyes. "It all bloody makes sense now."

"What does?" *What does he think of me now?* Ciaran knit his brows.

"We're two of a kind, aren't we? We both like things that are a little off." Shannon snickered. "We're both feckin' perverts." They both laughed loudly.

A loud creak cracked through the house from the direction of the hallway.

The laughing ceased.

Ciaran waited, listening for the slightest sound.

The soft patter of footsteps sounded from the hallway.

Ciaran's heart lurched. He glanced at Shannon. Would Da have seen or heard any of that?

The footsteps faded and the click of a door closing snaked into the room.

Shannon whispered, "This was a bad idea, Ciaran."

Ciaran rolled over onto his stomach, held up by his elbows, eyes wide. His heart thumped in his chest. "Yeah, you may be right."

Shannon focused on Ciaran. "Do you think he saw something?"

"I don't know. I hope not," Ciaran whispered.

"Maybe I should just go." Shannon made to get up.

Ciaran held him down. Even if his da heard or saw something, it was too late now. He needed him here. "No, I want you to stay with me. You said you would." He wrinkled his forehead.

"Damn, what if your da bloody saw something?" Shannon asked.

"If he did, having you stay won't change anything. Just stay, please." Ciaran pushed his forehead into his shoulder. He didn't just want him here, he needed him tonight. It felt like forever since they'd spent the night together.

"Oh, all right. Let me get cleaned up though." Shannon rolled to his back and sat up. "Damn it," he mumbled. He rose to his feet and made his way as quiet as possible to Ciaran's bedroom.

Ciaran waited a moment, then went into to the hallway, brushing by Shannon as he left the bedroom.

Shannon stopped and looked Ciaran up and down.

Leaning close, Ciaran whispered. "I have to clean up, too, you know." He smirked.

Shannon sighed, then padded back to their rumpled blankets.

When Ciaran had finished with the water-filled pitcher and bowl in his room, he came back to Shannon. A wave of fatigue washed over him. Too much had happened today. He needed sleep. He lay down on his side and reached an arm up under his pillow. He closed his eyes and sleep came over him like a warm blanket.

CHAPTER
EIGHTEEN
SHANNON

A loud clatter rang in Shannon's head. He jolted, then thrust himself up to sitting, fluttering his eyes open to scan his surroundings. *What the bloody hell was that?* His gaze rested on Mr. O'Kelly, standing by hearth, frying pan in hand, mouth gaping.

"Oh, Shannon, I'm so sorry. Didn't mean to wake you." Mr. O'Kelly said.

"That's okay. I um—" *Where's Ciaran?* Shannon's pulse quickened. He was alone with Mr. O'Kelly and if he'd seen something last night, he would have to face him all alone.

Mr. O'Kelly stood still by the hearth as if waiting for him to finish his sentence.

With a frown, Shannon looked at the blankets for a moment, then focused on him. "Wh-where is Ciaran?"

"Ah, he's out collecting eggs for our breakfast. I trust you had a good sleep?"

"Yeah." An awkward feeling rushed over Shannon. He stared at the blankets, toying with a fold in his fingers. What should he say or how should he act after what happened last night? Although if Mr. O'Kelly saw something he would have said it by now.

Mr. O'Kelly turned to the hearth and placed the frying pan on part of the insert. He clattered about, pulling out utensils and food.

Shannon relaxed his shoulders and let out a slow exhale.

"So, you must have been very tired to have stayed the night?" Mr. O'Kelly continued his pottering.

Shannon's chest tightened. He cut his gaze to Ciaran's father, his back to him. "Um, yes I was. I, uh...well, it was a very busy day for me yesterday, with my da taking me to Johnstown Bridge and all."

"Johnstown Bridge? What on Earth were you doing there?" Mr. O'Kelly's arms moved quickly around the hearth, preparing the meal.

"Ah well, my ma found a girl for me to call on." Shannon shifted in the blankets. Should he stand?

"A girl? You're joking me." Mr. O'Kelly turned around to face him, a knife in one hand and a potato in the other. He spread a wide grin on his face and chuckled.

Why does Mr. O'Kelly find that so amusing? Does he know about me? Shannon opened his mouth to say more.

The door slammed open with Ciaran standing at the threshold. "Morning, Shannon. 'Bout time you woke up." A wicker basket filled with eggs hung in his hand. He kicked the door shut with his foot and strode into the room. "Looks like there's a storm finally brewing out there. Did you see those clouds, Da?"

"I did. Looks like a nasty one," Mr. O'Kelly said.

Ciaran walked to his father and set the eggs close to him. "Here's your eggs." He came toward Shannon, then sat down, cross-legged, in front of him and smiled. "So?"

Returning the smile, Shannon said, "So bloody what?"

Ciaran dropped his gaze to Shannon's lips. His eyes dazed as if lost in thought.

The crackle of eggs hitting heated butter filled the room. The aroma of it wafted into Shannon's nose. "Smells lovely."

"Hear that, Da? Shannon says your cooking smells lovely," Ciaran called out. He took a quick glance at his father before facing Shannon again.

Ciaran dived forward, pecking Shannon's cheek with his lips, then quickly took his original position.

Gasping, heat flushed Shannon's face. His cheek tingled and he touched it. "Stop that," he whispered.

Ciaran gave him a devious grin while leaning toward him. "He can't see anything. Seems he didn't notice anything last night either," he whispered. "So, when are we going to see your da's lorry?"

"How about after breakfast? Is that soon enough for you?" Shannon rose up, smoothed out his rumpled clothes and strode to the table, then sat down with a sigh. So, all that worry was for nothing.

Ciaran stood, made his way to the table, and sat beside Shannon.

Mr. O'Kelly turned around with plates full of eggs and potatoes. After placing the plates in front of the young men, he brought them silverware and cups filled with tea.

"Looks lovely, Da." Ciaran dug into his breakfast.

"It sure does, Mr. O'Kelly. Thank you." Shannon brought a fork piled high with eggs to his mouth.

Mr. O'Kelly served himself and sat across from them.

"So, Da, you coming with us to see the lorry this morning?" Ciaran left his fork on his plate, watching his father.

Mr. O'Kelly gazed at his breakfast and furrowed his brows. "No, Ciaran, I have some business to attend to in town."

"Not at the pub again?" Ciaran wrinkled his forehead.

Mr. O'Kelly glared at his son. "Yes, at the pub. And I'll remind you to mind your manners at the table, young man." He ate, shoving his fork into his food and then to his mouth.

Shannon stared from Ciaran to his father. It was so much like the breakfasts he'd had in his own house with his parents. He took a sip of tea and struggled to think of something to say to change the somber mood. "Um, well, I'm sure whatever you're doing there is important."

"It is," Mr. O'Kelly said.

Ciaran glared at Shannon and kicked him under the table.

"Ow!" Shannon bent down to rub his shin, then threw him a threatening glance.

"Ciaran, if you're going to act like a bloody animal, then go out to the barn and eat with them." Mr. O'Kelly pursed his lips, fixating on Ciaran.

Oh, that was a good one. Shannon released a soft snicker, lowering his head. Sure, he was an animal, if only his father knew.

Ciaran sat forward. "Don't laugh, Shannon, it's not bloody funny."

Focusing on Ciaran, Shannon said, "You are a bit of an animal, you know." Would he understand the underlying meaning of his comment?

Ciaran spread a smug grin over his face. "Yeah? Well, so are you."

Mr. O'Kelly pointed his fork at each of the young men. "All right, that's enough, you two. Can a man eat in peace? I'd swear you two were brothers if I didn't know better."

SHANNON STROLLED beside Ciaran as they made their way to his front porch. He opened the door.

Shannon's mother and father sat at the kitchen table, teacups in hand and emptied plates in front of them.

"Good morning, Ma." Shannon tipped his head in their direction. "Da."

As his mother leaned back, she inspected him. "Where you been all night?"

Ciaran walked through the door behind him. "Oh, he was with me, ma'am. We had a bit of a problem yesterday and he stayed to help out. Guess we got tired and just fell asleep."

"Is that so?" His mother hesitated, grunted, and glanced at his father.

Shannon watched his father, his chest squeezing. He didn't like his mother's reaction.

His father rolled his eyes.

Shannon spread a smile over his face. Seemed he was still in good graces with his father.

"So, I suppose you're here to see the lorry?" His father stood and strode toward the young men.

"Yeah," Shannon said, nodding.

"Yes, sir," Ciaran said.

His father brushed by them on his way out of the door and they followed. "My, the sky is looking a bit dark today, isn't it, boys?"

Shannon looked up into the sky at the threatening clouds. The heavy air smelled of rain and felt thick on his skin. He peered skyward while he walked. When was the last time he saw clouds so dark?

They came upon the lorry and Ciaran ran his hand along the hood, his wide-eyed gaze taking in the vehicle. "Can I see the engine?" He let a broad smile play on his lips and glanced at Mr. Sullivan.

"Sure." His father went to the front and lifted the hood for him.

Shannon watched Ciaran bend over the compartment, pointing and carrying on with his father with regard to the workings of all the various mechanisms it contained. For some reason, these were things he just wasn't interested in.

"Shall I take you for a ride, boys?" His father's chest expanded a little farther and he placed his hands on his hip, grinning.

Ciaran straightened. "Oh, please."

Shannon stepped to the passenger door, opened it, and waited for Ciaran to join him.

Ciaran came around the lorry and scooted onto the seat.

As Shannon slid into the outside of the bench seat, he closed the door.

His father got in and pushed the ignition button, making the engine roar to life.

Chuckling, Ciaran beamed at his father. "Shannon, maybe you could learn how to drive it?"

Shannon leaned forward, looking to his father.

"Sure, son, I'll teach you." His father put the lorry in gear and eased it forward.

"Really, Da?" Shannon lifted his brows. Seemed he and his father were better than they'd ever been.

"Course. Maybe then you can drive yourself to Johnstown Bridge to see Melissa," His father said, while circling the lorry and starting down their dirt drive.

"What?" Shannon's heart pinched and he dropped his mouth open.

Ciaran flared his nostrils, glaring at Shannon.

"Ah well, it seems Mr. O'Doyle changed his mind. I don't know what really happened with you and her in that alley, but she really wanted to see you again. Seems she talked her da into letting you call on her again," His father spoke casually while driving the lorry down the road.

Shannon's pulse quickened. He glanced at Ciaran. Would he pick up on what his father had just said?

Ciaran stared straight out at the road ahead of them and stiffened.

A tight knot wound in Shannon's stomach. What should he say? Maybe, if he remained quiet, his father would just drop the conversation and he could make something up to tell Ciaran later.

Ciaran gave Mr. Sullivan a thin-lipped grin. "So, what's this about Shannon in an alley with Melissa?" Ciaran's throat dipped with a hard swallow.

"Oh, he didn't tell you?" His father straightened in his seat as if proud.

"Da!" Shannon's heart about stopped. He had to make his father keep quiet somehow, but how? He shifted in his seat to look at his father head on.

"Oh, Shannon, hush up," His father huffed.

Shannon whined, "But, Da."

"Shannon, let your da speak. I'm sure it'll be an interesting story." Ciaran pressed his lips together, flashed his eyes at Shannon, then squeezed Shannon's forearm hard.

Pain lit up Shannon's arm. Wincing, he ripped it away.

"Well, I'm sure you know Shannon's mother set him up with this girl from Johnstown Bridge. He was just supposed to lunch with her, but our shy little Shannon here—"

"Da, please..." Shannon wrinkled his brows. Nausea balled up in his gut.

His father leaned forward and glared at him. "What are you bloody going on about?" He came back into his seat, getting comfortable again.

Shannon stared at his fists, clenching in his lap, and gritted his teeth. *This is bad.*

"Anyway, as I was saying, apparently our shy little Shannon isn't so shy after all. When I got back from the hardware store, he had taken her into the alley." His father let a broad smile wash over his face. A chuckle rolled through his chest. "Seems he had her out there kissing and carrying on. Can you believe it, Ciaran?"

"No, I can't," Ciaran stared straight ahead, clenching his jaw.

Shannon stole a peak into his face. Tears glistened in Ciaran's eyes.

Shannon's heart ached. What would Ciaran do? *How will I explain what happened? The truth? Maybe, but would he believe me, now that I've already lied about it once?*

"Oh my gosh, I just remembered something I needed to do for my da. Can we go back now, Mr. Sullivan?" Ciaran's voice quivered with emotion.

"Sure, son." His father knit his brows and sent a nervous glance in Ciaran's direction as if sensing the sudden tension.

Silence fell on them while they bumped along the road and back up the drive to Shannon's home. It felt like it took forever, though it was only a few minutes.

As the lorry stopped, Shannon opened the door.

Ciaran thumped Shannon on the back.

Shannon pitched out, stumbling, then falling to his knees on the dirt.

Tearing out of the lorry, Ciaran sped down the path leading to the river.

"What's got his knickers in a twist?" His father stood outside the lorry, his hand on the open door.

Shannon righted himself and bolted after Ciaran. He had to catch up to him. He had to make him understand what really happened. He ran deep into the woods, keeping his focus on the blond head bobbing in front of him. His long legs propelled him forward at a quick pace. He could outrun him any day. He neared his target. "Ciaran, stop!"

Ciaran raced ahead of him.

Trees and brush flew past Shannon's peripheral vision while he chased him. His lungs burned. As he neared him, he groped out in front of him and snagged his shirt. He yanked, tossing Ciaran to the hard ground.

Cursing, Ciaran thrashed about on his back, sending dried leaves and dust all around them.

Shannon jumped on top of him.

Tears and dust stained Ciaran's cheeks while his frantic limbs fought to keep him off him.

Shannon scuffled with him, thrashing, and trying time after time to pin him down. Grunting, he worked a leg on either side of his writhing body and straddled him, arms pinned under his knees and chest under his hips. He panted.

Ciaran bucked his hips, crying out, attempting to thrust him off.

"Stop it, Ciaran, please." Shannon tussled with him.

"Get off me, you bastard!" With his eyes squeezed shut, Ciaran let out an agonizing sob and continued a slower struggle against him.

Shannon draped his whole body over him and held him tight, his body bouncing with Ciaran's now feeble attempts to throw him off. His breath hitched. Hot tears rolled down his cheeks. "I'm sorry, Ciaran," he wept, "I'm so sorry."

Ciaran slowed and lay still under him. "God, how could you do that? How could you bloody lie to me?" He freed a ragged breath. "What did you do with her?" He shoved Shannon off him.

Landing on his side, Shannon scrambled to right himself on his knees. Would he try to run away again? Silent tears tumbled down his cheeks. He fixated on him.

Ciaran rose to sit beside him with his legs stretched out. He glared at Shannon, then softened his eyes, wrinkling his brows. Growling, he said, "Tell me what you did with her, bloody all of it. Don't you dare lie to me again."

As Shannon freed a hitched breath, he reached a timid hand out.

Ciaran smacked it away.

Shannon recoiled, then wrapped his arms around his chest and hung his head. As a sob escaped his throat, he peaked at him. *He looks so hurt.*

"Tell me." Ciaran sniffled.

Shannon drew deep breaths. He had to find a way to sound less guilty than he really was. Slowly and deliberately, he said, "I-I did kiss her. I did take her into the alley." His words came faster. "But that's all I did. I had to, Ciaran. She made me. If I didn't, she was going to tell everyone I was-was, queer. Don't you see? I had to. I'd be run off."

Wiping his eyes, Ciaran creased his forehead. "What do you mean, she made you? She was going to tell everyone you're queer? How the hell would she know?"

Shannon straightened and sat forward, removing his arms from around his waist. "I don't know, maybe my sister, or, I guess there's been rumors going around about me all along. She told me she took a dare to see if they were true. I had to take her to the alley and prove to her I liked women. So, you see, I had no choice."

"But how did that prove to her you liked women? Anyone can just kiss someone."

Shannon stared at the weeds lining the path, his face heating. How could he admit the rest of it?

"Shannon? Tell me what else happened. I know you, you're still hiding something." Ciaran cocked his head, examining him. "Tell me." He pushed at Shannon's chest.

His chest aching, Shannon clutched at his shirt. *How am I supposed to tell him?* He tensed his brows and forced himself to look at Ciaran. "I had to get a stiffy. If I didn't, she wouldn't believe me."

"Ah, God, Shannon," Ciaran said while tilting his head back, looking toward the sky. He fixated on Shannon. "So what else did you do? Did you let her fondle you?"

"God, no, I just pretended she was you when I kissed her." Shannon watched him.

Ciaran spread a faint smile on his face.

The weight of Shannon's guilt lifted, and he wiped his eyes with the back of his hands, sniffling.

"Bloody hell, Shannon. I don't believe you sometimes, the things you get yourself into." Ciaran chuckled, shaking his head.

"Does that mean you're not mad at me anymore?" The aching in his chest lessened. Maybe it wasn't so bad after all.

"Damn, I should be. But you're just so bloody pathetic sometimes. Come here." Ciaran held his arm outstretched and drew him into his chest. "I sure love you, even if you are a bloody liar and a bad one at that."

Shannon closed his eyes, drawing his arms up. Being in Ciaran's embrace was like heaven after that horrible ordeal. "I love you, too, so much." Soft kisses pecked his cheek. He turned his face toward Ciaran's and pressed his mouth to his, their tongues tangling.

Ciaran roamed his hands over Shannon's lean chest beneath his shirt, stopping at a nipple, teasing, and pinching over the thin fabric of his undergarment until it hardened.

Moaning, Shannon arched his back. His cock swelled in an instant. "Ciaran, I want you," he said breathless.

Ciaran guided them both backward, onto the ground of dried leaves and grass.

Sprawling out on top of Ciaran, Shannon ground their hips together, rubbing delicious pressure and friction over his aching erection. He devoured Ciaran, kissing, and nibbling over his jaw and down into his neck. He bit and sucked down to the first button on Ciaran's shirt, then peered into Ciaran's face.

Ciaran's eyelids hooded over widened pupils.

Dropping down between Ciaran's legs, Shannon unfastened his trousers.

Ciaran planted his hands on the back of his head

Trembling, Shannon loosened Ciaran's erection from his trousers and underwear and took it in his mouth, fisting the base, sucking slowly, rhythmically. He loved being right here, tasting his lover, his Ciaran. He tipped his head to watch Ciaran.

Ciaran rocked his hips and groaned, wrinkling his brows. He clutched at Shannon's shirt and tugged at him. "Go faster, Shannon." His hips thrust harder, faster, egging Shannon on.

Bobbing his head, Shannon lapped at Ciaran's shaft, swirling the tip with his tongue.

Ciaran's body shook and a sharp moan escaped him.

Shannon ran his slick tongue up the front of Ciaran's cock, his desire humming inside him. He reached down, remembering what they did last night, and rubbed himself through his trousers. A delicious surge of pleasure rushed through him. He moaned against Ciaran's shaft.

Ciaran jerked his hips with the promise of a quick and urgent release. With a hard thrust, gasping loudly, he surged into Shannon's mouth, surrendering to release.

Lapping up his seed, Shannon licked and sucked while it burst into his throat. He wouldn't spill a drop. He kept on, until Ciaran slowed his hips and prodded him onto his back. He gazed deeply into Ciaran's eyes.

Ciaran gave him a lazy grin. "Now it's your turn." Ciaran dropped between his legs, unbuckled his belt, and unfastened his trousers. As he yanked fabric away, he lowered his mouth over Shannon's erection.

Ciaran enveloped Shannon's weeping cock with his wet, hot mouth. An intense sensation rushed his body. As he freed a loud groan, he bucked and clenched Ciaran's hair. "Damn, Ciaran, you've got so good at this."

Ciaran swirled the head of his cock with his tongue.

Releasing a new round of moans, Shannon thrust his hips. The tension in his groin coiled, a spring aching to be released. He grew sensitive. Pulses of pleasure rushed through him with every flick, every stroke of Ciaran's tongue. He fought against climax, biting his lip, wanting to savor everything a little longer.

Ciaran pumped quicker over him.

With his body trembling, Shannon drove hard into his mouth, surrendering, his climax surging over him. He clutched at blond hair. His toes curled. He writhed below Ciaran as exquisite spasms spurted his seed into Ciaran's lapping mouth. Each time pleasure dashed through him. He let his loud, needful moans fill the forest around them.

When it finished, Ciaran moved to hover over him and gazed into his eyes. "Damn, you are bloody loud, you know that? I'll bet all the animals scattered for miles around."

Shannon grinned and slapped Ciaran's arm. "Stop it."

Crackling sounded from a few feet away in the brush.

"What was that?" Shannon rounded his eyes and scanned the forest. Had his father followed him? He rushed to sit up, along with Ciaran, and fastened his trousers. He listened. Except for the gurgling of the nearby river and the occasional chirp of a bird, a quiet blanket fell over them.

Ciaran searched the woods for the source of the noise and

relaxed. "See? Told you. You scared the animals." Chuckling, he leaned in and gave him a peck on the cheek.

"Let's get going anyway. My da is going to be wondering what happened between us." Shannon rose to standing, brushed himself off as best he could and took another look around the trees and brush. Something didn't seem right. Anxiety formed in the pit of his stomach. He glanced at the ominous clouds looming above him, turning the woods around them a deep green. *Must be the storm.*

Ciaran took his hand and led him toward the path.

Shannon relaxed his shoulders.

"So what story shall we give your da?" Ciaran strolled, towing Shannon behind him.

Frowning, Shannon said, "I think it'd be best if I talked to him alone. It could be a very delicate situation."

Ciaran glared at him. "Just what are you trying to say?"

Sighing, he tipped his head back. "I'm not trying to say anything. Come on, Ciaran, just let me bloody talk to my father alone." Did he have to get put out by everything?

Ciaran hunched his shoulders. "Oh, okay. I just thought maybe I could, I don't know, help you in some way."

"Well, thanks, but I think it's best if I talk to him alone." Shannon looked ahead at the fork in the path. One direction led to Ciaran's house and the other to his own. He stopped and faced him, placing his hands on Ciaran's hips. "Okay, so I'll come back to your house when I've finished." He leaned in and placed a tender kiss on his lips.

"You sure you want to do this alone?" Ciaran studied his face.

"Yes, I'm sure. I'll see you in a little while. I'm sure it'll be fine." Shannon pursed his lips. He wasn't looking forward to this, but maybe his father would still be civil after hearing the news about Melissa.

Somewhere off in the distance, thunder rumbled.

"Hey, did you hear that? Guess it's finally going to rain," Ciaran said. "I'll see you later."

Shannon stood for a moment watching Ciaran stroll down the path toward his home. His chest squeezed. He had to think of an excuse while he walked back.

CHAPTER NINETEEN
SHANNON

Shannon trotted off toward his home, then slowed as a figure came into view. He squinted.

A man blocked the dusty path in front of him.

"Father Brennan," Shannon whispered, drawing near and eying the priest.

A white dress shirt and brown trousers hung on Father Brennan's stout build and wading boots covered his feet. A wicker basket hung around him at the waist and a fishing pole slung over his shoulder.

"Good afternoon, Father. Been fishing, I see?" Shannon rubbed his hands together.

Father Brennan gave a slow shake of his head. "Shannon, my son. I need you to come with me." He winced, as if someone did him a great harm.

"Something wrong?" Shannon's heart pounded in his ears. An alarm sounded in his head. His legs twitched for flight. *Something isn't right.* Maybe he should just take off and run home. No, that would look too suspicious.

Father Brennan stepped toward him, seizing his arm.

"Please, son, just come with me." He tipped his head in the direction of the path behind him. He tugged on Shannon's arm.

"Um, o-okay." *I have to go. I have no choice.* Shannon walked in silence, behind him, down the path toward his home and veered into the brush onto another trail. All the way, the priest kept a firm hold on his arm.

They walked into a clearing and Shannon looked over a motor car. *Where did he get the money for this?* It looked brand new. He examined it, a higher-end model with a black metal roof and windows closing in the carriage. The tires were white-walled and thin. He stalked toward it, Father Brennan's hand still wrapped tightly around his arm.

Father Brennan opened the passenger side door. "Please, get in."

Shannon nodded and slid onto the leather seat, taking in the smooth, new surfaces and smell of smoke and tannins.

Father Brennan placed his fishing gear in the back seat and climbed into the driver's seat. He started the vehicle. The engine purred. He put it into gear and drove effortlessly out to the main road.

Drawing deep breaths, Shannon struggled against a flurry in his stomach and his thrumming heart. There was no reason to be anxious. The man was a priest after all, not a monster. Memories of the nightmare he had on his trip with Ciaran flashed through his mind. He shoved them back, forcing himself to focus on the trees speeding by outside his window. "Um, where are we going?"

"Why, to church, of course." Father Brennan cackled and threw a menacing glance at Shannon.

Shannon's hair stood on end as a shiver worked up his spine. Why was he being dragged to church? Had his father requested another confession? It didn't make sense. "Why are you taking me there?"

"Because, Shannon, there is something you must see." Father Brennan fixated on the road, white-knuckling the steering wheel.

Shannon nodded slowly. "Oh." His mind sped through all the possibilities. Did he leave something behind on Sunday? Did Father Brennan know he left the church without saying his penance? He furrowed his brows, focusing on the perfectly new instrument panel while his mind reeled with questions.

They drove in silence through town and up the gravel drive. The tires crunched on small rocks. Cemetery gravestones jutted out from dry grass on either side of them. Father Brennan stopped the motor car to the left of the church.

Shannon peered out at the side of the old stone building. The heart-shaped leaves of the ivy surrounding it quivered. He opened his door and climbed out. A light breeze filled with the scent of rain ruffled his hair. He shifted his weight from foot to foot, watching the priest. Where were they going now?

With thin lips, Father Brennan approached, his gaze intense. "Follow me." He snatched Shannon's arm and hauled him toward the back of the church.

Shannon stumbled, then righted himself and ambled behind him, trembling, starting up inside him. Wherever they were going, it wasn't good. The thick clouds above only let the faint outlines of a shadow trail him. He followed the priest to a barely used path around the back of the church. He'd never been back here, never even known it'd existed. He ducked his head as low-hanging tree branches scratched at him and weeds whipped at his ankles. "Where are we going?" His voice cracked.

"You'll find out soon enough," the priest said without turning around, but stomping on.

A small clearing came into view. A flash followed by the close rumbling of thunder shook the sky as Shannon's gaze locked on a simple stone cross overgrown with ivy and moss. Fear shivered over his body. *An unmarked gravestone.* As his body shook, he glanced at Father Brennan. Oak and ash trees swayed thick, suffocating boughs overhead. "What's going on, tell me." His voice wavered. *This is not like Father Brennan, not like him at all.*

Father Brennan whirled around, facing him.

He winced. Pain shot up his arm. His vision blurred. *Something is very wrong!*

Father Brennan pointed a shaky finger to the stone cross. "See this gravestone, Shannon?" His voice rose to an unnaturally high pitch.

"Y-yes?" A flash blinded Shannon. Thunder cracked overhead. He cowered.

With almost burning blue eyes, Father Brennan curled the corners of his thin lips. He shook a gnarled index finger at the marker, his words hissing out of him. "This is what happens when you lie in confession. This is what happens when you let your demons take control. This is what happens when you fornicate with another male."

"Wh-what? But I-I didn't," Shannon whined. Hot tears spilled over his cheeks. He jerked his arm, but the priest's hold tightened. He stared at him, unable to move. *What the hell's going on?*

"Oh, but you bloody well did, Shannon, you did. I know, I saw it with my own two eyes." Father Brennan twisted his gnarled fingers to point at his own eyes, wide enough so the whole iris showed.

Shannon shook his head and a sob escaped him. He bit his lip to keep from weeping outright. It was time to face what he knew was true. "Wh-who is in that grave?"

"You know, Shannon, your beloved teacher, Mr. Flannigan. Oh, how his demon loved you. You've no idea. The wretched thing confessed to me how it couldn't stay away from you though it tried. It had to have you. Bloody thing even begged me to spare you." Father Brennan's eyes gleamed as if he'd gone mad.

"S-so you k-killed him?" Shannon freed a choked sob. Pain wrapped around his heart. *Oh God, Mr. Flannigan loved me. He never said goodbye because he was dead...Hold on, will the priest kill me, too?* He rounded his eyes, gasping, and stared at him.

"No, Shannon, I didn't kill him. It was the hand of God. It struck him down dead, sure as it will strike you down. We must go to confession. We must cleanse you of this demon now, once and for all."

Another flash and crack of thunder ripped through the heavy air. His nerves jolted. He thrashed and flailed, tearing his arm free. He dashed out of the clearing. Branches whipped and tendrils clawed as he sped up the path away from the church. He vaguely heard Father Brennan's calls and threats. All his senses focused on one thing. *Ciaran.*

He ran hard through town, lungs burning, not slowing while people stared and pointed at him. He darted onto the main road. Fear stabbed at his heart. Could the priest catch up to him in his motor car? He switched direction, heading into the woods.

While he ran, his chest heaved with deep, quick breaths. Bushes lashed his face. Raindrops fell around him. Tiny splashes pattered in the dirt, on the leaves, in his hair, taming the never-ending dust. His body could stand no more. He slowed his pace, striding quickly, in the direction of Ciaran's house.

As he approached, He searched around him, behind him, and calmed. Father Brennan wasn't anywhere. He lowered his brows, pinching his lips. What the hell had just happened? Father Brennan probably saw him with Ciaran down by the river. Mr. Flannigan was dead. *Most likely killed because of his love for me. He loved me.* His breath hitched as new tears stung his eyes. He wept while he walked, his shoulders shaking. His loud sobs echoed through the trees while the rain fell harder, covering his tears, cleansing his soul.

He walked on. It was obvious now what he had to do. He must leave. *Take Ciaran and leave this horrible place. Go back to Iona, back to Dublin and the pub, back to a place where I'm accepted.* Yes, they'd leave as soon as he returned. It would be all right. He'd have his Ciaran and they could be together with Iona. Numbness washed over his body as the rain drenched his clothes, running in rivulets down his face, dripping off his dark locks.

He came to the clearing between Ciaran's house and barn. He stopped for a moment, fisting his hands, taking calming breaths. This would be a difficult conversation. He trudged on through mud. Rain pelted him. A flash of light brought on the boom of thunder. He startled, then pressed on, almost to the door.

The door flung open. Ciaran ran at him. Puddles splashed underfoot as he tackled Shannon, almost knocking them over into the mud. He embraced him in a tight hold, covering his cheek with desperate kisses. "Where were you? I've been so bloody worried." He stopped and drew back, searching his face.

Shannon broke down, sobs ripping free from his throat, his chest heaving. He couldn't stop it. It was all too much. *Ciaran's here...Ciaran's here...*

"What's wrong? Are you crying? Oh God, Shannon, talk to me." Ciaran wrinkled his forehead, patting Shannon all over as if looking for something.

Shannon clutched at him, burying his face in his shoulder. Sobs racked his body. He couldn't speak, not yet. It was all too terrible. Lightning flashed overhead and thunder clapped around them.

"Please, Shannon, let me take you inside." Ciaran guided him up the stoop and through the open door into his house, then held him for a long moment, stroking the back of his wet hair, letting drips puddle below them.

Shannon calmed and pulled away, sniffling.

"Here, let me get you a blanket." Ciaran rushed to his bedroom and returned with one of the wool blankets they used on their trip. As he wrapped it around Shannon, he brought him to one of the chairs by the hearth.

Shannon sat down, frowned, then peeked up through wet bangs at Ciaran, standing in front of him. The rain made quick taps on the roof. Memories of Father Brennan and the unmarked grave came rushing back. He gasped. *How much time do we have until the priest shows up at the door?*

Ciaran startled. "What?"

Lurching forward, Shannon seized him by the wrists. His chest wound tight. "Ciaran, we have to leave. We have to go back to Dublin. Father Brennan, h-he bloody well knows. He knows, Ciaran! He saw us in the woods. He killed Mr. Flannigan and now he wants to kill me. We have to leave, now."

Ciaran shook his head, peering at him. "No..."

"Yes. Now. Before it's too bloody late."

Ciaran cocked his head, eying him. "I-I don't understand, what are you talking about? I thought you were going to see your da?"

Shannon shifted forward in the chair, swallowed hard and said slowly, "Listen to me. That sound in the woods? It must have been Father Brennan. He was on the path when I went home. He took me to a grave at the church. He told me he saw us together. He told me the grave was, was..." He choked out a sob. "Mr. Flannigan, he's dead."

Staring at him, Ciaran said, "He said he wanted to kill you?"

"Well, not in those words, but I'm sure that's what he bloody well intends. We have to leave, Ciaran. Iona said if we needed anything she'd be there for us. Remember?" Shannon gave Ciaran's wrists a shake. *He has to listen to me. We're in danger.*

Ciaran's lower lip trembled. His eyes glistened with tears. "But I can't leave my da," he whispered.

"Where is he now?" Shannon searched the room. There was no sign of Ciaran's father anywhere.

"He's at the damned pub in town again, getting bollocksed." Ciaran stared beyond Shannon. A tear tumbled down his cheek.

"You have to leave. He'll be all right. Look, we'll just write him a note, he bloody well knows where Iona lives, right?" Shannon tightened his hold on Ciaran's wrists.

"No, Shannon. I can't." He sniffled and pressed his lips together.

Shannon glanced at the floor. What could he say to get through to him? He must understand the gravity of the situation. He locked his gaze onto Ciaran's eyes. "Ciaran, you're not understanding me. We bloody well have to go, we have no choice."

Ciaran flinched, then wrinkled his brows. "No, you're not understanding *me*. I told you, I can't go. I'm staying here." He stomped his foot.

"You're not."

"I am."

Tears stung Shannon's eyes. Pain flooded his chest. With his voice shaking, he said, "No, you're not."

"I'm staying, Shannon." Silent tears rolled down Ciaran's face and he looked away.

"But that means..."

"I know."

"Ah, God, I can't lose you, Ciaran." Shannon jumped from the chair, the blanket falling, and seized Ciaran around the shoulders, yanking him into his chest. His sobs mingled with Ciaran's, filling the small room around them.

They clutched at each other, grasping for any part of the other they could reach while their grief took hold.

"Please, don't do this, come with me," Shannon said, burying his face into his shoulder.

"I'm so sorry, but I can't. My da needs me," Ciaran said, weeping.

"What if Father Brennan comes after you?"

"I'll be all right. Believe me. You said in Dublin you have to have faith in me? Well, I need you to do that now." Ciaran tightened his hold.

"I can't, Ciaran, not if it means losing you."

"You must."

Something snapped inside Shannon's head. It all became very clear. *I have to go to Dublin by myself. I have to leave him behind.* He quieted, his body becoming light, as if it could float away. Numbness washed over him again, taking away the pain, leaving only an empty husk where his essence once was.

"Okay." The words were faint, like someone spoke them from far away. He dropped his arms, becoming limp in Ciaran's hold.

Ciaran pushed Shannon in front of him and peered into his face. "Shannon?"

In a flat voice, Shannon said, "Yes, I have to leave now." Still, there was nothing. A flash broke through the gloom inside the house, followed by a low rumbling. It barely registered.

Ciaran screwed his face up and darted his gaze all over Shannon. "Listen, I still have some money from our trip. Let me get it for you." Ciaran trotted off into the kitchen, opened a small jar and pulled out a wad of notes. As he came back, he held them out. "Here." Tears welled up in his eyes.

Shannon stared beyond Ciaran in a daze.

Furrowing his brows, Ciaran studied Shannon, then stuffed the money into his front pocket. "Shannon, please tell me you'll be all right." Tears rolled down his already wet cheeks.

"I'll be all right." Shannon stared away from him.

Ciaran grabbed his arms and shook him. "Look at me."

Shannon slowly shifted his gaze to him. "I'll always love you, Ciaran."

Creasing his forehead, Ciaran dropped his mouth open. He yanked him back into his arms, clutching at his tall, but slender, frame once again. "Oh, God, Shannon, don't say that. Don't make it sound like I'll never see you again," he said, through choked sobs.

Shannon stood limply inside Ciaran's arms, still in a daze. "But you won't. I can never come back here."

"I'll come to Dublin. I'll visit." Ciaran buried his face in Shannon's shoulder, fisting Shannon's shirt in his hands.

"Maybe so, but we won't be together. It'll never be the same. You'll soon forget about me anyways," Shannon said, flatly. *I am dead inside.*

"How can you say that? I'll never forget you. I'll never stop loving you. I'll come to Dublin. I'll see you. We can be together then." Ciaran clung to him, rubbing his cheek on Shannon's shoulder.

Another bolt of lightning lit the house and thunder rumbled the eaves in the roof.

Ciaran flinched.

Shannon freed a faint chuckle. The haze faded from his mind. *This is what has to be. Ciaran can still have a normal life. It's better if we never see each other again.* "No, you won't. After I leave, you need to find a nice girl. You need to get married, run the farm, help your da. Do all those things you were always supposed to do. It's okay, Ciaran. I understand. If I could be normal, I'd do those things, too. But, I'm not." He shoved Ciaran away and strode to the door, hanging his head. He knew what must be done.

After running to him, Ciaran fell at his feet, snatching at Shannon's dark trousers. "No, it can't be. Don't say those things. Promise me you'll wait. Promise me you'll write. I won't be with anyone else. I won't marry. I won't..." Ciaran broke down in heavy sobs.

Shannon pried Ciaran's fingers loose from his trouser legs and opened the door. He stepped out into the storm and closed the door behind him, then strode from the house.

Ciaran called out to him. "Shannon Sullivan, don't you dare leave me like this. Don't you dare! I will not love anyone else. There will only be you...always be you..." Sobs filled the air, then grew softer.

I can't stop. I can't go back. It's over. Shannon walked on.

SHANNON TRUDGED on along the main road, soaked and shivering, for what must have been hours. Many horse-drawn carriages and motor cars stopped, offering to give him a lift, but he denied them. He just couldn't bring himself to be among people quite yet. His self-inflicted punishment wasn't over. As long as his body hurt physically, it masked the emotional pain, keeping him from feeling the raw ache in his heart. So, on he went until the road and forest around him darkened, the rain stopped, and his legs screamed for relief. He stopped and sat down on the side of the road, cross-legged, and waited for the next offer.

After a few minutes, the squeaky wheels of an old, horse-drawn cart rang in his ears as it pulled up and stopped beside him. He looked up. His heart jumped. Was it Ciaran? No, there were two of them. He squinted. He didn't recognize them in the darkness. He could only guess at who they were, and he was too heartbroken to care.

"Shannon Sullivan? Is that you?" The voice mocked him.

Staring off into darkness, Shannon wrapped his arms around his legs. Whoever this was, it wasn't good.

A brown-haired young man in a white shirt climbed off the cart and stepped toward him. He bent over, getting a closer view. "All alone, aye? And all bloody wet, for Christ sakes." He waved at the other young man still in the cart. "Hey, come here and look at this." He bent over him again. "Looks like a cat got your tongue, aye, teacher's pet?"

Shannon winced. They knew his old, familiar nickname. A host of old memories flooded his mind of sneers and cruel teasing. Of things children did to each other only when they thought no one could see, when they thought they couldn't be caught.

The other young man got off the cart and walked over to him. This young man also had brown hair, but his shirt was dark. It was the only distinguishing feature he had to tell them apart.

"Yep, it's the teacher's pet, all right."

The young man in the white shirt kicked at him, hitting his thigh.

Pain shot up Shannon's leg. He flinched, but remained still and quiet. It's not like he cared to fight back anymore. There was nothing to fight for.

"What's the matter with you then? You don't have that bloody knife on you tonight, do you?" the young man in the white shirt asked.

Shannon thought back. He hadn't carried his hunting knife in at least a year. He'd scared enough bullies off he'd didn't think he needed it anymore. No matter, whatever they did to him now didn't really matter. If they killed him at least he'd be spared the agony of living without his Ciaran. *It will be a blessing, really.*

The young men circled him like flying vultures preparing to land on carrion. "What shall we do with him?" the young man in the dark shirt asked.

"Let's have a go at him."

"Yeah, okay. He must be bloody pissed anyway."

The young man with the white shirt punched him on the cheek, knocking him sideways onto the road.

The other young man kicked at his limp body over and over, grunting each time. His friend joined him, pummeling him with malice and evil snickers.

Sharp pains pierced his back, his sides, his buttocks. He coiled up, groaning, and gasping in agony as they assaulted him, covering his face as best he could with his forearms. A blinding light flashed behind his eyes and darkness enveloped him. The pain was gone.

CHAPTER TWENTY
CIARAN

Ciaran dragged a chair from the kitchen table over to the window and sat down, then searched the grounds outside the house. He needed to be ready when either his father or Father Brennan pulled up to his house. Only the glow from an oil lamp on the table lit the room. He blinked and a tear meandered down his cheek. Seems he couldn't make himself stop crying. *Oh God, Shannon is gone.* It didn't seem real, didn't seem possible. Shannon was always there. Pain tore his heart in two. He clutched at his shirt over his heart as if it could ease it, somehow.

He sniffled and wiped his face. He'd had to stay. He had to make sure his father didn't give in to his drinking. *Shannon said he understood, but I don't think he really did. Why else would he tell me to find someone else? Like it was an option?* He shook his head, his vision clouding with fresh tears. *It hurt so badly to hear him say those things, to hear him give up on us like he did. Why can't he be happy with visits and letters? He seemed so strange before he left, like his spirit had just drained away.*

Ciaran scanned over the dark yard. *At least the rain stopped.*

Shannon, wherever he is, should be inside someplace warm and dry by now. Maybe he made it back to our inn?

As the night droned on, he grew drowsy, barely able to keep his eyes open. As his head dropped forward, he dozed off.

The whinny of a horse cut through the silence.

Ciaran bolted up in his seat, then rubbed his eyes and peered out into the darkness outside the house.

The cart and horse were there, his father climbing down from the seat.

Ciaran jumped up from his chair and dashed outside. "Da," he called out, running.

Sighing, Mr. O'Kelly frowned at him. He went through the motions of unfastening the horse from the cart and guided it into the barn.

Ciaran stopped next to his father and fell into step beside him.

His father gave him a stern glance, the one he'd use when he was about to be punished. In a low and firm voice, he said, "Ciaran, wait in the house for me."

"B-but—"

"Do it."

As Ciaran hung his head, he strode back into the house. Something wasn't right. Did Father Brennan speak to him already? *Does my Da know?* Once inside, he dragged the chair by the window back to the table and took a seat.

After stomping through the door, his father glanced at him, and slammed the door shut.

Ciaran startled. Da was *never* angry enough to do something like that.

As his father glared at him, nostrils flaring, he came to the table and took a seat across from him. "Bloody hell, Ciaran, what have you done?" he snarled.

Ciaran flinched, then opened his mouth to speak.

"I don't want to hear it. Father Brennan told me enough. Have you no idea how bloody awful it is to...I can't even say it. It's bloody disgusting. To think a son of mine could—could—with his best friend? Why would you do that? You're not queer, are you?" His father pounded his fist on the table, making it shake.

Ciaran's face flushed and his chest squeezed, his heart pounding. He'd never given thought to what his father would think about what he was doing with Shannon. *How can I ever explain it? Am I queer?* He hung his mouth open, staring at his father.

Mr. O'Kelly's eyes became glossy.

Pain rippled through Ciaran's heart. His breath hitched. *I'm to blame for Da's sorrow now. I'm a disappointment.* He hung his head and wept, tears dripping down into his lap.

"I'm sorry, son." His father got up and ducked into a seat next to him, then wrapped an arm around his shoulders and drew him to his wide chest.

Ciaran buried his face in his father's shoulder. *I don't understand anything anymore. It's all too confusing.* He just needed the comfort his father gave him for the moment. Soon though, his tears stopped.

His father released him and they both sat back.

Steeling a peek at his father, Ciaran said, "Da? I-I don't know if-if I'm queer. I just know that I, well, I love Shannon, so much. And he's gone, Da." His vision blurred. *Will I ever stop crying?*

His father wrinkled his brows and pressed his lips together. "I suppose it was bound to happen, you being so bloody close to Shannon and all." He sighed. "Funny, Iona always said it didn't happen that way. She always said her kind were born like that, interested in the same sex."

"Iona? Her kind? You know about her? About her female

lover?" He lifted his brows. He had no idea his father would know anything about her sexuality.

His father gave him a harsh glance. "Of course, I bloody well know about her. She was your mother's sister. We spent quite a bit of time together, all of us, in Dublin, before you were born." He tapped his head with his index finger. "You don't know it, but your mother and I were very modern thinkers." He sucked in a breath. "She told you about Sinead?"

Ciaran searched his father's face. He needed to say something, but no words would come. "Y-yes."

Shaking his head, his father lowered it. "Oh." He glanced at him and freed a long breath. "Truthfully, I blame myself. I didn't want to believe it when I saw you two sitting by the fire and all the other things."

Ciaran gasped. So, Da *had* noticed what went on.

"Where is Shannon now?" His father narrowed his eyes.

Ciaran gazed at him, taking him all in. He saw his father in a completely different way now. "H-he's gone. He just up and walked away in the middle of the storm. Oh, Da, he said Father Brennan was going to kill him. He said he was going back to Dublin to be with Aunt Iona."

"Father Brennan threatened his life?" His father scowled and clenched his jaw.

Ciaran leaned forward. He could tell him everything now. "Yes, Shannon said he showed him an unmarked grave where Mr. Flannigan was buried."

"Good God. Listen to me, Ciaran." His father grabbed his hands in his own. "You need to go, too. I want you to find Shannon. I want you to go to your aunt's in Dublin as well. You can't stay here, do you understand?"

"But, Da, what about you? I can't leave you." Ciaran furrowed his brows, his heart aching.

"Don't you worry about me. It's you who's in danger here.

They could do all sorts of things to you, including locking you away in jail or the bloody nuthouse."

"What?" Ciaran widened his eyes. In no way did his behavior warrant such treatment. *All I did was fall in love.*

"Listen. I don't want that bloody priest doing something rash. And I couldn't stand seeing you go through what poor Shannon went through all those years." His father shifted in his seat, looking away, then focused on him. "I wasn't going to tell you this yet, but I've been working a deal to sell the farm. That is why I've spent so much time in town." He gave a smug shake of his head.

"You what? You can't sell this farm. What about Ma's grave? How can you leave that?" The room spun for a second around Ciaran. Could he take any more surprises?

His father grumbled. "She's not really there, Ciaran. She's in here." He pointed to his heart. "This is where she still lives on. And I'll always have that with me."

Tears stung Ciaran's eyes and he blinked them back. "S-so what shall I do?" A heaviness fell on his heart. He'd have to leave his father, his town, his whole life behind.

His father looked down for a moment as if in deep thought, pursing his lips, then gazed into his eyes. "Here's what you'll do. At first sunrise, I want you to take the cart and horse—"

"But, Da—"

"No, listen. I want you to take the cart and horse and get to Dublin as fast as you can. You can take the rest of the money in the jar. I'll send another telegram to Iona, so she'll be expecting you. Look for Shannon on the way. I'm sure he can't have got far. I'll talk to his parents, too." His father looked him over as if assessing him.

"I gave the money to Shannon. He didn't take anything with him." His heart pinched. *Why did damn Shannon have to run off like that? Maybe if I leave now, I can find him.* His heart swelled with hope. They could be together, all of them. "I should go now, I'll just get the horse and ride all night until I get to the inn we stayed at. I'm sure he'll be there."

"No, it's too dangerous to be out there alone at night. Are you forgetting about the Black and Tans?"

"But—"

"Absolutely not. You'll get some sleep and leave in the morning. I won't hear another word about it."

"What about Shannon? He's all alone." Ciaran huffed, heat filling his chest. He wanted a say in the plans. He wouldn't be able to sleep anyway.

"Shannon can take care of himself," his father said, in a gruff tone.

"And I can't?" Ciaran shouted.

"No, you can't. I won't have you out on the road in the middle of the night. And now you have no money. I'll have to ask Shannon's parents for some before you go. Oh, what a mess this is." His father sat back and raked a hand through his thin hair. "Just go to bed for now. As soon as the sun comes up, we'll get started."

Ciaran sighed. He had to do as his father wished. But, his father knew best and was on their side. He rose from his seat, leaned over, and gave him a quick hug. "Goodnight, Da."

"Goodnight, son. I love you."

CIARAN FLUTTERED his eyes open to the first glow of morning illuminating his window. He'd only dozed off a few times all night, restless as he was. He threw the covers off and jumped out of bed, then pulled his clothes on, grabbed his already packed suitcase and sped out of his bedroom. He stopped at his father's door and rapped on it. "Da, you up?"

Grumbling and rustling came through from the other side.

"I'll get the cart readied while you go to the Sullivans'." Ciaran sighed. He absolutely did not want to face Shannon's parents after what had occurred. He was at least partially responsible for what had happened to their son. It would just be easier to let the parents handle all the details anyway.

He strode off through the house and out of the door. Thoughts of Shannon, finding him, holding him, kissing him, flooded his mind. *How I miss the bastard already.* He strode to the barn. A mist from last night's rain hung in the air. It looked like a different world— cobblestone walls glistening, leaves wet and dripping, muddy puddles below his feet.

He patted the horse on a white patch on her head. "Morning, Missy. You and I are off on another adventure." He bridled the horse and led her to the cart, still waiting where his father left it last night. As he neared the cart, his father left the house, walking at a brisk pace across the open area between their house and barn, onto the path leading to the Sullivan house.

He let a soft grin quirk his lips. He'd go and find Shannon. Everything would be all right. They'd find work somehow, live with his aunt and make love anytime they wanted. He'd planned it all out in his head last night when he should have been sleeping. It would be perfect. He fastened the horse to the cart and packed all the items he needed.

As Ciaran threw the last item into the cart, he caught his father in his periphery.

His father trudged down the path, furrowing his brows, thinning his lips, his shoes dripping with mud, and he held a suitcase.

Ciaran strode to him. "Da? How'd it go? Did you get some money?"

Stopping, his father looked at him and sighed. "It didn't go too well. They're pretty bloody upset. Shannon's mother especially. They did give me some money." He held a few notes out to him.

Ciaran took the notes and stuffed them in his front pocket.

"And his ma packed his things for you to take to him. They want you boys to write when you get there. I'd like you to send me a telegram. I have to know you're safe, son." His father flung the suitcase into the cart and gave him a fierce hug.

Ciaran's eyes blurred with tears. He sniffed them away. "I'll miss you, Da." His voice wavered.

"I'll miss you, too. And who knows? Maybe I'll be out there quicker than you think."

Ciaran released his father and searched his face. "You mean you'll come to Dublin, too? After you sell the farm?"

His father smiled, the first real smile since his mother died. "Of course, what else would I do? Definitely not staying around here."

Ciaran gave him another big hug, patting him on the back.

"You best be on your way now, son." His father pushed him away. "Go and find that boy you bloody love so much." Grinning, he patted his arm.

Ciaran's heart jolted and he stared at his father. "Wh-what?"

"You heard me, go on now." His father waved his hand at him. "I'll not say it again. It was strange enough the first time."

Ciaran stumbled as he walked to the side of the cart. He giggled to himself. Never in a million years did he ever think his father was so forward thinking. As he climbed up onto the bench seat, he stole a few quick glances at his father, then flicked the reins once and the cart lurched forward.

His father waved from the front stoop. Ciaran was on the road again.

Ciaran trotted the horse for a time in his haste to get to Shannon, but he was still only part way to the next town. With the excitement worn off, he grew tired and hungry.

He pulled back on the reins, making the horse whinny to a stop. He jumped to the back and rummaged through his crate for the bread he'd packed. He had to get something in his stomach. He grabbed the whole loaf, sat up, tore off a piece and stuffed it into his mouth.

While he chewed, he scanned his surroundings. An unusual quiet and peacefulness blanketed the road. Did the storm scare everyone off? The sun rose just over the trees in a cloudless sky, casting beams through the fine mist. Looking ahead of him, a dark mound caught his eye. *What the hell is that?* He let out a soft chuckle. *Maybe someone lost a sack of potatoes along the roadside.*

He continued eating, washing his food down with a little cold tea, then climbed back into the driver's seat. Slapping the reins on the horse's back, he started off again. As he neared the dark mound, the shape became clearer.

As he slowed the horse, his gaze caught on black boots and white skin underneath black hair. He yanked the reins back, stopping the horse. *No, it can't be.* Visions of his mother flooded his mind, lying cold and dead in their field, her body contorted in ways not seen in the living. He gasped and held his breath, paralyzed for a moment, staring at the body. "No, no, no, no…"

He shrieked, "Shannon!" He jumped from the cart and his feet flew over the ground to Shannon, lying still in the wet grass. "Shannon, oh God, oh God, Shannon, please, please, don't be dead, don't be dead," he said under his breath.

Picking him up, he yanked him to his chest, holding him there, rocking. *Don't look at his face. Don't look at his eyes. What if…what if they're like Ma's?* He rocked Shannon's lifeless body in his arms. He wouldn't cry. If he did, it meant his best friend and lover was dead and gone forever.

"Uh..."

What's that? It was faint, but he heard it. Heat radiated into Ciaran's body from Shannon's. *Shannon is alive—he's alive!* He dropped him low enough to peer into his face.

A beet red hue flushed Shannon's cheeks.

Ciaran brushed his hand over Shannon's face. It was clammy. Shannon had a fever, a bad one. He looked him over further. *How the hell did he end up on the side of the road?* Had he just collapsed from exhaustion? He skimmed the back of Shannon's head. A huge knot swelled under his hair. He pulled his hand away and looked at it. Dark, coagulated blood gelled between his fingers. "Who did this to you, Shannon?"

He picked him up with an arm under his chest and an arm under his knees, then brought him to the cart and heaved his body up and over the edge.

Shannon's body landed with a thud.

He winced. Maybe he should have been more careful. *Oh well, at least Shannon is alive.* He jumped into the back and ripped Shannon's wet clothes off. He needed to get him warm and dry as quickly as he could. He felt a lump in the front pocket of Shannon's trousers. He reached in and fished out the wad of money he'd given him. He furrowed his brows. Whoever attacked him didn't do it to steal anything from him. Shrugging, he stuffed the money into his own front pocket.

With a gasp, he shifted his gaze to Shannon's lean, naked body, taking in a host of nasty bruises, swelling and welts. *How he loved that body and someone tried to destroy it.* Heat surged through his chest, and he snarled, curling his lips, then stood up straight, raised his face to the sky, fists clenched, and let out a guttural cry, like a beast into the quiet morning. As he ran out of breath, he came to his senses and breathed in deep.

Don't think about it now. Just help Shannon. He crouched and tended to him, rummaging through his suitcase, finding fresh clothes. His touch was gentle and loving as he clothed him, placing a pillow under his head, blankets under and over his body and tucking everything all around him. He leaned forward and placed a lingering kiss on his lips. "I swear to God, Shannon, I'll never let anyone hurt you ever again. No matter what."

Ciaran checked Shannon's breathing, placing his hand by his mouth, and listened for a heartbeat. *All steady for the moment.* He slid into the cart's seat and slapped the reins down hard, three times, on the horse's back. The cart jerked behind Missy as she trotted off.

As Ciaran approached a town, he scanned the buildings. There must be a dispensary around somewhere with a doctor. He pursed his lips. Maybe one of the townspeople would know. He slowed the horse and looked for the nearest person, walking along the narrow street. "Excuse me, might you know where I could find a dispensary?"

A woman with wavy, blonde hair and large, blue eyes turned around. "Of course, just up ahead, take the first left. It's a two-story building made of brick. Can't miss it."

"Thank you, ma'am." He flicked the reins and was off again, taking the directions he was given. He soon found the building the woman had described. He tugged the reins, stopped the cart, and climbed down. He ran to the front entry, opened a heavy wooden door, and stepped inside.

A few people sat in chairs in a hallway, coughing, or silently watching him.

He took a deep inhale to calm his nerves.

A small, frail woman in a white dress, apron and cap came walking down the hallway, looking him up and down. "Can I help you?"

He shifted his feet, unable to hold still. "Yes, I need help, right away. You see, my friend is badly hurt. He's in a cart out front. He's unconscious. Please, get the doctor."

"Oh, I see. I'll get him." She hurried off.

Ciaran strode outside and climbed into the back of the cart to sit next to Shannon, groping under the blankets for his hand. He found it and squeezed tight. "Don't worry, Shannon, the doctor's almost here. You just hang on."

In only a minute or so, a middle-aged man with a white smock covering his shirt and tie, black loafers, and wire-rimmed glasses, hustled out of the front door and up to the side of the cart. He held a small black bag in one hand. "I'm Doctor Delaney. What's all this then?"

"My friend has been hurt. I don't know if I should move him." Ciaran glanced from the doctor to Shannon.

Moving quickly, Doctor Delaney climbed into the cart and crouched next to Shannon. "What happened?"

"Looks like he got beaten up. There's a nasty bump on his head, bruises all over and I think he's got a fever. I think he was left cold and wet on the bloody roadside all night." Ciaran winced. If only he'd been able to leave last night and not this morning.

The doctor opened his bag, pulled out a stethoscope and listened to Shannon's chest. He glanced at Ciaran and moved the stethoscope to Shannon's stomach. "Black and Tans?"

"Don't know, bloody bastards." He spat the words out. Heat surged in his chest, and he clenched his jaw.

Doctor Delaney thumped his fingers on various places of Shannon's body, took his temperature under his armpit and examined his head. He finally focused on Ciaran. "Listen, I'll stitch and bandage his head, but I think he's concussed. He's probably on his way to getting pneumonia as well from exposure. I don't see any fractures. Do you have any idea how long he's been unconscious?"

"No." Ciaran bit at his thumbnail, his pulse quickening. What were all those long words the doctor used? They didn't sound good.

The doctor frowned, placing a gentle hand on Shannon's shoulder.

"Will he be all right?" Ciaran drew deep breaths.

Looking directly into his eyes, Doctor Delaney's words were slow and deliberate. "It all depends on him. Is your friend a fighter?"

Ciaran let a slow smile work over his mouth. "Yeah, he is."

"Then there's a good chance he'll pull through on his own. But he should probably be in hospital. I'm sorry to say the closest one is in Dublin."

"Ah, well, I'm on my way there now. What should I do before we get there?"

"Keep his wound clean, keep him warm and dry and watch for any signs of the fever getting too high. If he starts seizing—"

"What the bloody hell is that? You mean having a fit?" Ciaran's heart pounded in his ears. *Shannon has to be all right, he just has to.*

"If he starts to shake with his eyes rolled back in his head or if he wakes up and then seems very confused, doesn't know where he is, that sort of thing, get him into a cold bath. It'll bring the fever down. Hopefully his lungs won't fill up with fluid."

"What?" Ciaran widened his eyes.

"Just keep his chest elevated, like this." The doctor rearranged the pillows, raising Shannon's chest.

The cart blurred and Ciaran's eyes stung. He fought to keep

the tears at bay while the doctor cleaned, stitched, and bandaged Shannon's head.

"If you're able, make sure to get some water in him, I wouldn't want him to get dehydrated as well." Closing his bag, the doctor stood in the back of the cart, looking down at him. "I'm leaving you with some extra bandages." He held his hand out. Wadded up gauze protruded between his fingers. "Please take care and good luck."

Ciaran took the bandages and let his arm drop. This was like a bad dream. So many things could go wrong.

"Are you okay?" The doctor studied him.

Ciaran took a hard swallow, then peered at the doctor. He had to keep his wits about him. "Yeah, I'll be fine. I just need to get him to Dublin."

"That's right." The doctor nodded once.

Ciaran's heart jolted. *I have to get back on the road now. I've no time to waste.* "Thank you." He rushed to the seat and waited only long enough for the doctor to climb off the cart before slapping the reins on the horse again.

Ciaran drove Missy hard, only slowing or stopping when it was absolutely necessary for her. He ate all the food he'd brought while the cart continued on, glancing back at Shannon for any signs of the shaking the doctor told him of or consciousness. Luckily, there were no Black and Tans on the road. He passed through the town they'd stayed at on their trip in the middle of the afternoon, but didn't stop.

As night closed in, it was increasingly difficult to stay awake. His body swayed and his head bobbed every so often. With darkness all around, only a sliver of moon lit the road. It looked as if it stretched on forever. He scanned around him. They were alone all right. No other travelers would be foolish enough to be out this late. The rolling hills glowed in the faint light and the still air held traces of wildflower scents. He searched the area again. There weren't many trees or much brush to hide behind if he came across a military lorry. But he needed a place to hide. He had to sleep eventually.

His body ached and his eyes closed on him time and again. Finally, he turned the reins hard, making the horse go off the road. Only a few hours' sleep, then he'd be okay to keep going. The cart bumped and shook over rocks and grass, going down a hill. He looked up at the road. This was good, out of sight of the road at least.

He stopped the horse, climbed down, and unfastened her, then led Missy to a nearby stream and waited. "That's right, girl, you drink up now. We still have a ways to go and I'll need you strong." When the horse finished, he brought her back to the cart, tossed her some hay from the back and tied her up.

He jumped into the back of the cart and lay down next to Shannon, then stroked his cheek and fingered the bandage wrapped around his head. "God, Shannon, don't you bloody die on me, you hear? I couldn't take it. I love you too much."

Shannon's brows tensed and his legs twitched, then he quieted again. His breathing stayed slow and steady.

Sitting up, Ciaran grabbed a canteen flask he'd packed. He looked at it, taking in the mottled aluminum sides. Last time he'd used it, he'd been out hunting with his father. It was way before he had any idea how Shannon felt about him, way before his mother had died. The world had seemed so different then, happy even. He'd looked forward to every morning, seeing his ma cooking over the hearth, going to school, and even doing his chores.

He'd had big plans. Smiling, he swirled the water inside the flask. He'd wanted to find Shannon a girl, a girl no less. He let a soft chuckle rumble his chest. He'd always thought if he found one for Shannon, then he'd find one, too, and they could settle down together. It seemed pretty silly now. How could he not know, not see it, Shannon always loved him. His attention drew to Shannon, and he leaned over, opened the flask and carefully dripped water into Shannon's open mouth.

Shannon sputtered and coughed, his chest thrusting upward. His eyelids fluttered, but never opened.

"Come on, luv, you need to drink this now." Ciaran tilted the flask a second time, watching while Shannon's throat dipped, drinking the water. "There you go, that's it." Shannon had to be somewhat conscious now. He screwed the cap on the flask, set it down and lay next to him with his arms and legs wrapped around him and his head resting on his chest. He fingered the folds in the blanket. "There now, just a few hours' sleep is all we need. Then we'll head into Dublin and Iona will show us where the hospital is. You'll be fine, Shannon. I'll make sure of it. Don't you worry now." He dozed off.

CHAPTER TWENTY-ONE
CIARAN

Something poked Ciaran between the shoulders, rocking him forward. He opened his eyes into darkness. The poke came harder, insistent.

"Bloody mick, get up will you?"

Ciaran whirled around and heaved up to sitting. He wiped at his eyes and looked around him. He counted five men, all in dark uniforms. One stood at the side of the cart, the moon glinting off the metal of the rifle. It was probably what they'd used to wake him. It pointed at him still.

"Put your hands where I can see them," the man with the rifle said.

Ciaran raised his hands over his head, his heart quickening. What else could he do? If he complied, they might leave them be.

"What about your friend there?" The man shifted the rifle to point at Shannon.

"Um, h-he's badly hurt, he can't even hear you." Ciaran shook. The British accents meant they were indeed Black and Tans, or at least British Army.

Another soldier jumped into the back of the cart, crouched down beside Shannon, and shook him. "Ay, this one's almost dead already."

Ciaran flinched. *How dare they touch him.* He held back the urge to lash out at the soldier. He'd wait, for now.

The rifle dipped for a moment, catching his attention.

"So, what you bloody micks been up to, ay? You been messing around the barracks lately? Maybe setting a few traps, trying to kill a few of the RIC?" the rifled soldier asked.

Ciaran shook his head. "N-no, of course not. I'm not involved with any of that. I'm just a farmer taking my friend here to hospital."

The soldier in the cart laughed. "A little bloody late, don't you think?"

Heat flashed inside him. Snarling, he whipped around to the soldier beside Shannon. "Shut your bloody hole, he'll be fine." The rifle plunged into his back, sending a sharp pain through his body, jerking him forward. He turned back around.

"Do not talk to the Queen's army that way or I'll have to shoot just for the fun of it." A wicked grin spread over the lips of the soldier holding the rifle.

The roar of an engine filled the night, and two lights came toward them from the direction of the stream. The soldier with the rifle hurried to stand in line with the others while they straightened themselves, holding their arms in salute. The soldier in the cart stood and did the same.

Ciaran took in the outline of the vehicle as it approached, the heavy armor and gun turret over the seating area. His breath caught. *A British Army, armored Rolls Royce.*

The vehicle stopped and a man got out and strode closer.

Ciaran eyed them all. By the way the soldiers behaved, he assumed the new one was an officer.

"What's all this?" the officer asked.

The man with the rifle said, "Micks, sir."

"Let's not use that sort of language around the natives, shall we?" The officer pulled his gloves off and slapped them to his hand. He walked a slow, deliberate circle around his men, glancing at Ciaran. "Now then. Are these the men we're looking for?"

"Not sure, sir," the soldier in the cart said.

"Well, do they fit the descriptions you've been given?" The officer asked.

"No, sir," the main with the rifle said.

"Then let's be off. We have work to do." The officer pursed his lips.

"What about the micks, sir?" The man with the rifle threw Ciaran a glare.

The officer strode up to Ciaran and looked him up and down. His gaze shifted to Shannon, lying haphazardly in the cart. "Hmmm, so sad, isn't it, to lose a friend like that."

Ciaran swallowed, then in a low and clear voice, he said, "He's not gone."

The officer waved his hand. "Leave now or I'll have you arrested for trespassing."

Trespassing? They're the trespassers. This is Ireland not Britain. Ciaran gritted his teeth. He wanted to say something nasty. He glanced at Shannon. Better not, it would be too risky.

The soldiers moved off, down the hillside, still searching for whomever set traps for them at their barracks.

Ciaran went to Shannon and confirmed he still breathed, and his heart was still beating. Tenderly, he straightened his blankets and checked his bandage. "Don't listen to them, Shannon. You'll be just fine. They left us alone and soon we'll be in Dublin." He stood and jumped out of the cart.

He fastened Missy up to the cart. "Bloody awful bastards," he mumbled. He took a sharp inhale. *Oh shite, I escaped with my horse, my cart and all of our money.* He spread a wide smile across his face. It would be all right.

A QUIET DARKNESS enveloped the streets of Dublin, so unlike the first time Ciaran had come through here. Of course, the sun had yet to come up and the street lamps were already out. He looked ahead to the boulevard. The stone buildings and cathedrals looked ominous in the darkness. The moon created a dull glow on their surfaces. The shops were all closed and shuttered as if afraid of the dark. The only sounds in the still, cool air were the creaking of the cart and the clops of Missy's hooves on the cobblestones.

But it was all right. He was almost there, and Shannon was still breathing. The air was cold enough for him to see a faint cloud of breath puff above Shannon's mouth every time he exhaled, a comforting sight.

He turned the horse down Iona's street, scanning the buildings. *Where is her bloody pub?* The street seemed miles longer than the last time he'd been here. His gaze snagged the sign above the pub's front door. *Finally.* His heart thrummed. He flicked the reins hard, making Missy trot. As he approached the pub, he looked up at a flicker of light from an upstairs window. *That's Iona's bedroom.* He pulled back hard on the reins and Missy came to a stop. The pub door creaked open while he jumped from the seat of the cart and into the back.

Iona, in her tattered white robe and slippers, walked out to the cart with an oil lamp in her hand. "Ciaran, dear, didn't you find Shannon?"

Ciaran hesitated at Shannon's side, about to tend to him. He turned to her, his vision blurring as he faced her. "He's here.

He's bloody hurt. Beaten up, I don't know by who. But we have to get him to hospital, he—"

"What? Oh my God, let me see him." She shoved the oil lamp at him in her haste to get to Shannon, then jumped into the cart. She knelt beside him, roaming her hands over him, checking him.

"The doctor said he is con, concus, I don't bloody well know." Relief washed over him. She'd know what to do.

"A concussion? He has a bloody awful fever, too. Let's get him into the bath. I'll need you to carry him upstairs while I get a block of ice from the pub." She thinned her lips.

"But the doctor said he needs to go to hospital." Ciaran came forward and leaned on the side of the cart, watching her prodding, and inspecting his Shannon.

She flashed her eyes at him. "No. People only go to hospital to die, and I am not letting this poor boy die."

"But the—"

"I said no, Ciaran. Get over here and take him upstairs. We need to hurry." She climbed down and glared at him. "Do as I say."

His heart pinched. She was scaring him. Was Shannon really that badly off? He stumbled over himself getting to the back of the cart, then unlatched the back panel, dropped it, and pulled Shannon down by his feet, sliding on blankets. While he positioned Shannon to be carried, his brows tensed, and mumbled words left his lips.

Ciaran drew him close, touching cheek to cheek for a moment. "It's all right, you'll be just fine. It's only a little bath. Then we'll tuck you into bed, right next to me. I'll be right with you, the whole time." He grunted as he picked up Shannon and brought him inside and up the stairs.

AUNT IONA HELD Shannon's ankles while Ciaran held him by the shoulders. "One, two, three, in you go." she said, swinging Shannon's naked body over the edge of the bathtub and into water with floating chunks of ice.

Shannon's body jerked as soon as they lowered him in. Teeth chattering, fists clenching, his eyes fluttered open for a second, dazed, and closed again.

She stood next to the tub and looked Shannon over. "Ah Jaysus, Ciaran. They sure did a job on him, didn't they? I wonder who did it."

Ciaran frowned, his heart aching. It was terrible seeing Shannon's bruised body shiver and shake in the cold water. "I don't know, but if I ever find out, I'll bloody kill them."

"Oh, you won't neither. You do that and you'll end up in jail. Just let it be." She placed her hands on her hips, studying him.

He peered at her. "Iona? Are you sure he shouldn't be in hospital?"

"Damn sure. All he needs is right here. Can't you see how he responds whenever you speak?"

"What?" He lifted his brows.

She pointed to Shannon's face. "See that? Every time you speak, he responds. He can hear you."

"No..." He watched, dropping his mouth open, as Shannon's brow clearly twitched with the sound of his voice.

"If you want him to get better, I suggest you get down there and talk to him. Tell him how you feel about him. He needs to hear it, now more than ever." She placed her hand on his forearm for a moment.

Ciaran dropped down to crouch next to the tub, taking Shannon's cold hand in his own. "I love you, Shannon. Come back to me, please, I need you."

Shannon winced. His chattering mouth moved as if trying to form words.

She left the room.

Ciaran set his forehead against Shannon's. "You have to come back. There's so much we have to do. W-we need to go and see the cathedrals. We need to see what's in all those shops. We have to make love again and again." His breath hitched.

Shannon's hand squeezed his.

His vision clouded. He blinked and tears splashed tiny drops into the frigid water below.

After a few minutes, Aunt Iona walked into the bathroom. "Time for you two to get to bed."

He swiped the wetness from his cheeks with the back of his hand and stood up, nodding.

CIARAN LAY NEXT TO SHANNON, completely bare, entwined in his limbs as best he could. Shannon's deep breaths and steady heartbeat filled his ears. A faint light came in through the guest room window. Morning came to Dublin. The bustle of motor cars, the clop of an occasional horse and hushed voices filled the air outside the open window.

A warm breeze blew over Ciaran, rustling Shannon's dark hair. He caressed Shannon's cheek with his fingers. A wave of fatigue swept over him, then his heart lurched. He was too afraid to close his eyes, too afraid to wake and find Shannon's breathing had stopped, his heart no longer beating.

I'll talk to Shannon instead. Keep him alive with my words. "Shannon, you remember the first time you kissed me? You were so scared, standing outside that hotel room. But all I wanted was you. Sure, I was a little confused. But deep down, I knew you were what I wanted."

Shannon turned his head toward him.

"I don't know exactly when I fell in love with you, but I bet it was right here in this room next to that silly lampshade Aunt Iona insists on keeping here. Sure, I always loved you, but I fell *in* love with you here. I've never been in love before. Did you know that? Never really knew what it felt like. But you showed me, Shannon, you...showed...me..." His eyes closed.

"CIARAN, wake up, please, we have to go. Father Brennan, he knows. He knows."

Tight hands shook Ciaran's shoulders. He fluttered his eyes open, then thrust up to sitting. *Shannon is awake.* He shook his head. *Is it real?*

Shannon looked toward him, sitting up in bed, eyes unfocused.

Ciaran peered at him. *Does he even see me?*

Beads of sweat ran down Shannon's pale face and mottled chest. His eyes were wide. His gaze darted around the room. "We have to leave now, Ciaran!"

"What? Shannon, you're awake." Ciaran drew him into his chest.

Shannon shoved him away. "Ciaran, listen to me, we have to go, now."

He stroked Shannon's arm. How could he calm him? "No, Shannon, we already left. We're at Iona's. We're in Dublin. It's all over, you're safe now."

Shannon knit his brows, then his eyes began to focus. "But we...I had to..."

"We're safe. Look around you. We're in Iona's house. We're

not in Drimnagh. See? There's the bloody feather lamp." Ciaran pointed to the red lamp on the nightstand.

As Shannon raised his hands to rub his temples, he hunched over. "Ah! It bloody hurts, Ciaran, my head. It hurts so bad." He rocked.

Ciaran wrapped his arms around Shannon's shoulders and pulled him into his chest. "Hush, I know, luv. Lie down and rest some more. I'll see if my aunt has something." He helped him lie down.

Panting, Shannon curled into a tight ball on his side.

Ciaran winced. *God, how he must hurt.* He climbed out of bed and grabbed his tan trousers, bunched up on the floor, then stepped into them, pulled them up and fastened them. He raked a hand through his hair while he made his way into the main room of the flat.

Aunt Iona ran toward him, dark trousers and a linen shirt clinging to her thin frame. "Ciaran, was that Shannon I heard?"

"Yeah. He's hurting pretty bad." Ciaran pursed his lips. This was terrible. Shannon looked so awful.

"I'll bet. Let me get some morphine. Hopefully he can take that now." She brushed by him and headed for the bathroom.

"Morphine? You have that?" He followed her, watching while she rummaged through her mirrored medicine cabinet.

She pulled a small glass bottle down, examined it and handed it to him. "Yes, I have morphine. It's a little old, but it should still work. Here you go. I'll get some water." She hurried off again.

He trudged into the guestroom, morphine bottle in hand, then looked Shannon over, his heart aching.

Trembling, Shannon curled up and panted, holding his head.

Ciaran stepped to the bed and sat on the edge. "Here, I'll need you to take this."

As Shannon rolled over, he cried out and returned to his original position.

Aunt Iona appeared in the doorway with a glass of water. She set it on the nightstand. "Oh, poor dear. Let me help you turn him."

Ciaran and his aunt both knelt down on the bed. They grabbed Shannon's body and rolled him onto his back.

Shannon tried to stay curled while they rolled him, taking sheets and bedding with him. "It hurts," he said, grimacing.

"Please, take this medicine. It'll make you feel better." Ciaran winced, watching Shannon.

Shannon carefully unraveled his body and sat up, groaning.

She held out the glass to Shannon.

Slowly, shakily, Shannon grasped the glass from her hand. He wrinkled his brows and thinned his lips, peeking at Ciaran.

Glancing at his aunt, Ciaran opened the bottle. Would this really work?

She nodded once. "Just give him one. If he needs more, we can always give him another."

Ciaran handed one small, white tablet to Shannon.

Shannon threw the tablet into his mouth, then tilted his head back and put the glass to his lips, taking long gulps of water. He finished and focused on Iona. "Can I please have more water?"

"Course you can, luv. I'll be right back." She took the glass from Shannon and left the room.

What should I say or do with him now? Ciaran scanned around the room, his pulse quickening. A warm hand rested on his arm. His attention drew to Shannon.

"Stay with me," Shannon said with tears brimming in his eyes.

"Of course, I will. I won't let you out of my sight, seeing as how every time I do you bloody well get yourself into a load of trouble." Ciaran forced a faint chuckle. Would that make him feel better?

Shannon spread a faint smile over his lips.

It worked. Ciaran offered him a grin, then leaned in and placed a lingering kiss on his lips.

Aunt Iona returned with a larger, water-filled glass. She stopped in the doorway. "Oh my, already doing that sort of thing?" Her eyes twinkled. She stepped to them and handed Shannon the water.

Shannon grabbed the glass and gulped it all down without stopping for a breath.

"Good Lord, you were thirsty, weren't you?" she said. "Listen, I've got a pot of stew on the stove. Ciaran, I know you've got to be starved. How about you, Shannon?"

Shannon shook his head. "I feel a little sick."

"All right then. Shannon, you rest some more while Ciaran and I have some supper," she said.

Ciaran peered at Shannon. "Um, can I eat in here, with him? I don't want to leave him just yet."

She cocked her head. "Yeah, sure, luv." She took the empty glass from Shannon and walked out of the room.

Returning his focus to Shannon, Ciaran said, "See? I'll stay right here. You just lie down and rest."

Shannon nodded.

Ciaran helped him under the covers. As he finished tucking him in, he leaned over, his hands resting on Shannon's chest. "I love you, Shannon Sullivan, and everything's going to be just fine."

Tears filled Shannon's eyes. He blinked and one rolled down the side of his face. He grasped Ciaran's hand and squeezed.

Ciaran wiped Shannon's tear away with his thumb. "Get some rest."

Shannon closed his eyes and let a faint, contented smile grace his lips.

After a few minutes, Aunt Iona returned with a wooden tray. Two bowls of stew, spoons, napkins and two cups of tea were set on top of it. She sat down next to him at the edge of the bed, glancing at Shannon. "Sleeping again?"

"Yeah."

She placed the tray on the floor in front of them and handed Ciaran a bowl of stew, spoon, and napkin. She took her own meal from the tray and straightened. "He'll be feeling no pain anyway, soon as that pill starts working." She sighed. "So that's a good sign, aye?"

"What's a good sign? He looked so bloody awful." He blew over the stew in his spoon.

"Sure, he did. But he woke up. That's a good sign. Looks like his fever broke, too. He's through the worst of it." She put a spoonful of stew into her mouth.

He stopped eating for a moment and gazed at her. "He didn't know where he was. I don't think he remembers what happened to him."

She nodded slowly, chewing. "Yeah, well, that's a bloody nasty bump on his head. Probably a good thing if he never remembers, seeing as how he might have been raped."

"Raped? You don't really—"

"Happens more than you think. Especially with boys like him." She stirred the stew in her bowl.

"What do you mean, boys like him?" He dropped his spoon into his bowl, staring at her.

"He's queer, Ciaran. Nothing wrong with it, you know. I just knew it the moment I saw him. Of course, I'm used to it, being part of the queer community myself. Maybe I just pick up on it easier than most. But he has a way about him, you know, sort of feminine." She chuckled. "Although he sure likes to hide it. He's such a sweet boy, you couldn't have found any better." She brought her filled spoon up to her mouth.

Heat rushed his cheeks. How strange it was, having this kind of conversation about Shannon with his aunt. He furrowed his brows, thinking over what she said while he ate. Sure, Shannon always seemed different to him, but he never really thought of him as feminine. Was that what attracted Mr. Flannigan to him in the first place? "You're right, I couldn't have found any better."

She lifted her brows. "What?"

He smiled. "I said, you're right. I couldn't have found any better."

CHAPTER
TWENTY-TWO
SHANNON

Shannon woke with a start, on his back, his head pounding. At least his head didn't hurt as badly as the last time he'd opened his eyes. He scanned his surroundings. *Where am I exactly?* It looked vaguely familiar, but he couldn't quite place where he'd seen these furnishings before. He tried to think back on what happened. Images flashed through his foggy head of Ciaran telling him he had to stay in Drimnagh for his father.

He moved his limbs. Sharp pain bolted through his body. He flinched, then touched the bandage around his forehead. Why on Earth was his head wrapped up? He gazed down. Ciaran's blond head lay across his chest. He smiled. *If this is a dream, I don't ever want to wake up.*

Stirring, Ciaran opened his eyes part way. He startled, widening his gaze, and raising his head. "Shannon, you're awake? And you're not in pain?"

"Um, not too much." Shannon knit his brows. "What happened? Where are we? Where is your da? Why do I have—"

"Bloody hell, Shannon, one question at a time, all right?" Ciaran propped on an elbow and gazed at him.

Shannon frowned, then curled his lips in a slow smile. Ciaran had told him some very romantic things. "So, you want to take me to the cathedrals and go to the shops, do you?"

Blushing, Ciaran lowered his gaze and grinned. "You did hear me."

"I guess so. It's all a bloody jumble though. The last thing I really remember is being at your house." Pain stabbed his heart. How destitute he'd been. "It rained, didn't it?"

"Yeah, it rained. It down poured and stormed even, and you went off in it, bloody left me. But I understand, you had to. Next thing I know, my da is telling me how he knows about us."

Shannon gasped, his heart pinching. "He knows?" He dropped his mouth open.

Ciaran brushed a strand of hair from his bandage. "It's okay. I know you won't believe this, but he actually doesn't mind, too much anyway. It's a long story."

Shannon fisted the bedcovers. His pulse thrummed. It didn't matter what Ciaran told him. How would he ever face Mr. O'Kelly again?

"My da spoke to your parents, too."

Shannon winced. "Oh, no."

"Yes, well, he said your ma was pretty bloody upset. But they did give us some money and your things." Ciaran nodded to the suitcase resting along the wall. "They want you to write them."

"What on Earth for? I can't believe they'd even care if I was alive now." Shannon looked away. What would he even have to say to his parents? They only told Ciaran's father to have him write to make themselves look good. They'd really disowned him. He knew it.

"Shannon, you're still their son, no matter if you're queer." Ciaran twitched the corners of his mouth.

Shannon threw him a glare. "What did you call me?"

Ciaran's face reddened. He toyed with the dark quilt, then met his gaze. "I said you're queer. You are, aren't you? I mean, you told me you always liked boys and well, Iona said you were."

Heat rushed Shannon's face. "I suppose I am, but you don't have to be so bloody blunt about it."

"I'm sorry. Iona says there's nothing wrong with it," Ciaran said softly.

Shannon snapped his brows together, peering at Ciaran. "We're at Iona's?"

"Yes we are and you're all right now." Ciaran beamed at him.

"Sounds like you and Iona have been talking quite a lot about me while I lay here almost bloody dead." Shannon huffed out a breath. This conversation was unnerving. It was too much after hiding for so long. A thought came to him. "Well, what does that make you then?"

Ciaran shrugged, giving him a wide grin. "I don't know, bloody mad, maybe. Madly in love."

Shannon gave him a playful hug, winced with pain, then pecked him on the cheek. "Please, tell me what happened to me."

Ciaran sighed. "So, my da sent me to find you, which I did, on the roadside, all bloody and beaten up. I took you to a doctor who stitched and bandaged your head." Ciaran pointed to his forehead.

Shannon fingered the bandage, then bit his lip.

"And I brought you here to rest and get well." Ciaran twisted his head toward the window. "And I think it's very early in the morning."

"I'm starving."

Ciaran grinned. "I knew you would be. I'll go and make you some breakfast. I think it's too early even for Iona to be up." He shimmied to the edge of the bed.

Shannon's heart pinched. He seized Ciaran's arm. "No, stay with me a little while longer." He didn't know why, but he needed him beside him right now.

Ciaran leaned over and placed a deep kiss on his lips. "Whatever you want. You sure you don't want some food? You haven't eaten in almost two days. Unbelievable, really, must be a bloody record." Chuckling, he entwined himself around Shannon, resting his head over his bruised chest.

Shannon held tight to him for a few moments. Hunger pangs racked his gut. "Um, maybe I would like some breakfast and to get cleaned up."

Ciaran lifted his head and studied his face. "Really? Cleaned up? You must be all bloody recovered then."

Coyly, Shannon said, "Enough. I think I still need you to take care of me though." Would Ciaran understand his meaning? Even though he still hurt, having him close like this hardened his cock. He leaned over, pulling him up to his face, and gave him a passionate kiss.

"Oh, you are a wicked one, Shannon." Ciaran ran his hand down between Shannon's thighs and brushed his fingers over Shannon's erection. "Really bloody wicked. I'd say you've made a full recovery."

"If you'd be kind enough to get me something to eat first, I'll let you do whatever you want to me." Shannon raked his teeth over his lower lip, desire shivering up his spine.

"Right." Ciaran climbed out of bed, pulled his trousers on, and strode out of the room.

Shannon flinched as he shimmied to the edge of the bed. His whole body hurt. It was like a carriage had run him over.

But he needed to get in the bath. The soothing water would be good for him.

He rose and stepped carefully to his suitcase, then turned it on its side and opened it. After grabbing a pair of trousers, he stood and made his way into the bathroom. It didn't matter if he was naked, no one was around.

After closing the bathroom door, he stepped to the white tub. Vague memories flooded his mind, sending chills through his body. *They put me in an ice bath.* He turned the tap and water flowed, making a tiny whirlpool over the drain. He winced as he leaned further down to close it.

He came up and gazed at his reflection in the small mirror. His face looked paler than usual, his hair matted on his head and dark circles rimmed his eyes. "Lovely," he whispered. He turned around. What was causing so much pain in his back? Gasping, he looked over numerous purplish blotches all over his body. He reached behind him and poked one. A dull pain pierced him. He flinched. "Ah, shite."

Facing the mirror, he unwrapped the bandage on his head. It unwound and fell to the floor. He fingered the stitches over the wound at the back of his head. At least the doctor left his hair alone. *Who did this to me?* He dropped his hand to his side. As he padded to the tub, he struggled to remember something from that night. *Why can I only remember the look on Ciaran's face when I left?* It was no use.

He stepped into the tub and lowered himself into the water, wincing as his back touched the side. He twisted off the tap and settled in, basking in the warm, soothing water.

SHANNON LAY on his side in bed with only the sheets to cover him. His trousers sat discarded on the floor. He looked at the sun streaming in through the window and listened to Ciaran and Iona's hushed voices for ten minutes while Iona prepared breakfast.

With a tray in his hands, Ciaran strolled through the doorway.

Shannon's stomach growled as he sat up.

Stopping next to the bed, Ciaran placed the tray over his lap. "Here you go. Seems Iona was up after all. She just didn't want to disturb us." Ciaran sat on the edge of the bed.

Shannon perused the tray. A huge omelette with beans waited for him on a plate along with a cup of tea. "You have no idea how good this looks," he said, his mouth watering. He dug in.

Smiling, Ciaran rested his hand on Shannon's thigh. "My da is selling the farm."

Shannon flicked his gaze to him, chewing with a full mouth.

"That's what he was doing in town. He was working a deal to sell it. Seems he'll be moving out here as well." Ciaran wrinkled his forehead and pinched his lips.

Shannon gulped his food down and took a quick sip of tea. "What about your ma's grave?"

After a sigh, Ciaran said, "That's what I said. But he's not concerned about that. I suppose we can always visit."

Shannon nodded. He doubted Ciaran would ever go back, the same as he would surely never go back. But he wasn't about to say so. "Sure."

Ciaran traced a soft circle on Shannon's thigh, then skimmed his fingers up to Shannon's groin. He parted his lips, his eyelids hooding.

Almost choking on his food, Shannon said, "Hey, Iona's up now."

"She won't bloody well mind. Besides, you made a deal,

and I brought the food." Ciaran came close and placed soft kisses and bites on his neck.

Shannon slowly closed his eyes, relishing in his touch. "Damn, Ciaran, I thought I'd never feel this again."

Pulling away, Ciaran glared at him. "Why did you tell me to go and find a nice girl and settle down? What sort of a bloody thing was that to say? I'd have visited you, you know. I'd have written."

Shannon dropped his jaw. *Did I really say that? Oh... Yes, I did.* "I uh, well, I just wanted you to have a normal life is all."

"Normal, aye? What is bloody normal anyway? Seems no one in my family has ever been like that. Why would I want to start?" With a wide grin, Ciaran slapped at Shannon's shoulder.

"Ow!" Shannon rubbed where he'd slapped him. "I'm still injured, you know."

"Ah, such a baby you are." Ciaran said.

"Am not."

"Are, too."

"Am—"

"Glad to see you feeling better, Shannon." Iona poked her head in, smiling at them.

"Iona, thank you so much for taking us in and helping me." Tears stung Shannon's eyes. Why he felt like crying all of a sudden, he hadn't a clue. Maybe seeing her made it all real somehow. He was safe and he still had his Ciaran.

"Of course, luv. I told you if you ever needed anything, you could always come to me." She leaned against the doorframe. "I've got to leave for a little while, I trust you two will be all right?"

Ciaran squeezed Shannon's thigh.

Shannon startled. "Yes, I'll be fine." He flashed his eyes at Ciaran.

"See you later then," Ciaran said to her. Ciaran faced him with a mischievous grin playing on his face.

She left.

"Hurry up and eat, will you?" Ciaran gave him a sly grin.

Stuffing food into his mouth, Shannon hungrily devoured every speck of it on the plate, while Ciaran watched. When he finished, Ciaran took the tray from his lap and set it on the floor next to the bed.

Ciaran stood and dropped his trousers to the floor, standing there naked, fixating on Shannon. He climbed over him, straddling him. "So, you said I could do anything, right?" he said in a low and seductive voice.

Shannon peeked down. Ciaran's erection stood tall, just for him. He smiled and sank a little farther into the bed. "Yes, anything."

Lowering the covers, Ciaran exposed his chest, then ran a trail of soft kisses and bites, starting at his nipples and ending at his navel.

Shannon arched his back, thrusting into nothing but sheets. Pain ached through his body still, but the pleasure Ciaran gave was worth it. He moaned low and deep as Ciaran lowered the sheets farther, Ciaran's tongue teasing the area between his navel and groin, Ciaran's cheek brushing against his erection. He placed his hands on the back of Ciaran's head, trying to put his mouth over his hard cock.

Ciaran tipped his head, grinning at him. "Now, now, you're supposed to just lie there and take it. Be a good boy and do as you bloody promised."

"Don't just tease me," Shannon whined.

Ciaran lowered his head and continued his assault on his thighs. With his tongue licking, mouth sucking, he dived into the crevice between Shannon's leg and groin.

Choking out a gasp, Shannon rocked his hips. "Please,

Ciaran." All he wanted was to feel his sweet mouth over him, sucking his cock, feeding his need. Desire pulsed inside him. He writhed.

Ciaran came up to hover over him, his pupils wide with obvious lust.

Shannon thrust in a desperate attempt for friction on his aching erection. "Please, Ciaran." He tensed his brows as an urgent need coiled inside him.

"That's right, beg me," Ciaran said, watching him.

"You are wicked, treating me this way after all I've been through." He spread a faint grin over his lips.

"You bloody well like it though, I can tell." Ciaran crushed his lips to Shannon's with a passionate kiss. He darted his tongue into his mouth, flicking and probing, doing to his mouth what he denied his erection.

Moaning into the kiss, Shannon thrust his hips, gliding his hand over his seeping cock in an attempt to pleasure himself. A pulse of sensation surged through him.

Ciaran slapped his hand away, pulling back. "That's mine."

"Then do something with it." Frustration built inside Shannon to a sweet tension. He thrust faster.

"All in due time." Ciaran smiled. "Wait here." He bit his lip. "And don't you dare touch yourself." He gave him a threatening glance, climbed off the bed, and trotted out of the room.

Sighing, he raised his arms above his head and tucked his hands under the pillow. What was Ciaran up to?

Ciaran stepped into the room with his hands hidden behind his back and a broad smile on his face.

Shifting his arms behind him, Shannon sat up on his elbows. "What have you got?"

Ciaran lifted a small bottle up for him to inspect, grinning like the Cheshire cat.

Shannon stared at the bottle for a moment. *It couldn't be.*

Mineral oil? "You didn't bring that bloody thing with you all the way from home, did you?"

Giving a slow shake of his head, Ciaran said, "No, I saw one in my aunt's medicine cabinet." Chuckling, he stalked closer to the bed, then climbed over him, straddling him. He unscrewed the bottle, poured the oil into his palm, and set the bottle down on the nightstand. As he gazed deeply into Shannon's eyes, he stroked slowly on his own erection. He closed his eyes, biting his lip, releasing a soft moan.

This is too much. He shifted and rocked his hips, holding onto Ciaran's thighs, driving his hard cock into the crevice of Ciaran's behind. He gasped as sensation surged through him. He thrust harder, faster.

Ciaran's body lifted with the force of his hips.

Shannon was so close to where he wanted to be, he could almost feel Ciaran's tight entrance around him. "Please, Ciaran, either you use that stuff on me or I'll fuck you without it."

Ciaran flashed his eyes open and focused on him. "Such language, my wicked lover. Actually, I'm going to fuck you, bloody hard." With a coy grin, he reached for the bottle again. His slick fingers fumbled a little with the cap.

Shannon drove faster into Ciaran's ass and sac.

"Stop that, I can't get the bloody thing open."

Shannon stopped thrusting. "Here, let me." He snatched the bottle from him, opened it and poured it into Ciaran's outstretched palm, then capped it and set it on the nightstand. Pleasure seared through his body as Ciaran's slickened fist worked over his shaft. Gasping, he pulled Ciaran down on top of him, forcing him to slide between his legs.

Taking ragged breaths, Ciaran's hands shook while he tilted to reach between them and slick Shannon's entrance. He pressed his lips to Shannon's, their tongue's tangling, while sliding a finger inside him.

Shannon bucked with the sweet sensation of Ciaran's finger entering him. It wasn't enough. He craved more, now. With heavy breaths, he said, "Do it, do it now." He slid his shaft along Ciaran's taut stomach, reveling in the pulses of pleasure rushing his body. Any pain he'd had vanished.

As Ciaran trailed hot, wet kisses along his neck, he withdrew his finger and nudged his solid cock against Shannon's passage.

Wrapping his legs around Ciaran's hips, Shannon tugged on his waist, driving Ciaran into him. Ciaran's thick cock hit the bundle of nerves inside him. A loud moan erupted from his throat. Ecstasy rushed his every nerve. The tension in his groin hummed with the promise of pure, raw release.

They rocked their hips as if each tried to dominate the other, grabbing and pinching at flesh, the sounds of pleasure escaping them.

Ciaran's body shook with each thrust of his hips.

Shannon's climax surged, a delicious eruption waiting for surrender. The sensation in his erection intensified. He couldn't hold on any longer. As Ciaran drove out and in, over and over, stroking his insides, he gave one good, hard thrust into his stomach. His seed spurted out between them, contractions racking his body. He cried out with the force of it all.

Ciaran dropped his head to the pillow, wrapping his arms tightly around Shannon. He thrust hard and held it, his body shuddering. With low, urgent moans, he withdrew and drove again, deeper, spilling his seed into Shannon's body.

Shivering, Shannon held him close. As his breath slowed, he relaxed into the bed. "Oh, how I love you." He tipped his head and placed a gentle kiss in Ciaran's hair.

"Not more than I love you," Ciaran said, muffled in pillow and skin.

Shannon smiled. *It really is all right. I have everything I ever wanted. Everyone else be damned.*

Shannon sat at a table in the corner of the smoky pub, waiting for Ciaran to return with tea and a pint from Iona. He hadn't wanted to make his head feel any worse, so he was the one who'd be drinking the tea. It was afternoon and about time he left the bedroom. As he scanned the pub, he noticed Dave and Colin, the two men Iona had pointed out the last time he was here. It made him smile to see them sitting at the bar, chatting with her, knowing they were just like him and Ciaran.

Ciaran strode to the table, leaned over, and placed a mug of tea in front of him, then set his beer down next to it. He took a seat beside him, gazing at him with a wide grin. "So what'll we do now?"

Shrugging his shoulders, Shannon shifted forward. "I suppose we'll have to get jobs."

A man in the corner said something incoherent but loud to the man sitting across from him.

Shannon glanced at them, then drew his attention back to Ciaran.

Ciaran scoffed, then sipped his beer. "I don't know a bloody thing about jobs except for farming. Chickens, horses and potatoes, that's what I know."

Shannon curled his lips in a sly grin. *I can't resist...* "Oh yeah? You know about mineral oil." Chuckling, he grabbed his mug and sat back.

"Shannon Sullivan, bloody behave yourself. I don't know why you get yourself all worked up about that. Like you never took your ma's mineral oil." Huffing, Ciaran shook his head, then drank more beer.

"I didn't."

"Ah, yes you did. You want me to think you're all prim and proper over there, never oiling yourself up. Well, I don't bloody well believe it." Ciaran flashed a glare at him.

Shannon sat forward, peering into his eyes. "I didn't, I tell you. She'd have clobbered me."

Staring a moment, Ciaran hung his mouth open. "What do you mean? How would she even know?" He snickered. "Did she keep tabs on the all the bloody oil in your house?" He held his pint to his lips.

Shannon thinned his lips. "Yes, she did."

Ciaran snapped his brows together. "You've got to be joking me." He took a quick gulp of beer and set it down, his gaze following his glass.

Fingering his mug, Shannon stared at the table surface. "She kept track of everything I did. Every time there was even a tiny stain on my sheets, she washed them. She checked my clothes, my underwear even. She was always searching my room, looking for something, I don't know what. Ever since she found out about what I did with Mr. Flannigan, she was bloody obsessed with keeping me and my room clean, like that would make it all go away. But she never let me talk about it. No, that was something I was forced to do with Father Brennan." The warmth of Ciaran's hand rested on his thigh. His gaze found Ciaran's.

Ciaran creased his brows, turning his lips down. "I'm sorry, Shannon. You know you can talk to me."

Gazing into his lovely, green eyes, Shannon took a hard swallow. He rested his hand over Ciaran's, on his own thigh. "Father Brennan told me." He swallowed again. "He told me Mr. Flannigan...he loved me." He blinked a few times, pain piercing his heart. It was strange, as if the loss happened yesterday, not five years ago.

Ciaran widened his eyes. "He did?" He squeezed Shannon's thigh. "Are you okay? You don't look so bloody well."

"I think I need..."

Ciaran lurched forward, knocking against the table, almost spilling his pint, and gave him a fierce embrace. "It's okay, Shannon. It's okay if you had feelings for him," he whispered against his cheek.

Shannon buried his face in his neck, wrapping his arms around him. His chest squeezed. He wanted to cry, but there were no tears this time. Maybe he was cried out.

After a few moments, Iona walked over to them. "Shannon, are you all right, dear?" She placed a hand on his back.

Shannon pulled Ciaran tighter.

Ciaran kept a firm hold on his head and shoulders. "He'll be okay. Just needs me, I think."

She sat down at the table, watching them, pursing her lips.

Shannon relaxed his hold on Ciaran.

Releasing him, Ciaran sat in his own seat. He grasped his hand under the table. "You okay now?"

Shannon tried to smile, but couldn't. Sighing, he looked to Iona. "I'm sorry, seems I'm still a bit of a mess."

"Oh come on, that's nothing to be bloody sorry about. I can't believe you're sitting down here already. You've been through so much." She glanced at Ciaran. "Both of you."

"We were just wondering. What should we do now?" Ciaran asked.

She smiled at them. "That's easy. Whatever you bloody well want."

EPILOGUE
SHANNON

A FEW MONTHS LATER

Shannon strolled out of the bathroom, feeling clean and refreshed, wearing a crisp, new, black dress shirt and trousers. The smell of bacon cooking made his stomach growl. As he strode into the kitchen, his gaze set on Ciaran and he covered his mouth, stifling a laugh about to burst from him.

Ciaran stood at Iona's stove, spatula in hand, red frilly apron covering his clothes. With a frown, his face flushed. "Stop it, right now, Shannon Sullivan. Or I swear I'll make you cook the bloody breakfast. I didn't want to get bacon grease on my new shirt."

Snickering, Shannon waved his hand and shook his head. "No, no, I'm sure you're a much better cook than I am." He sat at Iona's large dining table. "So, Iona left already?"

"Yeah, she wanted to get back early this afternoon so we could have the motor car." Ciaran returned to his duties at the stove.

Shannon grinned. It was obvious his Ciaran had planned

something for them. With deliberate slowness, he asked, "And what do we need the motor car for?"

Ciaran turned the bacon over. "Just you never mind. It's a surprise." He placed food from the skillet onto plates and brought them to the table, smiling at him. "Eat up." He went back, grabbed some cups filled with steaming tea and came back to the table, setting them down above the plates.

Perusing the meal, Shannon poked at the eggs. Somehow, they didn't look quite right. Bacon and toast rested on the plates as well. They, at least, seemed decent. He picked up a piece of bacon and placed it into his mouth. "Mmm, delicious, Ciaran. I definitely could not have done better."

Ciaran sat down next to him and shoveled an egg-filled fork into his mouth. He rounded his eyes and spit the egg onto his plate. "Oh, bloody hell, what happened to the eggs?"

"What do you mean? They aren't good?" Shannon cleared his throat and pressed his lips together, stopping a giggle.

"No. I wonder if they turned?" Ciaran took a quick sip of tea, then poked at the eggs.

"Don't you think you'd have smelled them? You were a farmer, you'd think you'd bloody well know that." Shannon smirked. How he loved teasing him when he got the chance.

"Oh, shut up. Well, eat the bacon and toast anyway. Then maybe we'll have some pudding." Ciaran waggled his eyebrows.

"I just cleaned up." Shannon offered a coy grin.

"Don't worry, I won't spill." Ciaran leaned over and placed a passionate kiss on his lips.

Closing his eyes, Shannon returned the kiss. He'd never tire of these kisses or of his Ciaran. When the kiss broke, he opened his eyes, remaining in a happy daze. "Can't believe it's been a month, can you?"

Ciaran shook his head, swallowing a mouthful of bacon

with some tea. "No. A month in Dublin and we've yet to really see it." He stared wide-eyed at him.

Shannon grinned. *He spilled it.* "So, you took the day off from the docks, made Kelly work the pub for me and arranged to use the motor car so we could see the sights?"

With his gaze falling to his lap, Ciaran said, "Yeah. Damn it, Shannon, it was supposed to be a bloody surprise."

He squeezed Ciaran's forearm. "Well, I don't know exactly where we're going so it's still a surprise. And you did a bloody good job on this breakfast, well, except for the eggs maybe."

Ciaran gave him a playful slap on the shoulder.

Shannon flinched.

"You're a real bugger sometimes, you know that? But I love you anyway." Ciaran turned his attention to his breakfast. "So did you hear from your ma and da?"

Frowning, Shannon set his fork down on his plate. "No."

"I'm sure you will eventually. My da says they were just shocked. It'll take them some time to get used to it all." Ciaran glanced at him. "Hey, my da sold the farm. I think he'll be coming out here in a few weeks."

"Really? When did you hear this?" Shannon scanned his face.

"Just yesterday, late. You were still working in the pub. Figured it could wait."

Shannon smiled and sipped his tea, washing down his toast. How good his life had become since the dreadful day of the storm. It didn't seem real. He'd healed, Ciaran found work at the docks, and he spent his time tending bar for Iona. He even had friends. Who'd have thought? He picked up his second piece of toast and took a bite. "So, what happened to that lamp we had in our room, the one with the red feathers? And I noticed all the doilies were gone."

Ciaran sipped his tea and placed the mug on the table,

spreading a wide grin over his lips. "My aunt finally let me put the bloody things in the study. Didn't you notice we have the lamp that was in there now?"

Glaring at him, Shannon shifted forward in his seat. "Ciaran, those things were Sinead's. I can't believe you'd ask her to move them."

Ciaran waved his hand at him. "Don't get your knickers in a twist, she didn't mind. Besides, it's our room now."

Shaking his head, Shannon said, "I don't bloody believe you sometimes. Is nothing sacred?"

Ciaran let a mischievous grin play on his face. His plate was empty, save for the tainted eggs. "No." He rose from his seat, stepped toward him, and straddled him.

Shannon peered up at him. "What are you doing?"

Ciaran came down, crushing his lips in a heated kiss. He rolled his hips, thrusting his erection against Shannon's stomach through his trousers. "Getting my pudding."

Scooting forward and leaning back, Shannon gave him a better angle to work with. He grabbed Ciaran's hips and pulled him forward and back, supplying friction to his own hardening cock. After a few moments, Ciaran shifted away from his stomach, continuing to rock over him.

"Touch me, Shannon." Ciaran moaned.

Shannon snuck his hand between them and toyed with Ciaran's hard shaft through his trousers. Ciaran really enjoyed this. Every time, it made him frantic with need.

Gasping in pleasure, Ciaran rocked his hips faster, tilting his head back. "Harder, rub me harder."

Shannon palmed him with more pressure and swirled his palm over the tip of his cock.

As Ciaran bit his lip, he clenched his eyes shut. A deep moan escaped from his throat, his hips moving faster still.

Shannon lost himself in the rocking hips and Ciaran's

heightened state of arousal. His thrusts became urgent, hungry for friction. Gasping, his sensitivity intensified, his climax building to a sweet edge inside him.

Leaning down, Ciaran kissed him, gliding his tongue over Shannon's.

Shannon stroked harder, more persistent over his shaft.

Panting, Ciaran writhed above him.

Pleasure pulsed over Shannon. Ciaran's rocking would drive him over the edge. "S-stop, Ciaran." He removed his hand from Ciaran's groin, gripped his hips and tried to halt his movement.

Ciaran persisted, shifting his hips over Shannon's, and rubbing their erections together.

The friction on Shannon's sensitive cock was exquisite, just the right speed and pressure to make him hum. The tingle of release teased him, and he struggled against it. He didn't want to lose control like this. He wanted more...skin-on-skin contact, Ciaran's mouth, all of it. Just as his peak surfaced, he shoved Ciaran sideways, onto the floor. He slapped his hand over the head of his cock and squeezed, keeping his climax from erupting further.

Ciaran looked up at him in a daze, panting. "Why'd you do that?"

Shannon shuddered, but gained control of himself. "I didn't want to do it that way." He raked his fingers through his long bangs, fighting to catch his breath.

With a sly grin, Ciaran rose up on his knees and crept toward him. "Oh? And what exactly did you want to do?" He snuck between Shannon's legs and lowered his head between his thighs.

Shannon placed his hands on the back of Ciaran's head.

Ciaran covered his erection with his mouth, then blew hot air through thin fabric.

As Shannon arched his back, he freed a loud moan. Having been so close, anything could send pleasure rippling through him. "C-Ciaran, stop."

Ciaran gazed up at him, his eyelids hooded, his pupils wide. "Come on then, what did you want to do?"

Flashing his eyes at him, Shannon said, "Get the oil."

"You dirty little bastard. You want to do that, right here, in my aunt's bloody kitchen?" Ciaran smirked.

Shannon bit his lip, desire shivering up his spine. "Yeah, right here."

With an almost unnatural quickness, Ciaran burst up and sped toward the bathroom.

Shannon stood and undressed. He'd be ready when Ciaran came back. He turned, completely naked, erection standing tall, then caught Ciaran trotting back through the arch to the dining table. He peeked at him from under his long bangs.

Oil bottle in hand, Ciaran choked out a chuckle. "Oh my, that's the best pudding I've seen in a long time." He stepped to him and set the oil bottle on the table. He placed both hands on Shannon's cheeks, then brushed his lips over Shannon's and came in to deepen the kiss.

The cool, hard edge of the table hit the back of Shannon's thighs and Ciaran's erection pushed through his trousers, against his hips. He wanted him inside him, now. Moaning, he broke the kiss. "Come on, what are you waiting for?"

Ciaran searched his face. He leaned over the table and swiped the dishes away, clattering as they mashed together. He shifted his attention to his clothing, unfastening, and unbuttoning until everything dropped away to the floor.

Shannon's hard cock ached.

Ciaran shoved him backward.

Shannon landed on the hard surface of the table with Ciaran holding him tight, breaking the fall. Ciaran's erection pressed flush against his entrance, making him squirm. He gazed deeply into his green eyes and lifted his legs over him, crossing his ankles behind Ciaran's back.

Pausing, Ciaran met Shannon's gaze. "I love you, Shannon."

Heat rushed Shannon's cheeks. "Not more than I love you." He watched while Ciaran came down hard on his mouth, lips parted, tongue penetrating and insistent. He thrust and groaned, trying to push Ciaran's thick cock inside him. They needed oil. He grabbed the bottle. "Please, just do it."

Ciaran lifted off him with a coy grin and unscrewed the cap, then took the bottle from him and poured it into Shannon's open palm.

Shannon stroked Ciaran's erection with his slick hand.

Moaning, Ciaran leaned over him, resting on his elbows. He placed soft, sensual, kisses over his mouth while Shannon stroked him.

I can't wait any longer. Shannon moved Ciaran's hard cock to his entrance and squeezed his hips with his legs, driving him partially in. He gasped, craving more.

Holding him tight, Ciaran drove all the way into him. He groaned, pulling out and pushing in again.

Shannon shifted and held steadfast with his legs. Ciaran drove in again and again, hitting his bundle of nerves, sending pleasure jolting through his body. "Oh, God, Ciaran, more." He freed a sharp moan, thrusting his hips in time with Ciaran's. His back rocked on the table surface. His erection ached for contact while his internal pleasure spot received stroke after stroke of Ciaran's hard cock.

Ciaran shook over him. Gasping, his thrusts became more insistent and ragged each time. "Shannon, I—"

"Hold on." Shannon snuck his hand between them and

pumped his seeping cock. Ciaran wouldn't climax without him. An intense wave of pleasure pulsed through him.

"Shannon, look at me." Ciaran propped himself on his elbows.

Shannon ripped his focus from their hips to Ciaran's face. Their gazes locked.

As Ciaran drove hard into him, his body shuddered with release. Keeping his gaze on Shannon's, he bucked and filled him, loud gasps escaping his mouth.

Watching him, Shannon surrendered to the surge of his own climax. He arched his back. As he pumped his stiff shaft, sweet contractions spurted his seed onto his chest. He cried out, losing complete control. As it slowed, his senses returned.

Ciaran lay on top of him, chuckling.

"What's so bloody funny?"

Ciaran raised onto his elbows and gazed down at him. "You are, you bloody animal. I'll bet they heard you all the way down in the pub. In fact, I'll ask Kelly when we go down."

"No, you won't." Shannon scoffed, heat flashing through his cheeks.

"Yes, I will."

"If you so much as—"

"You'll what?"

"I'll, I'll, put that feckin' red-feathered lamp and the doilies back in our room." He smirked.

"You wouldn't."

"I would. And I'd tell your aunt how you felt bad about taking them out in the first place." *Touché.* Shannon sniggered.

"Oh, you are a bugger." Grinning, Ciaran planted a playful kiss on his lips. "Ah well, let's get cleaned up then and wait for Iona downstairs." He pulled out and straightened.

Shannon climbed off the table and turned to look at it. "We sure made a bloody mess, didn't we?" He released a soft chuckle. The first time he'd been here, he'd never have thought that someday he and Ciaran would be making love on this table. He spread a slow grin over his lips.

Shannon hopped down the steps to the pub with Ciaran close behind. When he got there, he nodded to Kelly. He'd become fond of the tall blond over the last month. As he strode over the plank flooring to the mahogany bar, he caught a silly grin on Kelly's face. He took a seat on a leather barstool in front of him. "What are you smiling about?"

Kelly gazed at him with playful blue eyes. "Oh, just sounds like you and Ciaran had a—" He coughed into his hand. "Bloody good morning."

Gasping, Shannon dropped his mouth open.

Ciaran laughed, slapping him in the shoulder. "See? And I didn't even have to ask."

Shannon shifted his attention to Ciaran. "Oh, shut up."

"So what'll it be? A pint?" Kelly asked, wiping down the bar with a brown rag.

Shannon turned, taking inventory through the haze of smoke at the pub. A few men talked politics in the corner. He came back to Kelly. *It's almost lunchtime.* "Yeah, I'll have a pint."

"Me, too." Ciaran said beside him.

"Okay." Kelly grabbed two glasses and poured dark beer into them from a brass tap. "So, I hear you're going out in the new motor car today."

"Yes, we are." Ciaran grinned at Shannon.

"You over losing Missy then?" Kelly set the filled pints in front of them.

Ciaran frowned, fingering the top of his glass. "Yeah, I guess so. She did go to a bloody good man, and it made sense to buy the motor car. Not much use for a horse in the city."

Shannon watched him. How lovely his Ciaran was. He'd never tire of looking at him.

Cutting his gaze to Shannon, Ciaran slapped his thigh. "So shall I teach you to drive today?"

"What? You've got to be bloody joking. You know I don't like being in all that traffic." Shannon's heart lurched. It made him anxious just to think of driving the motor car. Driving the horse and cart on the boulevard was bad enough. With the motor car, he had gears and brakes to think about.

"Oh, come on. You have to learn some day. Right, Kelly?" Ciaran sipped his pint.

Kelly wiped the bar with the rag, giving him a smug grin. "Yeah, then you can get the bloody supplies and I won't have to do it all the time."

With a slow shake of his head, Shannon stared at his glass. "Maybe I should be drinking whiskey then." He brought the pint to his lips and took a few gulps.

"No, I don't want you all bloody bollocksed today," Ciaran said, leaning close to him.

The door opened to the pub and two men, one with short, chestnut-colored hair and the other a ginger, wearing dark trousers and cream-colored dress shirts strode in. He recognized them, Dave and Colin. They were large, gruff-looking men, dockworkers. They'd been the ones to help Ciaran get his job. When they saw Ciaran and Shannon, they grinned with a nod.

"Top of the morning, boys." Dave said, slapping Shannon hard on the back.

Shannon jerked forward. "Uh, morning. Although I believe it's almost noon."

Dave took a seat next to Colin on the other side of Shannon.

Ciaran leaned over and looked Dave and Colin up and down. "Why aren't you at the docks today?"

Colin leaned over. "Why aren't you?"

Ciaran chuckled. "I have a date."

"Really now? Did you know about this, Shannon?" Dave smirked.

Heat rushed Shannon's cheeks. He focused on his almost empty pint. It still seemed strange to talk so openly about his relationship with Ciaran. Even with men who had the same thing between them. "Yeah."

With a nod and a grin, Kelly piped in. "You should have heard them this morning."

"Yeah?" Dave asked.

Shannon widened his eyes at Kelly. "Don't you say a bloody word."

Ciaran laughed. "Oh, Shannon, everyone already knows what a loud bastard you are."

Shannon's focus shifted to Ciaran. "And how would they know that?"

Kelly mumbled from behind the bar.

"What?" Shannon glared at Kelly.

"I said, you're always at it with the feckin' window open." Kelly set his hands on the bar top meeting Shannon's gaze. "Always. At. It."

Shannon slapped his hands to the bar. *Bastards.* He opened his mouth to speak.

Iona appeared, strolling in from the side door of the pub.

"So, the motor car's outside ready for you." She plopped a handful of bags on the bar. "Morning, Colin, morning, Dave," she said, nodding.

"Morning, Iona. Been shopping, I see?" Dave asked.

Ciaran wrapped his hand around Shannon's and dragged him off his stool.

"Let's go," Ciaran said, walking toward the side door with Shannon in tow.

"Have fun, boys," Iona called out, waving.

"Thanks." Ciaran said.

"Hit the brake I say, hit the bloody brake!" Ciaran shouted.

Shannon's heart pounded in his ears. *Which foot pedal is the brake?* He slammed his foot down erroneously, hoping to hit the right one before he ended up in the middle of the intersection. With the motor car lurching to a stop, he sighed in relief. He looked up and down the street. Tenement buildings lined either side. Tall ash trees hovered above them, allowing only thin beams of sunlight to peek through. The few people strolling on the pavements stopped to watch them.

"Shite, Shannon, you're going to get us killed." Ciaran huffed and shifted in his seat.

"Well, don't make me bloody drive then." Shannon's heart pounded and his palms sweated over the wooden steering wheel. He looked around the black, carriage-style motor car, listening to the deep rumble of the engine.

"You have to learn. Today's as good a day as any." Ciaran placed his hand on Shannon's shoulder. "You okay?"

Shannon faced him. "No, I'm not. I thought we were going to see the sights? All we're doing is driving up and down this bloody street."

Ciaran grinned. "You have to be prepared for O'Connell Street."

"Oh, no, not today. I am not going to drive down bloody O'Connell Street. If you want to go there, you'll be the one driving." Heat filtered into Shannon's chest. He gripped the steering wheel tight, not able to look at him.

Ciaran squeezed his shoulder. "Ah well, it was worth a try I guess." He climbed out of the motor car.

"What are you doing now?"

"Move over, I'm driving," Ciaran said, walking to the other side of the motor car.

Huffing, Shannon slid over the puckered leather seat, taking care not to move any of the gears. He crossed his arms over his chest, looking out at the road and frowned. He'd never get used to driving a motor car.

Ciaran climbed into the seat, put the car into gear and drove down the street with little effort. "Come on, Shannon, you didn't do all that bloody bad."

"Yes, I did." Shannon scowled. Why was it so hard for him? Ciaran took to it right away.

Ciaran placed a hand on Shannon's thigh, driving out onto a boulevard.

The early afternoon sun shone down on them. Large, pillared, stone buildings with intricate carvings rose up on either side of the boulevard, littered with motor cars and horse-drawn carriages.

"You'll get it, you'll see," Ciaran said softly while he drove adeptly through the jumble of traffic.

Shannon's hair danced in the breeze and his stomach rumbled. "Ciaran, I'm hungry." He spread a soft smile over his lips. Ciaran was sure to tease him.

Ciaran glanced at him. "You mean that bloody breakfast I made didn't fill you up?"

"That was hours ago." Shannon rested his elbow on the vehicle door and scanned the shops on the side of the boulevard. An ice cream parlor came into view. His heart jumped. He smiled and faced him. "Ciaran, let's get some ice cream. I see a shop over there." He pointed just up ahead.

Ciaran stopped the car in traffic. "Yeah?" Grinning, Ciaran pulled the vehicle over to the side of the road.

When the motor car stopped, Shannon opened his door and climbed out, then met up with Ciaran on the pavements and strolled beside him, nodding politely at people passing by, to the ice cream parlor.

A bell rang as Shannon opened a red door with a glass insert. He held it, allowing Ciaran to enter first, then followed him inside. They walked over a checkered tile floor and passed metal parlor dinettes. His mouth watered while he inspected the brightly colored ice creams in their buckets behind a glass case. He stepped up closer to the case and peered at the various flavors. Cool air rushed over his cheeks.

Ciaran stood close beside him.

"What'll it be, boys?" a man behind the counter asked in a white smock with a silver ice cream scoop in his hand.

"I'll have strawberry, please," Ciaran said.

Shannon thought for a minute. Then a flavor caught his eye. He was no longer afraid to have exactly what he wanted. He spread a broad smile over his lips. "I'll have mint, please."

Ciaran turned to him. "What the hell, when did you start liking mint?"

Grinning at his beautiful Ciaran, Shannon said, "The day I was born."

WANT TO READ SOMETHING SIMILAR, but in modern times? Try stepping into the Mesa Boys universe.

When a skater boy rooms with a hot college nerd, sparks

fly. Will they give in to temptation? Read Catching His Fall to find out.

You can also try the prequel chapter for the series in which a bad boy skater has a bi-awakening with his roommate. Claim your copy of Catching Him.

Or, buy it on Amazon: Catching Him

CHRISTIE GORDON

THANK YOU

Thank you for reading **A Summer Without Rain**. Helping other readers find new books to enjoy is easy when you share a review. If you want to share your love for Shannon and Ciaran, please leave a review. I'd really appreciate it!

    Another huge help is recommending my work to others. Spread the word by giving this book a shout-out in your favorite book rec group if you like.

Find Christie and all her MM Romance books online at:
CHRISTIEGORDON.COM
Get exclusive content at Christie's Facebook reader's group:
Christie's Cocktale Cafe
Connect with Christie on social Media:

About the Author

Christie Gordon started writing gay and MM romance books after finding Yaoi fanfiction by accident and falling in love with it. She's always had stories in her head and always enjoyed writing, so she decided to try her hand at it and took up fiction writing classes at a local community college. She published her first MM romance book with eXtasy Books back in 2009. She enjoys writing about men discovering themselves, overcoming obstacles and finding love in the process, along with a happy ending. Visit her website for a complete list of her books.

Christie's day job is in the high-tech industry with a Bachelor of Science in Electrical Engineering and a Master's in Business Administration. She currently lives in the Phoenix, Arizona metro area but has also lived in the Bay Area of California and grew up in Minnesota. If she isn't writing, she's watching boys love dramas or creating digital artwork. She's also a mother of two young-adult sons, whose antics keep her on her toes. Her one-eyed rescue pug is always by her side, snoring the day away.

Printed in Great Britain
by Amazon

e143c45d-7383-4626-bde8-c52b45fb695cR01